D0068538

PRAISE FOR R.W.W.

"With a deft weaving of rock 'n roll, denim suits, AMC Pacers and nuclear-powered spaceships, Greene effortlessly recreates a 1970s America that could have been… The story becomes a ride as fast as an Oppenheimer-powered rocket and you won't want it to stop. Can't wait to see what comes next!"

Sarah J. Daley, author of *Obsidian*

"The action in *Mercury Rising* is compelling from the first chapter. Greene's skill at creating an alternate space-faring America in the mid-1970's is studded with the perfect amount of pop culture references, and his many-layered Everyman, Brooklyn Lamontagne, feels like a long-lost best friend. All this combines to lock you in for a thrilling story that's impossible to put down."

Ginger Smith, author of *The Rush's Edge*

"Everything I've come to love about Greene: impeccable story logic, fantastic prose, sly humor, and hope in all its glory."

Zig Zag Claybourne, author of *Afro Puffs are the Antennae of the Universe*

"*Mercury Rising* charmed and fascinated me. Greene has taken an absolutely wild premise and somehow made it fit like a puzzle piece into our own history and knowledge of the greater universe. It is unexpected and clever, heartfelt and funny, with big, conceptual penny-drop moments that hit the reader as hard as they hit the novel's weary protagonist, Brooklyn Lamontagne."

Chris Panatier, author of *Stringers* and *The Phlebotomist*

"Surprising, engaging, and with plenty of smart nods to society's bullshit, *Mercury Rising* is a slice of alternative history that reads like science-fiction Stephen King. A joy."

Dan Hanks, author of *Swashbucklers*

BY THE SAME AUTHOR

Twenty Five to Life
The Light Years

R.W.W. Greene

MERCURY RISING

ANGRY ROBOT

ANGRY ROBOT
An imprint of Watkins Media Ltd

Unit 11, Shepperton House
89 Shepperton Road
London N1 3DF
UK

angryrobotbooks.com
twitter.com/angryrobotbooks
Live Forever

An Angry Robot paperback original, 2022

Copyright © R.W.W. Greene 2022

Cover by Glen Wilkins
Edited by Eleanor Teasdale and Paul Simpson
Set in Meridien

All rights reserved. R.W.W. Greene asserts the moral right to be identified as the author of this work. A catalogue record for this book is available from the British Library.

This novel is entirely a work of fiction. Names, characters, places, and incidents are the products of the author's imagination or are used fictitiously. Any resemblance to actual events, locales, organizations or persons, living or dead, is entirely coincidental.

Sales of this book without a front cover may be unauthorized. If this book is coverless, it may have been reported to the publisher as "unsold and destroyed" and neither the author nor the publisher may have received payment for it.

Angry Robot and the Angry Robot icon are registered trademarks of Watkins Media Ltd.

ISBN 978 0 85766 972 8
Ebook ISBN 978 0 85766 973 5

Printed and bound in the United Kingdom by TJ Books Ltd.

9 8 7 6 5 4 3 2 1

MIX
Paper from
responsible sources
FSC
www.fsc.org   FSC® C013056

*To the 1619 Project and other scholars
who are iluminating our history and showing
what really happened.*

PART ONE
Mercury Rising

JANUARY 27, 1961

Commander Jet Carson shrugged into his flight jacket, assuming the weight of its fireproof fabric. The coat snagged on his gun belt, and he rolled his shoulders to settle it into place.

The woman in the bed across the room rose to one elbow, sleep-tousled hair falling in soft layers around her. The air got caught in Jet's chest. Twenty years married, and it happened every time he saw her. He crossed the floor in two quick steps and sat next to her.

She fluttered her hand over a yawn and blinked up at him. "Do you have to go?"

He smiled. "You always ask that."

"Always will."

He bent to kiss her. "Betty Brown." He kissed her again. "Betty Brown, you are mine, mine, mine."

She cocked her head. "I think you mean 'Betty Carson'."

"Girlfriend, fiancée, wife…" His eyes twinkled. "You'll always be the girl I met at the malt shop."

"And you'll always be the jerk leaving me." She faked a sigh.

Jet captured her chin and looked into her eyes. "I always come back."

"You'd better." She sat up in bed, the covers falling to reveal her camisole. "Level with me, Jet. Is this one dangerous?"

"Piece of cake, darling girl. A quick ride to the top to see if anything is coming our way." He grinned. "But I'll get out to Mars one of these days. It's only a day out and back with the new Oppenheimers. John's already done it twice."

"And everything John Dunne does, you have to do too."

He laughed. "Unless I do it first."

Jet blew Betty a kiss and made his way into the early-morning air. The Cape was twenty minutes away by car, but he could get there in half that on his motorcycle. He detoured to buy doughnuts for his prep crew and parked on a scenic overlook above the Cape. Looking at the rocket towers and gantries made him giddy, like when he was a kid and dreamed of being a spaceman. He winced. *Low-orbit patrols and scrambles. Not exactly what you imagined when you signed up.* This day's mission, something to do with an overnight meteor strike in Kansas, unexpected though it was, promised to be more of the same. Jet got back on his bike and continued to the Cape.

There were two taciturn guards at the gate instead of the usual friendly-faced singleton, and it took Jet a few extra minutes to clear security. He snagged a chocolate-glazed from the box and handed the rest of the pastries to a runner. "Get these to Big Swede." He pointed toward the launch bay with his doughnut. The runner hurried away without the usual banter. Jet watched him go, his mouth full of doughnut, head full of questions.

Pastry gone, Jet slid his hands into his pockets and strolled to the logistics office, where he stuck his head through the door without knocking. "What's in the wind, Mickey?"

The logistics chief tilted his head to look over the top of his reading glasses and leaned back in his chair. "Not a thing, Jet. They say get 'em ready, I get 'em ready." He held up his clipboard so Jet could see the cotton-candy pink of an ammunition requisition.

Jet whistled. "How ready are we talking?"

"Full load for everyone."

"Lot of firepower for a meteor."

"It is at that." He adjusted his glasses. "You don't look too broken up about it."

"Any day I chase stars is a good one." Jet pushed himself upright. "Everyone else in Brief?"

"Yeah." The chief stuck out his hand to shake. "Good luck up there. See you on the other side."

The elevator took Jet five levels down and dropped him off at the briefing room. The rest of his squad, the intrepid Eagle Seven, was already there. Carl White waved and pointed to a seat next to him. "What do you hear, boss?" he said.

Jet dropped into the seat. "Not much, but we're going up loaded for grizzly."

"Interesting." Carl nodded toward the podium, where the NASA bigwigs were gathering. "Maybe we're about to find something out."

Pad boss Guenter Werthner kept the briefing short and unusually vague: launch in two hours, form up in high orbit, and unseal a packet of formal orders. The thin-faced man straightened his bow tie. "That's all the information I've got, boys. This little trip originated at the highest level." He switched off the podium light. "We're out of time. Prepare your ships."

Jet leaned over to whisper to Carl. "Sounds like this might be worth getting out of bed for."

Carl frowned. "High orbit with all weapons loaded? I don't get it. Who are we going to shoot that far out?"

"Guess we'll find out at 1350." Jet clapped his pal on the back. "See you up there."

Carl nodded. "Good flying."

Jet took the monorail to the launch pit, where the crew was already hard at work on his ship. The aging LRF-15 stood on its tails, umbilicals attached at every port.

The crew chief appeared out of a bank of steam, wiping his hands on an oily rag. "We're making her good for you, Jet."

Sven Lindeson had a PhD in physics, but no one called him "Doctor". Some of the other eggheads insisted the pilots use the honorific, but Sven was always just "Sven" or "Big Swede" because of his height and broad shoulders.

Jet stuck out his hand, and Sven engulfed it in a paw like a catcher's mitt.

"Don't suppose you can tell me where we're going," Jet said.

Sven grinned. "Straight up. No sudden stops."

Jet faked a glower. "Then I just take a left at the Moon. Thanks a heap."

Sven ran a hand through his thinning blond hair. "Go see to your baby. After all this milk she may need burping."

Jet exchanged pleasantries with a few other members of the launch crew, but he only had eyes for his ship.

From seven paces back every red-white-and-blue foot of her looked as smooth as a car fender. Up close, Jet could see the seams, rivets, and too-frequent patches that made up her skin. *Ready for another show, girl?*

He circled the ship looking for flaws. He wouldn't find any – Sven's crew was top-notch – but it was part of his flight-check process, like kicking the tires before a road trip.

Jet had dubbed her *Victory* after their first mission, and she'd proved worthy of the name, surviving more than seventy-five combat and recon flights in near space. Two years before, one of the eggheads had saved *Victory* and her sisters from retirement when he pointed out how easy it would be to retrofit the aging long-range fighters with third-generation Oppenheimer Atomic Engines. The modification increased the fighters' straight-line range and speed, while maintaining their inherent toughness and maneuverability. There were younger, more sophisticated ships to be sure, but Jet wouldn't trade his girl for any five.

Jet climbed the metal staircase up to the hatch and ducked inside. A sliding door straight ahead led to a small bunk and refresher unit. The ladder anchored to the inside wall fed down to the power and life-support plants and up to the cockpit. Jet headed up and sank into the cracked leather of his pilot's couch. He flipped the switch to activate the control board and continued with the flight checks. Forty-five minutes later, he closed his flightbook and switched on the radio. "Sven, this is *Victory*. We're green as grass in here. What's it like outside?"

The clear-channel static sounded like a light rain, and Sven's voice cut it like an awning. "Forty more minutes to top off the tanks, and you'll be good to go. Want to come out and grab some coffee?"

Jet clicked his mic. "Negative on the Joe, but thanks for the offer. I'll grab a quick nap on the couch."

Sven chuckled. "Sweet dreams. I'll wake you before launch."

Jet grinned. He'd be up in plenty of time for final checks. Everyone on base knew about his habit of catching cat naps where and when he could. Jet draped a bandanna over his face and stretched out in the seat. He was asleep in seconds.

Twenty minutes later he was running through another, abbreviated, checklist. *Victory* cleared her final hurdles without a hitch and Jet pulled his acceleration straps tight while the launch clock ticked down in his earphones. He checked the seal on his helmet and watched the clock move from forty to thirty to twenty to twelve.

"Ten count!" the flight controller announced. "We're at ten!"

Jet flicked the safety cover off the launch controls and, at zero, stabbed the ignition button. Some of the other guys in the flight left the whole sequence up to the computer, but Jet wasn't about to let a glitch keep him out of the stratosphere.

The liftoff pushed him into the seat cushions, and the engine roar nearly blotted out the mission-control updates coming through the earphones.

"Eagle Seven is away!" the flight controller said. "Repeat: Eagle Seven is away."

At the computer's signal, Jet cut the launch engines and entered microgravity. Another switch uncoupled *Victory* from the booster ring, and the ship slid into orbit on her own power. Jet clicked his mic. "Everybody who made it up form on me, standard configuration."

He heard a chorus of "rogers", including one from a voice he hadn't expected. "I didn't think you'd make it back on time for this, Bullets," Jet said.

"Got tired of kissing babies," the voice said. "Figured I'd come along to make sure you didn't screw up."

Commander John Dunne had earned his nickname for his uncanny ability to attract enemy fire. He'd been on a meet-and-greet publicity tour when the mission alert went out, and Jet had assumed his seat would go to a backup. "Thanks for pitching in, Johnny Boy. Sorry to cut your vacation short."

The commander snorted in reply. John "Bullets" Dunne would rather be making garbage runs to the Moon than pressing flesh and smiling for the cameras in the Heartland.

Eagle Seven assumed formation and made their status reports.

"Looks like everybody made it to the top, boss," said Carl, Jet's wing man.

"Confirmed." Jet slid his hand down his right leg, feeling for the cargo pocket where he had put the sealed envelope. "I'm opening our orders." Inside the envelope Jet found a folded sheet of paper and a plastic punched card. He scanned the sheet. "Says here we're to park and wait for re-enforcements."

The radio burped static, then cleared to reveal the voice of Lt. Roger "Senior" Shaw, the longest serving member of Eagle Seven. "This is a turd fest, Jet. Some Congressman has his comb up about something, and we're here as a show of force."

"Could be, Senior," John said. "But maybe we should wait and see before we talk trash over an open channel. Little pitchers have big ears."

Senior grumbled something, but the static covered most of it up. He cleared his throat. "Sorry all you kids on Earth listening in with your crystal radios. Go America. Mind your mothers."

Carl laughed. "Senior apologizes to all the roosters in Congress, too."

Jet clicked the mic. "Look sharp, boys. Company's coming." He turned his attention to radar. Six bogies had entered range and were moving toward the Seven.

"What are they, Jet?" Carl said.

"I can't get a good read." He tapped the radar display. "Can you see anything, John?"

Static hissed for long seconds while he waited for the hero's reply. When John spoke, his voice was crisp, his earlier tomfoolery replaced with military precision and calm. "A squad of Reds, boys. Coming in fast."

Jet flicked the switches that activated his weapons systems and barked an order to the others to do the same. *Victory* responded to the new defense condition by tightening Jet's restraints and pulling the control rods a few more inches out of her reactor core. Instruments and dials in front of Jet crept closer to the red zone.

Jet worked his blindspots. "Anyone else have a visual?"

"Got 'em," Senior said. "Seven o'clock high. Six of them."

"Let's come about and get in their faces. On my mark."

Jet held his control stick in one hand and put the other on the attitude-control panel mounted on his armrest. "Mark."

The control thrusters fired on the ship's nose and tail, and Jet wheeled his ship around like a well-trained war horse. The Russian ships swung into view outside his cockpit.

"Do we engage, chief?" Carl said.

"Negative," Jet said. "We keep to the treaty. Sit on your hands until we know what they're up to." It had been two and a half years since an American had fired a shot at a Soviet, and Jet wasn't going to break the streak without a darned good reason.

The Russian ships matched their orbit, flying in precise formation. The drab green of their hulls reflected little sunlight, making them look more like patches on the sky than the high-tech military spacecraft they were.

"MiG 220s," John said. "Good-looking boats."

"They won't be so good looking if they try anything," Senior said. "I have the center one in my sights."

The radio squelched again, and a new voice entered the conversation in heavily accented English. "Good afternoon, Commander Carson. I am Commander Yuri Grishuk of the Soviet Space Forces." He chuckled. "For once you are here ahead of me."

Jet's adrenaline system went into overdrive. Yuri Grishuk was *the* Soviet ace, and there was no way he'd be flying unless he was expecting action. Jet took a deep breath and clicked the mic. "Greetings to the Soviet commander. To what do we owe the pleasure?"

Grishuk's voice was nonchalant. "A simple joy ride, commander. We wished to see if the stars were where we left them."

"They seem to be all here, gentlemen. Feel free to go home and make your report."

The static blended with Grishuk's chuckle. "I regret that I cannot. My orders dictate I remain."

A flashing light on the communications panel caught Jet's eye, and he switched his radio to the secure combat channel. John's voice was dry beneath the transmission's crackle. "What are they up to, Jet?"

"Not a clue." Jet rubbed his jaw. "You get more time with the bigwigs than I do. Have you heard anything?"

"Nothing like this." The radio fell silent for a moment. "This doesn't feel like an attack, though."

Jet squinted out his cockpit window, taking in the formation of the Russian ships. "Roger that. They're stacked too pretty for a dogfight. Pass the word, but tell the boys to stay awake."

"Copy that, Jet."

Jet turned his attention back to the Soviet commander. "How'd you like to tell us more about those orders of yours, commander?"

Grishuk laughed again. "They are much like yours, I suspect, comrade. Orbit and wait."

Jet stayed current on briefings and hadn't heard a thing about problems with the truce. His gut said Grishuk wasn't looking for trouble. "Confirmed. We'll just sit up here together and enjoy the view."

It wasn't a long wait. Within ten minutes a tone sounded, announcing an open-channel message from Earth. It was a powerful signal, a broadcast meant to be picked up nearly anywhere on the planet. It started with Douglas Edwards, anchor of the CBS News.

"It has been my honor to share with you, many times over, news of global importance," Edwards said. "In the last ten years alone we've watched together as mankind reached into space, settled the Moon, and set foot on Mars."

The anchor's voice was its usual practiced baritone, full of gravitas and warmth, but there was an edge to it.

"I come to you this evening, with full cooperation from our colleagues at the National Broadcast Company and the

American Broadcast Company, to the nearly one billion of you with access to my voice, to report we have definitive proof that we are not alone in this universe. But, after today, we might well wish we were."

Jet's jaw dropped. Edwards cut to a live message from President Kennedy. The president didn't mince words, either: Earth was under attack. A fleet from an advanced alien civilization, likely based on the planet Mercury, was on its way. The invaders had already struck the first blow, turning Freeport, Kansas and the Soviet city of Chekalin into glass-lined craters.

"Their intent is clear." The president paused, and the world held its breath. "Our intent must be equally clear. This is our planet. Our home. And we will fight for it with every breath, every beat of our hearts. Good luck to the pilots of the combined forces."

Edwards cut in again and introduced a live address from the Russian premier.

"Looks like JFK won the coin toss," Senior said.

"Looks like. Give me a minute." Jet switched to the command channel. "Carson to Cape. What can you tell me about this?"

The static held for a full thirty seconds. Jet was about to send the signal again when a voice cut in. "Jet, this is Sven." Static hissed. "This is what we know." He cleared his throat. "Correction: this is what we were told in the top-secret briefing we received just after your launch. Intelligence has known about these… Mercurians… for more than a year. Soviet intelligence, too, probably. The CIA has been trading messages with them, trying to get them to come in on our side."

Jet's fists tightened on his ship's controls.

"They've been talking us up, telling them how great Earth is. Practically invited them here. Nine hours ago, the aliens took out two cities and demanded our surrender."

"And we're being sent out, blind, to take on their invasion fleet."

"First contact. You're buying time for us to set up a defense." Static crackled. "Sorry, Jet."

"All part of the job." He switched back to the combat channel and filled the rest of the boys in on the conversation. The Secretary General of the United Nations was taking his turn at the global podium.

"Any word on fleet strength?" Carl said.

"Nothing. It's us and the Russians against who knows what. Speaking of which…" Jet flipped back to the open channel. "Commander Grishuk, this is Carson."

Grishuk's voice was terse. "We thought you had forgotten us, comrade."

"Not likely. You and your second come and join us on…" Jet recited the frequency of the Seven's combat channel. Once the Soviet pilots were in the loop, he briefed them on Sven's message. "You know anything about this?"

Grishuk's curses were in Russian but no less clear for it. "Spies and politicians! They will be the death of us!"

"That seems pretty darn likely," Senior said.

"Likely or not, we need to move, Jet," John said. "If we can't take out the enemy fleet ourselves, we need to buy time for a second-stage defense."

"Roger that. And that means meeting them as far away from here as we can." Jet slid the plastic punched card into *Victory*'s navigation computer, booting it up and programming in the course. The computer calculated the trip. "They're close."

"How close?" Senior said.

"North of Venus and moving fast if these intercept coordinates mean anything." The teletype machine began chattering. Jet tore off the top page and scanned it. "Looks like we're cleared to go, boys. Put your cards in and strap yourself down. Time to earn our paychecks."

"Let's just hope we don't have to cash them post-humously," Senior said.

"Yuri, your boys ready over there?" Jet said.

"Da, Jet. We are ready and awaiting your mark," Grishuk said. "We will set a little light burning when we get there so you can find your way."

"Alright, men, I don't need to tell you how important this is." He paused, waiting for Senior to cut in with some smart-aleck remark, but the veteran pilot stayed quiet. Jet's lips felt dry. He licked them. "Eat. Grab a nap. We need to be on our toes when we get to the other end of this. Carson out."

Jet craned his neck to see the glowing curve of Earth behind him. Ahead, the Russians were rotating their ships. Jet blew a kiss toward the planet. "Love you, Betty. See you soon." He clicked the mic. "This is Carson." He took a breath. "Light 'em up, boys. Mark."

The power of the atomic engine sent *Victory* hurtling out of orbit and beyond. Jet coded an "in-case-of" letter to Betty and sent it to Earth, care of Sven. Then he studied the mission files, rousing himself a few hours later when the ship emerged from hyperflight.

Victory came to a full stop at the rendezvous coordinates. Jet sent out a single radar pulse and counted the ships sliding out of the darkness around him. "Lucky thirteen." Every member of the Seven and all six Soviets had ended up in the right place at the right time. He opened the secure combat channel and dialed the power down to a quarter usual. "Looks like we made it. Yuri, how's your party?"

"Everyone is in attendance, comrade."

"Paint the Russkies as friendlies, guys. I expect they'll do the same." He paused. "No matter what's happening on Earth, we're all on the same side up here. We don't get this done, they'll be landing in Times Square in a couple of days. Red Square, too." Jet waited a full thirty seconds for questions that didn't come. "The Joint Chiefs have put me in overall command of the mission, with Commander Grishuk as my second. Sorry, Carl."

"What's the plan?" Carl said.

"We're going in hot. Four gees of forward thrust until contact. Watch your wingman. John, you're playing shortstop on this one. Hang back a ways and keep an eye on the action. Come in if you need to fill a hole. Otherwise, keep an eye on the big picture."

"Roger, Jet."

Senior's gravelly voice was tense. "What are we up against?"

"An unknown number of enemy ships with unknown capabilities. Intelligence says they probably need to breathe, so feel free to punch some holes in their hulls. Target cockpits, engines, weapons. The usual tactics. The Soviet ships are faster over the quarter. They'll go in first to see what cards the aliens are holding. We'll watch their backs."

"We will leave some of them for you to shoot," Grishuk said.

"I heard you Reds were big on sharing," Senior said. "Just like we're big on bailing people out after you get them in trouble."

"Keep it civil," John snapped. "We're all on the same side today."

Senior grumbled and moved his ship into position, covering Jet's five. The American ships were fitted with front-mounted projectile weapons, which could swing to cover a 120-degree arc ahead of the cockpit. Most pilots kept the guns locked, preferring to aim with the fighter's nose.

Jet triggered the mic. "Make sure your seatbelts are tight, men. Yuri's guys are going in at ten minutes; we're following at thirteen." *Lucky number thirteen again.*

The clock counted the minutes toward engine firing. At five minutes, Jet double-checked that the Seven's flight clocks were still synced. At ten, the Soviets lit their engines and blasted toward the invasion fleet. The next countdown started.

Jet put his thumb over the ignition button at ten seconds. The clock hit zero. "Here we go, boys! Look sharp!"

The acceleration pressed him into the couch, the only way to get a feel for speed in deep space. The stars weren't rushing by, the wind wasn't gusting. He was traveling at speeds unimaginable a decade ago, and he might as well be sitting in the training centrifuge back at base. Jet pushed the thoughts away and focused on his instruments. If the engagement ahead went as predicted, he'd be feeling something soon enough. "Light the scopes, boys. Long-range radar, half power. Let's not tip them off until we have to."

"Assuming they haven't seen us already," Carl cut in, his voice tight. "We've no idea what kind of tech they're packing."

"If they were all that far ahead of us, they could have taken Earth a long time ago. I doubt they know much more about us than we do about them."

"What the heck does the planet Mercury want with…?" Carl started.

Static flared and Grishuk's clipped voice cut in. "Grishuk here. We have them on our scopes, a hundred kilometers ahead. We see one large ship, more than a dozen smaller vessels. Escorts, we think."

"We read you, commander. One mother, lots of angry babies. What's your plan?"

Jet heard the smile in Grishuk's voice. "I plan to knock on Mama's door and ask to borrow a cup of sugar. I will let you know their answer."

"I'm starting to like you, Yuri. Try not to get shot."

Jet coded a message to Mission Control and advised them to stay tuned for further details. Those details came in seconds.

"Our visitors are indeed hostile," Grishuk reported. "They began firing before our weapons could reach them." Static flared, and the Soviet cursed inside it. "I've lost one ship already. Repeat: we're taking casualties."

"Received, commander. We're on our way." Jet's jaw tightened. "Alright, boys. Let's put the pedal down. Emergency boost to six-point-seven-five gee until we are in range. Radar at full."

Jet tried not to dwell on the Soviet ships – and the men inside them – fighting for their lives in the darkness ahead. The acceleration pushed him deeper into his seat, and there was movement on his long-range scope.

"This is going to get ugly fast," Jet said. "Carl, take your group and make it hot for the big one. Maybe you can draw some of those escorts away from the Soviets. One Flight, we're going straight in to assist. Weapons free, everyone, but keep an eye on your ammo."

"Confirmed," Carl said.

"ETA thirty seconds. John, hold back and keep your eyes on the forest for me."

"Roger, Jet. Don't forget to duck."

The big engines ate up the miles, and Jet felt the reverse thrust slow his ship to attack speed. High acceleration was for straight-line travel. Human physiology couldn't handle maneuvers at that speed, nor could their reflexes keep up.

"I see 'em, Jet," Senior reported. "How big is that thing?"

"Looks like…" Carl paused. "Little under nine hundred feet long. About the size of an Iowa-class battleship."

Carl's flight group shot past to engage the mothership, even as Jet's own One Flight targeted the escorts. Even though they came from a different planet, the enemy ships seemed to follow similar engineering plans: engines at one end, what looked like cockpits halfway along the gray barrel of their bodies. Near the engines, about ten feet of the underside of the alien hulls glowed like blue fire.

"Yuri, what's your assessment of their capabilities?"

The smile was gone from the Soviet ace's voice. "Less maneuverability. Less speed. More powerful weapons. Longer range. Well armored. We have hit them many times, but we are not hurting them."

"Roger that. One Flight, attack Plan Jitterbug. Strike and move. Keep them interested until we can figure out how to take them down." Jet's smile was grim. "But make them keep their big mitts off you. Our ladies only dance with nice boys."

Jet sent his ship into a barrel roll that put one of the escort ships in the center of his sights. He tapped the trigger, firing a burst of steel-jacketed projectiles. Recovery from the roll carried him past the enemy ship, and he whipped *Victory*'s nose around for a coup de grace. The enemy ship loomed in his cockpit window, firing even as Jet side-slipped to avoid whatever the aliens used as projectiles. The big gray ship zoomed by close enough to set off *Victory*'s proximity alarm.

Jet thumbed his mic. "You weren't kidding about them being tough, Yuri. I just hit one in the cockpit dead center, and it turned around and tried to bite me."

"Da. We've already tried all the usual targets. Many unusual ones, too."

"Tell your pilots to fall back to support for awhile. Let's see what we can do."

"Agreed."

Jet didn't wait to watch the Soviets pull back. He put *Victory* into a tight bank that took her to the edge of the dogfight and spun her around. He faced front just in time to dodge another attack by the ungainly escorts.

"They're persistent, *Vicky* girl. I'll give them that much." Jet fired his weapons again, and the projectiles bounced off his opponent's cockpit. "What the hell are these things made of?"

John's voice barked into Jet's earphones. "Jet, we just lost Carl."

Jet's chest cramped. "Any chance he ejected?"

"Negative," John said. "It happened too fast."

Jet put his ship into a climbing corkscrew to create distance between himself and his dogged attacker. "Give me something, John, What do you see?"

"I see them taking us out any time they tag us good," John said, "and us tagging them plenty but not doing any damage."

"Roger that." Jet opened a private channel to Grishuk. "Yuri, we're shooting blanks here. Got any ideas?"

The beginning of Yuri's response was lost to static. "– lost two more ships. Running low on ammo." Static flared again. "Suggest... withdraw and regroup."

Jet whipped his ship around as he considered the possibility. A strategic retreat would made sense on the ground, but in space there were few places to withdraw to. They couldn't even get more ammo without going back to Earth or the Moon. Jet put *Victory* into another dodging roll. "Withdrawing is not an option. We take them now, or they hit Earth right in the middle of *Gunsmoke*." There wasn't a mark on his alien antagonist, but he'd hit the thing at least three times. "What's that blue glow?"

"Readings say it's some kind of magnetic containment system," John said. "Maybe fuel. Maybe ammo."

"Magnetic." Jet summoned up old memories of college physics lectures about the natural forces. "Think we could weaken it if we heat it up?"

"You going to try to spacewalk with a pack of matches? Tech is working on plasma weapons, but they're barely off the drawing board."

"Comrades," Yuri broke in. "Not only our plasma

weapons off the drawing board, they are on our ships. New and very secret."

"What's the range?"

"Extremely short. Which is why we have not tried them against the invaders."

Jet rolled his ship again. "We can't do this all day. We'll triple-team him. I'll keep this one busy while Yuri makes a run on him with plasma. John, you come in here and throw some lead once things heat up a little."

"Roger that, Jet. I'll be in range in about forty seconds."

The invaders' ships weren't nearly as maneuverable, and the pilot Jet had been playing tag with wasn't any great shakes at the stick. Yuri came up under the alien fighter and unleashed a fiery plasma attack. The blue glow faded. Jet grinned. "Hit that son of a gun, John!"

The invader's ship went off like a firecracker, sending shrapnel and, Jet hoped, a surprised pilot into space. Jet howled in triumph. He thumbed his comm back to the combat channel. "Boys, we got one of them. The Russians have plasma weapons. Use them on that blue glow on the underside of their ships. When the glow fades, shoot the hell out of it. Attack in teams of three. One to distract, one with plasma, the other with projectiles." He let his speakers fill with battle howls and declarations of victory, then clicked his comm again. "Light 'em up, boys, and let them drift. If it doesn't kill them outright, maybe they'll run out of whatever they need to breathe."

Jet watched his scopes and listened to the chatter as the Soviets and Americans formed teams. He took a deep breath and let it out slow. He patted the arm of his flight seat. "We might make it home after all, girl."

In minutes, one of the red dots on his scope, marking unfriendly targets, disappeared. Then a few more vanished.

"It's working, Jet!" John announced. "We're whittling them down."

Jet and Senior paired off with Vladimir Krasnoff, another Russian ace. The Soviet flew in near silence, exhibiting an unearthly control and accuracy in his piloting. Working in tandem they took out four of the enemy ships in quick succession.

"When we get back to Earth, I'm buying the vodka, Vlad."

Jet heard a tight smile in the Russian's voice. "If you think you can afford my brand, commander."

There were no immediate targets on the scope, so Jet let himself relax for a moment and tried to get a look at the big picture. With John in the fray, he no longer had eyes in the sky to give him an overview. The scope showed far fewer unfriendlies then it had minutes before, but there also were fewer green dots marking the Soviet and American forces. He sent Senior in to fill a hole in another team. "We're still not winning this." He clicked his comm. "Vlad, let's fly in close to that mothership. See what she's up to."

Krasnoff acknowledged the order with two clicks of his comm and swung his ship into position to the right of and slightly behind *Victory*. Jet plotted a long, looping course that would take them on the edge of the battle and the rear of the mothership.

The alien craft was huge, far bigger than anything humanity had ever put into space.

Jet's comm crackled. "Most likely built in orbit," Krasnoff said, speaking precisely through his heavy accent. "Observe the superstructure. It would never survive a lift off from the surface."

There was a large opening in the side of the big vessel, just forward of the engines. Jet squinted at it, then clicked his comm. "That look like a hangar to you? Two o'clock low."

The shrug was in Krasnoff's voice. "Difficult to be sure from here."

The opening came clearly into view and abruptly the two Earth ships were under heavy fire from guns mounted around it. Jet put his ship into a corkscrew dive toward the opening. "Whatever it is, they don't want us near it. So, that's where I'm going."

Jet didn't wait to see if the Russian ace followed. This far away from command, it was every man for himself. He'd just have to hope the quiet Soviet was as interested in saving Earth as he was.

Half the telltales on *Victory*'s control panel went red. She was taking fire, absorbing hits along every surface. Jet gritted his teeth and gripped the control stick harder. "Sorry, girl," he said. "Wouldn't do it if I didn't have to."

A violent push threatened to send *Victory* spinning into the side of the mothership, and the other half of the telltales went red. Jet fought for control even as he triggered the switch that freed him from his ship's failing life-support system and left him reliant on whatever air and heat he could eke out of his flight suit. *Working on it, Betty. Working on it.*

Victory entered the hangar at an angle, scraping her port-side wing on the floor as she slid in out of control and throwing sparks. Jet could only hang on until she came to rest against an enemy fighter parked in the hangar. He shook his head to clear some of the fuzz and triggered his comm unit, mildly surprised that it still worked. "Yuri, this is Carson." He peered out his cockpit window for some sign of what to do next. "I'm inside the mothership. My boat's in rough shape. I'm going to see what kind of damage I can do from in here." He took a breath. "It's your mission now. See what you can do about getting everyone home."

The silence hissed, giving no indication that the signal had gotten through. Then Yuri's voice cut in. "Orders received, comrade. Good luck in there."

Jet twisted out of his safety harness and crawled down

the tunnel to the hatch. He patted a rung of the ladder. "Sorry, girl. Thanks for getting me down."

The hatch opened smoothly. Jet pulled his sidearm and exited into the alien hanger.

The only thing moving outside was Krasnoff, who had followed him in. The Russian was older than Jet had imagined, smaller, but a pleasure to see.

"I expect the defenses must be automatic," Krasnoff said. "Some kind of electric eye."

"Otherwise we'd be up to our ears in aliens." He nodded toward the Russian's ship. "She flyable?"

Krasnoff made a seesaw motion with his hand.

"How's your air?"

"Adequate. From what I know of American technology, we will run out at approximately the same time."

"There's gravity here." Jet poked his thumb toward the back of the mothership. "The engine room is probably that way. Let's find something that looks important and break it."

The two Earth men walked directly away from the gaping hangar doors. Neither Jet nor Krasnoff had to duck to get through the far smaller egress on the other side of the room, and both stood easily in the stark corridor outside. They headed down the corridor, boot heels thudding on the dull metal floor, toward what they hoped would be the engine room.

"There's some kind of atmosphere in here," Jet said.

"Do not get comfortable and remove your helmet." Krasnoff arched an eyebrow. "For all we know they breathe argon."

The two men walked on, making progress without firing a shot.

"I don't get it," Jet said. "Where is everyone?"

"Maybe they're all in the fighters." The Russian hummed. "Perhaps there is no one in the fighters, either."

"Robots?"

Krasnoff hummed again.

"Your side got them?"

"I have heard the Japanese do."

The engine room was empty, too. At the center of the large space was a column of energy, as big around as a redwood trunk, kept in check by a glowing blue field.

"More magnetism." Jet drew his pistol and pointed it toward the pulsing column. "What do you bet this won't put a scratch on that thing?"

"I have a plasma weapon built into my suit. Go. I will take care of this."

"No. There has to be a better way."

A wall panel beside the two men dissolved into gray static and cleared to show what appeared to be an egg made of gleaming metal. Jet winced as feedback squealed in his headphones. Out of the corner of his eye, he saw Krasnoff raise his hands to the sides of his helmet. The feedback dropped to a low hum and was replaced with a croaking, metallic voice. "Earth men, you may destroy this ship, but you will not stop us. Earth will belong to the Mercurians."

Jet recovered from his shock first. "What do you...?"

"Your resistance is useless," the egg said. "You are weak and divided. We will triumph easily!"

Jet craned his neck to look at Krasnoff. "He sounds like Ming the Merciless. What the hell is going on..."

"You have won yourself a small amount of time today," the egg shouted. "Use it to make peace with your gods!"

The voice fell silent, and the panel became inert.

"That tears it. I'll get word to Yuri and John. Tell them what's coming. You..." Jet gestured at the pillar of energy. "I'm sorry it has to go this way."

"This cannot end in a draw. I will give you five minutes before I fire."

Jet saluted the Russian and jogged back down the

corridor toward the hangar bay. Provided he didn't have to maneuver much, *Victory* could probably get him off the mothership and back to his men before he ran out of air.

Four minutes.

Three. Just another countdown. Nothing to worry about. He flipped switches to bypass damaged systems.

Two. Jet skipped the safety checks.

One. He got the ship off the deck and pointed toward the hangar opening.

Love you, Betty.

Zero.

PART TWO
Bad Blood

October 12, 1975

ONE

"Tellin' you, that ain't how it happened," Brooklyn said.

There was a yellowing *Playboy* centerfold pinned up behind the bar. Karla Conway. Brooklyn remembered the name – he'd swiped a copy of the magazine from a drugstore and kept it under his mattress for years – but the whole world remembered the pose. Dark eyes, dark hair, stretched out on a red-and-white-striped lounge, star-spangled seatbelt holding her in place, the big window behind her showing what the good old US of A looked like from the Eisenhower Space Station twenty thousand miles up. April 1966's Playmate of the Month. First naked lady in space. Some said the pictures were faked. Others claimed Rocky Shepherd, the first man to orbit Jupiter, was floating just off camera wearing nothing but a crew cut and a grin.

"We just saw the movie, Brook. It's a true story."

Brooklyn pulled his eyes off the pinup and focused them on his buddy Chris, who was riding the next barstool. Chris was growing his hair out like Rod Stewart's, but mostly it made him look like a Chatty Cathie doll with bad skin. Chris pushed his greasy bangs back with one hand like he was reading Brooklyn's mind.

"Ain't nobody on Mercury," Brooklyn said. "Know a guy says so."

"Guy's a moron, then," Chris said. "We've seen them. Cleveland's still smoking."

Brooklyn jabbed a finger at Chris "You seen them? You ever, in your life, seen someone from Mercury?"

"I seen–"

"Pictures. Drawings. Same shit we all seen." Brooklyn swallowed some beer and propped his elbows on the bar. "Duke says it's all made up. Says Nixon blew up Cleveland so he'd get re-elected."

"Bullshit. No way Duke Carlotta says that."

"Takes way more than a day to get to Mercury, dumb ass. No such thing as 'hyperflight'."

"They changed that part for the film ta speed things up. No one wants to see the dude who played Carson – whatshisname, John Savage – sleeping and going to the john for two weeks."

"Carl White ain't even a real guy!"

"They put him in the picture to make the NAACP happy," Chris said. "Saw it on *Merv Griffin* or something."

"Alright then, think about it." Brooklyn dredged up the details of *Mercury Rising*, the heavily promoted space opera they'd seen that afternoon. "Remember how the big heroes saved the day?"

"Americans went in close and softened them up with plasma blasters, the Russkies stayed back and blew holes in their fuel tanks. Then Jet Carson went in and blew the hell out of the mothership."

"Sure. Now, think about it. Mercury's right up close to the sun." Brooklyn ticked the planets off on his fingers. "Mercury, Venus, Earth, Mars, and then the other ones."

Chris nodded.

"So, it's hot there. Hotter than anything. How'd those little plasma things mess up their ships?"

Chris started to say something but let his mouth hang open instead.

"Another thing: magnets don't glow. Duke says the

government made the whole invasion up ta get Eisenhower his base on the Moon."

"Duke's crookeder than Nixon and Jake Molinas combined."

"Don't mean he's wrong. Gets people like you and me out of their hair, too. Sign us up, send us somewhere ta fight the alien menace that ain't really there, and forget about us."

"Maybe they make their ships somewhere else. Somewhere cooler."

"Where else? The Moon? Think maybe the Admiral mighta noticed something like that going on in his backyard?" Brooklyn rubbed the side of his head. "No. It's one of those – what do you call it – government conspiracies."

Chris drank some beer. "You been spending a lot of time with Duke Carlotta, Brook. Ain't healthy."

"Work for him. Why I don't make your mother pay for my company. He pays me, and I do her for free."

"Fuck you." Chris said. "You know she's probably in her thirties now. Maybe popped out a few kids."

"Who?"

Chris pointed at the pinup behind the bar. "Remember you had that one. She's probably fat now. Making apple pies for some Guido in Jersey."

"She was from…" Brooklyn squinted, forcing the memory. He'd read the interview printed with the picture a hundred times. "California somewheres. She ain't fat. Saw her inna stag film couple of years ago." Her eyes. That wide, knowing smile. The picture that launched six million erections and made space sexy. Karla Conway didn't owe anyone a goddamned thing, and if she ever needed someone to remind her of that he'd be happy to–

"You was crazy 'bout that space shit when we was kids, 'fore your old man died," Chris said. "You still think about going up there?"

Brooklyn centered his glass on the cheap coaster, a challenge considering the number of beers already sloshing in his gut. "Say it again."

Chris inspected the last inch of alcohol in his glass. "Joining up. Going to fight."

Brooklyn closed one eye to compensate for his doubled-vision. "I ever thought about joining the fucking United Nation's Extra-Orbital Fucking Forces and getting my ass thrown into orbit?" He shook his head. "You serious right now? Just heard me say it's all bullshit."

"David is. He's reporting next week."

Brooklyn rocked – the ground seeming to shift under his feet – but he pulled one hand from the bar to pick up his glass again. "Didn't know that." The glass was empty, and he set it back down. "Well, that's David, and I ain't him."

"I'm thinking about doing it." Chris swung around on his barstool, his knees brushing Brooklyn's legs. "I got nothing else, Brook. I got no job. I live with my ma. Anytime I want ta get laid I gotta find someone wants to do it in my car."

"You're not gonna do it. Know how I know that?"

Chris shrugged with one shoulder.

"Known you nineteen years, man. You're a good guy, but you been a pussy in all of them."

"Fuck you, Brook!"

The jukebox dropped the needle on "Dead Flowers" by the Rolling Stones. The song had been great the first fifty-five times Brooklyn'd heard it, but now it was four years past its day on *Hit Parade*. He caught the bartender's eye. "Mikey, you don't get some new music for that thing, I'm finding somewhere better to drink."

"Sure, sure," Mike said. "Good luck finding someplace that will let you in with those sideburns."

Brooklyn smoothed his sideburns with his free hand, one side at a time. His father screamed at him from the grave to get a haircut. "It's the style," he said. "Ma likes them OK."

"Your mother thinks the sun rises in your mouth and sets in your ass. It's no wonder you two don't have no jobs."

"Mind your business," Chris said. "Get me a beer."

"Which your mother is paying for." Mike pulled Chris's drink, leaving a four-inch inch head at the top of the glass. Foam slopped over the side as he set it on the bar.

Chris grimaced. "Put some beer in there next time."

"Pay for it yourself, you'd be amazed at what I do." Mike took the towel off his shoulder and tossed it on the scarred counter-top. "I gotta lie down a minute. Headache. Watch the bar."

Tuesdays weren't big nights at Mike's, and Brooklyn and Chris were the only ones in the place. Mike squeezed through the narrow door into the back room.

Chris took a sip of his foamy beer. "So, what do really think?"

Brooklyn ran his fingers over one of the many imperfections in the bar's glossy surface. He didn't have to see them to know what the scars spelled out. He'd put them there years ago with a bent fork and spent the next day sanding the scratches down and covering them with marine urethane. He'd done a piss-poor job, and the crude letters floated like ghosts just under the skin: B & C Forever. *Not hardly.* "You ain't cut out to be a spaceman. Hell, you used to get sick on the kiddie rides at Coney." Brooklyn rubbed his mouth. "Never could get you on the Cyclone."

"Least I'd get out of this shit hole."

Brooklyn waved him off. There was time when he'd thought of nothing but getting into space. He'd begged his mother to buy Wheaties so he could collect all the pictures of the astronauts and made models of American spacecraft. He even rigged a crystal-radio set so he could listen to broadcasts from orbit while his parents thought he was sleeping. He picked up Chris's glass. "Appears Mike might be awhile. Want another?"

Mike surfaced in time to close the bar at two. "Why didn't you get me up?" He blinked at the flickering neon Schlitz clock on the wall.

"You looked tired, Mikey." Chris zipped his heavy leather jacket and wrapped a scarf around his neck. "You were sleeping like a baby."

"An angel." Brooklyn got up off the stool and nearly fell, catching his elbow hard on the bar. "An angel baby." He was slurring and scrubbed at his lips with the back of his hand. "Teeth are numb."

"You OK getting home?" Chris said.

"Got money for a cab." Brooklyn swayed as he pulled on his coat. "It still cold out?"

"'Course it is," Mike said, "and let me tell you, I'm gettin' real tired of it."

The day after Cleveland died, its ashes started falling on New York City. The schools closed, but none of the kids went out on the street to play. Europe got its first dose about a week later as the debris slipped into the upper atmosphere and smeared the sky. A lot of it was still up there, going 'round and 'round, refusing to disperse due to chemistry or the stubbornness of the Forest City's ghosts. Whatever the reason, it was still fucking up the weather pretty good.

Chris lived a block away from the bar and the two men parted ranks at the door. Brooklyn weaved toward a taxi stand where a ratty fleet of robocabs – the folly of Mayor Marchi – waited for tourists who would never come so far into Queens unless it was by accident. He felt in his jacket pocket for the flat plastic cartridge that held his ticket home: directions and a prepaid fare written on magnetic tape. It wasn't there.

"Fuck." He stopped and stared stupidly at the cabs parked cold and empty ahead. Brooklyn backtracked to the bar and spent several minutes banging at the front door before admitting Mike must have headed upstairs to sleep. He checked his pockets again and found enough change for the subway. Five stops would put him close enough to his apartment to walk.

The closest station was twelve cold blocks west, and Brooklyn stumbled along on rubbery legs. The wind surged down the narrow street like a ghost train. He leaned into it, occasionally brushing the rough brick of a storefront with his right shoulder. Behind him, footprints wove through the thin snow cover, back and forth with his thoughts. Tricky Dick and the Cleveland Crater. Mick Jagger's pouting lips. David hadn't told him about his plans to enlist.

Mind your ma, or I'll tie you outside with a sign offering you to the Mercurians. It had been his father's favorite threat in the waning days of the early '60s, usually offered in a mock growl that had both terrified and thrilled his son. Brooklyn had been a good kid at ten and eleven, even at twelve, and it hadn't taken much more than threats to keep him in line. After his father died, two days before Brooklyn's birthday, things had changed. He'd made himself change, forced himself to grow up in spite of Ma's efforts to keep him a little boy.

Some wag had painted a Nixon nose – or a dick, it was hard to tell – on the "See Something Strange? Report It!" billboard at the end of the street. The menacing multi-eyed, multi-armed, now Nixon/dick-nosed alien on the sign had been there nearly as long as Brooklyn could remember. He rested his forehead against a shop window. Way too much to drink. The icy pane tightened his scalp and slowed his thoughts. Another half block, and the blue lamp marking the entrance to the subway came into view.

Warm, moist air blew up the entrance stairs, making the inside of Brooklyn's nose itch and his face burn. The heat came in waves, steady exhalations of fetid air. The fluorescent lights overhead buzzed as he descended. He stood on the platform and blinked in the unnatural mix of light and shadow, warmth and wet. It smelled like rats.

"Gimme a dollar."

Brooklyn peered fish-eyed around the dingy platform until he found the owner of the voice. The man – or woman, he couldn't tell – stuck one scabby hand outside a gray mass of blankets and old coats.

"C'mon," the thing said. "Pretty boy like you gotta have a dollar."

Brooklyn's stomach hitched, and he tasted bile and cheap beer. He shook his head. "Don't got any money."

"Give me a quarter, then." The bum stretched to tug at Brooklyn's pants leg. "You gotta have one. Pretty boy like you. Look at them boots."

The brown ankle boots were still new enough to shine in spite of the station's dimness. They'd set Brooklyn back $75, nearly half what he made in a week working for Duke Carlotta. The subway station seemed to spin slowly under Brooklyn's feet. He blinked owlishly as the thing's grimy fingers plucked at the long seam running down the outside of his leg. His stomach cramped, and he thought he might be about to puke all over the bum and his own new boots. He had a strange urge to lie down on the station floor to stop the spin, and curl up next to the thing. At least it would be warm.

"Give me $5," the thing said. "Suck your cock for five dollars."

Brooklyn swayed and reached a hand out to brace himself against the wall. He fought to focus his eyes on the thing's face. Man or woman? Did it matter? His vision filled with the thing's mouth, chapped lips opening and closing ahead of the yellow stubs of rotting teeth. The mouth smacked in a vile parody of an infant suckling. Was it even human? Brooklyn had played a lot of aliens & astronauts when he was a kid; everyone had. Off the aliens or they'd kill your mom and stick tentacles up your ass. They'd hold you down and fuck you to death, man, woman, and child. *Tentacles like cold sea jelly…*

The thing started scrabbling at the fly of Brooklyn's jeans. "Only take a sec–"

"The fuck off me!" Brooklyn said, taking a step back. His head was as brittle as glass, the beer fugue turned toxic by a change in the wind. "The fuck you doin' touching me like that? You want I should kick your raggedy ass up and down this platform?"

A second hand extended from the blankets. The thing raised them both, palms out. "Don't want no trouble, big guy."

"Show you some fucking trouble touch me again. Know who you're fucking with?"

Brooklyn reached into his back pocket and pulled out the plastic-handled switchblade Duke had given him on his first job. It was a cheap thing, but the blade was sharp. It caught the dim light of the station lamps as the spring flicked it out like a tongue. Brooklyn held the knife at waist level, like he'd seen the hoods in the movies do. "Touch me again I'll cut your fucking ears off!"

The thing's hands disappeared into its gray mass. "I won't touch you again! I won't touch you!" Its voice was higher now, more a screech than the gray rasp it had started as.

Brooklyn liked the way it sounded and took a step forward. "I should f–"

The shadows darkened and ran left as the train pulled in, its automatic pilot braking and opening the doors as it came to a stop. The waiting car was empty, and he had only moments before the train pulled away again. He flicked the knife closed. "Got some luck, buddy. Don't waste it."

He ran to the train.

TWO

The pounding was either coming from his head or the front door. Not for the first time he wished he had a laser blaster like Dirty Harry Callahan. Aim it at the source of the problem, pull the trigger, and, with a flash of light, no more problem. *Do you feel lucky, punk? Well, do ya?*

The pounding jimmied his eyes open, and the light leaking around the window shade was a spear through the head. There was a voice behind the din. He recognized it.

"Coming!" The shout sent another shock of pain into Brooklyn's skull, and he lurched to his feet, staggering toward the ruckus, dressed in his underwear. "Coming, goddamn it! You wanna wake up the whole fucking neighborhood?"

Brooklyn's bare foot crashed into the side of a cardboard box filled with car-audio equipment, and he hopped the rest of the way to the door. He slid the flimsy chainlock open and turned the knob. The door swung in, admitting the clammy world of the hallway.

The man there froze with his fist raised for the next assault. "Chris said he told you."

Brooklyn limped toward the kitchenette in the corner of his apartment. "Said you signed up to fuck around on the Moon, if that's what you're sayin'." He pulled open the refrigerator. "Beer?"

"Sure."

"Get it yourself."

Brooklyn fell into his battered armchair and peeled back the pull tab on the cold Schlitz. He dropped the tab into the beer and took a long drink. He held the can against his forehead.

"You're going to swallow one of those tabs someday." David closed the door behind him and stepped into the kitchenette to grab a beer. He pulled the shade up on the tiny window over the sink.

"Really gonna do it?"

David sat on the edge of the Murphy bed. "Ma's got a lot trouble right now. The sign-up bonus will be a big help."

"Won't help if some alien lights your ass on fire or you toss yourself out an airlock."

David grinned. "If this city ain't killed me, what can outer space do?"

"When?"

"Next week. Monday." David held up his hand. "I didn't want to get an earful from you. Afraid you'd be such a dick about it I'd have to slug you before I left."

"Still time." Brooklyn took another taste of the beer. The pull tab tinged around inside the can. "What about college?"

"It will be here when I get back. I signed up for a half term. I do five years, and the government will pay for most of it."

"And you'll be twenty-eight. Old man with weak bones. What's Maria say?"

"She yelled. Broke some dishes." David turned the beer can in his hands. "She says she'll wait. Five years, my body'll recover from that."

The Space Age was twenty-five years old, but the eggheads still hadn't figured out a way to keep low gravity from fucking over the Extra-Orbital Forces recruits. Wasn't so bad on a ship or a space station – most of them could be spun up to fake gravity – but ten years on the Moon or Mars might mean spending the next fifty in a wheelchair and body braces.

Brooklyn grunted. "Keep an eye on Maria for you."

"She can take care of herself. I'm more worried about you." David nodded toward a stack of boxes in the corner. "Selling encyclopedias?"

"Cigarettes. Guy I know gets them cheap."

"And hot stereos." David grimaced. "Heard you were working for Duke. Good way to find yourself in jail."

"Just small shit. Keeps the bills paid. Ma's, too."

"You could get a job."

Brooklyn crushed his empty beer can and tossed it toward a wastebasket already overflowing with dead soldiers. "There's a recession on." He sneered. "Or ain't you heard about that, Moon boy?"

"A month ago you were calling me 'college boy'. Can't come up with anything more original?"

"Give me a couple days." Brooklyn got up and shuffled toward the kitchenette. "Another?"

"Sure." David drained his beer and set the empty on the floor near the bed. "I'm serious about Duke, though. He's bad news. If your ma knew you were work–"

"She don't." Brooklyn sat back down and popped his second beer. "And she won't. Got enough on her plate." He took a long sip. "Where're we doing the goodbye party?"

"Where else? OK I put you in charge of the guest list?"

"Who else?"

THREE

Ralphy ViVenzio was trying to turn his bar into a night club, and it wasn't working so good. The velvet curtains hung up to create a VIP lounge in the back didn't do shit to hide the holes the after-work roughnecks had punched in the walls, and the single light-kit mounted in the middle of the ceiling didn't put a dent in the twenty-plus years of cheap cigarette smoke in the air. Ralphy had got himself a gold chain and some red bell bottoms and was making the rounds of the tables, playing host. Brooklyn squinted. The son of a bitch had even shelled out for a toupee.

Brooklyn scratched at the lipstick smear on the rim of his glass. No matter how much Ralphy dressed up *ViVenzio's* it would always be the same old pit.

"Beer tastes like piss," he said.

The bartender shrugged. "Tell you what. I'll piss in a glass, and you can try them out side by side."

"If I can't, I get my dollar back?"

The bartender pointed to a sign that showed a hand-drawn cartoon of a gnome flipping the bird under the words, "Complaints department".

Brooklyn saluted the bartender with the watered-down beer. "Classy."

The bartender sketched a mock bow.

Brooklyn sat the glass on the bar, ignoring the Narragansett coaster the bartender had tossed down. "That's The Way I Like It" by KC & the Sunshine Band was playing through the big dance-floor speakers. One of them was buzzing like a jigsaw, blown. Ralphy put a little disco swing in his step as he walked between tables, looking more like a farmer crossing a field of pig shit than the gigolo he dressed as. *ViVenzio's* would have gone out of business years ago had Ralphy not made it an open secret that he'd sell booze to underage kids and trade his detergent-cut coke for blow jobs.

Brooklyn felt someone sit on the stool next to him. "Hey, Brook," she said.

"Got my message?"

Carmen shook her head. "I don't think I can make it."

"C'mon," he said. "For old times? His last night on Earth?"

She gave Brooklyn the look, the one that said she still found him funny but no longer amusing. He spread his hands. "Look, no pressure. We were all tight once. Be nice to see you there."

"Did David say that?"

"Why I'm here."

"No funny business or guilt trips."

He raised his right hand, three fingers sticking straight up. "No funny shit. Scout's honor."

"The Scouts kicked you out."

"Nah, I quit."

"Right after you set fire to those guys' tent."

"Deserved it."

"They did." Carmen sighed. "Alright. Eight?" She put her hands on the edge of the bar.

"Yeah." Brooklyn looked around the room for a conversation topic that would keep Carmen around a little longer, but he had to reach outside it. "How's Stevie?" Steven was Carmen's little brother, and she'd thrown him a coming-out party two years before, on the fifteen-year anniversary of the day the Shrinks of America Club or whatever took being gay off their naughty list. At the party, Brooklyn had promised to take the kid out drinking when he turned eighteen. "He's gotta be close to–"

She pushed away from the bar. "I need to get back to work. They don't like it when I talk to friends while I'm on the clock."

"Friends, huh?"

She didn't answer, and Brooklyn didn't speak again. He watched her miniskirt travel back to her duty station.

"Pretty girl."

Brooklyn turned to see who had spoken and nodded a greeting. "Looked better."

"Ain't we all, pal. Ain't we all." The guy's real name was Peter, but Brooklyn had never heard him called anything but "Prick". He was a first-class scumbag, but he and Brooklyn ate from the same trough. His cold eyes didn't go well with Ralphy's new decor. "Glad I spotted you. Saved myself a dime."

"Whatcha need?"

"A beer. Then to see if you want to make some money."

"Delivery?"

Prick signaled the bartender. "Debt collection. You got a gun?"

"Not on me."

"Probably won't need it."

"'Probably' is a word for assholes."

Prick glanced around. "Lot of them in here. Wonder if they want to shut the fuck up and make some money."

"What're we doing?" Brooklyn said.

The man held up his beer and peered at the light kit through it. He nodded to the bartender. "Looks like it's all beer. Nice work." He took a sip and wiped foam off his lip. "Guy owes Duke some money. We're going to collect it."

"That it?"

"'Course it is."

* * *

The combination of fear sweat and polyester was like crotch rot in high summer, but the banana-colored leisure suit the guy – Galvano was his name – had on contrasted nicely with the black-and-white striped couch Prick shoved him onto.

"I told Duke I'd get the money," Galvano wailed. "I just need a little time."

"You hear that, Brook?" Prick grabbed a handful of the man's shirtfront, pulling tiny links of gold chain deep into marshmallow flesh. "He needs some time."

Brooklyn frowned. Prick knew better than to use real names on the job. He was either on something a lot stronger than beer or just didn't give a fuck what the man knew.

Prick slapped the sweating man hard across the face. "We'll give you a real good time, buddy." Galvano's nose was already bloody. "You owe the boss five Gs. Christmas is coming. Duke needs that money to buy something pretty for his ma."

Galvano sniffled like a weepy kid, and blood spread through his Burt Reynolds mustache. "I'll get you the money, I promise. Just give me a couple days."

Prick picked up the wooden baseball bat he'd leaned against the wall when they'd come in. The banana man hadn't shown a lot of smarts when he opened the door. If he'd thought they'd dropped by for a friendly chat, he didn't know much about Prick. The thug twirled the baseball bat in one hand like a baton. "You ain't got a couple of days, slick. You got today."

"I don't have the money," Galvano blubbed. "Please, Prick, just a couple–"

Prick brought the bat down slow and tapped it on the side of Galvano's knee. "Shh." He brought the bat around to tap the man's other knee. "Take it easy, pal."

The wide end of the bat shot neatly between Galvano's Scorpio medallion and belt buckle. The banana man bellowed and leaned over clutching his chest. Vomit splattered his brown tasseled loafers.

"Jesus, you're going to kill him!" Brooklyn said.

Prick grinned and spun the bat again. "He ain't dead." He grabbed the man's hair and pulled his head up. "You ain't dead are you, buddy?" Galvano's lips were rounded like he was trying to suck up life through a straw. He wheezed and shook his head. Prick smiled at Brooklyn. "See, he ain't dead."

Between the end of Brooklyn's nod and his startled cry, the bat came around again, smashing into Galvano's face. He fell off the couch, and Prick squared off, holding the bat like an ax. It came down three times, each blow sounding like Ma's meat tenderizer on a thick steak. Prick breathed hard. "Might be now, though."

"Fuck'd you do?" Brooklyn's voice was high, his balls drawn up tight.

"Duke's orders. Guess I was right about not needing a gun." Prick held the bat up, the wide end bumping the ceiling and leaving a red smear on the white paint. "Excalibur! Sword of kings, slayer of fuckin' dragons!"

Brooklyn looked hard at Galvano, whose blood was starting to creep over the lapels of his yellow leisure suit and onto the white shag rug. *The whole rug gonna turn red?* He watched the creeping stain until Prick snapped his fingers less than inch away from Brooklyn's nose. "Wake up, pretty boy. Time to work."

Brooklyn nodded, eyes still fixed on the body.

"I mean it," Prick said. "Get on it."

Brooklyn nodded again, and got his eyes to swing up to Prick's face. The killer smiled. "You need something to perk you up, or you going to be OK?"

A line of coke would be just the ticket. Just enough to take the edge off, sharpen his focus, but... "I'm OK."

Prick grinned. "Sure you are. Get going. We're looking for a gray box. About this big." He held his hands about as wide as a good-sized watermelon. "Plastic."

"The money there?"

Prick shook his head. "It's full of tapes. Eight-tracks. Whole bunch of them." He nudged the corpse with his toe. "But considering the looks of this fuck he's probably got some money stashed, too."

"Then why do we need the tapes?"

Prick grabbed the shoulder of Brooklyn's jacket and pointed at the dead man with the bat. "Duke wanted this fucker dead and the tapes in his hands." He pushed Brooklyn toward a door. "The money's a bonus, but only if we find it. Go."

Galvano's bedroom was yellow, like his suit. Yellow wood-paneled walls with two dark-walnut bureaus. Brooklyn pulled out every drawer and dumped the contents on the bed. The top drawer of the first bureau was full of sex toys, half boxes of condoms, and lube. *No accounting for taste.* The half brick of coke in the bottom of the second drawer explained Galvano's appeal. Brook pocketed the drugs but left the jewelry and watches. They looked cheap and might be easy to trace.

Prick poked his head in the door, waved, and strolled toward the kitchen whistling the chorus of "Rock the Boat" by the Hues Corporation.

Brooklyn found the tapes in the dead man's closet. He carried the box out to the kitchen, where Prick was going through the cabinets, and pulled out one of the tapes. David Bowie's *Young Americans*, brand new in the wrap. It was weirdly heavy. "The hell he want these for?"

"Fucked if I know," Prick said. "Get them down to the car. I'll clean up here."

"What about the money?"

"If I find it, I'll split it with you."

Prick wouldn't likely be so forthcoming but considering Brooklyn wasn't planning on fessing up to the half brick of cocaine in his pocket… "Alright," he said. "Hurry it up."

Brooklyn tried not to look at the dead man when he passed him for the last time but couldn't stop himself. There was a lot of blood on the white rug. It made him think of the tampons he'd occasionally find in the gutter as a kid. Chris, especially, used to like to whip them around by the string and wing them at his friends. "Pussy missile coming at you!" he'd say.

Better than a goddamned baseball bat.

FOUR

"I heard it on the TV," Ma said. "Walter Cronkite. He says the Admiral is expecting another big attack. There might even be a draft."

Brooklyn wiped his mouth with one of her second-best napkins. "Can't believe everything you hear on TV, Ma. The Admiral will say anything to get Congress to give him more money."

Ma flicked her dishrag at him. "Your father thought a lot of him. He listened to the Mars landing with you on the radio of his old Chevy, remember?"

Brooklyn had been five then. Sitting on the cracked front seat of the old car, watching his father smoke Lucky Strikes and search up and down the AM dial for the broadcast. "That was Dunne, Ma. The Admiral was the first man on the Moon. John Dunne went to Mars."

Ma hung her dishrag off the oven door. "I always get those two confused."

Always did. Probably always will. Lola Lamontagne remembered every one of her son's childhood friends, all of her husband's business contacts, and everything that had ever happened to any of the dozens of neighbors they'd had over the years, but she only had a passing interest in the world outside Queens.

"David's joining up," Brooklyn said. "Chris, too, maybe."

Ma took a piece of garlic bread from the basket at the center of the table and used it to clean the spaghetti sauce off her plate. "Talked to Sandy yesterday at the market. She told me about Chris." She took a bite of the bread. "I didn't know about David. Seems like only yesterday the three of you were tearing around here like your butts were on fire."

"Long time ago, Ma."

"Not so long." Ma put down the bread. "What about you? You thinking about heading to the Moon and leaving your poor mother down here?"

"You see me up there? Bouncin' 'round like some kind of goon?" He shook his head. "Nah. Got all the trouble I need right here."

Brooklyn started to twirl up another forkful of his ma's neighborhood-famous pasta, but it reminded him of the mess Prick had made of the banana man's head two nights before. He set his fork down and reached for his tumbler of water.

"You sick?" Ma said. "Most nights you've gone through three plates before I've finished one."

"Just saving some room. David's going-away party is tonight."

Ma snorted. "Like you're going to be doing a lot of eating down at Mike's."

"Hey, beer takes up space, too." Brooklyn grinned. "You should come down, Ma. Mike asks about you all the time."

Brooklyn liked the little smile that played on her lips. She was the best person on the planet, far as he was concerned, and Pop had been dead a long while. It was time she found someone to spend the rest of her life with.

"Talking that way about an old lady like me." Ma slapped him on the arm. "You should be ashamed."

"Forty-six ain't that old these days, Ma. Gotta lot of life left."

"We'll see," she said. "Clear if you're done, and I'll get the pie. You save some room for that?"

Troubles or not, there was always room for Lola Lamontagne's cherry pie. "Just one piece, though. Gotta meet somebody."

Ma raised an eyebrow. "Meet who? I thought you were going right to the party."

"It's nothing. But I got to do it before I head over to Mike's."

Ma put a fat slice of pie on the table in front of her son. "Someone I might know? Ramona's daughter is home from college." She pointed to the half-gallon of vanilla ice cream she'd pulled from the freezer.

Brooklyn shook his head. "Beatrice? Shit, no, Ma. She's, like, twelve years old or somethin'."

"Don't swear at the table. You miss the part where I said 'college'?"

"Just a guy, Ma. Owes me some money for helping him move. That's all."

"I wish it was Beatrice. Or someone. You spend too much time alone since..." She sighed.

That was the cue. Once she got talking about Brooklyn's relationship status, she'd move on to summarizing every damned thing happening on her "stories", the soap operas she watched every afternoon. Brooklyn stuffed the final forkful of pie into his mouth and rose to his feet. "Someday, Ma." He leaned over and kissed her on the cheek. "Lots of grandkids. Promise."

"We'll see."

Brooklyn walked to the door and put his hand on the knob. "See you at Mike's later?"

"Maybe. Wish David luck for me."

Brooklyn's ma lived on the third floor of a battered brownstone, about four blocks from where Brooklyn had parked his car. He hated that she had to climb stairs with her groceries, but the little house they'd lived in when his father was alive was far in the past. A Haitian family was living there now: Mom, Dad, and two rowdy kids.

The old neighborhood hadn't changed much, though. The city had thrown up Bell panels and wind turbines everywhere, sucking up sunlight and breeze to offset the energy crisis. Mostly they worked. Ma said she barely lost power more than a few times a month now and usually only at night.

Prick was waiting in the parking lot, the interior of his gray Pontiac heavy with cigarette smoke. "Where the fuck you been? I was starting to think you didn't want to get paid."

Brooklyn got in the car. The door complained as he pulled it shut. "Eat dinner with my ma on Sundays."

Prick pulled an envelope out his jacket pocket. "Count it."

Brook thumbed through a stack of worn bills. "Three times what we agreed in here."

"Your share of the Galvano's money. Found it in a coffee can." Prick sucked on his cigarette. "Besides, I got another job for you."

"Gotta be somewhere tonight."

"Not a problem." Prick jerked his thumb at the back seat. "You can take it with you."

Brooklyn craned his neck to see the box of eight-tracks from the banana man's house. "Hell am I babysitting it for?"

"Duke got word he might get raided tonight, and I got better things to do than lug that shit around." Prick nodded at the money. "You want that or not?"

There was enough in the envelope to cover Ma's rent for the next six months. "How long do I keep it?"

"Just until tomorrow." Prick lit a cigarette off the first. "Maybe the next day. The boss calls me, and I call you. Good?"

Brooklyn didn't miss the not-so-subtle reminder about the thug pecking order and his place in it. He put the cash in his pocket and opened the car door. "Pop the back lock for me."

Prick leaned over and unlocked the back door. He saluted Brooklyn with one finger. "Have fun at your party. Tell your pal to watch his ass up there."

* * *

Brooklyn gave the trunk of his car a good whack to clear the ice off it and set the box of tapes on top of the stereo parts and junk souvenirs inside.

The wad of bills in his pocket pushed against his leg as he dropped behind the steering wheel. He hadn't slept well since Prick killed the banana man but had to admit the night's activities had paid better than fencing car radios and smuggling cigarettes. *More money in being an asshole than a chump.* He adjusted the rear-view mirror, and the face he saw there seemed to agree. He looked tuff. Once he found a buyer for the half brick of coke, he could take a couple of weeks off, catch a show or two.

Brooklyn's car, a worn but game '68 Cougar, grumbled when he prodded it, but he held the pedal down until the engine burst into an outraged roar. He let it warm up for a couple of minutes, twirling the dial on the radio until he found Al Green singing "Let's Stay Together". He hummed along, joining Al on the chorus, singing to Carmen maybe. At first, she'd liked his wild ideas and crazy schemes, but none of them had worked. The last straw had been the old punched-card computer he'd lugged home and tried to wire into the apartment's electrical system. The thing had been the size of a refrigerator, and he'd had a half-baked idea to use it to run an Italian lottery and as a house comptroller like the one on *The Partridge Family*. What he got was an electrical fire and an ultimatum. Carmen hadn't been bluffing, and she moved out a week later. *Keep on lovin' you whether, whether, babe.* He put the car in gear.

Cars were lining both sides of the street by the time he got to Mike's, so Brooklyn took a right into an empty lot half a block down. The warm air inside the Cougar darted into the cold night as he opened the door. He pulled the collar of his jacket close around his throat and reached back inside the car, worming his arm into the back seat to get David's present – a blowup doll he'd picked up because of its vague resemblance to Maria. She'd probably find it funny, which was good because she'd own it once David shipped out.

The snow squeaked with each step. More was falling, and Brooklyn was grateful to get inside the heat and light he found when he opened the door to the bar. "Lola" by the Kinks, a song he liked to tease Ma about, met him halfway over the threshold. He hung up his jacket and maneuvered to the bar.

"Who the hell's paying for all this?" Mike looked beside himself. Mike's Pub was rarely busy. Now the bar was covered in empties, but he probably hadn't seen a wallet come out all night.

"Aw, c'mon, Mike," Chris said, winking at Brooklyn. "David's going to the fucking Moon to fight the alien menace. Where's your patriotic spirit?"

"In my wallet with the dead presidents," Mike said. "Who's paying for all the booze you little shits are drinking?"

"Relax, Mikey." Brooklyn pulled out a wad of bills. "I got this."

Mike's eyebrows leapt up his forehead. "Who died and made you a Rockefeller? I know it wasn't your old man."

"You ain't the only one with a job." Brooklyn stuck two twenties in the bartender's shirt pocket and put the rest of the money back in his jeans. "Keep pouring, and we'll send David off right."

"I'll give you the family discount – a quarter a draft."

"Real sweet of you. I'll make sure Ma hears about it."

Mike polished a clean spot on the bar. "We dated a little in high school. She ever, ya know, mention me?"

"All the time. Just today at supper. Said she'd like to see you."

Mike made the spot shinier, eyes on his work. "You'd be OK with that?"

"Ain't pretty, but you'd be good to her." Brooklyn laughed. "It's Pop you gotta worry about. One bad step, and he'll come back to get you."

"I can handle Al Lamontagne." Mike slung the bar towel over his shoulder. "Maybe I'll give her a call."

"Do that, Mikey. But gimme a beer first."

Brooklyn put his back to the bar. The place was as packed as he'd ever seen it. Maria was supposed to get David there by nine, and most everyone else had come at eight to decorate and warm up. He caught Carmen's eye – she was talking to some of her old friends from the neighborhood – and lifted his glass in salute. She looked good. Happy. He still missed her like crazy, but she'd been right to leave. He was going nowhere fast. *Least nowhere good.*

"Dead Flowers" came on the jukebox again. Brooklyn frowned at the machine, a kindred spirit. Carmen had moved on. David and maybe Chris were heading out. He and the jukebox were staying put, playing the same damned songs over and over again.

"I have been looking for you, Lamontagne. Where are the tapes?"

Brooklyn didn't recognize the man who'd come to stand next to him at the bar, but he didn't like his looks. His face was sickly, almost waxy, but he was thick-bodied like a weight lifter. Brooklyn shook his head. "Missed it. What'd you say?"

The man's sneer showed teeth and gums like cheap dentures. "The fucking tapes. The ones you and your pal took from Galvano."

Brooklyn drained his beer and put the empty glass on the bar. "No idea what you're saying." He started to walk away, but the man grabbed him by the elbow and squeezed.

"Your pal Prick said you had them. He told me right where to find you."

The stranger's grip was painful and wrong, like his finger bones were on the outside instead of buried in his sallow flesh. Brooklyn worked to shake him off. "The fuck off me, man! Gonna get hurt."

The man jabbed Brooklyn in the side with something hard. Brooklyn froze.

"You got the idea, shit heap. Now tell me where the tapes

are, or I decorate the people in front of us with your guts."
The stranger jabbed harder. "This thing makes a big hole. Your
friends will be able to use you as a punch bowl."

Brooklyn had to bite his lip to keep from crying out. "In my
car. The trunk."

The stranger pushed him forward, one hand clamped on
Brooklyn's elbow, the other digging the gun deep into his side.
"Stop to talk to anyone, I kill you both."

Brooklyn was sure his eyes were as big as plates as the stranger
propelled him across the room, but no one noticed. Halfway
to the door, the stranger twisted the barrel of the gun like he
was trying to bore a hole. His grip cut off the blood supply, and
Brooklyn could feel nothing below his throbbing elbow.

The dark outside tore at him, pulling him out of the light
and warmth of the party. The future was clear. He'd open
the Cougar's trunk. The stranger would replace the box of
tapes with Brooklyn's body. Brooklyn would spend the last
seconds of his life gagging on the smell of his own intestines
and drowning in blood. He wondered how long it would take
someone to find his corpse.

He led the stranger to his car.

"Open it," the stranger said.

A thin layer of snow already covered the trunk lid. "Key's in
my right pocket. Need my arm back."

The stranger's grip released like it was spring-loaded.
Brooklyn shook his arm to force the feeling back into it and
tried to figure the odds of surviving the next sixty seconds. He
had a better chance with two hands certainly, but–

"Open it." The stranger didn't raise his voice, but the relative
quiet of the street outside the bar made it ring. There was a
snap to it; he was used to being obeyed.

Brooklyn dug into his hip pocket and pulled out his key
ring. The trunk lock always stuck a little, and he had to jiggle
the key to move the latch. The lock squeaked, and Brooklyn
lifted the lid.

"Lift it out," the stranger said. "Slowly. Carry it around to the hood."

Brooklyn reached into the darkness of the trunk, feeling for the bottom of the box. His hand struck cold metal – a tire iron – and a plan formed. Pull the iron, knock the gun away, and take the tall man down to the icy sidewalk. The only play he had left. Brooklyn gripped the tire iron in his fist and took what he imagined would be his last breath. He tensed.

"Hey!"

Both the stranger and Brooklyn turned to look for the source of the shout, but Brooklyn recovered first. He lifted the tire iron and swung it at the gun in the stranger's hand.

He missed and went sprawling into the snow. The stranger turned and leveled the gun at his face. Brooklyn's pants heated up with piss, and he squeezed his eyes shut.

Someone grunted with effort, and feet shuffled. Brooklyn fluttered his eyes open.

David had the stranger's wrist in his hands and was forcing the gun to point at the night sky. "Get up and help me with him!" The stranger took a step forward, and David gave ground rather than being knocked off his feet. "He's strong as fuck!"

David's face was red with effort and frustration, but the stranger's flat, shiny face showed nothing of the strain he must have been under, or of the pain he should have felt when David kicked the side of his leg.

"Goddamn it! I can't hold him."

Brooklyn still had the tire iron clutched in his numbed hand. He lurched to his feet, took three running steps, and brought the metal bar down hard, aiming for the side of the stranger's head. Without looking, the man caught the tire iron in his free hand and pulled, yanking Brooklyn off balance and throwing him aside to land face down on the icy pavement. The tire iron clattered into the shadows.

Shouts from Mike's. People were coming. Brooklyn pushed himself to his hands and knees and tried to shake his head clear. *Get up. Go low.* A knee-level tackle should put the stranger down no matter how strong he was. It always worked on the tall ones; their center of gravity seemed to be somewhere in their necks. Once the mook was down, he and David could keep him there until the cops showed.

ZARRK! A green light flashed as Brooklyn rose to his feet again, the flare blinding eyes widened and enhanced by the adrenaline rush. He put his hands over his face and tried to blink his eyes clear. His vision was filled with afterimage. Several sets of feet pounded toward him.

"Are you alright?" Chris grabbed Brooklyn's wrists and pulled his hands away from his face. Maria was screaming. Someone was throwing up.

David lay on the cold ground, steam rising from a crater burned into his chest. The stranger was gone. So were the tapes.

FIVE

The bottom of the top bunk was barely two feet above his face, and Brooklyn had a clear view of the graffiti penned there by the prisoners who'd come before. There were dozens of handwriting and artistic styles in the nine-square feet he could see without turning his head.

"Hear about the belt got arrested?" one wag had written. "It held up a pair of pants."

"Why the white guy the scariest one in jail?" wrote another. "Becuz you no he really did it."

Ha. Biggest joke of all was Brooklyn Lamontagne. He hadn't been in custody more than a couple hours before a dead-eyed dude weaseled up and warned that saying "Duke Carlotta" to anyone in a uniform or a cheap suit would be a good way to earn a shiv to the throat. "Stay cool, asshole," the dude rasped before melting away to the other side of the big holding cell.

Week two of staying cool involved a transfer to Rikers Island. Brooklyn's court-appointed lawyer swore the bad old days when rape and assault (*Don't drop the soap!*) were considered just desserts for being put in a cell were over, but Brooklyn got the feeling the bulls didn't much care what the inmates did to each other, prison reform be damned.

At first, the top bunk had been occupied by a red-faced man who wept constantly and kept promising someone named

Sharon that he'd never do "it" again. The next week, Brooklyn had a cellmate who spent most of the night hours jerking off into a sock. He finally caught a few days' break in week four with a con named George Milton. Small, sad, old guy, who looked like he'd split his years behind bars and working a plow somewhere. "Jail's better'n it used to be," George said, "but watch yerself. Real bad 'uns come in all friendly, get close ta ya before stickin' the knife in." George was gone a few days later, replaced by another sad sack who swore up and down he was innocent.

Week after Thanksgiving, Brooklyn could look at the graffiti without really seeing it. *Yer mothers fucking an alien!* He needed a way out not a cheap laugh.

Circumstantial evidence. The words meant little in a case involving someone like Brooklyn. No job he could talk about, an apartment full of stolen merchandise, his sweaty fingerprints all over a brutal murder scene. Whatever Prick had meant when he said he'd clean things up, it hadn't involved hiding their identities. Dumbass had even kept the bat. Cops had found it – *sword of kings, slayer of fuckin' dragons!* – in the trunk of Prick's car, his body behind the wheel, the scorched remains of his head riding shotgun in the seat beside it.

Brooklyn had managed to stay stony at the bail hearing until his mother took the witness stand to beg the judge to show mercy. "He's a good boy," she'd said. "He's all I have!" When she collapsed in tears, he'd wept, too, and didn't care who saw him do it. *Fuck them for making her go through this.* David was dead, and all the cops could think to do was finger him for murder of the banana man. They'd even tacked on a possession-with-intent charge because of the coke they'd found in the glove compartment of the Cougar. *Fuck them and fuck me.* The judge set bail higher than Brooklyn could reach with a housepainter's ladder. The court-appointed attorney, a skinny old fart with a fringe of hair, responded with an exasperated sigh. "Sorry, kid."

The cops had tried to pin Prick's death on him, too, but couldn't make the timing come out right. Brooklyn's lawyer flashed his coffee-stained dentures after that hearing. "Least we got that one." A charge more or less wasn't going to matter much. He was on the hook for Murder One, anything else was window dressing.

A bull named Tomlin banged on the door with his nightstick. "Lamontagne, you gotta visitor."

Brooklyn swung his legs around and stood up. "Who is it?"

"Cheryl Tiegs. Said she's looking for a first-class loser to take to a party." He gestured Brooklyn forward. "Turn around and put your hands through."

The cuffs bit hard on Brooklyn's wrists. Wouldn't have mattered if he'd complained, so he didn't. "Man or woman?"

"Mineral." Tomlin imagined he was a funny guy and calling him on it was a good way to get jabbed in the gut with that nightstick of his.

"Yeah?" Brooklyn said. "Bigger than a breadbox?"

The bull opened the cell door and let Brooklyn through. "You better hope so, cuz any baby of yours would be one ugly bastard."

Babies ain't minerals. Tomlin was also a moron but pointing *that* out would really hurt. Brooklyn held his tongue and let Tomlin herd him to the visitor's room.

Brooklyn had made two good decisions the day David died. First one was leaving most of the roll Prick gave him in the hidey-hole on the roof of his apartment building. Second was using his one phone call on Chris, telling him to get his ass up there to get it. That's why Ma looked sad and worn, not homeless and hungry.

Brooklyn slumped into the seat in front of the dirty window and picked up the phone. "Don't need to come all the way out here, Ma." An hour or more by bus and train, once a week, every week. No way she'd take a robocab, get driven around by a machine, even though the subways were automated too. *Getting frisked by security, bulls goin' through her purse.* His stomach rolled.

"I talked to your lawyer yesterday," she said. "He's a nice man, but I didn't understand half the words he said."

"That's the point, Ma." He ran his free hand through his hair. It was getting shaggy. "Judges and lawyers talk like that so no one else knows what they're sayin'."

"He said you're holding back. I got that much." She grimaced. "I'm not asking you to be a rat, Brook, but maybe just give them a little something. A name. It don't even have to be–"

"Can't do that, Ma. I..." He shook his head. "Just can't."

"Duke Carlotta's nothing but a crook!" Her face colored up. "He wouldn't piss on y–"

Brooklyn held up his hand. "Don't know Duke Carlotta, Ma, and if I did, I wouldn't expect him to save the day. Don't work that way." *Might sing loud and clear if I thought I'd live through it.* His hand fell, and he put on his best "get outta trouble" smile. "Boob tube in here's on the fritz. What's goin' on with your stories?"

She took the peace offering. The storyline on her favorite included an affair and an unwanted pregnancy, and the father was an alien disguised as a human. Whenever he was alone on camera his eyes glowed red and cheap-looking tentacles came up behind him. They both laughed at the description. Before she finished the rundown, the time-running-out light flicked on.

Ma cleared her throat. "Something I want to say. Chris told me you've been payin' some of my bills."

Brooklyn's throat worked. *That son of a–!*

"He didn't volunteer it. I had to dig it out of him. It's all 'Mrs. Lamontagne this, Mrs. Lamontagne that' with him. Some of you kids still respect your elders." She passed her hand over her eyes. "I just want to know. You do this for me? Is this my fault?"

Razor blades all the way down to his stomach. He could

barely speak for them. "Ma, no..." He blinked back tears. "One-time thing. Just in the wrong place at–"

"You get out of here, things are going to change, Brook." Her mouth firmed. "I'll see you next week. I love you." She hung up the receiver.

Four of Duke's guys had been killed the night of David's party. A straight line to Prick to the parking lot outside Mike's.

Brooklyn blinked, really seeing the bottom of the bunk for the first time in days. A faded message caught his eye. It was written in brown and smudged, probably blood. He brought his head up and squinted to see it better. "Your fucked," it said.

Yeah, probably.

"Didn't kill him," Brooklyn told his lawyer. "Prick done it."

The lawyer rubbed his glasses clean on his tie. "You were there. The police have all the fingerprints they'll ever need."

I'da worn gloves if I knew Prick was feeling violent. "Didn't know he was going to fucking kill him."

"What was on the tapes?"

"Don't know."

"Why did Prick want them?"

Brooklyn took a deep breath. "Look, Prick said we was going to get some money from the guy. Scare him a little."

"Scared him to death looks like."

"That was Prick!"

"Who told Prick to kill Galvano?"

"Nobody."

"Was it Duke Carlotta?"

"Don't know no one named that." Brooklyn leaned back as far as the cuffs would let him. "What if I was at Galvano's place the day before? What if I broke in to steal the coke?"

"Did you?"

"Would it help?"

The lawyer grunted. "It'd help if you quit lying to me, kid."

"You know I didn't kill no one." Brooklyn's eyes ached. He hadn't been sleeping well.

The lawyer looked steadily across the table at him. "So, you didn't kill him. The way you were going you would have killed someone eventually."

The streets only kept paying those who were willing to keep raising the stakes. He'd been playing mostly penny ante but… *Raise 'em.* "Guy who killed David," Brooklyn said. "Why ain't he in this?"

"No one knows who your gunslinger is. The police aren't even convinced he exists."

"Lot of people saw him. Maria told the cops what he looked like."

"You and she used to be an item."

"For a fucking month back in fucking high school!"

"It's enough to make a jury wonder about her credibility as a witness. Prosecution might hint you killed David, too. To get her back."

"You seen the pictures." His mouth tightened. "Everything in his chest was gone. Burned up. What does that? Nothing I got."

"Your gunman isn't in this, Brooklyn. This is your trial. We need to prove that you're innocent or too stupid to have known what you were getting into." The lawyer signaled through the window at the guard. "Might be able to get them down to accessory. We'll talk again soon."

Brooklyn looked at the man. The harsh light overhead reflected off the lawyer's glasses making him seem eyeless. "I going down for this?"

"They have your prints and a dead body, and you're not helping me out much." The lawyer herded his papers into his leather briefcase. "A lot of what we have are good feelings and wishful thinking. Guess we'll see."

SIX

The guard walked Brooklyn down the line of cells and through two security doors before taking a right to the visitor's room. A row of wall-mounted metal stools stuck out like tongues in front of grimy windows and dirty telephones. If he leaned in enough, the pressed-wood partitions would offer something like privacy. He sat as far back from the window as he could and picked up the phone.

"Hello, Brook."

"Hey, Carmen."

She'd changed her hair since David's party. A shorter cut, less feathering. She was wearing a wide-collared white shirt under a tan leather jacket. She looked good until she took off her sunglasses. Then she looked tired and maybe a little sad.

"What happened to your face?" she said.

"Know me, babe. Can't get along with anyone."

"Same old Brook."

Silence fell, but the conversation continued in their eyes. Brooklyn saw her maybe thinking about all the times they'd laughed and had sex in their old apartment, one time in the kitchen after he'd chased her there wearing nothing but a vampire cape and a pair of plastic fangs. The times it had been his turn to cook dinner, and he'd welcomed her at the door with a takeout menu. *We were so young, and now I am so damned tired.*

"You look skinny," she said. "You eating OK?"

"'S'alright." Brooklyn couldn't tell if the spit the chef added to the thin soup as he ladled it out made it better or worse. The chef did it right in front of him and added a big shit-eating grin. Bon appetite, he'd say, just like Julia Childs on TV. "Helpings are a little small."

She nodded.

"You still working for Ralphy?"

"Quit." Her face changed. "Got a new job in an office downtown. Tax accountants. I have a desk and everything."

Carmen had done a year in secretary school before he convinced her to move in with him. "Good. Real good," he said.

"I'm going back to school, too. They'll help me pay for it."

"Deserve it. Deserve a lot of things. I..." Brooklyn's hand reached out, almost involuntarily, and hit the thick glass between them. He pulled it back. "Carm. Sorry for everything. All of it."

Her eyes brightened in a way Brooklyn knew too well. He'd made it happen dozens of times, letting her down again and again. "Brook..." She cleared her throat. "Don't. That's not why I'm here."

Brooklyn's chest was tight. "Shoulda done better by you. By everyone."

Carmen put her hand on the glass, smearing the prints of so many women who'd visited so many men in similar circumstances. Brooklyn was ashamed to see her there; it hurt almost as much as seeing Ma through the dirty glass. "It wasn't your fault. David wouldn't blame you either."

Brook didn't answer. Every step he'd taken in recent months, every decision, had led to his friend lying there in the icy parking lot. He put his hand on the glass, too. Only an inch or so kept them from touching. "Love you, Carm. Always have."

A buzzer sounded, marking the end of the visit. Carmen

stood, her hand still gripping the phone. "It wasn't your fault, Brook," she said.

The line clicked, the call automatically cut off when the time was up.

Carmen said something else, but Brooklyn couldn't hear it. It might have been, "I love you, too."

Might have been something else.

Tears didn't make things any easier on Rikers Island, no matter what the chaplain said. Brooklyn was recovering from a fight with a couple of guys who had time to kill and nothing better to do. A punch to the throat had sent the biggest guy gagging to the ground. The two bulls who responded to the disturbance did a lot more damage with their nightsticks, made Brooklyn move like an old man. The bruises were starting to yellow at the edges.

Chris waved from the other side of the glass. "I'm real sorry your ma found out."

He'd cut his hair. It made him look older. Brooklyn cleared his throat. "How'd that happen, exactly?"

Chris squirmed. "Landlord's jacking up the rent. Property manager couldn't get hold of you so he went right to her."

Pop's death benefit only covered about half her bills. Brooklyn had been secretly making up the other half for years, convincing Ma she had rent control. It was hard to believe he'd kept the wool over her eyes so long. *Maybe I didn't. Maybe she didn't have no choice but to play along.* "How much?"

"Doesn't matter. She says she's not living off dirty money anymore."

No way in hell she's gonna hang onto her apartment without help, an' I'm none at all in stir. Squeal on Duke, I'm dead. There's–

Chris spread his hands. "What can I do?"

"Probably nothin'." Brooklyn narrowed his eyes. "Thought you were joining up."

One shoulder went up, dropped. "Got a job with my father. Entry-level. Working the floor at one of his dealerships."

"You hate your old man."

His face colored. "Green's thicker than blood, I guess. I needed a job, he had one. Guess I'm staying put. Better than ending up dead or in a wheelchair."

The UN's Earth Defense drew mainly from countries that'd skipped the space race. The EOF was for citizens of the superpowers – the Soviet Union, America, and China – and it needed boots on the Moon and Mars. Anyone coming back from ten years of that would have a helluva hard time in Earth gravity. *David dies, then Chris backs out. Local recruiter must be getting desperate to make his quota.* A childhood of Wheaties boxes and model spaceships… Brooklyn wondered if he could still fake enthusiasm for it. He signaled the guard. "Good to see ya, pal, but I gotta cut this short. Need to talk to my lawyer."

"Got them down to accessory," the attorney said. "Plead guilty, and they'll drop the possession charge, too. You'll do eight to twelve years if you keep your nose clean. Lot a life left after that."

Brooklyn grunted. "Ma loses her apartment, has ta fend for herself. I don't get stabbed to death in the shower, I come out an ex con nobody wants to hire."

"Best I can do. If you're smart, you'll let me do it."

"Got an idea to go with it," Brooklyn said. "Need you to talk to Duke Carlotta for me."

"Thought you didn't know him." The attorney folded his arms. "The time for bullshitting is past, son. Rubber's about to hit the road, and you're the little thing between them that gets squished."

"Help me slip out, then. Been playing Duke's game the way he wanted. Ain't said a word to no one 'bout him. Time he greased this a little. Bet he has some bigwig on his payroll I can get a good word from."

"Threatening Carlotta's just going to get you killed."

"Ain't crazy. Just giving Duke a chance to get me out of his hair for a good while." Brooklyn felt sick, but he couldn't see another way through. "Want to join the EOF. Full term. Ten years." *An' I hope ta hell Duke's right about the aliens.*

PART THREE
Squeeze Box

January 27, 1976

SEVEN

The dust was a physical force, adding weight to the bus with every mile and slowing it to a straining series of lunges and recoveries. Since they'd left the airport behind, the driver had stopped four times to send guys out to sluice down the windshield with water from one of the half dozen milk jugs racked behind his seat. The water turned the dust – some of it surely the remnants of Cleveland on yet another trip around the world – into mud, and the windshield wipers spread it translucent across the glass. When the driver could see well enough, he set the bus jolting ahead another few dozen barren miles. An autopiloted bus wouldn't have needed a clear windshield, but the EOF short-sheeted its ground operations to make up for the billions it spent in space.

Fucking Texas. Dirt, a shitty airport, and not a cowboy in sight. Just miles of flatland and thirty-three douche bags, dipshits, and dropouts on a bus with no air-conditioning. The other riders were so quiet and still in the heat that Brooklyn wondered if they might be dead. Maybe the ride was the first test to weed out the weak from the ones who'd make it "upstairs", as the recruitment officer had called it. *The fuck's the rush?* They'd be in Texas for six months before the survivors flew to the Arctic for stage two. Plenty of time to wash out.

The bus driver had timed his trip well. The training camp

71

was just visible on the horizon when he stopped the bus and ordered Brooklyn and another of the more-lively-looking recruits to pour the last of the water onto the windshield. An hour later they were through the gates and the driver was yelling at them to get on their feet, off the bus, and into a ragged line outside.

A recruit coming down the stairs on Brooklyn's heels stumbled, nearly sending them both to the bare ground. Brooklyn's hand shot out to catch himself, and he turned to curse out the man, a red-headed beanpole in denim overalls, who'd stumbled. "Watch what the fuck you're…!" An asteroid hit the side of Brooklyn's face, knocking him to the ground he'd so narrowly avoided seconds before and jarring whatever else he'd been about to say out of his skull.

"The Admiral doesn't like that word, trainee." The voice seemed to come from fifteen feet up and a quarter-dimension away. "Better get it out of your vocabulary."

Brooklyn's vision cleared in time to see a short man in fatigues gesture to the redhead. "Help him up and get him in the line."

Red leaned over and offered a hand, but Brooklyn slapped it away. "Don't need your help."

The trainee shrugged and fell in with the rest of the men. Brooklyn pulled himself to his feet and stood at the end of the line nearest the bus door. There was blood in his mouth, and he spat it into the dust. The short man in fatigues was at the other end of the line looking over the new arrivals. He walked halfway up and put his hands behind his back. "What do you think, Sergeant Trask?"

Trask was a little guy, too, with a thin scar running up the left side of his face. "Looks like a kindergarten trip to the zoo, Major Conkey." He squinted at a recruit whose feathered hair and Paul McCartney mustache had wilted badly in the heat of the bus. "But uglier."

"I suspect you are being too kind." Conkey walked until he was standing in front of Brooklyn. "Sergeant, do you believe any of these men will be worth sending up to the Admiral?"

"Too early to tell, sir." The wiry little man shrugged. "Maybe a few."

"I'll leave you to it then." Conkey nodded at the line of recruits. "Welcome to the Extra-Orbital Forces, gentlemen. Pro Terra."

The barber grinned.

"This get you off or something?" Brooklyn's newly-shaved head felt like a peach.

The barber's grin twitched but refused to disappear. "Better watch the mouth, Frenchy. Someone's gonna want to fill it with a fist."

"Like to see them try."

The barber grinned harder, exposing a gold tooth in the far left corner of his mouth. He had thick knuckles. "Like to see it myself. Get the hell out of here."

Brooklyn pulled his issue cap out of the back pocket of his fatigues and jammed it on his head. As he walked past the men still in line, somebody wolf-whistled. Brooklyn whirled. "The fuck was that?"

Brooklyn surveyed the men's faces. From the neck down, dressed in their gray fatigues and T-shirts, they looked like they'd all come out of the same machine. Above the neck most of them were still human, eyes bright, hair brushed. One man even had a beard. *He's really going to get the barber hot.*

No one in the line moved. Probably most of them hadn't heard him, or none of them cared. They just stood there swapping jokes and chewing nicsticks.

Least you could say "fuck" in Rikers. Brooklyn took his place and stared at the toes of his boots. Jail had left a mark on him. Nothing too bad had happened, but he felt like he'd been stripped naked and rubbed raw. Being in a crowd, especially one made up of rowdy men, was jangling every nerve.

The training group entered the barber cubicles in sixes, walking through the door as mods, punks, hippies, straights, and surfers and coming out as would-be EOF guardians.

"Look! It's the dark side of the Moon."

Brooklyn's eyes flicked off his boots in time for the laughter. There were several black guys in the group, but the one who'd just stepped away from the barbers was by far the darkest. The man's teeth flashed in a broad grin when he spotted the source of the jibe. "If I the dark side, you must be Pink Floyd." He pointed at the trainee who made the crack and lunged, stopping with his finger an inch or two from the white man's nose. "Boo!"

The joker flinched so hard he nearly fell over

The grin slid into a laugh. "Dark Side. Never had a cool nickname before. I'm keeping it, Floyd. Next time you say it, keep your face straight."

It took less than an hour to get the trainees through the barbers' chairs and into another ragged line outside. The sun was hot. The sky was jaundiced. The New York City air was soup by comparison.

"Lamontagne!"

Trask pronounced his name wrong, like "Cagney" instead of "pain", but Brooklyn quit rubbernecking. "Yeah?"

"You mean, 'Yes, Sergeant', don't you, trainee?"

Yeah, I seen The Dirty Dozen. "What I meant. Yes, Sergeant."

"Square those shoulders up and say it like you mean it, trainee."

Brooklyn shifted his posture an inch or two. "Yes, Sergeant."

"I can't hear you, trainee." Trask stepped nearer until his face was nearly close enough to kiss. "I'm concerned about your conviction, Trainee Lamontagne. This where you want to be?"

"Not really, Sergeant!"

Trask stepped back a pace and gestured along the line. "Where would you rather be than protecting your planet from an invading force?"

"With a hot chick and a cold beer, Sergeant!"

The sergeant turned and paced down the line of men. The sun beat at the back of Brooklyn's neck, the newly exposed skin there starting to burn. Trask walked back to the center of the line and stood, hands clasped behind his back. "I'm going to turn you wastes of food into something useful." He pulled a short riding crop out of a sheath strapped to his leg. "Lead off, Lamontagne. Fifteen times around the perimeter." He slapped the riding crop into the palm of his left hand. "I'll let you know if you aren't going fast enough."

They were still running three hours later. Brooklyn had puked twice and was thinking he might do it again. Trask had hardly broken a sweat, even though he'd been jogging up and down the line the entire time, cracking heels and the backs of calves with his crop anytime someone looked like they were slowing down. One trainee had collapsed. Two corpsman lifted the downed man onto a stretcher and carried him away.

The men huffed and puffed back into the center of the base, and the sergeant called a halt near a shipping pallet loaded with duffel bags. "Line up for inspection, boys! Ten-hut!"

Brooklyn forced himself to stand up straight. A jeep pulled up in front of the line, and the major swung out of the back. "How's it looking, Sergeant?"

Trask offered a crisp salute. "Thirty-two city boys and softies, major."

"Down one already."

"Yes, sir. He collapsed about halfway through the break-in run. He's in the infirmary. Docs washed him out."

"Seventeen more to go." Conkey walked down the line of red-faced men, looking them over from the toes of their dusty boots to the slick crowns of their heads. He stopped in front of the black man with the dazzling grin. "How are those boots feeling, son? Any pain?"

Dark Side stared over the major's shoulder. "No, sir. No pain at all, sir."

"Three hours into it and one of you is already going home." The Major raised his voice so all the men could hear. "By the time you launch, we'll have cut you down to fifteen." He stopped in front of Brooklyn. "Some of you can't afford to miss that boat. Some of you," he glanced at Dark Side, "might be better off dying where you stand." He nodded to Trask. "Put them to bed, Sergeant. Tuck them in."

The kid with the red hair was a slow study. "Bet you never saw it coming. Open-hand slap to the side of your head and – POW!" He clapped his big paws together. "You were on your ass. Never even seen my pa hit that hard."

Brooklyn continued to stare at the bottom of the bunk above him. It was free of graffiti.

The springs of the adjacent bunk complained as the kid sat down. "Thomas Young. Friends call me Tommy. I'm from Oklahoma."

"Don't need no friends named Tommy," Brooklyn said. *Real bad 'uns come in all friendly, get close ta ya before…*

"Call me Tom, then." He hummed. "Heard the sergeant call you Brooklyn. That where you're from?"

"Where my pop wanted me to be from. Moved in with my ma's folks in Queens before I was born."

"Good thing they didn't name you Queens." Tommy lay down on the bunk and slid his hands under the thin pillow beneath his head.

Brooklyn craned his neck to see him. "Look, pal. Don't expect me to be buddy-buddy or all GI Joe about this bullshit. It was either join up or end up somewhere worse."

The kid chewed his nicstick. "Ever know someone who got up there?"

"Have you?"

"Couple." The bunk creaked. "My older brother and his best friend joined up 'bout six years ago. We got letters for a while."

"Then what?"

"Missing, then declared dead. There's nothing underneath their headstones. Nothing to bury. Their ship failed to report, fell off the scope. Guess they're still floating around out there somewhere."

Brooklyn's heart gave a hard couple thumps. A guy with red hair like Tommy's tumbling through space forever, a scream maybe frozen into his face. "You still joined up."

"Pa said it would make a man out of me." He chewed. "'Sides, it was either this or look at the world from the seat of a tractor for the rest of my life."

"More options than that. It's a big world."

"Not so big in Oklahoma." Tommy covered a yawn. "Morning comes early. Gonna try to get some sleep." He rolled over on his side, facing away from Brooklyn.

Brooklyn returned his attention to the bottom of the bunk. *Big world 'less you keep slamming doors on it. College, SLAM! Carmen, SLAM! Ma, SLAM! David. For fuck's sake, Earth.* In a year, it might be him floating frozen in space, eyes wide with terror or blown into jelly from explosive decompression. All because of the banana man. All because of Prick.

Nah. That ain't right. He'd taken Prick's money, gotten David killed. There was a price for that. Ten years in space, bones and muscles falling apart in low gravity, or prison. *Least Ma will take the money this way.*

Morning began with a whooping siren. Trask let it sound for ten panicked seconds before shutting it off and striding to the center of the big room, boot heels thudding against the wood.

"It is oh-four-thirty. You will get out of your bunks. You will make up your bunks. You will dress, and you will shave. You will be standing in front of your bunks at oh-four-fifty for inspection. Are we clear?"

Even the guys who were only half awake managed to mumble an affirmative. Satisfied, the sergeant turned on his heel and left the room.

Brooklyn rubbed his temples. He hadn't slept well. With no wall to put his back against, he'd felt vulnerable and exposed. "Feels like I just went to bed."

Tommy was already lacing up his boots. "I've been getting up like this all my life. Least I won't have to milk anything today."

Brooklyn's face was still stinging from his tepid-water shave when he stood in front of his bunk for inspection. The sergeant entered, followed closely by the major.

"Attention!"

Boot-heels scuffed on the wooden floor as the men in the bunk room brought their feet together and squared their shoulders like they'd seen in the movies. Brooklyn stared at the end rail of the bunk across from him.

Trask and Conkey moved down the double line of men. Occasionally, the major mumbled something, and the sergeant wrote on his clipboard. The two men passed in and out of Brooklyn's range of vision.

"Thank you, Sergeant." The major's footsteps receded, and Brooklyn heard the thin door shut.

"At ease." Trask consulted his clipboard. "Wood. Addison. Trent. After PT, you three will come back here and remake every bunk while the rest of us go to breakfast. Maybe you'll get enough practice in to learn how to make yours right." The message met with a mixture of groans and laughter. "Outside. Start it off with sixty jumping jacks. Young, you count them off."

The history teacher they met after lunch was a graying man with a neat mustache and a tweed jacket. He'd written "Thank you for your service" on the chalkboard and underlined it. Next to it was his name: Professor Mark Rhineberg, Captain USAF retired.

"Good afternoon. Let's try this out." He tapped the line with a piece of chalk. "Counting down, three-two-one. Go."

It took six more countdowns to get it said the way he wanted it: in unison, bright-sounding, and earnest.

"Any questions that don't involve why we just did that?" he said.

Pink Floyd raised his hand. "The EOF ain't even a dozen years old. Why're we taking a class on it?"

"Not enough history to bother with, you mean." Rhineberg nodded. "In the early morning of January 27, 1961, a small fleet of alien spacecraft destroyed two Earth cities but were chased away by the combined high-orbital forces of the United States and the Soviet Union. You all know that, right?" He surveyed the room with his eyes, collecting a mix of nods and grunts. "Anyone know the names of the pilots who died up there? And I'm not including the guy they made up for the movie."

"The black guy," Pink Floyd said.

"Carl White. In truth, there were no black fliers in Eagle Seven. But there also wasn't really a Guenter Werthner who served as launch-pad boss. The real launch-pad boss was Clayton Winters, who was black, but didn't make it into the movie. Any ideas why?" He walked to the back row of desks and stopped in front of Brooklyn. "How about you?"

"Guy who played White, Billy Dee Williams, said he was added to keep the NAACP happy," Brooklyn said. "Saw it on *Cavett*."

"I saw that, too. A factual response, but it doesn't answer the question about Clayton Winters." He adjusted his glasses to look at Dark Side. "Do I know you from somewhere?"

"Wanted posters at the Post Office?" Dark Side smiled. "Film's director took out Winters cuz someone paying the bills didn't want to see someone looks like me giving orders to white pilots."

"And there's your answer." He smiled at Pink Floyd. "Still think you don't need a history class? How many of you gentlemen have been to college?"

A couple of guys raised their hands, Dark Side included.

"When Sergeant Trask isn't running you into the ground

and training you within an inch of your life, you'll be here with me or one of my colleagues. Math, physics, history, math, physics, history... until you learn it to our satisfaction or wash out."

Tommy's hand shot up. "Can I ask about 'thanks for your service' now?"

Rhineberg stroked his mustache with the knuckle of his index finger. "Aliens showed up in '61. Scared the hell out of everybody. Blew our minds. Panic in the streets. We knew for a fact that we weren't alone in the universe. We'd barely made it to Jupiter and all of a sudden we were facing war on an interplanetary scale. Most, if not all of you, were just kids then, and I doubt you remember much."

Brooklyn had been ten. Old enough to understand that something bad was happening and be grateful that his family was safe within the thick walls of Our Lady of Sorrows on 37th Avenue. He'd spent the night tearing around with the other kids while the adults worried their beads and hovered around the black-and-white TV Father Manuel set up in the community room. The next morning, they went home safe, and the world started living with one eye on the sky.

"What happened next?" Rhineberg said.

"Treaty of '63," Dark Side said.

"Close enough for now. To provide for the common defense blah-blah-blah members of the United Nations Security Council put all the nukes under lock and key and dissolved their armed forces to create two new, unified military organizations under UN control."

"That when you retired?" Pink Floyd said.

"Bet you're not the type to hang around and read the credits." Rhineberg smiled tightly. "The United Nations had some progressive ideas about how war should be conducted and armed forces should be organized. Lot of US military retired after '63. Lot of those guys still resent that it happened and think we would have been better off going it alone, American-style." He pointed to the phrase he'd written on the board. "You will doubtless meet some of them, and they might try to draw you into an argument. Maybe even start a fight with you. This is how you are going to respond when you meet anyone who served under the old system. Let's try it again. Countdown, three-two..."

EIGHT

Brooklyn was recovering from morning PT when Trask singled him out in week two.

"Lamontagne," the sergeant said, still murdering the pronunciation, "get over to the med center. It's your turn to see the shrink."

"Yes, Sergeant." They were going reverse alphabetically; "L" had to come up sooner or later. Counseling was mandatory in the EOF, once a month and more if needed. Tommy had told him what the questions were like.

"Double time, Trainee!" Trask said.

Brooklyn launched into a jog, some easier to do than it had been the week before. The shrink's office was the first place Brooklyn had seen in several days that was not painted EOF blue and white. A heavy desk was in the corner against the wall, the shrink in an armchair in the middle of the floor. He motioned Brooklyn into one just like it.

"Larry Gephardt. You must be Mr Lamontagne."

"No name, rank, and serial number here?"

"Not unless you want it." Gephardt had a folder on his knee.

"That part of the test?"

"It was. Congratulations, you passed." Gephardt's hair wasn't regulation length.

"Unless you decide I'm crazy and wash me out."

"The Admiral is very particular about what kind of people he wants in space. It's a dangerous place." He patted the folder. "Your file is already thicker than most."

"Because of jail."

"The Admiral doesn't like surprises." He smiled. "That said, everything you tell me is confidential. I won't tell Trask. I won't tell the major. If I wash you out, it's a simple form. No whys or wherefores, just an unimpeachable 'no and thanks for your time'."

"Had a shrink as a kid for awhile. After my pop died. We played a lot of basketball."

"I applaud your mother for getting you into therapy," he said.

"You guys got real popular after '61. Shingle on every street corner."

"Change an entire planet's perspective on the universe, most people are going to need someone to talk to." He put a notebook on top of the folder. "I watched the tapes they made of intake here. You seemed pretty defensive. Were you assaulted during your time in jail?"

Brooklyn's stomach turned sour. "Few scraps is all."

"It's ironic, but had you made it to prison you'd have been better protected. Prison is for rehabilitation after all. Rikers is a warehouse with bars."

"It's a shit hole," Brooklyn said.

"You're not in any danger of such things here. No hazing. No abuse. No assault. The major is a stickler for the rules, well-educated, and a thoroughly modern thinker. I am proud to serve with him."

"He hit me in the face because I said 'fuck'."

"Imagine what he'd do to someone who broke one of the big commandments. His wife, a colonel I believe, runs the women's training camp. She is equally intolerant."

"Bet they have great pillow talk."

The shrink chuckled. "Got some questions for you. Short

answer. How do you feel about working in small spaces?"

"Don't have a problem with it."

Gephardt made a note. "Ever experienced vertigo?"

"Only when I drink too much."

A note. "Do you believe in God?"

"Not really. That a problem?"

"There are a lot of learned beliefs and behaviors that will get you discharged. That's not one of them." He shifted his leg. "Tell me about Mr Galvano."

Yeah, Tommy didn't warn me 'bout that one. Brooklyn took a deep breath. "Can't do that one short, doc."

NINE

Tommy huffed along beside Brooklyn. "Why we running so damned much? Running don't even work on the damned Moon."

Brooklyn saved his breath. Two months in, it was getting easier to eat the miles and not feel like they'd be coming back up as soon as he stopped. A couple of days before they'd had to tough out the "test" – a series of pushups, situps, and runs that determined whether they'd stay in basic or go to "fat camp" for four extra weeks of PT.

All the guys had passed, the resilience of youth making up for the fact that a lot of that youth had been spent fucking around. Brooklyn swore every beer he'd ever drunk was sitting on his back, laughing while the sergeant stood over him, stopwatch in hand, and counted out pushups

Tommy had been assigned as his battle buddy, which meant they had to go everywhere together. It wasn't so bad. He was a good guy, might even be cool if he didn't talk so damned much. The kid had gotten sweet on one of the other recruits, a tall blond guy from California, which gave Brooklyn a couple hours off before lights-out every evening.

The mess hall came into view on the right. Brooklyn slapped Tommy in the chest with the back of his hand. "Last lap," he said, panting. "I get there first, you have to stay quiet for a full hour after chow."

Tommy grinned and picked up his pace, easily pulling out in front of Brooklyn as they headed into the home stretch. Brooklyn kept his pace steady. He had no chance of beating the long-legged farm boy, but he'd bought himself fifteen minutes with nothing but the sound of his booted feet and rasping breath to keep him company. The constant togetherness was the worst thing about the gig so far; the guys did everything together: running, eating, sleeping, showering. The only private space was the toilet, and loiterers usually found themselves on cleaning duty.

Brooklyn ran and felt pretty good. He bitched constantly about the heat, all the guys did, but he felt like it was paring him down. Burning the shit away. Prick, the banana man, even David – it was starting to feel like it happened a long time ago.

The sergeant was waiting for the men in front of the barracks. Brooklyn had been running somewhere in the middle of the pack, and he checked his watch as he stutter-stepped to a halt and took his place in line beside Tommy. Five miles in forty minutes. Not bad.

"Beat you," Tommy whispered.

The back of the pack was right behind. When the men were all assembled the sergeant walked the line for a cursory inspection. Brooklyn heard something about pugil sticks before the sergeant reached into the back of his jeep and produced the mailbag. He tossed it to Dark Side. "Get your mail and then get to chow," he said. "Dismissed!"

Dark Side pulled a stack of mail out of the bag and started to shout out names, pausing once to stuff a thick envelope into his back pocket. "Lamontagne!" he said.

Brooklyn stepped forward to receive his mail: a postcard from Mike the bartender and a letter from Carmen. The postcard was one of those cheap tourist things that showed the New York skyline, a jagged gray underbite against a blue sky.

Brook,

How's tricks? Me and your Ma drove upstate last weekend to do
Ash Wednesday with your Aunt Rhoda. She's good. Your Ma, I
mean. Rhoda is sick but not too bad. Your Ma had a good time.
She told me to say "hello" to you and that she misses you. Well,
that's all the time I got. Keep your head down, buddy.
- Mike

Carmen's letter was longer, the familiar loops of her Catholic-
school cursive packed tight on two pages of text. Brooklyn
read it twice before crumpling it into a ball in his fist.

The padded end of the pugil stick caught him under the edge
of his helmet and knocked him into the dirt again. He rolled
to his feet with a roar and swung his own stick wildly at the
sergeant's head. The sergeant barely seemed to move, but
something hit Brooklyn in the small of his back, and he was
back on the ground with a mouthful of grit.

"That, gentlemen, is how you don't want to do it." He
motioned to Tommy. "Help your buddy up and get him back in
line. Who's next?"

The wild anger had vanished as fast as it had come, and
Brooklyn took the help Tommy offered. Tommy kept his hand
on Brooklyn's shoulder as he limped back into line. They
watched as the sergeant calmly took down the new volunteer
with a leg sweep.

"Watch your balance," the sergeant said. "Next."

The sergeant took down five more trainees before tossing
his helmet into the jeep. "Grab your gear and pair up. Let's see
what you can do."

They beat the shit out of each other for the next three hours.
After facing the "friendly" bouts offered by their battle buddies,
the sergeant had them switch partners twice. In the last hour,
he organized a tournament with a final match between the

best of the winners, which ended up being Dark Side, against the best of the losers, Brooklyn.

Brooklyn dashed sweat from his forehead with his forearm before pulling on his helmet and facing the other man. Dark Side looked entirely too comfortable, holding his pugil stick loosely in one hand. The sergeant blew his whistle, and the match started.

Dark Side closed the distance almost before Brooklyn noticed. He thrust his stick out desperately like a pool cue, catching the taller man in the chest by surprise and scoring the first point. Dark Side smiled slow and came in more carefully the next time. Brooklyn came to seconds later, staring up at sky and surrounded by boots.

"What happened?" he said.

"You forgot to duck. Dee swung right across and caught you on the side of the head." Tommy helped Brooklyn sit up and offered him a canteen. "You going to be alright?"

Brooklyn got to his feet slowly, waiting to feel dizzy or sick but nothing like that happened. He took a long swallow of water. "Looks like it."

"Sergeant wants you to get checked out anyway. You want me to go with you?"

"I'm good." Brooklyn stacked his protective gear and racked his stick before crossing the courtyard to the medical building. The doctor there checked his blood pressure, shone a light in his eyes, and pronounced him healthy enough to return. He handed Brooklyn a bottle of pills. "APC."

Brooklyn stared blankly at it.

"All-Purpose Cure. Aspirin. Come back if you start throwing up."

Sleep came hard that night. Brooklyn lay still and listened to the guys sleep. After weeks sharing space, he could recognize most of them by snore. He rolled to his feet, careful not to shake the bunk above and padded toward the bathroom.

"Hark, who goes there?"

The challenge was nearly whispered, but Brooklyn almost pissed himself in surprise. "The fuck wants to know?"

A wide grin flashed in the shadows near the wall. "I know who you be, Brother Brooklyn. The Dark Side is the fire guard, and the fire guard sees all."

Fire guard wasn't all that hard a gig but woe betide the man who fell asleep during the two-hour shift. Brooklyn knew some guys played solitaire to keep themselves awake. He usually read magazines when it was his turn, but Dark Side... Tommy was friendly with everyone and had called him Dee... was just sitting there being quiet. "About to see me take a piss."

Dee chuckled, the laugh barely rising above a whisper. "Good tussle today. Knocked the wind right out of me with that first poke." His shoulders rose and fell against the shadows. "Got a little mad. Might have hit you a little hard back."

"Don't even have a headache."

"Good," Dee said, "but you ain't sleeping."

"Got a letter from home. My girl – well, a girl – she's seeing someone. Getting married."

He sucked his teeth. "Tough road."

"Started down it a long time ago." Brooklyn made his hands relax. "You got mail, too."

"My lawyer. Had some business to finish. Ends to tie. That kind of thing."

"You in stir too?" Brooklyn's eyes were getting used to the light, and he could pick out more and more of Dee's face. He looked thoughtful, maybe a little sad.

"You are looking at a certified threat to the domestic tranquility of the United States of America." Dee might have been quoting something. "College educated, radicalized by the Black Panther Party, and set on a course of civil disobedience and destruction. Pissed off a few governors and a couple congressmen. Lawyers made a deal, and here I am."

"Watched a guy kill another guy with a baseball bat."

"What was that like?"

"Didn't see it coming."

Dee grinned. "Me neither."

"Sorry, man. Ain't like me to be so nosy. Just curious, that's all."

"Curious, not friendly?"

"Don't pay to make a lot of friends right now. Ain't all going to make it."

"Could be right. Maybe go back and sleep on it." Dee waved his arm to indicate the sleeping men. "Seems to me you got all the friends you don't need right here."

PART FOUR
Take the Money and Run

June 22, 1976

TEN

Brooklyn met Tommy's parents at the graduation ceremony. They'd driven the family pickup a night and a day to see their middle child in the uniform that had led to their oldest son's death. They didn't seem anything but proud. *I lost an older brother or sister up there, no way Ma would be smiling if I joined up.* Brooklyn couldn't decide if he was looking at heartland patriotism or redneck dumb ass.

An older man in a sharp suit showed up for Dee. He introduced him as his mentor and martial-arts teacher, George Cofield.

Brooklyn got a handful of telegrams, from Ma, from Mike, from Carmen. One from David's girlfriend Maria. No one showed up in person. Nobody he knew had the money to waste for a trip to Texas, and he hadn't invited them to.

Major Conkey made a speech – it wasn't long, mostly congratulations and remember all the hard work – but Brooklyn found a bit that stuck.

"I cut my teeth in Korea, fighting the Communists before I even understood what a Communist was," Conkey said. "Now, we're allies with them against something bigger. Maybe Earth and the Mercurians will be allies against an even greater force someday."

Brooklyn had to wonder what could be a bigger enemy than

a planet full of technologically-advanced extraterrestrials, but allowed it was possible.

Conkey continued. "And what, when alliances can change so quickly, are we really fighting for? Country? Family? Security? Peace?" He swept his eyes over the assembly before him. "I know my answer, but I believe it's something that every one of you must answer for yourself. Good luck out there. Do us proud."

Graduates were given two weeks liberty before their flight to the Arctic. Brooklyn watched the other survivors pack their duffels and head out for parts unknown. He had no idea what to do with his time off. It would take three or four days to get to New York City by bus. It might make more sense to go to Austin or New Orleans and blow off some steam there.

Tommy slammed into the room and dropped into his usual bunk. "I'm headed out tomorrow. Riding back with my folks. They wanted to go tonight, but I told them I wanted to grab a beer with some buddies. You in? I can get us a ride into town."

"Be a fool not to," Brooklyn said.

The town, fifty miles away, wasn't much of one, but it had a few restaurants, a couple of bars, and a movie theater, so it beat the hell out of the base.

The bar Tommy picked was full of cowboys near as Brooklyn could tell. Worn boots, mustaches, and big hats. The women with them all looked like country singers. Most of them could probably sing "Stand By Your Man" without looking at the liner notes.

Brooklyn and Tommy were wearing fatigues. The corporal they borrowed the jeep from said it would make them irresistible to the locals. "They love a man in uniform over there," he said. "They'll be on you like flies on shit."

They'd attracted a lot of attention – everyone in the place seemed to be staring – but none of it looked like lust.

Brooklyn nodded at the bartender. "Beer and a shot." He jerked a thumb at Tommy. "Same for this guy."

"You boys from around here?" The bartender filled the order as he spoke and slid them in front of Brooklyn and Tommy.

Brooklyn picked up the shot glass. "New York. Charles Atlas here is from Oklahoma."

"Farmer?" the bartender said.

"Third generation," Tommy said. "Mostly dairy and corn."

The bartender wiped at the bar with his towel. "Mostly beef around here. And oil. And bullshit." He leaned toward them and lowered his voice. "You should drink your drinks and go down to Manuelo's. Guardians aren't too popular here, an' some of these boys ain't too keen on all their tax dollars headed to United Nations. Hell, some 'em think the UN did Cleveland."

"We can handle ourselves," Tommy said.

The bartender shrugged. "Just a friendly piece of advice."

Brooklyn and Tommy clicked their shot glasses together. "To the Moon."

The cheap whiskey burned going down. Brooklyn sipped his beer. It wasn't as cold as he was used to, but it was the first he'd had since David's party. The booze would hit him hard, and he knew he should take it slow, but he tossed it back and ordered another. He put his back to the bar and turned to watch the crowd, fresh beer in hand.

The crowd was still eying them, even the guys playing pool in the corner. A tall man in a dirty leather vest stepped away from the pool table. "You boys real soldiers or is you astronauts?" He leaned hard on the first syllable of 'astronaut', drawing it out until the insult was more than clear.

The bartender spoke up. "We don't need trouble tonight, Bill. You remember what happened the last time."

Bill rested the thick end of his pool cue on his shoulder. "No trouble." He turned and spit on the floor. "Just want to know who I'm drinking with. Had a cousin in Cleveland, and these fellas look like they made out alright from that."

This ain't good.

Tommy grinned. "You got us, Tex. We're here to drink all your beer and take your prettiest kin to the Moon with us."

The two men the cowboy had been playing pool with picked up their cues and stepped forward to stand beside and just a little behind their buddy. The bar got quiet and the locals nearest the bar moved away like a hammer was about to fall right where they were standing.

"Mighta gone a little too far, Brook," Tommy said. "But what do you say? Semper fi?"

"That's the Marines, you asshole," Brooklyn hissed. The EOF motto, *Pro Terra*, "for the Earth", would be an inappropriate battle cry in the situation.

Three against two, as long as nobody else got feeling rugged. Entirely possible, even before all the hand-to-hand training. The crowd of onlookers was the wild card. If he and Tommy roughed up a local hero, there was no telling what his buddies would do. It was a bad bet. Brooklyn held up his hands. "Sorry, boys. New in town. Don't want no–"

Bill took another step forward. "Don't give two shits what you want. Why don't you two just bounce out of here?" He moved his hand up and down in a slow, sinuous wave pattern.

Brooklyn put his nearly full beer back on the bar. "You heard the man. Let's go."

Tommy smiled. "We'll just finish these up and–"

The cowboy whipped the fat end of his pool cue down, knocking Tommy's beer out of his hand. The glass shattered on the floor. "Appears you're about done."

Tommy looked at the spilled beer and nodded slowly. He craned his neck to see the bartender. "Some butthole spilled my beer. Can I get another on the h–"

"Don't you do it!" Brooklyn yelled.

Tommy turned in time to dodge about half the force of the pool cue. The other half caught him in the side of the neck and sent him stumbling backward against the bar.

Brooklyn's swing missed, but the knee he thrust into the

cowboy's crotch didn't. Bill bent double, and Brooklyn took him down with a flying tackle. They both hit the floor hard. Brooklyn's head swam with surprise. All those hours of hand-to-hand training, and the skills deserted him in the heat of battle. He reverted to brawling tactics and threw an elbow into the cowboy's face. Something hard hit him in the back. The cowboy's friends had arrived.

"Goddamn it, Tommy!" Out of the corner of his eye, Brooklyn saw one of Bill's reinforcements hit the floor. Tommy remembered his training just fine. "All I wanted was a fucking beer!"

Brooklyn stood, leaving Bill the cowboy where he'd fallen. The man Tommy had taken down was getting to his feet. *Two on two. Even odds.*

Four more men came out of the crowd of onlookers. Brooklyn raised his hands and dropped into a combat stance he'd learned in training. It looked cool, but he figured it wouldn't hold up past the first punch. "Take the three on your side. I'll take these assholes." *This is gonna hurt.*

"My, my… Look what the white boys are doing."

The voice was clear and deep, and the action froze around them. Brooklyn saw a familiar shape slip through the crowd and approach the bar. "Dee."

"Comrade." Dee smiled and saluted the bartender. "How 'bout dealing a brother one of those beers?" He was still wearing his suit from dinner.

The bartender worked the tap. "This ain't your fight, son."

"Maybe." Dee raised the glass to Tommy and then Brooklyn. "*Pro Terra,* boys." He winked at the bartender. "But these fools will get themselves killed without me." He moved like a dancer into a comfortable-looking foot-forward stance with his right arm extended and smiled at the cowboys. "Let's do this 'fore my beer gets warm."

* * *

"We looked around base for you, but they told us you were already gone."

Dee put the jeep in gear and pulled out onto the street. "George took me out to dinner. He's staying at a hotel here in town."

"Should have brought him with you," Brooklyn mumbled though the dishrag pressed to his nose. Cowboy Bill had caught him with a kick to the face. His nose wasn't broken, but it sure as hell wasn't happy.

"He doesn't drink," Dee said. "'Sides, six or ten hicks against the three of us? George would have called it a fair fight and let it play out."

Tommy had a cut on the side of his head that was bleeding down onto his collar. Dee had taken a punch to the eye that was starting to swell some. "Sorry if we fucked up your plans," Tommy said.

"Long as I make my flight tomorrow all is well," Dee said. "I'm persona non grata on the East Coast and LA, so George is flying me out to Seattle to talk to some of the brothers and sisters there. Teach a couple classes, get laid, eat some real food."

"Brook's still looking for something to do," Tommy said. "I said he could come stay with me."

Brooklyn pulled the rag away from his face. His nostrils were plugged, but the bleeding had stopped. "Not looking for charity. Just don't feel like being much of anywhere for a while."

Dee shifted gears and took a quick left onto the road leading back to the base. "Ride up to the airport with me tomorrow. You can rent a car there, wander the American wastelands like the dude in *Kung Fu*."

Brooklyn resisted the urge to probe his nose. *All I seen of the Earth is New York and Texas an' I might be leaving it for a decade.* "Not a bad idea. Could find a couple of shows to go to."

"Just don't get in any more fights," Tommy said. "You kind of suck at it."

TWELVE

The dink at the Fort Stockton rental-car place talked up the electrics, but Brooklyn balked after reading the specs. "Seventy-five miles per charge?" He tapped the sticker on the window. "Won't even get me outta the desert, man. You tryin' to kill me?"

The dink muttered some shit about quotas, commissions, and federal subsidies, and grudgingly revealed the gasoline-powered options. The winner was an AMC Pacer in "Mellow Yellow" with way too much window glass. It looked like a fishbowl on wheels, heavy, slow, and all the grace of a cinder block. Brooklyn handed over his cash-cartridge.

His first stop was a supermarket where he picked out a Styrofoam cooler and filled it with cold cuts, bread, beer, and ice. The eight-track/radio combo in the Pacer worked just fine, and the little car gummed on the miles while Brooklyn caught up with the Hit Parade. He heard most of Steve Miller Band's new record *Fly Like an Eagle* on some deejay's play-it-all-the-way feature but lost the signal halfway through the second side. He came in range of a different station in time for the last two-thirds of "Afternoon Delight" by the Starland Vocal Band and all of Gordon Lightfoot's "The Wreck of the Edmund Fitzgerald". The next song was some trash about moonlight by a band called Starbuck. Brooklyn's mood was only saved when he found a station playing "Shout It Out Loud" by KISS. The Pacer's speedometer struggled up to its maximum ninety miles per hour.

It was good to be free and on the road. Good to be alone for awhile.

He stopped for gas in Odessa, Texas, and had a bologna sandwich and a couple of beers in a parking lot at the Junior College. Women in blue jeans and side parts, already five years out of style in Manhattan, walked to and from classes with their soft-looking boyfriends. One dude was wearing a denim jacket over his tanned bare chest, completing the outfit with a peace medallion, mutton chop sideburns, and John Lennon glasses. Brooklyn would have bet the rest of his beer that the kid either changed clothes before he went home every night or got his ass kicked anytime he left campus.

He unfolded the map he got at the rental place and measured the distance to Oklahoma with his fingers. *Four, maybe five more hours to the border. Couple, three more to Oklahoma City.* Stop there, find someplace to get a drink and park for the night. Move on the next day.

A plan without many details. Two weeks until he had to be somewhere. P-Funk was playing in Detroit, and Cleveland was sort of on the way to New York. Brooklyn fired the Pacer up and pulled it out of the parking lot. The tuner needle stopped on "Devil Woman" by some British whiner named Cliff Richard. It sounded more like a cry for help than the sexy ode Cliffy was probably shooting for. *This the way music is going, I'm probably better off on the Moon.*

Brooklyn cranked the volume and hit the gas.

He spent the night parked at a CR Anthony's Department Store outside Oklahoma City. The Pacer's "high-performance" bucket seats didn't make for the best sleeping, and he woke up stiff and aching. He did some calisthenics and ran around the lot a couple of times before going inside the store for clean underwear and socks. He emerged with a road atlas, Eagles'

Their Greatest Hits (1971-1975), AC/DC's *High Voltage*, *Destroyer* by KISS, and *2112* by Rush. *Clean socks and bad radio be damned.*

A cashier smoking outside the store directed him to a bank where he turned some of the funds on his cash-cart into actual money. Most of the mom-and-pops he'd been in didn't have a cart reader, and there was a lot of road between cities. He had plenty of scratch even with diverting a good chunk of his pay to his ma. Helped that he no longer had rent to pay and hadn't been anywhere or seen anything to spend it on in months.

Downtown Oklahoma City was an armpit. Billboards bragged the construction of a massive shopping area called "The Galleria", but when Brooklyn asked where it was, a middle-aged lady in cat-eye glasses said the money had run out years before.

"We got a real nice parking garage out of it, though," she said. She pointed Brooklyn to a hamburger joint for lunch, and he bought a postcard of the Biltmore Hotel to send to Ma and Mike.

"They're tearing it down next year," the counterman said, handing over the postcard. "Spent like $3 million on the damned thing in the '60s, and now it's coming down to build some kind of a garden."

"Like a food garden?" Brooklyn said. "Tomatoes and shit?"

The counterman answered with a mournful shrug of his shoulders and went back to cleaning the grill.

Brooklyn drove through a town called Chandler on his way out the city, and stopped at a store for a Coke and to see the street fair setting up on both sides of the tired-looking roadway. Temperature in the shady spots was eighty-plus and the air was bone dry.

"What's the occasion?" He searched the tiny store's cooler area for a bottle opener.

"It's one of them new twist-offs." The proprietor had lead-colored hair and a set of dentures to make a rat proud. "Whadaya mean 'occasion'?"

Brooklyn took a slug of the cold soda and used the bottle to point toward the roadway. "Outside. Some kinda local holiday?"

"Nothing to celebrate 'round here, son. Everybody living on Family Security and not much else." The old man frowned. "That outside is the swap market. Runs all day, every day. Pretty much ev'ryone in town has a table. Probably find yourself a helluva deal on somethin' or other."

"My ma's on EffEss."

The old man scoffed. "Everyone gets EffEss, boy. It's like grits. What you can afford to put on top of 'em makes the difference."

Brooklyn drank some of his Coke. His ma had gotten Family Security since Nixon put the program in place in '69, but the yearly payout hadn't gone far then, and even with the bump in '72, it didn't stretch much further now. "Everybody in town's out there, huh?"

"Near 'nough. Place ain't exactly boomin'." He shooed Brooklyn out of the store. "Natty Dodge down on Union and Tremont sells the best pie around. Git yourself a slice 'fore you head out."

Now he knew what he was looking at, Brooklyn saw desperation everywhere. The street tables were loaded with past-their-prime kitchenware, hand tools, sports gear, crafts, canning, old books, and baked goods. Whatever would fit in the back of the car for the trip from the house to the main street. The vendors were selling or swapping among their neighbors and hoping a windfall – a tourist, maybe, flush with outside cash – would show. *An' here he is.*

Brooklyn's fatigue pants and dirty T-shirt were well within the bounds of the local dress code, but something about him was flashing "outsider" in grimy neon. Every vendor he passed made an effort to rearrange their wares to best affect.

"Lot of life left in this," said a bottle-blonde woman pushing a blender at him. "Make yourself some of them ice-cube drinks."

R.W.W. GREENE   103

Brooklyn made a show of looking at the blender and the other things on the woman's table: a room's worth of window curtains, a set of pots and pans, a few bowling trophies, a couple of work shirts, a rundown pair of size-eleven work boots...

"How much for this?" He held up a tree-shaped air-freshener, still in its plastic package.

"Dollar," she said.

They made the exchange. Brooklyn put the tree in the cargo pocket of his pants. It wouldn't hurt the Pacer to smell a little better. "Which way is Union and Tremont? Guy in the store said the pie there is worth checking out."

The woman's face screwed up in disgust. "Wouldn't eat that pie if my life depended on it. Diseased for sure."

"Kind of disease you get from pie?"

"The kind you get from fucking other people's husbands." Her face reddened. "Little whore's over that way if you want to get yourself a piece. Can't miss her."

Brooklyn passed a table where two old ladies were dickering over a package of toilet paper and one where the vendor was wiping down a display of what looked to be jars full of green baby dicks. She caught him looking and smiled. "Pickled okra," she said. "Right out of my garden."

"Think I'm allergic," Brooklyn said and kept walking, every step weighing a little more than the last. So much of the economy and attention were geared to fighting off the alien menace, a lot of people were being left behind. Knowing it and seeing it laid out were two different things. *Duke'd find all the cheap labor he needs right on the street here.*

Couple of kids on rusty bikes zoomed by, chasing each other.

"You're in the EOF, right?"

Brooklyn turned his head to face the question. Thick guy in his fifties. Balding and bitter-looking. "Yeah."

"Recognized the pants. Did six years in the Marines."

"Thanks for your service," Brooklyn said automatically.

The man waved it off. "Squeezed in between Korea and all the space shit. Never fired a shot off the range."

"Still, you were ready. That means somethin'." *Probably that you couldn't figure out something better to do with your life or got yourself stuck like me.*

"You on leave?" the man said. His table was mostly hand tools and paperbacks with grim-faced, armed men on the cover. Enshrined at the rear was a set of *Playboy*-branded highball glasses and coasters with pictures of Hugh's Bunnies on them.

"Two weeks. Then up to the Arctic for training. What do you do?"

The man spread his arms. "You're looking at it. Haven't worked steady in five or six years. Feds came through a while ago with some work programs. Took every damned test they had and nothing."

"No jobs?"

"Plenty of jobs, none of them in Oklahoma. I'da moved for one, but they said I didn't have the right attitude." He counted off on his fingers. "I don't like gays, immigrants, communists, and coloreds. I admit it. That mean I ain't worth giving a job to?"

Brooklyn kept his eyes on the pornographic coasters. It seemed safer.

"This used to be America." The man was warming up. Probably he hadn't had a new audience in a while. "We had freedom. Then the UN – the goddamned globalists – took over, and we just bent over and let them fuck us! Fucking Kennedy. Fuck all the Kennedys! Wishtahell Oswald had been a better shot. I'd been in Dallas that day," he brought an imaginary rifle into position, "POW!"

"Guess things are tough all over," Brooklyn said. With his attitudes and age, the angry man could have been his father.

The man jabbed his finger at him. "White man's being left behind in his own country! You wait and see, pal. We're going extinct! Then what do we do?"

Lie down with the rest of the dinosaurs. "Gotta get going, man. Good talking to you."

The man's face cleared. "Hey, you wanna buy those glasses and coasters? I saw you looking at them."

Natty Dodge was in her early thirties, wearing hip-hugging blue jeans and a Bob Dylan T-shirt well. "You're new," she said when he approached her table.

"Just passing through. Heard you had good pie."

"Mr Calhoun tell you that? Old guy in the store?" She smiled. "He's on the town council. Still feels bad about bringing me down here. Always points people in my direction."

"You a baker?" Brooklyn said.

"High-school teacher, or I was. Council put it all on video this year to save money. Fired most of the staff. Kids come in now, someone takes attendance and presses 'play' on the VCR. A thoroughly modern education."

"Did some of that when I was a kid," Brooklyn said. "Had a couple history classes that way."

"If you can learn about conjunctions and multiplication from a cartoon, who needs a teacher? I only finished my master's degree five years ago, and I'm already obsolete."

"Surprised you're still here."

"Oh, I came in ready for the long haul. Moved everything from California, bought a house, joined the garden club, adopted a dog. The works."

And now you're stuck. "Where's the dog?"

Her face clouded. "Next-door neighbor poisoned her. Thought I was sleeping with her husband and figured she'd show me. Tried to get me fired for my 'radical' teaching methods, too. Her husband was screwing around on her long before I came to town, but it's always easy to blame the outsider."

"Burn your house down for you." Brooklyn was only partly

joking. His experience with arson was limited, but he had the gist. "You could take the insurance and run."

"Not quite there, yet. But I'll let you know." She smiled. "Want some pie?"

Brooklyn bought two half pies. One chocolate chess, the other strawberry-rhubarb. The fruit pie was the better of them. He ate a quarter of one, then the other, and tucked the leftovers in with the glasses and coasters in the back seat.

THIRTEEN

The further north, the grayer the skies. Interstate 44 led to St Louis, Missouri. He rode up to the top of the arch, and caught a Cardinals/White Sox game at Busch Memorial Stadium. The Cards lost badly. Brooklyn didn't give a shit. He was in the stadium mostly just to have someplace to be, grab something to eat, and take a piss without committing a crime. He splurged on a grubby room in a Motel 6 for the shower, and washed his socks and underwear in the sink.

At breakfast he met a teenager in a leather jacket who swore up and down he could "hack" his cash-cartridge, make it seem like it had more money on it, for a fifty-percent cut. Their conversation ended when the kid's mom showed up and made him carry their luggage out to the family station wagon. "Now, Kevin, and I don't mean later!" The kid wrote his phone number on the napkin and slid it to Brooklyn on the way out. He tossed it out with the rest of the trash.

Ten hours on I-70 put him in sight of the Cleveland Crater, which really was still smoking. Brooklyn found a place to park and got out of the Pacer to walk in close. The sun was going down, and he put a beer in each jacket pocket.

On April 7, 1972, the city of Cleveland had a population of about 750,000 people. There'd been a fuel-shortage protest downtown earlier in the day, and some unknown number of protesters stayed in the city for dinner and to see the sights. The big national news of the day was a hijacking. The guy had held eighty-odd passengers and the flight crew at gunpoint until he got his $500,000 ransom, then he bailed out of the plane somewhere between Denver and LA. He was never found. *Probably never got looked for. Feds had plenty else to do after the eighth.*

The next day, the population of Cleveland was near-enough zero, and a cloud of ash and dust was spreading east. The color of the sky changed. The rain fell oily and gray, and Central Park withered. The Boot – a roughly shoe-shaped asteroid about the size of an Egyptian pyramid – had hit hard enough to speed up the planet's rotation some. Smartasses started saying a day just wasn't what it used to be. The debris cloud dimmed the sun, dropped temperatures all around the world, and spawned the acid rain that was currently eating up the northeast. The rock with Leningrad's name on it fell short and landed in the Baltic, wrecking and flooding the city but not quite killing everyone.

The suburbs and little towns around Cleveland mostly cleared out on their own. The Feds bulldozed everything in sight to keep people away. But memory and mourning only lasted so long. *Now, someone's probably selling T-shirts and tickets. Gilded chunks of meteor and building rubble as paperweights.*

Two miles in, Brooklyn squeezed through a hole in a chain-link fence and headed toward a cluster of campsites set up in the ejecta. A woman waved at him.

"Hey, brother! Come sit down! Room enough here for everyone." She was young, maybe mid-twenties. "Want some pot?"

"Not right now." Brooklyn sat in the lawn chair next to hers. There was a tin can full of cigarette butts in front of it. "Who else is here?"

She peered over her shoulder at a tent set up a few yards away. "My boyfriend's taking a nap."

Brooklyn tugged one of the beers out of his pocket and pulled the tab. "So, this is it."

"The beginning of the end. Tony – that's my boyfriend – and I come out here just about every weekend to wait."

"Wait for what?"

Her eyes widened. "The Mercurians! They made the hole. Only a matter of time before they come down here and park something in it."

Brooklyn took a sip of his beer. He'd forgotten to buy ice the last time he stopped, so it wasn't all that cold. "The hell you want them back for?"

"Help us solve our problems, man! Racism, sexism, global warming, acid rain!" She grinned wryly. "Or wipe us all out. Depends on who you talk to."

"Seems like they might be more interested in killing us than teaching us." Brooklyn drank some more warm beer. "Million people died right there, and I can't fucking believe I'm saying that." He scrubbed at his mouth. The beer thought about coming up. "Fuck. Hard to imagine going up against something can do that." *An' that's supposed to be my job.*

"God sent the flood. The aliens sent the Boot."

"Sound like a priest."

Her face screwed up in mock distaste. "I went to Vassar, man. Class of 1973. Anthropology. I just want to be one of the first to talk to them when they get here."

There were half a dozen more tents set up in the area, seven or eight more people in view. "Looks like you might be in the first ten or so."

"That's because it's Friday. Tony likes to get here early to get a good spot. Wait until tomorrow night." She laughed. "That's a real party."

Brooklyn hiked back to his car to sleep and stopped at a phone booth to check the Yellow Pages. In the morning, he bought a tent and a sleeping bag and set them up near Tony and Holly's campsite. He refilled his cooler with ice and beer.

The crowd at the crater was starting to grow. He set up his lawn chair next to Holly's. "Thanks for saving me a spot."

Tony was wearing wire-framed glasses and an EOF fatigue jacket. One shoulder of the jacket lifted irritably.

"Were you in?" Brooklyn said.

The face Tony made could have curdled ice cream. "Do I look like a fucking pig asshole to you? Those motherfuckers will fuck it up for all of us."

Holly put her head on her boyfriend's shoulder. "Tony doesn't like the military."

"Noticed that. Just wondered about the coat."

"Skin of the fucking oppressor, man!" Tony snarled. "I wear it as a trophy."

Brooklyn opted not to ask whether Tony had killed someone for the skin or just bought it at a second-hand store. "Brought beer," he said. "Hope you guys like Iron City."

"Only if it's cold," Tony said.

"Cold as long as the ice lasts," Brooklyn said.

He sipped beer and chatted with Holly while the rim of the crater slowly filled with hippies and robes-and-cults types. Peddlers worked the crowd, selling drugs and craft items, soda pop, beer, bootleg eight-tracks, and cheap souvenirs. Women in tie-dyed skirts danced to pipe-and-drum music. A guy whose black-leather chaps framed his pale, bare ass jiggled by and waved to Holly.

The sun was starting to beat down hard, and Brooklyn spent two bucks on a cheap cap with an "I Survived the Cleveland Crater" patch glued to the front. It both amused and disgusted him. If the aliens had taken down the World Trade Center he might have been the one out there hawking shit. He cut the patch off and stuck it in his pocket.

Tony got up to talk to a group of similarly dressed men gathered about fifty feet away. They were passing a joint around and complaining about The System. Tony glanced back at Brooklyn with a dark scowl on his face.

"He always this pissy?" Brooklyn said.

"He thinks I want to fuck you," Holly said. "Thinks I want to fuck everyone."

"Do you?"

She made a moue. "Depends on how mad I am at Tony. Right now, no."

"Healthy relationship."

She flashed a grin. "You're in the EOF, aren't you? You've been dancing around it all day, not wanting us to know."

A group of guys in tie-dye shirts were setting up risers for a stage. "I'm not here to spy on you, if that's what you're worried about. I just wanted to see the place."

"I don't care if you are, but don't let Tony know. He'll get all self-righteous about it. Start complaining about all the money going to the EOF that could be going to schools and hospitals." She sighed. "He really doesn't care about schools and hospitals, but that's his shtick."

"What's yours?"

"I hope to get a doctorate out of this." She nodded at the friendly chaos around them.

"So you're the spy," he leaned back in his chair, "and you don't really think the aliens are going to come down and solve all our problems."

She pointed at the crater with her foot. "Helluva way to say 'hello'. My father's in the EOF. We don't really talk anymore, but he's right about this."

"Why don't you join up? Chicks make the best pilots, or so I've heard."

"The drugs are better here, and I don't like the hours in the EOF." She squinted toward the stage. "Is that Jerry Garcia?"

Brooklyn pulled his cap low. It was even cheaper looking without the patch, but it hid his military cut. He walked out toward the edge of the crater and looked down.

It was easily the biggest thing he'd even seen. Bigger than Manhattan from the Empire State Building. He'd read somewhere that the Boot had hit Cleveland so hard it made a bulge on the seafloor on the other side of the world. It blew the city into powder, threw the powder into the air, and let it fall wherever gravity and wind currents decided. The shockwave had decimated whatever was left. The Cleveland Indians had been playing in Boston the night before, and the TV reporters had asked members of the team for their comments about losing everything: wives, girlfriends, kids, homes, sponsors... The Indians' pitcher punched out a reporter during the live broadcast, ending the segment with a scrum of flailing limbs and camera gear.

The crater was deeper than the Grand Canyon. An interviewer from *Rolling Stone* had asked Evel Knievel if he'd considered jumping it, and the daredevil had called the reporter a "fucking, insensitive moron" before walking out.

Duke Carlotta believed Nixon had blown up Cleveland to get re-elected and that the Mercurians were a big hoax to get the world's wars under control. *Duke might change his tune a little if he saw this fucking thing.* It was hard to imagine man could engineer something so vast and terrible. *But we ain't fighting each other no more.* In his mind's eye, the New York City skyline exploded in atomic fire. His mother, Carmen, Chris, Mike... everyone he cared about burned. If the alien invasion were a hoax, even if a million people had to die now and then, maybe world peace was worth it.

Brooklyn lifted the ball cap to scratch his head. He'd started the road trip wanting to be nowhere and ended driving to a site that was inarguably Somewhere. Its impact was right there in front of him, too big to take in.

He walked back to where Holly was sitting, probably writing the Great American Academic Journal Article in her head. "When I first got here, you said something about pot," Brooklyn said.

She squinted at him. The sun was getting low behind him,

and he was probably little more than a shape against it. "Got something better than that," she said. "You ever done A&A?"

"Never heard of it."

Holly rose from her chair. "Let's go see Dr Tim."

Dr Tim was an owlish-looking man with thick glasses and a shock of white hair. He'd set up a large canvas tent, almost a pagoda, about a quarter mile clockwise on the rim from Holly's campsite. He frowned when he saw her.

"Too soon!" he waved her away. "Your last treatment was less than a month ago."

"It's not for me, silly!" The graduate student had put on her stoner mask again. "It's for my friend." She pulled Brooklyn into the tent. "He's a guardian."

"Have you been in orbit?" Dr Tim's attention sharpened, and he spoke quickly. "Beyond the Earth's magnetic field? Have you experienced weightlessness?"

Brooklyn held up his hand to forestall more questions. "Just got out of basic training. Won't be going up for another six months." *If ever.*

The doctor's face soured. "No matter. Have a seat." He gestured to a comfortable-looking recliner.

"What's A&A?" Brooklyn said.

Dr Tim glanced at Holly. "It's short for acid and acupuncture. Some of the young people I treat call it that, but really I use psilocybin. Have you heard of it?"

"Shrooms."

Dr Tim nodded. "Found in nature. Perfectly safe."

Brooklyn sat up to see Holly. "So your idea of a good time is to let this guy stick needles in you and then trip your balls off?"

"It's hardly recreational," the doctor scoffed, "it's therapeutic. It helps you deal with addictions, old trauma... There's some indication that it can treat combat stress and battle fatigue."

"What if I don't have any of that?" Brooklyn said.

"Then it just clears you out," Holly said. "Opens your mind, gets you ready for the next thing. Whatever that is."

The North Pole. It was hard to see how a ride in the doctor's magic recliner was going to help prep for that. "Anyone ever have a bad reaction to this, doc? Like brown-acid-level bad?"

The doctor shook his head. "It's a guided trip. I will be right here with you the whole time. Your friend can stay, too, if you wish."

Brooklyn's previous experiments with psychedelics had been more interesting than earth-shattering but... "Alright. How does this work?"

"First some paperwork. Do you mind answering a few questions for my research?"

Dr Tim brought the chair to about half recline and covered Brooklyn chest to toes with a patchwork quilt. He told Brooklyn to put his arms on the arm rests. "Palms up, please."

He unrolled a piece of cloth. "These have been sterilized, of course." The acupuncture needles glinted inside. "I am going to put seven of these into each of your hands. Two for each chakra. This will open up your energy flow and prepare you for the trip. Do you understand?"

"How bad this gonna hurt?" Brooklyn said.

"I spent several weeks training with Dr Gim Shek Ju the last time he was here. He said my technique was impeccable." The doctor pulled the first needle from the roll out. "This one is for your crown chakra. It goes here at the tip of your thumb." Brooklyn barely noticed it going in. The doctor pulled out another needle. "This one is for the crown chakra point on your other thumb."

Brow, throat, heart, solar plexus, sacral, and base followed. Brooklyn felt none of it. Needles bristled from his hands. The chair was comfortable, reclined perfectly so there was no pressure or pinch anywhere. "Now what?"

"I have distilled the psilocybin into a tincture with grain-alcohol base." He held up a tiny bottle. "Or I can make a tea."

"Do shots or sip tea?" Brooklyn said. "Shots all day, doc. Lay it on me."

Brooklyn downed the tincture and closed his eyes to wait for it to kick in. He might have fallen asleep. "Will you sit by him?" he heard the doctor say. "I want to take some notes."

Holly boarded the stool next to the recliner and put her hand on Brooklyn's arm. "You are perfectly safe, Brook. The doctor is here. I'm here. Everything's cool."

Brooklyn opened his eyes. He felt good. Muzzy, maybe a little sleepy. "'M OK." He yawned. Holly's aura was showing.

"You are on a search for yourself, Mr Lamontagne," the doctor said. "Are you thirsty? Would you like to listen to some music?"

Brooklyn drank the proffered water. It was silver cold and delicious. The glass felt like mercury on his lips. "Whadda ya have?"

"How about some jazz? A friend of mine in Japan sent me a new Miles Davis album. It hasn't been released here." Dr Tim busied himself at a side table. The speakers on the battery-powered turntable were tinny, and he kept the volume low.

"Sounds orange," Brooklyn said. "The trumpet sounds orange. The drums are blue."

"I'm going to record this session," the doctor said.

Could get into this cat. The melodies were complex, the musicians having a conversation that the listener could never quite get the details of. It was like eavesdropping on strangers in a bar made of polished obsidian. With great cocktails. And a bonfire.

"Don't think this is working." Brooklyn frowned. "Don't really feel anything."

"Just relax," the doctor said. "Give up your expectations and see what happens."

"We're here, and you're safe," Carmen – no, Holly – said. "Just remember that." Her voice dropped to a murmur. "He said he didn't have any trauma. Maybe this is all you're going to get."

"Everyone has trauma," Dr Tim said.

Miles began a long trumpet solo. The orange notes licked like flames around the room. *Fire!* Brooklyn's pulse shot up.

"Here we go," the doctor said.

Let's show him what the aliens will do to him!

On a plane to South Carolina to visit an aunt and uncle he'd met for the first time at Pop's funeral. Brooklyn hadn't even been a Cub Scout, and Ma'd spent way too much money on a tent and other shit for the trip.

"The boys will have a wonderful time together!" the aunt said through the red lipstick staining her teeth.

The cousins, older, covered in badges and ribbons, hadn't wanted him there and demonstrated it whenever they could. Noogies. Wedgies. Indian burns. Monkey bites. Tiny cruelties that grew after the family station wagon's left them at the campsite.

Boy Scouts are good at knots. "Do they still sting when they're dead?" one of them asked.

"Let's find out," the older cousin said. "Let's show him what the aliens will do to him."

Cold fish jelly, tentacles splaying as they fell, rained down on his body, stripped naked and tied like a sacrifice on the beach. Hundreds of jellyfish had come onto the sand to die, and dozens of them ended up on his bare skin. And they burned! No one had come to save him then.

We're here, Brook. You're safe. Her voice was purple, blending into the pale violet of the saxophone and surrounding the fire on all sides. The flame was a lighter, his dead father's Zippo, packed for the trip and applied liberally to the side of his cousins' tent. Now his scream was audible in bright orange-red trumpet tones. *Fuck you, guys!*

The orange died to embers. To falling ash. To snow. *Brook! Goddamn it, I can't hold him!*

He tried to get up. He'd tried. Surely, he'd tried. Rescue his rescuer, his friend. David. The tire iron clattered and slid into the dark. Brooklyn hit the ground, pants already full of piss, waiting for the plasma heat to burn. *ZAAARK!* David reduced to matter and memory.

It wasn't your fault, Brook. The purple lady was back. She had MaCarmenHollyPopTommyDeeChrisMariaDavid's face. The Purple Lady had a billion eyes, ever watching. The Purple Lady had a billion arms, ever holding and defending. Her roots went deep into the ground of every planet, especially–

You're safe, Brooklyn, she whispered. *It's OK.*

It really was.

Brooklyn floated awake and stretched his arms and legs in the chair. "How long was I sleeping?"

"A while. Dr Tim's gone out for a walk," Holly said. "You want some water?"

The water was more cool than cold. The doctor probably hadn't invested in as much ice as Brooklyn had.

"That was it?" Brooklyn said.

Holly smiled.

"That was some real bullshit."

FOURTEEN

Brooklyn had a mild headache and three hours of his life had gone missing, otherwise he felt OK. He walked with Holly back to the campsite and popped one of his beers. It was still very cold.

"How are you feeling?"

It wasn't the first time she'd asked. "Fine. Like I took too long a nap."

She nodded. "That sounds about right."

"See anything weird when you did it?"

"I talked to my grandmother the last time. She died when I was eight."

Tony was waiting in his lawn chair. "Where the fuck have you been?"

Holly rushed to him and planted a huge kiss on his cheek. "We went to see Dr Dream!" She was a helluva actor. She could shed thirty IQ points between one sentence and the next.

Tony frowned. "That shit will rot your brain if you do too much."

"Oh, it wasn't for me. I just watched." She looked at Brooklyn and winked.

"Yeah, I was in the hot seat," Brooklyn said. "You ever done it?"

"I don't need my mind expanded." He sneered. "I read."

The sun went down over the bandstand. The bearded guitarist was not Jerry Garcia, but he was pretty good. The other members of the band kept up OK, and they played mostly covers. Brooklyn threw a ten in the hat when it came his way. It was easy to be generous when basic needs were met. He had a place to sleep, food to eat, beer to drink, and a pretty girl to talk to, as long as he ignored the scowls and glares Tony threw his way. Baiting him further might have been fun, but the drama wouldn't be worth it.

Women in long, soft dresses spun like flowers along the rim of the disaster, their hands twisting like smoke to the rhythm of whatever song the band was finding its way through. Shirtless men with long hair thumped along behind them, hoping one of the flowers would float in their direction. Holly handed him a joint, and he pulled the smoke deep into his lungs. Held, held, held it and released it into the universe like a prayer. *Shortest prayer in the English language*, Pop used to say. *Fuck it. Outta my hands, outta my control. Fuck it.*

Brooklyn filled his lungs again and got up to dance with Holly.

It was probably 3am. when he yawned and bid the little group he'd been hanging with goodnight. "When you folks going back?"

"In the morning" was the most common answer. A long drive back to real life and a few hours to kill before bedding down for the start of the work week. Most would put their head down and grind, then come back to the Crater the next weekend. Real life is where they slept; the Cleveland Crater was where they lived, man.

"I'll walk you back," Holly said.

Tony looked like he wanted to say something, but he kept his mouth shut.

"Why are you with that guy?" Brooklyn said when they were out of earshot.

"Utter convenience," Holly said. "My grant covers housing

but not transportation. He has a car and is headed in the right direction. It won't last long."

"Don't know that it's worth it, sister. Cars are pretty cheap." They stopped in front of Brooklyn's tent. "Want to come in for awhile?"

"Not unless I want hear Tony pouting all the way back tomorrow." She smiled. "I just wanted to check in. Make sure you're still OK with everything."

"With Dr Dream? No problems."

"You might feel a little low in a couple of days, but it's just the shrooms. Be easy and do something nice for yourself."

"That from experience?"

She shrugged. "Doing something nice for yourself is generally a good idea. Go to a movie. Get a steak. Get laid."

"I'll take your advice."

She kissed him on the mouth. "Good luck up there, Brook. Thanks for your service."

As if I have a choice. "Not a done deal yet. I can still fuck things up at the Pole."

"True. But I have a feeling about you. EOF brat, remember? I think you might be OK." She smiled. "Stay groovy, spaceman."

Crater Fest was packing up around him when Brooklyn slithered out of his tent the next morning. Tony and Holly were gone, the holes of their tent stakes and divots from the legs of their lawn chairs the only evidence of their existence.

Except for the Purple Lady.

He might have dreamt about her, but the night images were cloudy and thick. Brooklyn scraped through the fire pit to find some embers and put water on to boil. His camping-supply run had included a jar of Taster's Choice instant coffee, his ma's favorite, and he needed it badly. He sat back on his heels to watch the pot.

"You don't look like them others."

Brooklyn shielded his eyes with his hand and looked up. The man was in his fifties, heavyset, wearing a Korean War veteran cap.

"You need a shave, but that haircut says military," the man said.

"Extra-Orbital Forces," Brooklyn said.

"US Army. Twenty-Fourth Infantry."

Brooklyn nodded like he understood the significance and responded by rote. Prof Rhineberg would have been proud. "Thanks for your service. Want some coffee?"

"Don't mind if I do." The man hunkered down by the campfire.

Brooklyn's road supplies included a sleeve of Styrofoam cups and he shook two out. He spooned in the instant coffee and added hot water. "Don't have cream or sugar, sorry."

"Don't need it." The man took a sip of the coffee and grimaced. "They say no coffee is bad coffee, but this instant shit comes close. Weak sauce."

"I think they add napalm and cocaine to the coffee in the mess hall." A soldier's joke. Shared pain or inconvenience. "My name's Brooklyn."

The man chuckled. "Chuck. Brings you to the Crater?"

"Had some time before the next phase of training." Brooklyn grunted. "Guess I just wanted to see it."

"Take a look at what you're fighting for." Chuck nodded. "This it?"

Good question. "Just a big hole in the ground."

"It's a graveyard. Maybe the biggest one ever," the man said. "There was some talk about building a memorial. I suppose they'll get to it eventually."

"You from here?"

"Never been to Cleveland in my life, but I been to the Crater dozens of times. Come out here just about every weekend."

"For the party?"

"Clean up afterwards." Chuck snorted. "Look at all this shit."

The rim was littered with cast-off bottles and packaging. Trash. "Clean all this up yourself?"

"Nah. Got some buddies who come up from the Veterans of Foreign Wars post. We clean up, drink a few, curse at the kids, wonder what the world is coming to... Good times."

"The parties bother you?" Brooklyn readied to disavow participation. He hadn't expected to find one, after all.

"Bother me?" Chuck rubbed his face. "Guess not. 'Preciate it if the little shits picked up after themselves, but I can't begrudge them having a little fun. You're only young and stupid once. I sure in hell had my chance."

"The kids..." *Jesus, I'm only a few years older than them!* "Kids told me the aliens are going to land here someday and tell us how to solve all our problems. You believe that shit?"

Chuck held his cup out for more coffee. "Don't know what I believe anymore," he said. "Thought I knew what I was fighting for when I went to Korea. Turns out it was something way different. By the end, the only thing I gave a shit about were my buddies. Lot of them died over lines someone in Washington, DC drew on a map."

"Crater's way more than lines on a map."

"'Tis. This big ol' hole in the ground has us all peering at the sky waiting for the next Boot to fall." He tugged his cap to settle it on his forehead. "Makes me wonder if someone's tying our shoelaces together while we're all looking in the wrong direction. Fool me once, shame on you. Fool me twice, and I'm the stupid fucker with his feet tied." He sucked the last few drops of shitty coffee out of his cup and rose to his feet. "Nothing here to fight for, but graveyards ought to be kept nice. Give me your cup, and I'll toss it for you."

"Got a few hours," Brooklyn said. "Lemme help you clean up."

A week later, Brooklyn found a good spot to park and piss, with a pretty good view of the Manhattan skyline. The city was tall and alive, full of stupid, ugly, beautiful, brilliant people going about their lives, eating pizza, drinking beer, fucking up relationships, dancing around their problems, and waiting for the next shoe to drop. *Cancer, eviction, heart attack, cheating spouse, alien invasion, pregnant girlfriend, bad day at the track… there's always a fucking shoe. Big shit or small shit. Everything happens.*

It wasn't hard to imagine as a crater. As a kid, he'd sometimes wished it would happen. Seven million people dead as Cleveland. It wouldn't matter to them who dropped the next rock. Dead was dead was dead. *Fuck it, man. I'm just trying to keep my ass out of jail.*

There was an appointment in central New Jersey coming up. Drop the Pacer off at the rental place and get a lift out to the EOF Engineering Station in Lakehurst. Tommy would be there, and Dee. A few others he'd met in basic he gave a shit about. Brooklyn put his hands on the small of his back and rubbed at the tension there. The skyline was gray and dirty. *Tired, like me.* He turned to hunt up a payphone.

Ma bustled around her kitchen. "You'd told me earlier, I coulda had dinner for you!"

"Wasn't sure when I was gonna be by, Ma." *Or if.* "Relax yourself and take a load off." Brooklyn was two glasses into a Queens' tap-water reunion.

She pushed errant hair off her forehead with the back of her wrist. "Let me call Mike an' tell him I can't make it first."

The water hit the wrong pipe. "You gotta date?" He captured her hand before it found the receiver on the wall. "Save it. Take you out to breakfast tomorrow and catch you up. I'll give Chris a call 'n' see if he wants to grab a couple tonight."

"Where will you sleep?"

"Leave me a key, an' I'll crash on the couch." He grinned. "Want I should wait up for you?"

"Brooklyn Villalobos Lamontagne!" She flushed. "That's no way to talk about someone's mother!"

"So, should I?"

A little smile played on her face. "No, but I'll be back in time for breakfast. Late breakfast."

"Lunch at *Juquila*?"

"Probably safer." She patted his arm. "You sure?"

"Hundred percent. Sack out on the couch for an hour or so, meet up with Chris." The corner of his mouth lifted. "Probably spend the whole night jawing 'bout our sinful mothers."

"You!" She hip-checked him toward the living room. "Try not to wake you up when I leave."

She succeeded. Rousing at eight, he found a note on the table and a twenty-dollar bill. *Sandwich in the icebox for you. Happy your home! – Ma*

Chris said he wanted to meet at Neir's Tavern on 78th Street. The Pacer was in a good parking spot, so Brooklyn took the bus as far as he could and walked the rest. The city felt good under the soles of his boots.

"Hell you want to meet here for?" he said, spotting Chris at the bar. "No one in here under forty!"

Chris slapped him on the back and shook his hand like he never had. He'd put on weight and looked like he'd stepped out of a Sears catalog. Denim cut like a suit and a wide-collared yellow shirt. "Jesus, they sure beat the shit out of you!"

Brooklyn's ma had hung onto a few of his things. The fatigue pants and graying t-shirt had been replaced with jeans and a work shirt he'd been meaning to toss. The jeans fit OK, but the shirt hung loose in places and bound in others. He ran his hand over his head. Two weeks hadn't done much to make his hair look less military.

"Didn't expect to see you around here for awhile." Chris ordered them beers.

"Had some time to kill before I went north." He spread his arms. "Thought I'd see America." The woman he met at the

P-Funk show in Detroit had been the highlight. They'd run hot and crazy for about forty-eight hours straight before crashing on park benches for the night. She'd been gone by the time he woke up, leaving nothing behind but memories and the Motörhead tattoo she'd talked him into getting on his shoulder.

"A lot's changed." Chris sniffled. "You heard about Carmen, I guess." He nodded to himself. "Moved out of my mom's place. Got my own."

"Still workin' for your old man?" Chris's pop was a scumbag but hid it well. Most of the money he made behind the scenes got cleaned up through his car dealerships and real-estate interests.

"Right-hand man, almost."

"Explains the suit."

Chris tugged at the neck of his shirt absently. It gaped a couple of buttons at the top, showing off his pale chest. "Appearances matter."

"Bet your dad doesn't like it."

Chris drank some beer. "He doesn't like anything that's not gray or black and uncomfortable."

"You happy?"

"That s'posed to be a thing? I'm making money, got an apartment, door with a lock. Girl I'm seeing pretty regular." He shrugged. "Sounds like happy, don't it?"

"How's your ma?"

Chris consulted the beer glass again. "We ain't talking much. She's not too pleased I got in touch with him."

"Never did have a good word for him. Stories she used to tell, I don't blame her."

"She mighta been, whatayacallit, exaggeratin'. He done alright by me. Got a new wife, 'bout our age. Done alright by her, too."

Angry, son-of-a-bitch, abusive, and womanizer were the words Chris's mom used the most often when describing her ex. *Maybe he's changed.* "Good to see you on top of things, man."

"You, too, Brook." He smiled. "Knew you'd come out on top of this shit. Always do."

Brooklyn drank some beer. *Right on top of the shit. Truer fucking words, pal.* He slid a newspaper-wrapped package to Chris. "Got you a present. Guy I got 'em from says they're collectible."

PART FIVE
The Rubberband Man

November 25, 1976

FIFTEEN

Every day at Arctic Base 1 had been a cold one. *No reason the last bit would be any different.* Brooklyn cleared his throat. "Hoping to go for computers, sir."

Captain Houston scanned the papers on his desk. "Your math scores are decent but not optimal."

Brooklyn was sitting so straight his back wasn't touching the chair. "Like to be a tech, sir. Solder-monkey not a programmer."

Houston pointed at a row of numbers with a stubby finger. "Your PT scores are pretty good. Could put you in with the drop troopers. With a combat bonus, the money would be better."

Drop troops spent their time training for a fast-deploy, planet-based war that wouldn't come unless the Mercurians landed on Mars or the Moon or Earth without destroying it with rocks first or, far less likely, the EOF figured out a way to invade the hottest planet in the solar system. *Lots of ways to die as a drop trooper.* "I'll shoot if a target shows its face to me, sir, but the troops are a younger man's game." Brooklyn could keep up OK in training, but at twenty-five he'd lost the edge in reflexes and response time. He'd considered intelligence – he had some experience on the shady side of things – but surviving the Arctic had half convinced him that, if he kept his head down, he'd make it through his term intact. "Might as well learn something useful."

"What do you know about computers?"

"Had an HP-2115 wired into my apartment as comptroller, sir. Worked until it caught fire."

"How long was that?"

"About three minutes, sir. I also built an Altair 8800 from a kit. It's back in the barracks."

"What have you done with it?"

"Made it whistle."

"IBM made a computer sing fifteen years ago."

"I made it whistle the *Andy Griffith* theme song. Least as I remembered it, sir. Also turns my coffee maker on and off."

Houston signed the form. "Computers it is, specialist." He handed the paper to Brooklyn. "I warn you, though. You wash out of tech training you'll spend the next nine years polishing the domes from the outside."

"Yes, sir." Brooklyn stood.

The short hallway between the captain's office and the base's primary hub had been carved directly out of the Arctic ice. With death from exposure a near certainty for anyone who stayed long outside unprotected, training in the ice and snow was the next best thing to the Moon.

Tommy was waiting in their shared bunkroom. "What'd you get?"

"Computer tech. You?"

"Weapons. Ships and tanks."

"An' while you're charging in guns blazing, I'll be keeping the Admiral's computers humming."

Tommy pshawed. "Least I won't electrocute myself crawling around inside an antique mainframe."

The door hissed open. Dee walked in, beating his hands together to warm them up. He stripped off his parka and dumped it on his bunk. "Scout. Just the way I wanted it."

"Fast and helpless?" Tommy said.

Dee's teeth flashed. "Long hours away from punks like you. Just me and the stars."

Scout ships were fast as hell in a straight line. They were sneaky, too, but there wasn't much a scout pilot could do if they attracted unwanted attention. By the time the pilot could get the ship slowed down enough to change direction, the Mercurians might have him.

"Let me guess." Dee pointed at Tommy. "Mr Big-Gun-Dick-Substitute." He moved his finger to indicate Brooklyn. "Captain Computer Jockey."

"Got it in two, pal." Brooklyn opened his locker and reached inside his spare boots for a flask. Despite the cold and the regulations, enterprising base personnel had found a way to open a market with the Soviet base fifty miles south. The Russians got American music and pornography, and the American officers got homemade vodka. In spite of his intentions to keep his nose clean, Brooklyn had found his way into the black market and made himself useful.

"A week to go." Brooklyn drank and passed the flask to Tommy.

"A week to go."

Dee took a long drink when it was his turn. "Leaving tomorrow. Month of advanced training in South America then up to Eisenhower."

"Don't need to be sober for the flight," Brooklyn said. "Let's do something 'bout that."

The Soviet vodka was easy on its drinkers. The old comrade who made the stuff was an artist. Even so, Brooklyn felt tender around the edges when he woke up to Tommy shaking him.

"You hear me?" Tommy said. "I said he's gone!"

Who's gone? The answer swam to the forefront. "Dee? Know he's gone, man. We got him to his plane." He held his watch in front of his face. "Two hours ago. Hell you waking me up for?"

Tommy's face was flushed like he'd run ten miles. "His plane went down, man! A storm kicked up about seventy miles out. The pilot sent a mayday then nothing."

Brooklyn sat up, wincing at the dull pain in his head. "Anybody out looking?"

"Not until the wind drops. The colonel ordered the base sealed."

"What's the temperature out there?"

"Negative ninety. Get your pants on, and let's go see the captain."

"You're drunk," Houston said. "I can smell it on both of you."

"We were drinking, sir. Stopped a while ago," Tommy said.

The adrenaline had burned out the residual fugue. The APC they'd swallowed on the way out of the bunkroom would take care of the rest.

"There are twelve men on that plane, sir," Tommy said. "They deserve a rescue attempt."

Houston paced his quarters, a room no less spartan but twice the size of the one Brooklyn shared with his friends. He stopped in front them. "Son... I understand what you feel, and I admire your concern." He frowned. "The winds are at a hundred per hour plus out there. A rescue party would never make it."

"We trained for worse than this, sir," Tommy said. "The suits can take it. Give Brook and me a Sno-Cat. We'll bring them all back in."

The captain looked at his desktop without seeing it. "I want to, but I can't. The colonel has locked us down tight for the duration. Clears up some, maybe we can go out tomorrow."

Brooklyn's jaw ached from clenching.

"They'll be dead by tomorrow, sir," Tommy said.

"And you won't be." The captain stood. "You're dismissed, gentlemen."

Tommy spun on his heel and stepped to the door, Brooklyn close in tow. The captain spoke again before they could touch the doorknob. "They're already dead, boys." He made his face stern. "There's nothing you can do."

* * *

Tommy pulled gear from his locker and tossed it on his bunk. "We need a 'Cat, suits, and a dozen evac bags. What else?"

Brooklyn stopped pacing. "Hell you talking about?"

"I'm not waiting till tomorrow."

Brooklyn shoved his hands into the pockets of his jacket. "You heard Houston. Nothing's surviving out there. It's the North Fucking Pole!"

Tommy shook a woolen Union Suit under Brooklyn's nose. "And we're going to the damned Moon in a couple of weeks! How much worse can it be?"

"Relax a minute. Crack a bottle, and we'll talk this out. Dee and them got all the gear they need to survive. Probably got his feet up in the seat writing an essay about it by now."

"You sure about that?" Tommy's face was fire-engine red. He jabbed his finger into Brooklyn's chest. "You just said no one's going to survive out there. You're chicken shit!"

"Careful, is all." Brooklyn raised his hands, palms out. "Dee's my friend, too, but I get busted for something I'm going to jail, man."

"He's gonna die out there!" He threw the suit of long underwear at Brooklyn. The red wool hit the floor and pooled between them. "Fine. Stay here if you want. Be safe."

Brooklyn chewed his lower lip. *Dead is dead. Possibly alive is... something else. God damn it.* "I'll get the Sno-Cat, the suits. Grab whatever else we need and meet me at the kitchen docks in twenty minutes. He picked up the red suit. "Gonna end up in the shit for this."

"Keep your fingers crossed." Tommy smiled a little. "Might just freeze to death."

Top speed for a military-modded Sno-Cat in the Arctic was about fifteen miles per. The blowing snow brought it down to seven. The windshield wipers were working furiously.

"I can't see a fucking thing," Tommy said from the passenger seat. "How's it on your side?"

"Same snow here as there. Lost sight of the base at less than fifty yards." Brooklyn squinted into the near whitewash ahead. "This is going to take some doing."

"The radar's not showing anything."

"Watch the road. See something I don't, yell your ass off."

Crevasses, huge cracks in the ice sheet, could be hundreds of feet long and dozens of feet wide, easily capable of swallowing the thirty-foot Sno-Cat and its passengers without a burp. Brooklyn's eyes didn't leave the limited view outside. He could maybe see fifteen feet ahead before the blowing snow scrubbed away the details. At thirty feet there was nothing but white.

There was no road, just ice in flat plains or hills and valleys created by tides and the shift of tectonic plates. The Sno-Cat churned forward gamely, its big engine gulping diesel, its treads leaving deep tracks behind. The blowing snow covered them almost immediately.

"How long before they notice we're gone?" Tommy said.

"Wasn't real sneaky when I grabbed this thing. Anyone's paying attention they'll see it's missing." He smothered a yawn. Adrenaline only went so far. "Don't see the sense in sending someone after us right away. Ain't like we got a lotta places to go."

"We got the fuel for this?"

After two hours of travel the fuel needle trembled an eighth of a tank under the 'full' mark. "Depends on how far we gotta go."

"I'll make some coffee."

They settled in for the ride the best they could. Brooklyn tense at the wheel and Tommy dividing his concentration between the map and radio beacons he was juggling. They switched places after five hours and again after ten. At eleven hours, Brooklyn took the vehicle out of gear and shook his arms out. "Plane's last known location. See what the locater says."

Tommy switched the box on, and the two men held their breath. Thirty seconds passed. Tommy fiddled with the dials. Forty. At forty-seven they heard the telltale ping of an emergency beacon. Brooklyn's breath escaped in relief. "How far?"

Tommy scribbled on the dash-mounted clipboard and checked his figures. "Fifteen miles." He pointed south-southwest. "That way."

"Down to a little more than half a tank. Plus the reserve." Brooklyn rubbed at his face, wincing at the scratchy feel of his beyond five-o'clock shadow. "How's the terrain that way?"

"Pretty rough."

The pings grew louder and closer together. When it became a steady tone, Brooklyn slowed the big machine to a crawl. "See anything?" After nearly twenty hours in an Arctic blizzard, the wreck would look like any other hump of snow.

"We should have grabbed a thermal-imaging camera."

Brooklyn scanned the snow field ahead. "That look like a plane's tail to you?"

Tommy studied the spot Brooklyn was pointing to. "Could be. Might just be a big chunk of ice."

"Let's get suited up and go see."

The Arctic environment suits were kissing cousins to the gear they'd use on the Moon. Insulated, helmeted, and heated, the only things they lacked were a set of chemical rockets and oxygen tanks. The changes took the weight down from a hundred-twenty-five pounds to seventy. They struggled into their suits and helped each other run safety checks. "Just like training," Tommy said.

"Yeah, maybe." Brooklyn opened the door to the outside. The sudden cold took his breath away in spite of the suit's heating elements. He rocked backward as the wind battered at his oddly-weighted body. He took a couple steps to stay on his feet. "Don't get cocky here. End up on our asses it'll be murder getting back up."

"You lead, I follow," Tommy said.

They set off slowly, lifting their feet as little as possible to avoid getting caught off balance by a sudden gust. The gray metal of the plane's tail came into focus, mostly buried. "I'll check it out," Brooklyn said. "Get back to the 'Cat for the sled and the bags."

Tommy crackled an affirmative via his suit's short-range radio and turned back. Getting the flatbed snowmobile off the back of the Sno-Cat was a one-man job and would make transporting the crash survivors easier. Brooklyn moved forward, reminding himself to stay slow and careful. It seemed an eternity before he could reach out with one heated gauntlet to brush snow off the plane's skin.

As crash landings went, it hadn't been a bad one. The plane rested on its belly, the few windows well over Brooklyn's head. Keeping one hand on the plane, Brooklyn walked away from the tail looking for a way in. The C-130 had taken off with seven passengers, five crew, and a load of trash and broken equipment the United Nations had decreed should not be left to clutter up the Arctic. The planes were usually a hundred feet long from nose to tail, but this one ended in jagged metal about fifteen feet ahead of the wings. Brooklyn chinned on his radio. "Looks like the cockpit's gone. She's broken open."

His receiver blew static for a few seconds. "Any survivors?" Tommy's voice was small, and not just because of the tinniness of the speakers.

"Don't know yet."

Brooklyn stepped into the hole left by the missing half of the plane. The wind stopped buffeting, making it eerily quiet inside the suit. His helmet light shone on empty seats, each coated in white frost. They looked like something made of marble. *Like walking into a tomb.* He shuddered and walked further into the plane.

Not all of the seats were empty. "Got bodies." He counted, his helmet light flickering over the seated statues. "Two... No. Three of them."

A stiff wall of canvas separated the passenger section of the plane from the cargo hold. Brooklyn pushed past it and played his light over the boxes and crates. He activated his radio. "Get the sled here. Fast!"

"How long they been unconscious?" Tommy said.

Brooklyn glanced back at the stretcher racks. Dee and the other survivors were strapped down and zipped into self-heating evac bags. "Had a fire, but it was out. Probably just went to sleep an' nobody woke up to check it." He put the Sno-Cat in gear and started a wide turn away from the wreck. "Gonna do a circle around the plane, see if we can spot the nose."

Three sets of dog tags chilled the inside of Brooklyn's shirt pocket. The bodies would keep until a retrieval team could come out and get them. He drove a quarter mile out and made a left turn to start the circle. Tommy leaned toward the windshield, as if the extra six inches he gained would make it easier to spot the rest of the plane.

"In this shit they could be right beside us and we'd never know," he said.

"Try the radio."

Tommy twisted the frequency dial to the emergency channel. "What should I say?"

The left side of the 'Cat jumped as its tracks hit something more solid than snow. A rock, maybe. Or wreckage. Brooklyn growled. "Just tell them we're here."

Static hissed in response. Tommy repeated the hail every couple of minutes. Brooklyn kept an eye on the odometer.

When the numbers reached one-point-six miles, he took the Sno-Cat out of gear. "Oughta be something like a circle if my math is right."

"Now what?"

Brooklyn drummed on the steering wheel with the heels of his hand. He took in some air. The storm showed little sign of letting up. "Back to base. The guys may be warm now, but they ain't out of the woods. Captain Houston said they might send out an S&R party today. Maybe we'll meet them on the way back." *An' hold our hands out so they can put the cuffs on.*

The Sno-Cat's cabin lurched.

"The road's getting rougher," Tommy said.

"Ain't no damn road." Brooklyn clenched his teeth. "It's the wind. Storm's picked up." He rolled his head to stretch his neck. "Figures the trip back would be worse." He glanced at the fuel gauge. "Usin' a lot of diesel heading into the wind like this."

The needle showed a quarter of a tank.

"How far?"

"Fifty or sixty miles, maybe. Hard to tell." He stopped the 'Cat. "Take the wheel for a minute. I gotta piss."

Their forward motion continued while Brooklyn staggered toward the rudimentary latrine in the back of the vehicle. He nearly fell twice as snow and ice shifted underneath the machine's metal treads. On the way back, he stopped to check on the survivors. Dee's skin was gray and clammy, and his breathing shallow. His right foot had frozen in blood to the floor of the plane; he'd probably lose it. Brooklyn checked the pressure bandage on the wound and resealed the bag. The other men were in similar condition. Brooklyn checked the power levels on all the evac bags and headed back to the cockpit.

"How we doing?" He dropped into the co-driver's seat.

"Decent. How are they?"

Brooklyn grunted in response. "Gonna grab a catnap. Wake me up in half an hour, and I'll let you have the next one."

Brooklyn arranged himself in the seat as best he could and closed his eyes. Inside his head, the constant thrum of the big diesel morphed into a beat. "Walk on the Wild Side" by Lou Reed, maybe. Brooklyn ordered a beer and looked around for a likely lady. And there she was, on the wild side if there ever was one. Her lavender dress clung to her like an afterthought and barely came to the middle of her tanned thighs. Brooklyn grinned and walked down the bar to where she sat alone.

"Nice dress," he said. "Talk you out of it?"

She tapped her cigarette into the glass ashtray in front of her and opened her mouth to speak. Then she punched him in the face.

Brooklyn woke with his cheek mashed against cold glass. "What…!?" He heard Tommy swearing beside him and turned his head to see his friend to the left and slightly above him. Tommy's face was white.

"We're in a hole. Gonna roll!"

Brooklyn clawed for his seatbelt. "Reverse it! Put it in reverse!"

"I did!"

The Sno-Cat tilted alarmingly as Brooklyn stood. He grabbed a roof strut and pulled himself to Tommy's side of the cab. "I'll try to put some weight in the back!"

The 'Cat's engine was in the middle, a pivot point. Brooklyn struggled to reach the back corner opposite the shotgun seat. His buck seventy wasn't much, but maybe he could weigh down the rear treads enough to get them engaged and pull them out of danger.

The floor tilted again and Brooklyn lunged for the next support. He reached into an overhead compartment for a heavy toolbox and held it to his chest. Another lunge took him as far as he could go. "Reverse it! Rear treads. Full power!" He jumped in place, hoping the extra push would be enough to let the tread find purchase. He lost his grip on the box and barely noticed when it hit his foot. "Reverse it!"

The Sno-Cat trembled as its rear treads struggled for purchase and slowly, by agonizing inches, pulled itself out of the hole. The transmission screamed as the deck leveled. The big engine shuddered and stalled.

The wind, momentarily lost in the sound of the big diesel and the pounding in Brooklyn's ears, surged.

"You alright?" Tommy said.

Brooklyn swallowed hard against pressure rising from his gut.

"Brook! Are you alright back there?"

Brooklyn took a slow breath. His foot was killing him. "Let's not do that again."

"It's not starting, man." Brooklyn slapped the center of the wheel with one gloved hand. "The hell you do to this thing?"

Tommy flushed. "I didn't do nothing, Brook. Just put it in reverse and floored it when you said. I didn't–"

Brooklyn waved his hand tiredly. "Sorry. Know it ain't your fault."

"It's getting cold in here."

"Get a lot colder we don't this thing running." He rubbed his face. "The evac bags are good for another four hours."

"We only used four of them. We have eight more."

Twenty hours of heat in the unused evac bags. Maybe. Without heat in the Sno-Cat, the bags would be fighting to keep the occupants warm against something a lot colder than cabin temperature. The outside gauge read negative ninety-two.

Tommy stood. "Get on the radio and try to contact Arctic One. I'll go out and look at the engine."

The suits' batteries had nearly recharged. Brooklyn helped

Tommy with the suit, and the kid went through the door as fast as possible to keep whatever heat remained inside.

"The wind's worse than before," he transmitted. "Gotta be hurricane force or better."

"Gauge says it's steady at eighty."

"Gauge appears to be fucked up. Hold on."

Brooklyn rubbed his arms to warm up and maybe just to comfort himself.

"Lost the instrument package," Tommy reported. "The dish is gone."

"How long ago?"

"No way of tellin'," Tommy said. "We could be anywhere." The biggest part of the instrument pack was the receiver that allowed them to triangulate their location. "It's all gone. Even the radio antenna." It might have been easier if they'd fallen into the crevasse. Even if they got the engine going, there was no way to tell if they were heading in the right direction. "We're completely off the map."

Brooklyn got a glimpse of Tommy's helmet as he crunched around to the engine compartment. "Don't even know what the hell I'm looking at," Tommy muttered.

"I didn't copy."

"Coming back in," Tommy said. "Not a damned thing I can do here."

Brooklyn dropped back into the driver's seat. Tommy had covered his red buzz cut with a gray wool watch cap. "How far do you think the radio signal is going?" he said.

"Without an antenna?" Brooklyn warmed his face with his hands. "Couple miles maybe. Even right outside I lost some of what you said."

"The sled's good for fifty miles. I could head out in a suit. Maybe find some help."

"Got any idea which way to go, Magellan?"

"Beats the hell out of waiting here to die."

"Maybe. But not yet. Let's get a couple of hours sleep first." He yawned. "I'll check on Dee and the others, and we'll each get about four hours. You sleep, I stay on the radio. Then vice versa."

"Some food would be a good idea, too."

"Bring you back something."

Tommy devoured a boxed MRE meal then crawled into one of the stretcher racks for a nap. Brooklyn stood radio watch, transmitting a mayday every fifteen minutes or so. When four hours passed, he woke Tommy up and the two of them moved the crash survivors into new evac bags.

"They're not looking good," Tommy said.

"Look better than they did when we found them," Brooklyn pulled himself onto a stretcher and tried to get comfortable. "Least they won't notice when we're all freezing to death."

He closed his eyes. He heard Tommy at the radio, sending out distress calls, at least twice before he drifted off. He woke to Tommy shaking him.

"Any luck?"

"Nothing." Tommy said. "Cabin temperature is down to freezing."

Brooklyn slid out of his bunk. *I ain't sitting here and waiting to die.* "Sled it is then."

"I was the one driving. I should go."

"We don't even know if you was driving in the right direction." Brooklyn opened an overhead compartment and pulled out an MRE. "Let me eat something, and I'll head out. You outweigh me by fifty pounds. Sled'll go further with me."

The MRE was one of the new ones, it contained some kind of noodle and hamburger dish, along with cheese and crackers and a chocolate bar. It all tasted like preservatives but Brooklyn wolfed it down – a fast two-thousand calories – and climbed back into his suit.

"Try to stay in contact and send out a mayday soon's you

get somewhere with more altitude. Signal might go farther."
Tommy patted Brooklyn's helmet. "All sealed up."

"See you soon."

"You better. I'm not getting court martialed alone."

Brooklyn shuffled to the back of the Sno-Cat and tripped the switch that lowered the snowmobile to the ground. It, too, was fully charged, capable of fifty miles of travel at thirty miles an hour depending on the age of the battery and the temperature. Batteries and cold didn't go so good together. Brooklyn sat awkwardly in the saddle. He chinned his mic. "I'm off," he said. "Keep the kids alive for me."

He twisted the throttle slowly and moved away from the stranded 'Cat. He twisted harder and picked up speed. The sled hummed like an electric razor. *Gonna die on this stupid thing.* He headed deeper into the storm.

SIXTEEN

"So, big hero."

"That what I am?" Brooklyn leaned forward in the shrink's armchair. "Seems like I'm the guy about to go back to jail."

"Could be." This shrink's name was Shapiro. He had a lot of letters after his name on his desk plate, but he didn't want to be called "doctor". It was "Shapiro" or "Shap". He was a big dude with two fingers missing on his left hand. "How do you feel about that? Four guys live and you go to jail. Fair trade?"

Brooklyn had made it barely two hundred yards from the Sno-Cat before running into a Soviet checkpoint. Explanations were made, aid requested, and within an hour he and Tommy were sitting down to a hot bowl of borscht. Dee lost the foot, but everyone they pulled out of the fallen plane had survived.

Brooklyn's legs jittered up and down. He made an effort to still them. "It's a trade. Don't know about fair."

"Would Specialist Michaels do it for you?"

It was always weird to hear Dee's real name. "Maybe. Probably." *Dead is dead. Living is opportunity.*

"This may be the biggest act of altruism in your life, Brook. You've come a long way." He glanced at the pile of papers at his elbow. "Dr Gephardt said you had the potential."

"Guess I know what I'm fighting for now," Brooklyn mumbled.

"What was that?"

"Nothing." Brooklyn sat up. "We done here? I gotta pack or something. Colonel wants to see me and Tommy at 1400."

"We have a few more minutes. How are you feeling in general? Bad dreams? Panic attacks?"

ZARK! A green flash of light. David on the ground, staring up at him. "Just regular dreams. Nothing Jim Morrison would write a song about."

Shapiro turned in his chair to look at the poster above his desk. "You ever see The Doors in concert? I saw them in Asbury Park in '68. Best show I've ever been to."

"Listened to all the records. First one was the best."

The shrink nodded. "You know, it's possible your little shroom trip in the Crater did you some good. Lot of people in my line of work think Leary is on to something."

"Nixon wasn't a fan. Makes me like him more."

"Same." Shapiro crossed his arms. "President Carter seems a little more open to it."

"How'd you lose those fingers?" Brooklyn had asked the question at every session. Shapiro's answer was different every time.

The shrink looked at his hand. "You know, I really don't remember." It rang true somehow. "Looks like you've run out the clock, man. Good luck with the Colonel."

Brooklyn stood at attention and felt like he was going to pass out. *Go to jail. Go directly to jail. Do not pass Go. Do not collect...*

In spite of the chill in the room, sweat beaded between his shoulder blades and ran down his spine. He'd figured on either ending up dead, in jail, or a hero, and the EOF was taking its sweet time about deciding which one it was. He and Tommy had gotten a warm welcome from the other trainees, but everybody above corporal was giving them the cold shoulder.

Their names showed up on the duty roster as soon as the doc had cleared them but...

"You disobeyed orders. Endangered yourselves. Damaged a half-million dollar vehicle." The colonel leaned back in his chair. "The only point in your favor is the fact you brought those men back."

"Not all of them, sir," Tommy said.

"Not all of them. But four people are breathing and taking up space in the hospital today because of the two of you. Fortunately, that's a big point." He threw his pen on the desk. "Even so, you both should be sent packing with six weeks in the stockade as a bonus prize. And for you, Lamontagne, that would mean going straight to Attica."

"It was my idea, sir," Tommy said. "I talked him into it. Said he'd be a coward if he didn't go."

Brooklyn flushed red. "That's bullshi–"

"Brooklyn tried to talk me out of it. I didn't listen. I wanted to be a hero, sir."

The colonel slid open a drawer in his desk and removed two small boxes. "It seems to have worked." He tossed the boxes on the desk. "Those are yours. Don't expect a ceremony because you won't be getting any."

"What are they, sir?" Brooklyn said.

"Airman's Medals. Pick them up."

Brooklyn picked up both boxes and handed Tommy the one with his name on it. Inside each was a gold medallion on a short blue-and-gold ribbon. On the front of the disc was a kneeling man wearing a winged helmet. On the back was etched the words "For Valor".

"Congratulations, men. You are bona fide heroes." He stood and offered his hand to both. "You've also been reduced in rank and pay grade." He looked hard at each man in turn. "You play you pay, gentlemen. You're both very lucky it worked. Is that understood?"

"Yes, sir," Tommy said.

Brooklyn spoke up about a half second behind. He couldn't take his eyes off the medal. The yellow part of the blue-and-yellow ribbon was the same color as Galvano's living room. He squeezed the medal in his fist, wishing it had points so he could feel it bite into him.

"Dismissed. You're still heading up to Eisenhower Station with the rest of the company." The colonel smiled. "Looks like you made it through."

Back in the hallway, Tommy thumped Brooklyn in the chest. "Can you believe it? A damned medal. Wait till I tell my pa!"

Brooklyn nodded absently. His father would have been proud, too, and he knew Ma would be beside herself, but it didn't feel right to gloat. The next check he sent home would have less in it, and a piece of jewelry wasn't going to change that. "You do that." He slipped the box into his pocket.

Back in their shared bunk, Brooklyn slipped the medal into an envelope and wrote a quick note.

Maria,
This should have been David's. I'm never going be able to make that right. I think about that a lot. Every time you look up and see the Moon, I'll be thinking about that.
Brook.

Brooklyn addressed the thing. It would take a couple of weeks for the letter to get to Queens, and he'd be in a very different place by then. He leaned back in his chair. *Bang-zoom. To the fucking Moon, Alice.*

PART SIX
Flight '76

SEVENTEEN

Earth's moon had inspired countless chants and songs since humankind had taught itself to make such things. The month Brooklyn Lamontagne took up temporary residency on Rikers Island alone, The Meters were opening for the Rolling Stones' European Tour with an original song called "Mister Moon" and Starbuck was rolling in cash and playing *American Bandstand* off a little ditty called "Moonlight Feels Right".

Brooklyn saw the Moon a few days before Christmas 1976 from the window of a slow-poke shuttle carrying seventy-two souls from Eisenhower Station. He and Tommy had spent two weeks on the station throwing up and floating around to get their space legs. No song he'd heard measured up.

But even that was nothing compared to what Brooklyn saw the next day, a view of a full Earth coming up over Mons Agnes. He would remember that view until the day he died.

PART SEVEN
Boogie Nights

December 14, 1977

EIGHTEEN

"Lamontagne, how far are you from Post 12? Report."

Brooklyn slowed his rover to a crawl and squinted against the glare that always found its way past his polarized helmet. The next distance marker was less than fifty yards ahead. "Looks like another twenty-four miles, Freedom. Repeat. Twenty-four miles out from Post 12 on a direct bearing."

He parked the rover. Freedom Base wouldn't have called him just to say howdy. He wasn't important enough. A year on the Moon and he'd spent most of his time driving from outpost to outpost to service computers. He'd logged more miles in the low-powered moon rover than he ever had in his Cougar. It was the perfect gig. Lots of quiet, little stress, and he was mostly left to his own devices. Not an alien in sight.

He stood up in the cockpit and stretched his back as much as the vacsuit let him. If he had anyone handy to bet with, he'd have put money on a recall. Freedom would order him to come back, retrace the ninety-eight miles he'd already gone to pick up a piece of equipment someone needed.

"Lamontagne, proceed to the twenty-mile marker and set up your shelter. A courier will meet you with a package of upgrades."

Brooklyn hummed. That was a new one. He'd spent hundreds of nights in the inflatable shelter packed into the back of the rover, so that was nothing. A special courier with computer parts, that was something else. "Freedom, kind of upgrade we talkin' about?" he said. "Wanna make sure I got the right tools."

Static crackled. "The technical sergeant says you'll be all set. Standard kit only."

"Roger that, Freedom. Drive four more miles then tuck myself in for the night."

Brooklyn dropped back in the seat and flipped the catch on a box jammed between the rover's seats. He pulled a tape out at random and plugged it into the eight-track player he'd jury-rigged into the dash. He flipped a switch, and the music played through his helmet speakers. Brooklyn twisted the accelerator and the little rover picked up some speed along the dusty road.

At the twenty-mile marker Brooklyn pulled onto a wide, flat space one of the EOF road crews had carved into the lunar rock. He checked carefully for any "sharps" that might have been thrown up by micrometeor impacts and rolled out his inflatable cabin. The tough little dome was erect and pressurized within fifteen minutes, and Brooklyn crawled through the airlock to shuck his suit and bed down for the night.

The furnishings inside the dome were rudimentary. The first time he'd crawled inside one he'd been reminded of the inflatable bounce houses at Coney Island, but instead of red, blue, yellow, and fun, the EOF inflatables were a uniform dusty white and covered with warning labels and little cartoons advising the occupant to watch out for "sharps" and to "keep your emergency bottle handy".

Brooklyn reached into his coveralls and pulled out a flask of the vodka he was becoming known for Moon-wide. He toasted the warning signs, his Soviet distillation guru back on Earth, and took a long drink. It was smooth as hell, filtered three times through a cast-off urine-processing system. The system was designed to make piss palatable, but it did a far better job, in Brooklyn's experience, of making his hooch smooth. He had it on good authority that a few bottles of his best had ended up in the Admiral's liquor cabinet.

Brooklyn set the heat to sixty-four degrees Fahrenheit and unrolled his sleepsack on top of the inflatable bench that served as a bunk. With the Moon's gravity, he would have been comfortable sleeping on the rock outside, but stretching out in the inflatable was the closest thing to lying on a cloud he could imagine. He reached into a pocket in his bunk and pulled out one of the magazines he kept there for just such occasions. Brooklyn sipped vodka and read until the magazine fell from his hand. He turned off the light.

He woke around midnight, the thin screech of the airlock alarm rousing him from a formless dream. Brooklyn blinked sleep from his eyes and kicked out of his sleepsack in time to see a bulky figure crawling through the front door. His stomach leapt into his mouth. *A parking lot and a cold voice. Crushing fingers.* The thing stood, the polarization of its helmet obscuring whatever was inside. *Just a person. All it is. A man in a can.* There was no sign of rank on the suit, not even unit markings. The thing raised its hand to its helmet and the visor opened with a hiss of escaping air. "Lamontagne?"

Brooklyn nodded, his mouth dry. The courier was female, lean-faced, with close-cropped hair. There were plenty of women on the base, many of them pilots. They adapted well to the lower gravity and were, by and large, better fliers than men. But Brooklyn's duties seldom put him in the vicinity of them, and hardly ever in such close quarters. He imagined he could smell her, which, considering the stink factor of the average vacsuit, was entirely possible.

The courier was carrying a gun-metal gray box and set it down to remove her suit. Underneath she was wearing issue coveralls, also without sign of rank or unit number.

"I salute you or what?" Brooklyn said.

The courier smiled. "You can if you want to. I outrank you, but I'm outside your chain of command unless I want to be."

She put her suit behind the dust curtain in the corner and carefully rested her helmet on top of it. "Your choice."

Brooklyn flipped the barest hint of a salute. "Brooklyn Lamontagne."

"Hero of Arctic One." She smiled. "I'm Sierra Ramos." She stuck out her hand. "Special operations."

"Spook?"

"Right now I'm a delivery boy." She pointed to the case. "Upgrades."

"Hardware or software?"

"Both," she said. "You're going to retrofit some lookout posts with magnetic storage." She nodded at the case. "Few eight-drives in there, and a little something extra."

"Know about the eight-drives," Brooklyn said. "On the schedule for early next year. All the card-readers are being replaced."

"We're moving the timetable up on a few so we can test the new software."

"What's the rush?"

"That's need to know. And you don't." She smiled. "I'll handle the software once you get the drive installed." She looked around the sparse furnishings of Brooklyn's inflatable. "You got anything to drink around here?"

Brooklyn pointed at the water reclamator. "Help yourself."

"I was hoping for something a little stronger. I read your file. The real one."

Brooklyn stepped past her to his suit and lifted the flap on his toolbelt. He handed Sierra his backup flask. "Finest on the Moon," he said. "Made it myself."

Sierra let herself fall onto the inflatable bench across from the one Brooklyn usually slept on. She did it without hesitation, without even looking to make sure she was on target.

"Good to get out of that suit." She flipped the top off Brooklyn's flask and took a swig. "Smooth."

"Handle yourself like a Lunatick," Brooklyn said. "How come I never seen you around?"

"Just got here. I travel a lot." She stretched like a starfish. "A month ago I was on Mars. Next month, who knows. I go where the work is."

"You travel solo?"

"Modified scout ship. It's parked about fourteen klicks from here." She sipped more vodka. "You got enough water in there for me to clean up a little? I must reek."

"Spare a few gallons," Brooklyn said. "Schedule has me back on base in a couple of weeks."

Sierra glided back to her feet and walked to the tiny refresher unit built into the back of the shelter. She looked back over her shoulder. "No peeking, guardian."

Brooklyn stared after her, not sure whether she was giving him signals or not. *Been awhile. Doesn't beep, buzz, or short circuit, I don't know how to interact with it.*

He could hear her inside the refresher, careful splashes of water and low singing. Brooklyn thought he recognized it. *Low Rider?*

"Need help reaching your back?" he said carefully.

Sierra poked her head out of the refresher. "I wouldn't say no." The sponge spun in its slow arc toward his head. It squished and splattered when Brooklyn snagged it out of the air. She laughed. "Maybe you ought to skin down so you don't get water all over yourself."

That's a signal.

Sierra ducked back into the refresher and started singing again. Brooklyn nearly fell over himself struggling out of his coveralls.

She met him at the refresher door and slid slickly against him. "Let's work on the front first."

They split an MRE and a self-heating flask of coffee for breakfast. Sierra inspected her suit dubiously. "Doubt I'll need all that armor on this job. Give me a hand stripping it off?"

EOF vacsuits were modular, the basic structure not much bulkier than a diver's wetsuit. Kneepads, boots, heavy gloves, pads, and plating could be added as the work required. Brooklyn's suit had extra layers of tough fabric to guard against the Moon's highly abrasive regolith. Most of it had to be replaced anytime he returned to base. Sierra's suit was fitted out for combat, ceramic plating anywhere it could stick and reinforced joints.

"Hell you wear all this for?" Brooklyn held the suit up while she removed nearly three quarters of the fittings.

"Protocol. Had to be ready in case you weren't human."

He smiled. "I look like I got extra arms?"

"I had to get your clothes off to be sure. Protocol."

"Seriously?" His mouth was hanging open, and even in the low, low gravity he couldn't get it shut.

She buckled an equipment strap so it wouldn't hang loose and snag somewhere. "Let's go, guardian. We're burning Earthlight!"

The gases inside the inflatable went back into the tanks and Brooklyn folded the thing into the cargo box at the back of the rover.

"Neat," she said.

"Never seen one of those before?"

"I like antiques." She skipped around to the driver's side. "Hop in."

Brooklyn was more than happy to ride shotgun in the rover and in the conversation. Sierra shouted in delight when she spotted his collection of tapes and poked through it with the blunt fingers of her vacsuit.

She kept the space between them full. He'd never met anyone who talked so much without revealing anything. After an hour of travel, pulling up beside Listening Post 12, Brooklyn wouldn't have been able to write a paragraph about Sierra Ramos with a gun to his head.

They teamed up to get the parts and tools inside the post, and shucked most of their suits to work.

"Hell's this thing?" He turned a brushed aluminum casing in his hands.

"Guess," Sierra said.

"Can I open it?" She didn't object so he removed the screws from the bottom of it and slid off the top. He hummed while he traced circuits. "Short-wave transmitter and receiver... Encoder, demodulator... Some kind of modem?"

"Bright boy. If I had a cookie, I'd give it to you. These will give us the ability to access the lookout posts remotely, even update the programming."

"I can't see this doing more than three-hundred bits per second. Might be quicker to send out a tech."

"Not if we can access and update all of the stations in range at once. They'll be able to communicate with each other, too, pass the changes up and down the line. Adjust on the fly."

"Until it all crashes because of a software bug or an overload."

She crossed her arms. "Focus on your soldering and let us worry about the software."

"You're the boss." He opened his tool case. "Might wanna look at a book or something. 'S'gonna take awhile."

Sierra leaned in to inspect his work. "Is this the first of these drive refits you've done?"

"Nah. Did habitat and sanitation control when I got up here. Been working my way out ever since." He patted the new interface. "This thing is already obsolete. IBM's working on some kind of three-and-a-half-inch high-density storage thing. More than a meg each. Eight tapes worth of data on something 'bout the size of a business card."

"The EOF is better than the Air Force and Navy used to be, but most of its R&D is still weapons based. Always looking for a bigger gun instead of a better brain." Sierra reached into the

gray case. She pulled out one of the eight-track tapes inside
and slid it into the interface. A red light came on and motors
whirred. "These are high-density storage. Lot fancier than the
ones you put in the sanitation system." She sat back. "Now,
we'll see how good your work is."

"Work's just fine," Brooklyn said. "Finest training off Earth.
What's on those things?"

"New search protocols and coding for the remote access. Just
be glad we can do this with tapes now and not punched cards."
The light went green, and Sierra pulled another tape from the
box. She slid it into the second of six interfaces Brooklyn had
installed. "They'll make response and analysis a lot faster."

Brooklyn leaned over to look into the case. There were
four eight-track tapes remaining. Gray, labeled only with
classification numbers. He picked one up. *Heavier than a normal
one. Reminds me of... David Bowie?* He turned it over and over in
his hands.

"Hey." Sierra had her hand out. "I need that one now."

He handed her the tape, his mind still somewhen else. A
box full of tapes and a spreading pool of blood. "Ever seen a
Mercurian?"

"Never seen one alive. Supposedly, we've taken a few
prisoners, but that's way above my clearance." She rubbed at
the back of her neck. "The one I saw was pretty chewed up.
Like a jellied squid, all arms. They evolved deep in the cracks
in the planet's surface, as far away from the heat as they could
get."

"I got the briefing."

She smiled. "Sometimes I forget who I'm talking to. These
days I'm as likely to be working with a civilian as military.
Space is getting pretty crowded."

"Think it's real?" Brooklyn folded his arms. "Plenty of people
say it's all bullshit. Aliens. Invasions. Just another way to keep
us all under control."

"You believe that?"

He offered the smallest of shrugs. "Less than I used to, maybe."

"I'm a fucking spy, Brook. It's my job to do sneaky shit, and I'm telling you there's no way in hell Kennedy or anyone could have gotten all the ducks to line up for something like this."

"Okay."

"It's a real as you are."

Brooklyn knelt to avoid her eyes, pulled another tape from the case and hefted it. *Young Americans.* The weight was the same. "My file say anything 'bout why I'm up here?"

She nodded. "Accessory to murder charge. Considering who it was, I don't hold it against you much. Galvano was a sneak for hire. Mostly corporate espionage. Some government work."

"File say anything about the tapes?"

She shook her head.

"Lemme tell you a story."

"You got yourself mixed up in a whole lot of shit, didn't you?"

Brooklyn swallowed. "Checked out?"

She slid down the wall to sit on the floor across from him. She'd spent the last twenty minutes in the radio room speaking in hushed tones to someone on the other end of her call. "What I'm about to tell you is classified. Way over your head, OK? Court-martial and treason charges if you say a fucking word." She frowned. "There's some evidence the Mercurians can disguise themselves to look like people. It's not very good, but apparently it can pass in a crowd."

Waxy, sickly face. A crushing grip that felt almost... inside out somehow. David. Brooklyn felt hot and cold all at once. "So the guy who...?"

"Don't know what the story is with the tapes, but we're passing the question up the line. No one has any idea why a Mercurian would be shooting people outside a bar in Manhattan."

"Queens."

"Whatever." She rested her elbows on her knees. "Someday all this shit will be digitized and searchable. I'll be able to program a couple of words into the computer, and it will give me every article or report on the planet about it. Or send me a message if something I'm looking for pops up."

"Someday."

"I can't imagine what we've missed because we didn't know we should be looking for it." She closed the gray case and started putting on her suit. "You want to keep talking or get moving? Sooner we get this done, sooner we can pump your dome up again."

Half Earth is a romantic sight from the surface of the Moon.

"What's the weirdest thing you've seen up here?" Sierra said.

Brooklyn shifted his arm to use it as a pillow. The cartoon on the ceiling right above him advised him not to waste water "Picked up a hitchhiker once."

"Civilian?"

"Yeah. Colonist." He stretched and clenched his toes. It felt good. "A kid. Maybe fifteen or sixteen. She'd had a blowout with her parents and decided it was a good idea to walk to see a friend at Tranquility."

"That's more than a hundred miles!"

"One-twenty-eight if you stick to the road. It's doable if you're prepared. She wasn't. Had about an hour of air left when I found her. Drove her the rest of the way and radioed her parents."

She whistled. "Had a lot of blowouts with my family, but I always had somewhere to go and didn't have to worry about running out of oxygen on the way."

"Colony prefabs are real small. Not a lot of room to sulk or shut yourself up and crank the music." He shifted position. "'Bout you?"

"Name it, I've seen it." She laughed. "I infiltrated a cat-smuggling ring once. Earth to Mars. That was pretty good. But the weirdest thing," she hummed, "probably the Belt. How's your Russian?"

"Bad to worse."

She nodded. "If you're thinking about going out there, you'd better pick some up. The miners are mostly Chinese and Soviet dissidents. It was an easy way to get rid of them. Pack up the intellectuals, poets, and artists, send them out past Mars to pound sand. There are at least seventeen publishing houses out there. Entire asteroids have been painted to look like things from Earth. There's one that looks like Nikita Khrushchev with Mickey Mouse ears. They work all day and hold literary salons at night. It's gorgeous and sad and nuts all at the same time."

"Like to see that."

"Eat your Wheaties and do your homework, buddy. Santa might take you there for Halloween." She prodded him. "I'm ready to sleep. Time to go back to your own bed."

"This is my bed. The other one is yours."

She pulled her legs up to her chest and shoved. Brooklyn sailed off the inflatable and landed on the floor. "Try that in Earth gravity," he said.

"I'd still win," she said. "Shut up and sleep tight. Don't let the moon rats bite."

They hit posts 13 and 14 the next day. The work got quicker each time. Sierra slotted the last eight-track and stood easily. "That should be it. We'll know in a few minutes if it worked." She glided to the small radio unit on one side of the outpost and adjusted some dials. She slipped on one of the headsets units. "Hush now." She flipped a switch and pushed the send button. "This is Charlie looking for an Angel. Angel, are you there?"

Sierra released the button and waited. She repeated the hail.

"This is Angel, Charlie. We on schedule?" The man's voice was clear, telling Brooklyn his transmitter was powerful and close by.

She glanced at the interface where the last light had just gone green. "Looks good to go. Try it out."

"10-4."

"Is that coming from the base?"

"Orbit. One of mine, not one of yours."

One by one the 8-tracks whirred, backward and forward, and then the lights went green again.

The voice from orbit cut through the static again. "That's it. We have control. Nice work, Charlie."

Sierra pushed the button. "Always a pleasure. See you back on the ranch." She shut down the radio and stood. "Looks like you wired it right. Once your little refit is finished next year, the posts can work together under one control without having to send some tech out with a bunch of punch cards every time we want it to look in a new direction." She patted the computer. "It will be better at analysis, too. Fewer false alarms. Better early detection. If we had it a few years ago we might've saved Cleveland. At least evacuated the population."

Seven hundred thousand people. It might have showed on his face.

"You do what you can. Mission accomplished today," she said.

"Just those three posts?" Brooklyn said.

"Pilot program. Give a girl a ride back to her ship? I got places to be."

"Least I can do is give you a lift."

"Good. Otherwise I'd have to steal your car."

They lingered at Post 14 long enough for Brooklyn to harvest the results of the vacuum still he'd installed there, and they spent one more night together in Brooklyn's inflatable before driving out to Sierra's ship.

"There she is," she flourished, "the mighty *Fourcade*."

"Tiny." A cockpit area half the size of the inflatable coupled to the drive system of a scout.

"Courier class. Basically two phone booths mounted on an Oppenheimer. Crazy fast. Really uncomfortable unless you like small spaces. Which I do."

Goodbyes are awkward in spacesuits. Worse, Brooklyn wasn't sure if he should send her off with a hug, a handshake, or a salute.

Sierra settled the matter. "I wrote my personal contact code on your bunk this morning. Only use it if you have something interesting to say."

"You're the one headed off into the wild black yonder," he said. "Here it's just me and the Moon dust."

"Don't get too comfortable, Lamontagne. There's a war on. Things can change in a heartbeat."

"Try to remember that." He tossed her a half salute half wave. "Be careful out there."

"Where's the fun in that?"

Another ten days of dusty moon roads went by under the rover's wire-mesh wheels before Brooklyn passed back through security at Freedom Base.

The inside of his suit had long since started smelling like a dirty sock, and by the end of the duty cycle opening the thing up to some nice, fresh vacuum had been sounding better and better. Brooklyn pulled his helmet off and ruffled his flat hair with a dusty gauntlet.

"You think you'll remember how to talk to people?" a lanky guardian said. "Been a while since you've seen civilization."

"Manage OK," Brooklyn said. "Any messages?"

He handed over a slip of paper. "Just came in. Says you're to report to personnel at 0600 tomorrow."

Time enough for a shower, some dinner, and a night in his bunk, though likely he would have slept better on the surface.

Tommy snored like a chainsaw in low gee. He climbed out of his suit. "Get this cleaned, will ya. Smells like Nixon's scrotum."

Most of Freedom Base was underground – long-timers liked to say they were dug in like 'Lunaticks' – but enough reached through the lunar surface that base designers had opted to put a dome over it. All the comforts of home with, at the moment, a view of Earth hanging right overhead. Looking up it made Brooklyn feel like he was falling so he kept his eyes on the horizontal. Twenty rookies skipped by in formation, getting their Moon legs and learning how to move around the lunar surface without falling on their faces. Brooklyn nodded to a civilian contractor he knew vaguely. The man was sitting alone at a table outside the Luna Café. He motioned for Brooklyn to join him, but Brooklyn pretended not to see and didn't stop.

An elevator took him down four levels, and a hundred yards of hallway and two rights took him to his front door. It slid open at his touch. No locks on the Moon. He and Tommy had come up with a way to signal to the other in the event they were "entertaining". The big red-head was sort of seeing a guy named Mack who worked in the motor pool, but Brooklyn hadn't met him.

Tommy looked up from his desk where he was doing paperwork. "Hey, Brook. Staying long?"

"Hard telling." Brooklyn tossed his bag on his bunk and sank into the desk chair opposite Tommy. "S'posed to report to personnel in the morning. You eat?"

Tommy shook his head.

"Let me get cleaned up, and you can take me out to dinner."

"What's in it for me?"

"End to your fucking loneliness. And some beers, if you're lucky."

Brooklyn stayed in the shower a long while. He'd been out nearly a month this time, not his longest stretch by far, but long enough to accrue a deep well of unspent hot-water rations. His fingertips were as wrinkled as Red Fox by the time he left the shower stall and dried off. Tommy was still at his desk, and he waited while Brooklyn shrugged into an off-duty coverall.

"What do you think personnel wants?" he said.

Brooklyn laced up his boots. "Kept my nose clean." The left boot lace broke with a snap. "Cleanish. Maybe they want to give me a promotion. You heard anything?"

"Lot of new faces around here. People are saying the Mercurians are headed this way again."

Brooklyn tied the broken ends of the lace together. "Who's saying it?"

"Just people. You know, around."

Brooklyn stood up. "Yeah, well... How many times we heard that since we got up here?" He stretched, relishing the feel of clean clothes on clean skin. "Believe it when I see it." *Feels different after talking to Sierra, though. Aliens disguised as people.* He shook off a sudden chill.

"Just telling you what I've heard. Speaking of which..." Tommy reached under the desk. Velcro rasped as Tommy pulled out the notebook he'd stashed there. "We got orders. You bring any back with you?"

"About ten gallons. Hit the stills behind 14 and 15 on the way in. It will be a good batch once we blend and water it."

"I'm down to my last crate. People upstairs been drinking like they're worried about something."

Brooklyn rolled out of bed early the next morning, hoping an extra shower would kill the psychic stench of weeks spent in a spacesuit. Feeling slightly more civilized after, he went to mess and drank enough coffee to bring himself within human parameters. He was standing outside the personnel office at ten minutes to and waited twenty minutes to be seen. *Nice to see the military is holding to form.*

"Got new orders for you, Lamontagne," the staff sergeant said as Brooklyn came through his door, "and you need a haircut."

Brooklyn ran his fingers through his hair. "Out for a few weeks this time, Sarge. Get on it as soon as I leave here."

The sergeant nodded, seemingly mollified, though her hair didn't look strictly regulation, either. She handed Brooklyn an envelope. "Three days of R&R at Tycho, then you're to report to the *Baron Friedrich von Steuben*. Deep-space patrol boat."

"Must be a mistake, Sarge," Brooklyn said. "I'm a tech not a flyboy."

"You're still a tech. Now you're a tech on a patrol vessel. Twelve to twenty-four weeks. Get out there, see the solar system, tell your grandkids that Pop-Pop was a real spaceman."

"The hell am I supposed to do up there?"

"Same as down here. The *Baron* is one of the early deep-space ships. Most of her systems are still working off punched cards. You'll be bringing her into the '70s."

It will be the '80s in another two years.

The staff sergeant held up her hand. "Read the packet. Nothing in it I don't know, and I don't know anything beyond it."

Brooklyn flipped the envelope over and looked at the back. It had been opened and resealed with tape. First-class security. "Guess that's it then."

"Guess so. Good hunting, specialist."

Brooklyn offered a salute just in case someone was keeping track. "Sic semper Tyrannus," he muttered. He turned on his heel and left the room, his new orders bunching up and wrinkling in his grip.

Six months in deep space. As a kid, he might have thrilled to the idea, but now it only made him sweat. It had been more than a decade since an Earth ship had seen any action, but the accident rate on patrol vessels was high.

Brooklyn opened the packet of orders and scanned it. There wasn't much there that the staff sergeant hadn't already told him. His updated service record was included as a plastic punched card, which he'd be expected to present to his new commanding officer when he reported. Brooklyn put the card in his thigh pocket and rolled his orders into a tube.

Tommy was up and gone by the time Brooklyn got back to their shared room, so he typed out a note giving directions on how to maintain their little enterprise while not putting anything on paper that might cause them problems later. He tucked the note into Tommy's well-thumbed Bible, a place they had arranged in advance as a message drop. Their enterprise was going to take a hit no matter what. Tommy had a numb tongue when it came to blending. *Good fucking luck, buddy.*

NINETEEN

When the entertainment magazines did features and photo spreads on the Moon, they focused on Tycho. It was Disneyland in a sloppy three-way with Times Square and Hollywood. Movie stars, including Elizabeth Taylor and Jane Fonda, had houses there, claiming the low-g made them age slower. Prostitution and gambling were legal, booze was cheap, and big names flew in for concerts. Brooklyn's travel package included two tickets to an ABBA show.

It was a twelve-hour train ride under the regolith from Freedom Base. The bullet-shaped subway car was packed with guardians looking to blow off steam for a few days. Fraternization was inevitable, and some couples had to wait months for their duty schedules to line up to get a weekend away. Brooklyn tried to sleep, but paranoia kept poking him awake.

Mercurians in disguise. Stolen software. Spies caught with their pants down. The signs were all pointing to something. *Shoulda told Tommy. Should tell Mike to take Ma out West for their vacation. Maybe tell everyone to avoid the big cities for a while.*

Brooklyn shifted in his seat. The couple behind him was cooing at each other, and the two guys ahead were talking about hitting a bar in the red-light district. When the train stopped, he followed the crowd to the hotels and checked in.

There was a neon-looking Mexican place a couple of blocks from the hotel, and he took the morning paper there for coffee and huevos rancheros. He was immersing himself in all three when he heard someone call his name.

"My man!" Dee strode across the room, hand out and smile in place. They slapped five.

"The hell you doin' here?" Brooklyn said.

"Same as you. Breakfast and taking a load off." He waved to the waitress. She looked enough like the woman who'd greeted Brooklyn at the door to be her sister. The whole family might have been flown up together to work. "Came in for repairs and a refuel."

"Wasn't sure you were still in," Brooklyn said. "We lost track of you."

Dee pulled up his pant leg to reveal an artificial foot and shin. "Doesn't affect my flying and poses no problem at all in micro. You are looking at the master and commander of the EOF scout ship *Bessie Coleman*. Just coming back from a trip 'round Mercury, but you didn't hear that from me."

"What'd you see?"

"Not a damned thing. You want a beer?"

"It's not even 10am."

"Might be midnight in Manhattan."

They ordered beers. Dee slapped a *Rolling Stone* magazine on the table. Paul McCartney was on the cover. "Page seventy-nine."

"Got an album out?" Brooklyn turned pages. "'The Dark Side of the Interplanetary Cold War'," he read. "Are you in this?"

"Wrote that."

Brooklyn tapped the byline. "That's not your name."

"I'm a threat to domestic tranquility. That's my," Dee waved his hand, "my nom de plume. I can say things like that now. Became a French citizen few months ago."

"What's it about?"

"Racism, inequality, class warfare. People being left behind. The usual modern dystopia."

"Thought the Kennedys put an end to all that."

"You don't believe that." Dee stretched his legs under the table. "Kennedy Administration changed some laws. Didn't change people."

Brooklyn put his newspaper on top of the magazine. "Elected a black guy vice president last year. Carter-Jackson won pretty easy."

"But in the election after that or next one, they'll elect a bona fide bigot to compensate. Some hat-wearing cowboy who'd soon as call me a monkey as give me a medal." He looked around for the waitress. "What're your plans for tonight?"

"Two tickets to see ABBA. Wanna come?"

"Be your date if we go down to the red-light after."

"Deal," Brooklyn said.

ABBA and Tycho's biggest strip club had a lot in common – 'space-age' costumes, weird lighting effects, and unnaturally bouncy performances.

Dee ordered another martini. "This not as much fun as it used to be. Must be getting old."

The stripper was doing a pole routine that would have been impossible in Earth gravity. The tables around the stage were filled with singles and couples, looking more like folks at a circus than people at a peep show. It was too clean. More showy than raunchy. Even the VD warnings were chipper and polite.

"Probably my fault," Brooklyn said. "Don't get a lot of practice talking to people these days."

"You think *Bessie* got a built-in speakeasy?" Dee's eyebrows shimmied up his forehead. "Barely enough room in there to change my mind. Few books and a typewriter only things 'tween me and the abyss."

"You love it."

"Yeah, kinda." He sucked his teeth. "Be nice to have a lady along though."

"Long spacewalks under the stars."

"Like to have the female perspective on my pages, too. Got a manifesto in the works."

"Under the fake name?"

Dee ate the olive from the martini. "Part of my redemption arc. Come back to Earth a big hero. Go on Dick Cavett. Couple of book tours. A nice professorship somewhere. Live a life long and politically radical."

"Better plan than I got."

"Which is?"

The stripper held herself away from the pole with one arm and stretched out in low-gravity like a pornographic flag. Brooklyn cocked his head to see better. "Sit here, drink, hope this chick doesn't fall on her cooch."

Dee flew out in the morning, and Brooklyn wandered down to the water park. Swimmers dropped like leaves from the high-dive board and the resulting splashes lingered like upside-down chandeliers.

He chatted up two women from the Tranquility Colony, both in their early thirties and giddy to be away from their husbands and children. They had the lanky, pasty look of longtime Lunaticks. If their kids were Moon born, the little nippers would never be able to safely visit Earth.

Helluva thing to do to a kid. Brooklyn kept the thought to himself and listened to the women talk about life in Tranquility ("boring") and their hopes to meet ABBA before they headed back. "Bjorn is gorgeous," one of the women said. "I've half a mind to find his hotel and invite him to one of our key parties."

"You could come, too," her friend said to Brooklyn. "Fresh meat is a treat."

"Sorry," Brooklyn said. "Headed out to a patrol ship."

"Maybe when you come back." She wrote her communications code on a napkin before they headed back to their hotel to nap. Brooklyn balled up the napkin and stuffed it into his pocket. He used the teletype machine in the pool locker room to punch out a message: "Got anything to do with my sudden transfer?" He put Sierra's communications code on it and drank another three hours' worth of cocktails while waiting for an answer that never came. *Maybe the question wasn't interesting enough.*

Brooklyn wasn't much of a swimmer, but he put enough of himself in the pool to call it good and went back to his hotel for room service and a couple of aspirin. He found the napkin in his pocket and punched in the Tranquility woman's comm code. He signed it "SOS".

She responded right away and invited him to join her and her friend at a disco in an hour. "We have quaaludes! Hee-hee!" she added.

What the hell, I'm on vacation.

PART EIGHT
Don't Let Me Be Misunderstood

January 9, 1978

TWENTY

Brooklyn's headache would not be denied no matter how much he darkened the sunglasses he'd picked up at the hotel gift shop. It was way too soon to have developed symptoms from any Moon cooties that might have rubbed off the Tranquility Twins, so he chocked his general malaise up to the pills and cheap hooch that fueled the one-night stand.

He would have given many dollars to curl up in his smelly inflatable for a couple of days and sleep it off. Instead, he was following arrows and poorly translated signs to his new assignment.

Brooklyn pulled the nearly opaque glasses off his face to search for his ship's name on the final sign, a blackboard really, covered in smudged English, Cyrillic, and hanji. *There it is...* He followed the arrow to the ship's assigned dock.

The *Baron Friedrich von Steuben* was an early long-range patrol ship, launched in 1958, back when the US and Soviets were still space racing. Brooklyn had looked over the ship's blueprints on the way up from Tycho. It was over-engineered and cramped. Most of the ship was a five-spoked wheel that could be spun up to simulate as much as 150 percent of Earth gravity. The wheel rotated around a fixed central hub, where the command bridge and engines were located.

Brooklyn had gotten his first look at the thing during his

ride up to Red Star Station, the Chinese government's primary contribution to the Earth defense effort. The station, too, was a spinning spoked wheel and just thinking about the possible centripetal forces involved made Brooklyn want to puke. He presented himself at the *von Steuben*'s docking airlock with little enthusiasm.

Tommy got there first. The big red-head was leaning against the wall, chewing a nicstick, and otherwise taking up space near the door. "Cool shades."

"Come a helluva long way to see me off."

He patted the breast pocket of his jacket. "Orders came through yesterday. Gave me the option of riding up from Freedom or spending the night here and going up with you."

"Who's mindin' the store?" There was a contingency plan to keep the distilleries going in case both of them had to be away from Freedom for a while, but Brooklyn didn't like it. It meant turning the whole operation over to their junior partners without much guarantee of getting it back.

Tommy lifted one shoulder. "EOF didn't fly us up here to make booze."

Brooklyn dropped his duffle bag in line with Tommy's. "Shoulda told me you were in town. Bought you a drink or five."

"I came out here with Mack. Sort of a going-away party. Believe me, we drunk plenty." He tossed the nicstick in the trash and popped his knuckles. "Mack's the one suggested I apply for the transfer."

"You asked for this?" Brooklyn's eyes bugged. His roommate had it pretty good on the Moon. Lots of training and security drills, sure, and far too much mandatory exercise and centrifuge time for Brooklyn's taste, but Tommy slept in his own bunk most nights and had full access to base entertainment and food.

"You and me joined up for different reasons, Brook. Saw the ship, saw a way to be useful. 'Sides, Mack knows a couple of guys on the *Baron*. He says I'll find it interesting."

"Like, how interestin'?"

"All gay crew. Women weren't allowed in space back in the '50s, and guys didn't like to be out so long without them. Idea was they'd fight harder for lovers than they would for pals."

"'Less they all got together, broke up, and hated each other's guts."

"Didn't happen. Mack says a lot of the original crew is still there. EOF can barely pry them off even once they reach mandatory retirement."

"So, no women."

Tommy slapped him on the knee. "An' you're probably gonna be the only guy up there who misses them."

Brooklyn and Tommy parted ways inside the *Baron*'s airlock, and he presented himself to his duty station. The officer-in-charge slid his service record into his reader and hummed as he read. "Never served on a ship before, eh? Still, you have a lot more suit time than a lot of our guys." He scratched his head. "Looks like they barely let you out of it. I'm going to recommend we cross-train you in emergency response."

"Works for me."

"Your tools and parts came up yesterday. I'd suggest you open everything right away, while we still have time to fix all the fuck-ups. One time they sent us three crates of raincoats instead of rations." He chuckled. "Still have mine."

Brooklyn slid his sunglasses back on. "When we headed out?" *Say, "never". Tell me this is all some big fucking mistake.*

"Two or three days depending."

"Pal told me there are no women on the crew. That even legal anymore?"

"The *Baron* is sort of special case." He smiled. "You get as many 'firsts' and commendations as this old boat has, brass tends to let you be."

"Kinda 'firsts'?"

"Bunch of farthests and fastests. Some hairy stuff before the mutual-defense and aid treaties were signed. Rescues, escorts, sneaky ops... You name it. If you're about to leap into some shit, you want the *Baron* beside you."

"Try to avoid that kind of shit, personally," Brooklyn said. *But don't it just find me anyway.*

The *Baron Friedrich von Steuben* carried about half the contingent of a modern deep-space patrol boat; subsequently the crew had twice the work. Everyone had multiple assignments, including the ship's third officer, Paul Carruthers, who also served as its doctor. Carruthers had the O'Jays' "Family Reunion" playing in his office when Brooklyn showed for his readiness physical.

"I'm in charge of the damage-control team, too." The doctor looked up from the printout of Brooklyn's service record. "So, we'll be seeing a lot of each other. Speaking of which, take off your clothes."

Brooklyn hesitated. He'd had a weird couple of days in basic when he thought Tommy might have a thing for him. When he sussed out what Brooklyn was fretting about, Tommy had laughed his ass off and made it clear he didn't find him remotely attractive. *Lesson learned: Bein' gay don't mean you find all men irresistible.* Brooklyn unbuttoned his coveralls. "Never had a, you know, a gay doctor before."

Carruthers washed his hands. "You never had one you know of. I'm just hoping heterosexuals keep everything in the same place. Hate to find out your head is where your ass is supposed to be."

Brooklyn got down to his jockey shorts. "Go easy on me, huh?"

The doctor poked and prodded for twenty minutes. "You got pretty soft on the Moon. No muscle tone at all, but we'll toughen you up." He gave Brooklyn a list of supplements to take and a physical-training regimen. "You can get dressed, but keep an arm out for me."

Brooklyn scanned the printouts. Lots of laps around the ring and daily workouts. "Gonna kill me, doc. Ship gravity can get up to six or seven times what I'm used to."

"And you've been shirking your workouts and centrifuge time." Carruthers popped an eyebrow. "Don't bother denying it. Start slow. Walk the laps if you have to." He held up a pill bottle. "Black beauties. Uppers. You might want these. In moderation they're fine."

Prick had liked the speedy stuff. Brooklyn wasn't above the occasional recreational bump, but regular use was a scary idea. He waved the bottle off. "Think I'll stick to caffeine."

"Bet you a week's pay you'll be back here with your hand out the first time you pull back-to-back shifts." The doctor set the bottle on the examination table next to Brooklyn. "If that leaves with you, I'm going to assume you want a prescription."

Brooklyn slipped the bottle into the pocket of his coveralls. If everyone on the ship was on them, odds were some of the guys weren't getting as much as they wanted. He hadn't seen a place yet that didn't have some kind of around-the-back market.

Carruthers filled a syringe. "This will put some muscle back on that scrawny frame of yours." He laughed at the expression on Brooklyn's face. "Relax, my young friend. This isn't junk off the street or something they pulled out of a horse to make your chest swell and your balls shrink. It's my own design. Make a man out of you in a month." He stuck the needle in Brooklyn's arm. "You'll get another of these next week, one more the week after, and that will be enough to keep you lean and mean for life." He smiled. "Provided you don't live too long."

Brooklyn slid off the table and pulled the top of his coveralls back on. "Thanks, doc." He offered a salute.

The doctor ignored the gesture. "Save it for the Moon or one of those fancy new ships." He opened a folder on his desk and pulled out a punched card. "Shove that in the mailroom terminal and it will print out your work schedule. Your primary assignment is an all-around computer upgrade. Parts came in on the shuttle yesterday."

Brooklyn pulled on his boots. "This is going to be quite a project. Any chance I can get a crew to help me out?"

"Doubt we have the manpower for a crew." He washed his hands at the small sink. "I'll check with the captain, but I bet the best we can do is give you an assistant."

"Skilled?"

"I assume he can change a light bulb on his own." He cleared his throat. "You're on light duty for the next couple of days, and I'm through with you. Go get something to eat – it'll make the injection sit easier – then go get the lay of the land."

Brooklyn's watch was still set for Moon standard. "What time is it now?"

The medic took off his lab coat and hung it on the door. "Time for me to get a drink. I'd invite you to come along, but the captain frowns on me drinking with the enlisted men." He slid the door open. "Close this up when you leave?"

Brooklyn nodded, fighting to keep his reaction to the informality off his face. Freedom Base was hardly West Point, but there was enough spit and polish left to remind the guardians they were military. He closed the examination-room door behind him.

Already, his joints were aching and his feet hurt. His heart was hammering, too. Station Red Star kept its spin to half-Earth gravity, but that was three times what Brooklyn was used to. *Really should have exercised more.* He made it as far as the hallway before he had to rest and asked directions of the least-threatening-looking person he could see.

"Ain't met you before," the man said. He was nearly a head shorter than Brooklyn and built like a rail. "Long-term?"

"Temporary assignment. Computer refit. Name's Brooklyn Lamontagne."

The spacer grunted. "Frank Lewis. Came out here with the ship. Never went back."

"Nearly twenty years," Brooklyn said.

"Good countin'." Frank motioned for Brooklyn to follow him down the low hallway. At the next junction they moved to the side to let by four guys ferrying a crate along.

Brooklyn tried to catch his breath. "Weird there being no women on board."

"Heard one of you was coming on. Feel like a piece of meat in a lion cage?"

"Did some time in jail."

Frank's craggy face softened some. "Ain't like that here. No one'll mess with you if you don't want. Don't be an asshole, you'll get treated just fine. Get me?"

Brooklyn nodded.

He gestured down the hallway again. "Mess is right down here."

Someone had done a fair job of making the mess hall homey and cheerful. Someone had hung white Christmas lights here and there, and the gray girders and panels were covered with smears of paint, just thick enough to suggest color rather than bring it to life.

"Had to smuggle the paint in at first," Frank said. "Little jars concealed in our duffels. Captain set it up. He's been here as long as I have." He stuck his hand out. "Grease monkey. Never mind 'bout rank. That doesn't matter much 'round here."

"Pleased to meet you." Brooklyn accepted the hand. "Sounds like you and me might be neighbors."

Frank's face cracked in a grin. "Long Island. Can't lose the accent."

He waved to a couple of the men dining and led Brooklyn to a table against one of the walls. "Eat with us." He smiled at the man already sitting there. "We'll get you up to speed on what's what around here."

Brooklyn followed Frank through the chow line, filling his tray with an assortment of pastes and glops, then to the table. Frank sat next to the other man and waited for Brooklyn to join them. "Henry, this is Brooklyn Lamontagne. Brooklyn, this is Henry."

"Good to meet you." The tray seemed to weigh a hundred pounds. Brooklyn sat it down gratefully and slid into a seat. "Came up from Freedom with a pal, but he's working the guns."

Frank split open a dinner roll and filled it with a slice of something pink. "Brooklyn's straight, so try not to fall in love with him."

"Do my best," Henry said. "Haven't had one of those on board in a while. Could be tough."

Brooklyn tried to summon the energy to eat. "My pal's gay. One I came up here with."

"You ever see him kiss anyone?" Henry said. "Hold another guy's hand? You ever double date with him?"

"Spent most of my time out on the surface." Brooklyn put his head in his hands and waited out a dizzy spell.

"Back in the '40s, eggheads said the best way to crew deep-space missions would be to use married couples," Frank said. "Better morale and more stability over long deployments. But women weren't allowed to serve, an' ships weren't set up for babies. Some West Point brain dug up a paper on the Sacred Band of Thebes, these elite warriors in ancient Greece."

"All gay," Henry said.

"Anyway, these guys supposedly fought like hell 'long side each other because they were lovers. Someone got the paper in front of Eisenhower, and his people put the program together."

"They didn't have to look too far for recruits." Henry put his elbows on the table. "I was already in the Navy. Bring the fight to the Russians and live out of the closet? It was like a big, flying party. I'd never seen anything like it." He took a swallow of water. "Most of us are paired up by now. Frank and I been together almost twelve years. Captain married us," he frowned, "eight years ago?"

"Didn't know you guys could get married," Brooklyn said.

"We do our jobs, we can do just about anything we want out here," Frank said. "Part of the appeal."

After dinner, Brooklyn had the want but not the will to check in with Tommy. His ankles were swollen and bruised looking, and his head swam sickeningly. *Half-way 'round the damned ring. Might as well be a hundred miles in this gravity.*

His bunkmates worked the night shift, so the room was empty when he arrived. Someone had crammed a narrow cot into the small space and pushed it right up next to the built-in bottom bunk. Brooklyn pushed it as far against the wall as he could, putting a twelve-inch gap between the bunk and the cot he expected to be sleeping on for the next six months.

The wall above the cot had been inexpertly painted into a landscape scene. The colors were all slightly off, but the representation of the mountains and sunrise, something he hadn't paid much attention to even before he left Earth made his eyes burn.

Brooklyn stripped down to his boxers and climbed onto the creaky cot. His back brushed the wall and fearing for the safety of the mural, he wriggled forward a few inches. Balanced on a knife edge, he fell asleep.

There was a man standing over him when he next woke, looking down at him over a jutting gut. "You're in my bed, kid."

"It's just for one night, Raul. Let him be," someone else said.

Brooklyn caught a flash of hairy ass as it swung into the top bunk. The man named Raul grunted. "Tomorrow you take the top bunk. We share the bottom."

The mattress Brooklyn was lying on was rock hard, but he was grateful that he wouldn't have to move. Every part of him ached, every breath was an effort.

He heard the unmistakable sound of a good night kiss, and Raul slid into the bottom bunk. "Sleep tight, kid. Welcome to the *Baron*."

Brooklyn tried to squirm closer to the wall, mindful of the painting. It probably wasn't a good idea to steal your hosts' bed and deface their art in the same night. His chest tightened. Trapped in a small space, c-force pinning him down like a fucking butterfly… *Ain't like that here*, Frank had said.

"Know I'm not gay, right?" Brooklyn's voice sounded ridiculously young and scared in his own ears.

"Get over yourself, and go the fuck to sleep," Raul said.

Brooklyn's watch alarm woke him to the snores of his cabin mates, and he heaved himself off the cot to dress. There was a fairly recent Grateful Dead poster on the wall that he hadn't noticed the night before.

The doc's PT plan called for three laps of the ring every morning, at whatever pace got him through. Halfway through the first lap he was ready to crawl. His legs were on fire, and he bent over, hands on his knees to catch his breath.

A steady stream of morning runners pounded down the metal hallway past him.

"It's better if you keep walking or at least stand up straight," said a man coming to a stop beside him. He had lapped Brooklyn twice already and glowed with health. "Lets your lungs expand better."

Brooklyn had no energy to comply with the advice. The man patted him on the back. "Come on. I'll do a rest lap with you."

"Crushin' me like a fucking bug."

"Bugs are better built to take it." The man cracked his neck. "It's going to be worse when we're underway. Cap likes to spin us up to one-hundred, one-twenty sometimes. Says it keeps us in shape."

The man slung a towel around his neck and started at a slow walk down the hallway. Brooklyn shuffled about a half step behind him.

"Terry Mehic, one of the pilots on this rig." He held out his hand.

Brooklyn wiped his sweaty palm on the leg of his shorts before reaching for the shake. "Brooklyn Lamontagne. Computers."

"Cap says you're going to keep this boat flying another twenty years."

"Don't know about that. Got some things that will make navigation and acceleration more efficient. Probably help your targeting out, too." He gestured limply at the metal walls. "Can't do much about the rest of it."

"You don't need to do anything about the rest of it," Terry said. "We like the *Baron* just fine the way he is. His namesake was Prussian nobility, hired by George Washington himself to whip the Continental Army into shape."

Brooklyn stopped and leaned against the wall. "Newer ships have more room. More shit to do."

"You ever been on one of them?"

"Just the Moon shuttle."

Terry thumped one of the gray metal walls with the side of his fist. "There's not much extra room in him, but he's built strong. Real steel, not asteroid alloys and plastic. Rather be flying around in this tin can than anything they've launched in the past ten years."

Brooklyn nodded, uncertain what to say.

"Besides, the *Baron* is home. Been up here with him nearly fifteen years. Don't know what I'd do on a bigger ship."

"You'd get used to it."

"Maybe, but now I don't have to. If he lasts another five years, I can fly him all the way to my retirement."

The more he talks, the less I walk. "An' after that? Back to Earth?"

"Mars, maybe. The colony will need pilots. Maybe out to the Belt. Get my own ship, do some prospecting. Get rich and buy myself a nice asteroid somewhere." He looked at his watch and stuck his hand out to Brooklyn again. "Gotta go. Piece of advice. It's a small ship. You don't need to run around telling all the guys you're not interested in them. You keep it up, we're going to think you don't like us."

Brooklyn paled. "Just wanted ta–"

Terry waved it away. "Everyone up here knows hitting on straight guys is way more trouble than it's worth. We don't get extra points for making a conversion."

Brooklyn felt a crazy urge to defend his attractiveness, prove to Terry that he was plenty desirable, but it vanished in a wave of exhaustion. "Fair enough."

"Hey, I'll drop by tomorrow same time and do a couple of laps with you."

Terry jogged ahead and disappeared, and Brooklyn shuffled on. *Need a fucking walker by the end of this.*

Three laps equaled a mile, and by the time Brooklyn finished, nearly ninety minutes had passed. There weren't any lines for showers, but nor was there hot water. Brooklyn washed the sweat off under a thin spray of water, each wince-inducing drop hitting him like a falling penny.

He dried off. The bottoms of his feet were bruised from the thrice as heavy impact on the metal deck. He popped one of the black beauties and a couple of APC.

His work coveralls had come up from the Moon with his tools, so he'd only had to ask the *Baron*'s quartermaster for underwear, T-shirts, and socks. The items came in the same standard brown as they did on the Moon, and slipping into them brought on a wave of sadness. His coveralls were blue, a contrast to the gray the rest of the crew wore. *One more way to stand out.*

Brooklyn shuffled to the mess hall for breakfast and then down to his assigned work space to meet his new assistant.

"Bob Murphy," the guy said, offering his hand for Brooklyn to shake. "Murph works. You gotta girlfriend?"

Brooklyn blinked. "Nothing serious."

"I do. Write her every day."

"Lucky lady." The small cargo hold was packed with crates just up from the Moon. A lot of it was food and other supplies, but the computer project took up two pallets right near the door.

Murph rubbed his hands together. "Tells me how much she loves me every time she writes. Wanna see a picture?"

Brooklyn wobbled. "Wanna lie down. Sooner I get all this looked at and inventoried, sooner I can."

"I got you. We gotta stick together, you and me." He slapped Brooklyn on the shoulder, nearly forcing him to his knees "Watch each other's back."

"Back's just fine, man. Let's just get to this."

Brooklyn slipped the pen into his clipboard. "This will be our staging area. Other cargo will be unpacked and broken down in the next couple of days. Give us plenty of room to work."

Murph wiped sweat off his forehead. "'Zactly what're we doing, boss?"

"Upgrades. Give the nav system faster processing. Replace the card readers with eight-track drives. Install some new programs." He prodded a medium-sized crate with the toe of his boot. "This is the big one. Five-megabyte hard drive. Install it, shield it, install the software... Ever worked with one?"

"Barely understood a word you said," Murphy said.

"Got some reading to do, then." He searched out the smallest crate. "Those should be the manuals. Crack that open and get learnin'."

Murph grabbed a pry bar off a wall rack. "I'm sure glad you're here, pal. It's going to be a lot easier to—" He interrupted himself with a grimace.

"Easier to what?"

"Just glad you're here."

Brooklyn stayed up to meet his bunkmates, Cliff and Raul, and they shot the shit a while. Cliff was from Minnesota, Raul from New Mexico, and although they'd only been aboard the *Baron* six years, they'd been together longer than Brooklyn had been out of high school. Last time they'd had leave on Earth, they'd indeed followed the Dead around for a couple of weeks. Raul was the artist and also part of the ship's emergency-response team.

Terry was waiting outside when he got up for his shuffle the next morning. "Didn't think you were serious 'bout coming back," Brooklyn said, using the corridor wall to stretch.

"You'll push yourself harder if you work out with someone else. Get in shape a lot faster."

The morning doses of APC and speed had taken the edge off the pain, and Brooklyn managed a steady hobble for the first lap. Terry made it more challenging for himself by dropping and doing a hundred push-ups every ninety-degrees. "You're already looking better than yesterday," Terry said. "Wish the fuck I was still in my twenties. I could live on barbed wire and bull piss back then. Bounce back from anything."

Brooklyn was feeling anything but better. Climbing into the top bunk the night before had taken three tries and a final desperate lunge, and getting down hadn't been much easier. "Hope the hell I bounce back. It's going to be a long six months if I don't."

Terry cleared his throat. "Asked around about you. Heard you might know something about vacuum stills."

Brooklyn chuckled. "Knew there had to be something like that around. Thought it might be the Doc making hooch to wash down with his pills."

"Carruthers is an opportunist, not a producer. Doesn't mind if people get hooked because it gives him something he can hold over them. Got a few friends of mine in his pocket that way. I just want the crew to have a nice drink or two at the end of the day. Nothing wrong with that."

"Not a thing. Where's your baby?"

"I'll show you after you get off shift," Terry said. "Just wanted to find out if you were interested."

Terry changed the route on the second lap and led Brooklyn to a small gym just forward of engineering. "We call it the Y. Figured we could spar a little. Best way to get back in shape." He handed Brooklyn a pair of gloves.

Brooklyn looked at them dubiously. "Barely lift my arms, man."

"Barely's good enough. It will be like starting in the eighth round."

"I'm not really trained," Brooklyn said. "Just what we did in basic."

"I'll give you some lessons. Take it out of whatever you're going to charge me to look at my still. Get your feet apart." Terry demonstrated. "Like this. Bend your knees. You want your weight to be on the balls of your feet." He adopted a lazy-looking stance. "Don't tense up."

Brooklyn tried to relax but waiting for Terry to take a poke at him didn't help.

"Keep your hands up but loosen your shoulders. Now move toward me."

Brooklyn took a listless step toward Terry, swaying as he did so. Terry dropped his stance. "You really don't know much about this do you?"

"I been in a lot of fights." Brooklyn flushed embarrassment. Adrenaline kicked in, and his muscles felt loose. "Could knock you on your ass right now." His accent, diluted from a year and a half away from the neighborhood, surfaced.

"There's the fire. Got ya feeling a little testy." Terry grinned.

"I'm sure you been in a lot of brawls. And maybe you could kick my ass on the street, but not in the ring." He dropped into his stance again. "Get your gloves up."

He stepped toward Brooklyn, the top of his body moving like it was on rails. Brooklyn put his hands up and bounced on his toes like he had seen the boxers on television do.

"Don't bounce." Terry slid to Brooklyn's left. "You're wasting energy and taking your hands out of line."

Brooklyn scowled and threw a right that sailed right past Terry's head. He didn't even bother to dodge.

"See?" Terry said. "You bounced it out of line."

More heat rose to Brooklyn's face, he threw a left this time, a jab. Terry moved his head a fraction of an inch and avoided it. "Better." He feinted a right toward Brooklyn's head. "But you're telegraphing. I can tell by your shoulders when you're about to swing."

Brooklyn moved backward, crossing his right foot over his left. Terry stepped in with an uppercut that slid through Brooklyn's guard and just barely touched his chin. Brooklyn lurched in surprise and off balance, fell on the floor.

Terry grinned. "You don't want to cross your feet." He demonstrated and extended his hand down to Brooklyn. Brooklyn took it and let Terry pull him up.

"Show me that again," he said.

For the next three minutes – all Brooklyn could take – Terry showed him how to box. He stuck to the simple: movement back and forth, foot placement, and how to get around the floor. "Better," Terry said, clapping the younger man on the back. "We got a couple of guys up here who can show you some other styles, too. Karate. Some judo. We hold open fights about once a month. You keep training you might be able to get in there and hold your own for a little while." He nodded at the wall clock. "But I need to get in a real workout before my shift."

Brooklyn panted, fighting a wave of nausea. "Thanks for the lesson."

"Same again tomorrow?" Terry said.

"Bet you got better things to do."

"It's good to go over the fundamentals again. I learn something new every time I train someone." He flipped Brooklyn a salute. "No trouble at all."

Brooklyn hobbled back for a quick shower and a fast meal before heading to the cargo bay to meet Murph. The squirrelly little guy was leaning against a stack of opened packing crates, chewing a nicstick when Brooklyn arrived.

"You started early," Brooklyn said.

Murph tossed the empty stick to the deck. "Might start spending even more time down here. Set a cot up."

"Suit yourself. There's a lot of work to do." He collapsed onto a stool. "Finish reading all those manuals?"

"Didn't understand a word of them."

"What was your specialty?"

"Demolitions."

"Not much use on a ship."

"Not much use planetside, either." Murph held up his hand. "Got the shakes. Too little for a clean discharge. Too much to work with bombs. Been banging around since."

"Medical discharge might start looking pretty good once you spend a couple of days in the crawlspaces. Sixty-three junctions on this boat, and we can't get to any of them from this side of the hull. Gonna spend the next few months inside the ducts like rats. Can't replace the junctions without dry docking or leaving the ship floating, so we're going to string the new equipment in parallel. Leave the old wiring in there. No point in ripping it out."

"You just point and grunt, I'll follow along." He smothered a yawn. "Hey, got some Playboys back in my bunk you can borrow you get bored. Whole bunch of them. Move 'em in here when I set up my cot."

* * *

The *Baron* uncoupled from Red Star Station that night and moved away on a cloud of thruster gas. When it reached a safe distance, the pilot of the old ship switched to the Oppenheimers and moved smoothly out of lunar orbit and into a course toward the inner planets. Brooklyn was so damned tired he didn't notice a fucking thing.

TWENTY-ONE

Tommy made like he was having no trouble adjusting to the ship's spin, but his face showed the lie whenever he moved quick. "I said you needed to exercise more, man." He flexed. "This is a lot easier than a day in the centrifuge."

Brooklyn concentrated on not dropping his fork. "Got nearly five years on you, junior. Just gonna take me awhile." Tommy was second shift at the big guns, which meant his breakfast just about lined up with Brooklyn's dinner. "Make any new friends over there playing space ranger?"

Tommy took a long swallow of orange juice-analog, his Adam's apple working. He set the tumbler down and wiped his mouth on the sleeve of his gray coveralls. "Tell you what. It's been a whatayacallit, a revelation." He spread his hands. "No worry, no questions, no tiptoeing around. A lot of them are coupled up already, but I see a single guy here, I know. There's no dancin' around, looking for signals to see if he's in the club."

"Sort of signals?" Brooklyn said.

"It took me years to learn them. I'm not giving them away for free."

"Imagine there ain't a lot of how-to-gay classes in Oklahoma."

Tommy laughed. "Even after the APA took it off the crazy list and Kennedy made it illegal to discriminate, folks in my

197

hometown gave anyone who came out of the closet a hard pass. My parents still don't really understand. Mom keeps hoping I'll meet a nice girl and give 'em grandkids."

"Carry on the family name."

"Got two younger brothers to handle that." He smiled bigger than Brooklyn had seen. "Tell, ya, man, feels like I've come home."

Brooklyn knocked at the door of the shrink's office for his first appointment and stopped short on the thin carpet inside. "Thought you were a pilot."

Terry smiled. "Certified for both. I'm one of four or five guys who work in here during the week. Ship's not big enough for three shifts of full-time shrinks, and there's not much for a pilot to do once we're under way." The counseling office wasn't far from the gym where Terry had been giving Brooklyn boxing lessons. It was a small room with a desk and two comfortable chairs.

"So all that walking and teaching me how to fight...?"

"Just me being neighborly. I didn't know it was my turn to catch the new guy until yesterday." He tapped the ubiquitous folder. "If you're uncomfortable working with me, you can ask for someone else. No harm, no foul. The doctor-patient thing will still apply. Everything in that folder stays need-to-know."

"Shot a lot of hoops with my first shrink. Said it was part of his process. Beating the shit out of each other part of yours?"

"Could be. You feel better don't you? You sure in hell look better than you did last week."

Either the exercise or the doctor's injection had kicked in, and Brooklyn was feeling a little closer to normal. He could walk his three laps without stopping and had started working with weights. He'd also spent several hours on Terry's vacuum distillery, with hopes that the next batch would be something special. "If I say something during a workout, is it gonna end up in that folder?"

"Like," Terry pretended to write in the air, "'patient assisted me with my against-regulations still'? Maybe. Depends on whether you say something crazy."

Brooklyn frowned. "Just weird. Never hung out with anyone who knew so much about my shit."

"I won't bring it up outside this room unless you do. Past is past. A punch is a punch."

"We'll give it a shot." He took a seat. The captain was ramping up the c-force slowly, and everything weighed about forty-five percent of what it did on Earth. Uncomfortable but increasingly bearable.

"Good." Terry uncrossed his legs. "So, how are you adjusting to life on the *Baron*?"

Brooklyn wheeled a cot into his workspace in the cargo hold.

"Get tired of life in Fairyland, too?" Murph said. He'd moved his bed into the converted cargo bay the week before and covered anything that held still in Playboy pinups. Murph was starting to remind Brooklyn of Dee's first battle buddy, Dex. A lot of the other trainees had been like Brooklyn, the EOF was a ticket out of their old lives. Some of them joined up because of family legacy or out of a half-baked idea of patriotism. Dex just wanted to kill things. He had a "Remember Cleveland" tattoo on his left bicep and was always talking about slaughtering "the Mercs". *Talked about so much it was like he was trying to convince himself what his target should be.*

Brooklyn shoved the cot into a corner and unfolded it. It was a little chilly, but there was plenty of room "Nah. Just didn't seem fair. The guys've been together eight years. I was cramping their style." *And Raul snores like a fucking chainsaw.* He'd left a thank-you note and a jar of the new distillation in their quarters. "This'll do fine. Shrink approved and everything."

* * *

Dr Carruthers pulled his eyes away from blood sample under the microscope. "This is very interesting, specialist. Were you exposed to much radiation during your time on the Moon?"

The examination table was chilly under Brooklyn's ass. "Spent a lot of time on the surface, but kept an eye on my dosimeter. Never got into the red zone. You sayin' I got cancer or something?"

The doctor smiled. "Nothing like that. My treatment is simply working better than expected."

"Because of the rads?"

"Possibly. How do you feel?"

"Fine. Get tired and achy toward the end of the day."

"Are you using the stimulants I prescribed?"

"Some. Mostly I'm drinking a lot of coffee."

"Your heart appears to be in good shape, and your bones and muscles are adapting nicely to the higher gravity." He pulled a bottle off a shelf and tossed it to Brooklyn. "Calcium supplements. You lost a lot on the Moon, those will put it back." He stood. "Wait there. I'll prepare your injection."

Brooklyn stayed seated while the medic went back into his small office. Every doctor's office in the EOF had the same posters. Stay clean. *On it.* Guard against loose women. *Probably a joke here.* Re-enlist! *No fucking way.* VD – A Sorry Ending to a Furlough. *The Tranquility Twins were nuts, but they were clean.*

"Here we go." Carruthers came back in with his syringe. "I made a few adjustments. I'm curious to see what it will do."

Brooklyn frowned. "Not sure how I feel about you turning me into a guinea pig, doc."

"Nonsense. I've forgotten more about biology than anyone on Earth has learned. Give me your arm." The doctor administered the injection. "Anything else to report? No? Then we'll see you next week."

TWENTY-TWO

Brooklyn shouldered his tool bag and tossed a roll of cable to Murph. He put on a headlamp and gestured to the wall panel. "Yank that off and let's get this started."

Brooklyn's maternal grandfather had worked as a welder at a shipworks. He'd gotten asbestosis from working inside battleship and submarine crawlspaces and died coughing on the orange couch in his living room. Brooklyn had been about five when the old man died, but he remembered that couch and some of the stories his grandfather used to tell about the job, especially the one about finding a coworker who had crawled up inside a ship and smothered to death when his air line crimped.

The space between the *Baron*'s inner and outer hulls wasn't much bigger than those naval crawlways, but Brooklyn didn't mind small spaces. For the most part, they made him feel like he was in a fort or protective shell. *Maybe I should have been like Dee, gone out for a scout ship.*

Brooklyn pulled a rebreather over his mouth and nose and ducked into the hole Murph made in the cargo-bay wall. He consulted the schematic slid into the plastic sleeve on his coverall arm. "Looks like we're headed up toward the alpha spoke first." He was on his hands and knees inside the curved crawlspace. Even through the insulated gloves and boots he imagined could feel the chill of the vast space outside. "Keep an eye out for leaks. Might as well throw on a few patches as we go."

Brooklyn let the cable play out behind him like a tether. It was Murph's job to secure it, wrapping and labeling it against the old wiring, most of it installed before the ship had left Earth.

It's damned dusty in space. They don't tell you that in training. On the Moon, it was regolith. Shit got everywhere. Here, years of habitation and the ship's aging ventilation system had left a thick layer of shed skin cells and other detritus inside the crawlspace. "Bring a vacuum cleaner along tomorrow, and we'll try to get some of this up," he said. "This ain't clean-room work, but we might as well go through the motions. Make a note to tell the life-support crew that their ventilation ductwork needs an overhaul."

Brooklyn quit talking and focused his energy on moving. He weighed about sixty-five percent of what he did on Earth that day, and for someone used to Moon gravity, crawling fifty yards was still a chore. He pulled himself along until he reached the junction. "We're here. Still with me?"

"Catching up," Murph said. "All you got to do is crawl. I got to crawl and tie everything up."

"Be here for a while. Give you time to get caught up and maybe take a break." Brooklyn flipped the junction box open and whistled at the obsolete tech he found inside. It might have been one step up from the computer that had set his apartment on fire and driven the last nail into his relationship with Carmen. "Plenty of room in here for the new circuitry. Crazy to think how much we've been able to miniaturize everything since we started working with the Japanese."

Murph didn't answer, but Brooklyn heard him muttering somewhere in the darkness behind him. The new circuit board was about the size of his palm. Brooklyn pulled the drill off his belt to make a hole for the new cabling and conduit pipe. The drill was rechargeable, good for nine or ten holes.

"You bring any extra batteries for the drill?" he said.

"You didn't tell me to." Murphy sounded defensive.

"Didn't think to. Got one extra. Hopefully it will last us until lunch."

He drilled the hole, careful not to cut into the existing circuitry. The old hardware had to work until Brooklyn could make it redundant by switching to the new. The next time the *Baron* came in for a refit, a team would take the old computer core out and replace it with something more modern. Though, likely, considering the state of the vessel, that something would be less than top of the line and most likely used. Even so, the improvements would probably double the old boat's effectiveness.

"Where no man has gone in a long fucking time." Brooklyn adapted the catchphrase of a TV show he'd gotten into as a kid. It lasted a single season, overshadowed by everything humanity was actually doing in space. It was hard to get excited by rubber-masked aliens when the news was filled with reports about alien invaders, Mars, and the asteroid belt. The show had been replaced by a still-popular soap opera about asteroid miners. It was one of his ma's stories, and her correspondence usually included long-winded summaries of her favorite episodes. Sometimes, it was hard to distinguish them from the neighborhood gossip she also shared.

He snapped the new circuit board into place and soldered the connectors onto the new cable. The connector was new tech, too, held in place by a threaded sleeve rather than a cap and miles of electrical tape like the old days.

"How you feeling back there?" Brooklyn said. "Not too cold? Getting enough air? No hypoxia?"

"I'm fine," Murph said. "Where's the next one?"

Brooklyn shone his headlight on the map on his sleeve. "Another fifty yards forward. That will bring us out," he fumbled with the mechanical scrolling mechanism on his map sleeve, "near the mess hall. Or close enough."

"Think we'll get there in time for lunch?" Murph said.

"Might surprise some people we came out the wall there, but I think so."

"I wonder if we could rig creepers to make this easier. Grab some wheels off a couple of the pallet jacks."

"Good idea," Brooklyn huffed. "They do this with robots on the big ships. Little toaster-looking things. You leave them right inside the conduits in case you need to run new lines."

"Don't suppose you brought a couple of those with you?"

"Crawlspaces aren't designed for it. The *Baron* reminds me a lot of Freedom. Spent weeks in those old conduits when I first got there. Colder than this, and creepy as hell. They're pressurized, but you're crawling around on the actual Moon surface. Pure regolith. No way to keep that shit out of your clothes. Itches like a son of a bitch."

"Never been on the Moon," Murph said. "My first deployment was to Eisenhower. Spent nearly a year there, then out to the Belt. Did a year on a security detail there."

"How was that?"

"Busted up fights. Arrested a lot of guys on drunk-and-disorderly charges. Not much to do out there other than drink and watch movies."

Brooklyn held up his hand to signal a stop. "You hear that?"

Murph stopped moving and both men strained to hear. It was just a whisper of a sound. A hiss in the conduit ahead.

"Sounds like a pinhole," Murph said. "Where is it?"

"Up ahead somewhere. Dust probably clogs it up sometimes, might be why no one has noticed an O_2 leak." Brooklyn took his left glove off and tried to find the leak via the air currents.

"Kick up a little of that dust ahead of you," Murphy said. "Wait and see where it drifts."

Brooklyn swept his hand across the steel wall to his left, stirring up a sea of dust motes. They glowed and swirled in the light of his headlamp before juking right in a sudden eddy of escaping air.

"Got it." Brooklyn crawled forward another few feet and

brushed his gloved hand against the right panel. The whispered hiss increased in volume. "Weird shape. It's bigger than a pinhole. More like a gash." He touched it with his bare hand. "Almost like a tool gouge."

Murphy tugged on Brooklyn's boot. "I got a patch."

"Let me brush it clear first. The dust is crusted with something, like it got wet." Brooklyn scrubbed at the plating around the hole to get the area clean then slapped the patch into place. The hiss of escaping air stopped immediately. "We're going to want to report that. Hole's big enough that the captain might want someone to take a walk outside for repairs."

"Find the number on the plate," Murphy said. "Make it easier for the repair crew to find it from the other side."

Brooklyn brushed away more of the dust, scrubbing away at the scab-like crust that had formed around the leak. "Some of this is dried like cement." He scrubbed harder. "Here's the number." He read it off to Murph then checked that he got it. "Alright, let's keep going. We time this right, we can pop out of the mess hall wall in time to be first in the chow line. "

Brooklyn resumed his crawl forward. The crusted dust under his hands felt thicker and cracked when he touched it. "Should report this as a liquid leak, too. Something must be wrong with the plumbing in the mess."

"If we're really lucky we're crawling through dried shit," Murphy said. "Be glad you're wearing a respirator."

"Ain't shit." Brooklyn ran his hand over the shape that had materialized out of the gloom ahead of him. The boot shifted enough that Brooklyn could feel the weight inside and attached to it. The other boot was a little ahead, like the owner of the feet had tried to crawl away from his death. Brooklyn's gorge rose. *Wish it was, but it ain't.*

"Yang was his name."

Murph's breathing sharpened.

"Sir?" Brooklyn stood more or less at ease in the captain's office, Murphy beside him.

"Specialist Gary Yang. He came on late last year. We thought he'd jumped ship on us, deserted, when we were in the Belt. It happens sometimes."

"Did you try to find him, sir?" Murph said. "Or did you just write him off while he was rotting away in the wall?"

The captain's eyes narrowed. "The Belt's a big place, Mr Murphy. We made appropriate inquiries then left it up to the local administrators. They would have let us know if he'd surfaced."

"Sure surfaced now, Captain," Brooklyn said. "Big as life." *Not what I mean to say.*

"And thanks to you, we can close the book on a chapter that's been open too long," the captain said. "A suicide."

Murph flushed. "Just crawled into the wall like a rat, I guess. Shot himself." He glanced at Brooklyn. "Funny how that happened," his mouth twisted, "Captain."

The look on the captain's face sucked all the light and air out of the room. Brooklyn was struck dumb and paralyzed. He was amazed Murph wasn't rendered immediately into ash.

"I spoke to you this morning purely as a courtesy, gentlemen. And as a courtesy, I'm going to chalk that outburst up to your emotions and advise you to remove yourself from my presence with all due haste. Dismissed."

The service was held in the mess hall the next morning, an open casket in respect for Yang's Catholic faith. Attendance was mandatory for everyone off shift. Yang had been well-liked during his short time on board. A solid, friendly guy who did his job well and liked rock music and comic books.

The body in the box, decked out in dress blues and made up for the occasion, had been well-preserved in the thin atmosphere inside the hull. It looked like it had belonged to a professional wrestler, thick-necked and broad-shouldered.

"Being near that leak made him swell up or something,"

Brooklyn's former roommate Cliff whispered. "He worked out but nothing like that."

The captain said some words, his mustache bristling with solemnity. The chaplain, some denomination called Unitarian Universalist that Brooklyn had never heard of, said a prayer that didn't mention Jesus at all. A guy with big shoulders played Taps on a bugle.

The chaplain closed the coffin and blew it out the airlock to float around with Tommy's big brother and all the others who'd died in space.

Floating around forever and ever. Brooklyn shuddered, shoved his hands in his pockets.

The end.

TWENTY-THREE

"A corpse in a crawlspace." Tommy shook salt onto his egg approximations. "I swear you could set yourself on fire on a submarine."

"Probably not all that hard to do. Lot of flammables on a sub." Brooklyn cupped the back of his head in both hands. "Don't want to think about it. Reminds me all the shit can go wrong out here. Shook me up some."

Tommy narrowed his eyes. "You're filling out, man. I think you're bigger than you were in basic."

"Doc gave me some shots to help. You didn't get any?"

Tommy chased the eggs with a piece of toast. "Probably a different doctor for second shift. Wish ta hell I had a shot. Still not feeling a hundred percent."

Brooklyn was. Maybe a hundred plus some. He chalked it up to finding the body. Being around death did that for some people. Other people... "Guy with me went right off the rails 'bout it."

Tommy covered a frown with his coffee cup. "You're talking about Bob Murphy."

"Know him?"

"Heard of. He used to work on our side of things, but the chief chased him over here a couple of months before you and me showed up. He hooked up with a couple guys and went on a big self-flagellation kick afterward. Hates us, hates that he is us. Guess his parents really fucked him over. Gave him to a cult when he started talking about being gay, an' they tried to pray and beat it out of him. Tied him up, burnt him with cigarettes."

"Jesus!"

"Yeah, pretty sure he was in the name of the cult."

Brooklyn hummed. "Never expected to hear something like that come out of you."

"Some of the guys here have pretty fucked-up stories, man. Real sad they had to come all the way out here to get somewhere safe." Tommy huffed. "Guys say the captain's got a thing for strays. Pulled Murphy in as a favor to his shrink."

That night, the teletype in the work area unexpectedly pinged and rattled into action. Brooklyn ripped the long sheet of paper off the machine and carried it back to his cot. He snapped on the reading light. He was having trouble sleeping anyway. Bad dreams about Galvano and finding bodies in weird places.

The first block of text was a message from Ma, sent special priority. Mike had proposed, and they were getting hitched. "Hope you can make it!" Brooklyn rubbed his face. If he put in for leave now, he might just. *Be nice to see her happy. Be nice to have some help with her bills, too.* He'd have to talk to Mike about that. Ma wasn't likely to be interested in living above a bar. At the end of the paragraph she added a p.s.: "Saw Carmen at the market. She's expecting a baby and sends her love." He read the p.s. a few times, and each one of them hurt.

The second message was addressed to the "Young American" and signed "Low Rider".

Sorry, pal, you aren't that special. Took our problem all the way north. Sherlock Holmes and Hercule Poirot are on the case. Charlie's Angels are going long. Don't call me unless you're pregnant (again).

He read the thing three times. *The fuck is Hercule Poirot?* Sherlock Holmes was a detective from old movies. Charlie's Angels was an obvious reference to Sierra and the people she worked with. The "problem" had to be the disguised Mercurian and the tapes. A detective is looking into the problem? Had Sierra been Angel or Charlie? Didn't matter. She was going long, whatever that meant in spy talk.

Brooklyn crumpled up the printout and tossed it in the trash. *Not my job.* His life had been shit since those tapes came into it. *I did my bit. No more sticking my neck out. Get done, get home.*

"That was the last dose." Dr Carruthers set the used syringe aside. "You've put on thirty pounds of lean muscle. Your respiratory efficiency has doubled, and your metabolism is faster than a teenage boy's." He pulled a scalpel out from somewhere and slashed the outside of Brooklyn's wrist. The skin parted cleanly.

Brooklyn pulled his arm away. "The hell, doc?!" He clamped his hand around the cut to slow the blood.

"Science, Mr Lamontagne. Science. I'll bandage that, and you'll keep it on until you come back in two days. And then we will see what we will see." He cleaned the wound with an alcohol swab and covered it with a bandage. "It's barely a scratch."

Brooklyn made a fist, feeling the pull of the bandage and the sting of the cut. He caught a glimpse of himself in the reflection of the paper towel dispenser and did a double take. There was no mirror in the cargo bay, and the one he used for shaving was so small it only showed part of his face at a time. He flexed his biceps and tightened his stomach muscles. *The hell? I'm built like Carlos Monzon!*

"How're you doing with Bob Murphy?" Terry said. They were on their third lap of the morning, holding a steady pace toward a six-minute mile at seventy percent of Earth gravity.

Brooklyn sucked in extra air to reply. "Good worker. Does what I ask him to."

"You know his story?"

"Enough. He one of yours?"

"I think you've been a good influence on him. Normal guy, OK with everything here. Might be what he needs to help him accept himself."

Some of the guys here have some pretty fucked-up stories. Brooklyn kept his mouth shut. Lola Lamontagne's blue-eyed boy was a good time, he was free with cash when he had it, but he was no one's idea of a good influence. Or potential father. *Tommy had to convince me to go out and save Dee, for fuck's sake! Terry's the kinda guy wouldn't think twice.* "Savin' people is your thing, man," he said. "I'm just doin' my time."

"We watch out for each other here."

Brooklyn got a little red in the head at that. Wasn't enough that he was a billion miles from home on an antique spaceship. Wasn't enough that he was pullin' corpses out of crawlspaces and crawling through miles of conduit, risking his ass so a bunch of old farts could play house on the final frontier. Now they wanted him to be big brother to a fucked-up asshole who hated himself and was afraid to go in the showers in case he fell in love with someone. He'd been acting like getting in shape, getting acclimated to the ship, making friends mattered, when he should have been focusing on getting the job done and getting the fuck back to the Moon. Better yet, getting back to New York where life was speeding by without him. *Got my own fucked-up story to deal with.*

Brooklyn didn't bother to shower after his run. He swallowed two more of the doc's pills and headed to the cargo hold. Murph held up a Thermos in greeting. "Coffee. Help us beat back the cold in there a little better."

Brooklyn pulled the access panel off the wall opposite. "Let's just get to it."

They replaced two junctions before breaking for lunch and two more before the end of shift. Brooklyn washed down another black beauty with coffee and a mess-hall sandwich and spent the hours after dinner fastening connectors on the cable ends to make the work go faster. He studied the central processor and hard-drive installation manuals to make sure he could do the work without a hitch. His fingers were raw with solder burns by the time he stumbled to his cot and fell into an exhausted sleep around four in the morning.

He skipped his workout and downed a couple more pills with his coffee. He'd hoped to get out of the mess before Terry made it in, but the older man caught his eye and nodded before sitting at a table on the other side of the room. Murph was dancing like a puppy when Brooklyn arrived in the cargo hold.

"The other guys don't think Gary killed himself. They were surprised when he ran off."

"Whadda you care?"

Some of the light went out of his face. "I knew him. Wasn't a pal, exactly, but–"

"Ain't got time for stories about your boyfriends."

"I ain't like that, and you know it." Murph's face darkened.

"Yeah, whatever. Just do me a favor and let me know if you start feeling amorous around me. I'll give you a thirty-second head start before popping you the yawp. Now, shut the fuck up and let's get to work."

Terry caught up with him at breakfast the next day.

"I'm running alone for awhile," Brooklyn said. "Later in the day."

Terry shrugged. "Suit yourself. Any particular reason?"

Because I ain't what you think I am, and I'm not doing your shrink job for you. "Just want to finish this job and get the fuck off this ship"

Terry's mouth worked. "Coming by the gym later? Or is that off, too?"

Brooklyn plowed through the disappointment he saw in Terry's face. "Gotta make up some time."

"Like I said, suit yourself." He turned to go. "Did I say something to set you off?"

"It ain't about that." Brooklyn held his hands up. "It's just..."

"Cool, man." Terry gave him a two-finger salute. "I'll be around if you change your mind."

TWENTY-FOUR

Dr Carruthers worked at removing the old bandage. "You've done nothing to it?" The medic examined the wound site with a magnifying glass. "It's completely healed. There's not even a scar." He stroked his chin. "I wonder if you could regenerate a limb."

Brooklyn pulled his arms and legs out of the doctor's reach. "Not interested."

"What about a toe? For science. Imagine what the EOF could do with–"

"Fuck science, man. And fuck the EOF." Brooklyn made a grab for his coveralls. "You ain't cutting anything off me."

Carruthers frowned. "Very well. Just another couple of vials of blood then. And maybe a tissue sample."

Brooklyn tensed.

The doctor's eyes rolled. "A very small tissue sample."

Tommy leaned against the corridor wall and folded his arms. "Seems to me I'm looking at a Class-A asshole." The skinny Oklahoma hayseed from basic training had been replaced by a confident, take-no-shit bear of a man. He even had a beard started, filling in the Middle-American space between his nose and burly chest. "Murphy started some shit over here and almost got his ass handed to him. Now you're telling me you're the one set him off."

"EOF trained me to fix computers, not people, man. Don't see how any of this is my problem."

Tommy's left boot joined his shoulders on the wall. "Is that why you came all the way over here? You want me to back you up on this?"

It was near midnight, ship time. Brooklyn had ventured into the unknown world of the gunners' quarters in hopes of finding his battle buddy and getting him to do just that. "Murph ain't my problem."

"No, you just made him someone else's." Tommy's foot dropped back to the deck. "You fed right into the crazy he's wrapped himself in. He came over here with some truly foul shit in his mouth an–"

"Shoulda known you'd take their side. Ever since we–"

Despite all the recent fight training, Brooklyn failed to see the big fist coming. It hit the left side of his face and sent him spinning to the floor. Tommy stood over him, shoulders loose and hands open. "How...?" One second he'd been standing, the next... *Did I have a stroke?* His arms and legs wouldn't work.

"If I weren't on your side I wouldn't bother telling you when you're being an asshole," Tommy said.

Brooklyn regained enough control to pull himself to a seated position. The pain in his face helped him figure it out. "You hit me." Even the major hadn't tagged him that hard. If he were a cartoon, birds would be flying around his head. "Fuck you do that for?"

"Guess."

"It's what shrinks are for, man. They got the training for this. I'm just–"

"The only guy on the *Baron* Bob Murphy didn't see as a threat. Stop being a selfish prick, Brook."

Tommy stomped off some point after that, and it took Brooklyn a while to get to his feet. *Hayseed rung my bell good.*

Oughta put him in the ring with Terry. His brain went in and out a few times on the way back to his bunk. He used the shaving mirror to get a look at his face. It was already swelling and purple. *Stop being a selfish prick.* He opened the bottle of uppers, most the way through what should have been a thirty-day supply. *Prick had always liked the speedy stuff.*

God damn it. He tossed the bottle in the trash. *Point fucking made.*

TWENTY-FIVE

This right here is why you ain't 'sposed to be pals with your shrink.

Terry was wearing his counselor clothes. Issue khakis, spit-shined boots, and a button-up shirt. His neck was too thick for the top button.

"You've missed a couple appointments," he said. "How you been?"

"Alright." *This feels like talking to Carmen after we broke up. Like either one of us is ready to get up and run anytime.*

"You look good. Been keeping up with your workouts?"

Brooklyn's eye had healed as fast as the cut the doctor made. He cleared his throat. "Terr... I'm... S'pose I freaked out when you said I could be a good influence on Murph."

"Ah." Terry looked confused. "This is when I'm supposed to say, 'go on'."

"I ain't a good guy. I got my best pal killed, and was ready to let another one die, too. No one should follow my example."

"I see." Terry tented his fingers on his knees. "We've all let people down. Done things we shouldn't."

"I'll talk to Murph."

"That's something a good guy would do."

Brooklyn ran his hand over the top of his head. "It ain't gonna help."

"Do what you can. Might help you both."

Brooklyn nodded. "Think I should start seeing a different shrink, though."

"Yeah, probably. I'll see who's available."

Brooklyn hooked the test box to his end of the cable and waited as Murph swarmed up the ladder behind the cargo space. In a few minutes, Murph yelled down. "I'm here. Let's get this over with."

Brooklyn turned on the tester, fingers mentally crossed that the idiot light on the front would show green instead of red. "It's good! Move up to the next one!"

Murph started swearing again. Most of it was pro forma. It was fairly easy work, assuming a lack of claustrophobia, and the job would look good on his record. Maybe get him onto a new training path now that demolitions had been denied him. Murph climbed higher and they repeated the test. The idiot light showed green again.

"Alright!" Brooklyn said. "Move to the right, and I'll follow you up."

The vacuuming and the new filters the life-support crew had installed in the air system were paying off. The dust was largely gone, and the crawlspace was starting to look like it should. Brooklyn climbed up to the second junction and waited until Murphy reported that he'd reached his destination. The light glowed green again. "Good! Now you move down, and I'll follow."

They chased each other like that for the rest of the day, testing all the cable and conduit they had put into place. It all checked out. Brooklyn slid out of the wall and back into the cargo bay.

"Check the other side tomorrow." Brooklyn tucked his toolbelt into the storage cart he'd been using as a work bench. "Doing good work, Murph. Coming to the fights tonight?"

Murphy shook his head. "Everyone will be there, and I can

have some peace and quiet. I might watch some TV and turn in early."

Brooklyn was tired enough that a similar evening was tempting, but he'd told Terry he'd check out the fight and Tommy had the night off. "Suit yourself. But drop by if you want a couple of beers. My treat."

"If it were just you." Murphy put his own gear in the ad hoc work bench.

"They're just guys. Look…" Brooklyn ran his fingers through his hair. He'd need a haircut soon to keep it regulation. "What I said about Gary and you was stupid. I was an asshole. You're a smart guy, hard worker. Sure he was, too. That's what matters. The super-macho, I-hate-gays bullshit gets old. Exhausting to me, can't imagine how it must wear you out."

Murphy's face was red. He looked like he might be about to cry. Or scream with rage. *Hard to tell with the Irish.*

"Just be yourself," Brooklyn said. "Change your mind about the fights, I'll see you there."

Murphy closed the top of the box. "Have a good night, boss." He flipped Brooklyn a lazy salute.

Brooklyn took a quick shower and met Tommy in the mess hall. He spotted the table he wanted.

"My pal Tommy," Brooklyn said. "Known him since basic. Likes to shoot shit."

Terry stood up to shake Tommy's hand. "Any friend of Brook's and all that."

Tommy grinned. "Mosta Brooklyn's pals are crooks. What does that say 'bout us?"

Tommy fived and shook with Frank and Henry then Terry introduced them to the rangy black guy at the corner of the table.

"Me and you got lots in common," the man said to Brooklyn. He winked at Terry. "You the only straight man on the ship, I'm the only Muslim."

"You'd be Ali." Brooklyn stuck out his hand. "Terry says you're the only reason he's not in love with me."

Ali laughed. "Good to know I got competition. Means I can be extra sweet to him without him thinking I'm up to something."

"Anytime you're sweet, I know you're up to something," Terry said. "Ali is from New Jersey, but he's been all over the place. He's the one who can teach you some judo to go with your stand-up fight."

"First rule is, don't let the bastards get you down." Ali shrugged. "But I can show you some things make it more likely you can get up again."

"Are you fighting tonight?" Brooklyn said.

Ali shook his head. "I'm too pretty for that. Terry is the only one of us dumb enough to mash his face up against all the fists on the ship. He's defending his crown next month."

Brooklyn raised his eyebrows. Terry blushed. "Ship champion five years running. Thought I told you about that."

"Maybe you forgot," Brooklyn said.

"Didn't want you to get too nervous when we were sparring. Challenger is Roger Hanson in engineering. Big dude. Hits like an elephant. I've defended against him twice." Terry grinned. "Every once in a while he starts feeling lucky and takes a shot at the champ."

"Big, dumb and slow," Ali ruffled Terry's hair. "Just the way I like them."

Brooklyn was about to crack a joke when an alert siren went off. It whooped in the big space, and the captain's voice echoed throughout the room. "Battle stations," it said. "All hands to battle stations!"

TWENTY-SIX

Brooklyn strapped himself into position above, under and beside the other members of the emergency-response team. Suited up and strapped in nose to nose, shoulder to shoulder in the microgravity of the *Baron*'s central hub, the members of the team were like eggs in a carton, ready to hatch when the shooting was over to set the ship right, or as right as could be had without a dry dock.

Brooklyn shifted to make his bandoleer of tools and hull patches fit more comfortably under the safety belts and waited. Tommy would be strapping in and checking weapons on the rim of the wheel with his gunnery team.

"Was anyone up on the bridge when the alert was called?" The speaker, a crewman named Robinson, was strapped in somewhere near Brooklyn's left foot, but his voice was loud and clear courtesy of the team's emergency channel.

"I was bringing coffee up," said another voice. Tom or at least T-Something. A slight man who worked as chef's assistant in the officers' mess. The perfect size for sliding around inside the ship's hull in search of punctures and holes.

"Is it an attack?" Robinson's voice was high and strained.

Dr Carruthers, in full third-officer mode, cut through the chatter. "There's no attack. Freedom picked up an unidentified signal out this way, and we're heading out to investigate it.

Calling battle stations is the fastest way to make the ship ready
for hard acceleration."

"How many gees we gonna do?" Brooklyn said.

"Probably all of 'em," Raul said. "Feel that vibration building?
That's the Oppenheimers, and they're about to push real hard.
Save your breath for, ya know, breathing."

Brooklyn had trained with the emergency-response team
twice since coming on board the *Baron*. The repair procedures
weren't much different than those at Freedom Base, and he
knew vacsuit operations backward and forward. Mostly, he
just needed to know where to go and how to avoid getting in
the way. The doctor had assigned him a locker full of gear and
a place to sit, and ordered him to practice getting in and out of
the pod a few times.

The acceleration alarm sounded and Brooklyn ran through
his limited high-gee training. There wasn't much use for
it on the Moon or on a shuttle, but it was a different story
when on a battleship in a hurry to get somewhere. The alarm
sounded twice more, and an elephant plonked its ass down on
Brooklyn's chest.

"Don't fight it." Raul was panting. "Makes it. Worse. Breathe
into. The space you have."

Brooklyn ran song lyrics through his head, computer
schematics, the names and faces of women he'd slept with…
anything to keep his mind away from his feelings of panic and
suffocation. Launches and acceleration were the worst part of
space travel.

After an interminable time, the pressure stopped.

"Everyone make it through?" Carruthers said. "Check each
other."

"Robinson's out cold," the chef's assistant said. "He's
breathing though. I think he's waking up."

"Look over your gear while I wait for orders."

Brooklyn inventoried his bandoleer by feel.

"Alright, we're good," Carruthers said. "I'd like Misters

Lamontagne and Robinson to stay seated and suited. The rest of you are dismissed." He pulled the knife switch on his arm rest, and the pod cracked open like a clam shell.

The rest of the emergency-response crew unbelted and floated free of the pod, slipping around and over teammates in the micro-gee. In less than a minute they were packing their gear into the storage lockers.

"The captain would like us to walk the outside of the ring and check for damage before we spin it back up," the doctor said. "I picked the two of you because one of you has the most experience in vacsuits of anyone I've seen and one of you has the least. I will leave you to figure out who is who." He unbelted and pushed off toward the airlock. "Shall we?"

Brooklyn and Robinson followed him through the lock and out onto the hull of a ship. The doctor rested his fists on his hips. "What a lovely day for a stroll." He pointed at a distant point of light. "Earth. Never been there myself, but I hear it's nice." He stepped onto one of the spokes connecting the hub to the ring. "This way."

Even if he was a first generation Lunatick, math doesn't work out. "How long you been on the *Baron*, doc?" Brooklyn said.

"Five years last month. My eighth birthday is in April, and it took me a couple of years to establish my identity and credentials, so that makes sense."

"Did you say eighth birthday, sir?" Robinson's voice cracked.

There was a lot of empty space looming in every direction, and the spoke they were walking across wasn't much more than six-feet across; it would be easy for a rookie to get vertigo. Brooklyn wasn't feeling so great himself. Bouncing around the Moon was one thing. Down was down, and there was a lot of ground to land on. Here... *Here you'd fall forever.*

"Did I?" the doctor said. "Well, it must be true."

"You feeling OK, doc? How's your gas mix?" Brooklyn said.

"Lovely. Clean, cold... Not a single particle of testosterone, fecal coliform, or thioalcohols. It's a literal breath of fresh air. A vast improvement over that filthy ship. I should do this more often." He laughed.

Brooklyn chinned the switch to change his radio's frequency to that of the command bridge – safety regs said any sign of psychosis had to be reported ASAP – but the channel was either dead or his radio was busted. He switched back. "Robinson, see if you can raise the bridge. My radio might be busted."

"Not necessary," the doctor said. "Your radio also is not working, Mr Robinson, but mine is just fine. I've told the captain that everything is proceeding as normal, and he cleared us to walk the outside of the ring."

"He's right, Brook. My radio only works on this channel."

"That's gotta be against regulations, doc. We should head back."

"Nonsense." Carruthers stopped at the edge of the ring and turned to regard the men following. "My radio is working perfectly, and as I am the officer in charge of this expedition, that's all that's required. Boots charged up?"

The electromagnets in the soles of their boots were what allowed them to walk so blithely across the hull. The indicator showing the status of Brooklyn's boots was a healthy bright green.

"Green," Robinson said. He was breathing faster than he should have been. Burning through his O_2 supply and risking hyperventilation.

"Let's go then." The doctor turned around and walked down the curve of the ring to the outside edge. Brooklyn and Robinson followed. The hull there was devoid of windows, just a long stretch of steel panels with occasional access doors. *How many miles have I put in running on the other side of this thing?*

"Mr Lamontagne, your predecessor also was an enormous help to my research. Mr Yang was a lovely young man. Sadly, his reaction to my experiments was not as positive as yours."

Cold fingers traced the back of Brooklyn's neck. "You saying those injections made him off himself?"

"What injections?" Robinson huffed. "What're you guys talking about?"

"I was forced to fake his suicide in haste, which is why he was so easily found." The doctor chuckled. "In truth, I had forgotten about the whole thing until he showed up in my morgue. Organic brains are funny old things."

"Is that the guy we had a funeral for?" Robinson said.

"I've had more time to plan for this." He hummed. "This will go much better."

The charge light on Brooklyn's boots turned red, and a buzzer sounded in his helmet.

"Shit!" Robinson said. "My boots just..." His body jerked and came off the ring, beginning a slow spin in reaction to the gasses jetting from the hole in the suit's chest.

"Some friends of mine are coming this way. Unfortunately, I used a forbidden technology in my last two batches of serum, and it would not go well for me if they found us together."

A hammer blow hit Brooklyn in the upper chest, and the oxygen sensors in his suit screamed. He stumbled backward, losing his footing. He twisted to find a handhold, but the ship was already out of reach. *This ain't good.* The escaping air pushed him into a tumble. His chest was hot and cold at the same time.

"It's nothing personal, specialist. I didn't know Robinson to piss on him, but the story works better with him here. His clumsiness and experience caused you both to fall from the ring, and I was, alas, unable to rescue you." The doctor's voice was crystal clear inside Brooklyn's helmet. "This must seem terribly unfair to you, Brooklyn, but we were here first."

Brooklyn couldn't find the breath to respond.

"Damn it!" the doctor said. "I should have gotten that toe!"

PART NINE
Runnin' on Empty

February 1978?

TWENTY-SEVEN

"You're safe," she said. "Relax a minute and let me do this."

The air smelled like eggs gone bad, but the thick ointment the scarred woman was smearing all over Brooklyn's body stunk worse.

"The sulfur dioxide in the air is aggravating the rash. This will help." She closed the ointment tin. "Made it myself. You don't want to know what's in it." She took his hand. "Hospital Corpsman First Class Jillian Milk. Just call me Milk. If you have pain, I can give you morphine, but it might make you itch even more."

"I'll take the pain." Brooklyn squeezed her hand gingerly. His joints were on fire, but the urge to scratch was worse. "Brooklyn Lamontagne, but you probably got that from my tags."

"Didn't know how to pronounce it. Demarco," she used her chin to point at the tall man working off to the side, "gave it a shot but didn't even come close."

"Did better than you," the man rumbled.

Milk leaned closer to Brooklyn. "Demarco is a lowly hospitalman apprentice, but he's picked up a few tricks. He's from New Orleans but can't cook or play the trumpet."

"Can't dance, neither," Demarco said, "so don't ask me."

Brooklyn's head ached, and he was somehow both hungry and nauseous. "How long I been here?"

"A day and a half or close to it," Milk said. "You were unconscious all of yesterday. Do you know what happened?"

The *Baron* and the call to battle stations. Then... an old Jimmy Clanton song his ma used to hum-sing while doing the dishes. The Purple Lady gathering him to her chest and cradling him in all of her arms. "Think we were attacked." The room he was in looked like it had been fashioned from sheet-metal scraps and hull plates, but someone had painted it a uniform shade of off-white. "I was on the *Baron*... and we had an alert." Darkness. "It's gone. Can't remember a damned thing." *Jesus, Tommy!* He raised up to his elbows.

"Don't try to force it. It might come back on its own." Milk's voice was a rasp, maybe damaged by the same thing that had scarred her face.

"Did anyone come in with me?" Faces and names lined up in his head. Tommy, Frank, Ali, Terry, Murph.

"Kid named Robinson, according to his tags," Demarco said. "Didn't make it."

"Robinson." Brooklyn rubbed his face. "Worked with him in emergency-response. Decompression get him?"

"Didn't help, but 'twas the bullet that killed him. Close range in the chest. Show you where we planted him once you're on your feet."

Brooklyn sank back on the mattress. "The hell are we?"

"We call it De Milo," Milk said.

Demarco sucked his teeth. "Seemed better than calling it Hell."

"Kind of name is that?" Brooklyn said.

"What you name the place where aliens dump your ass when they don't need you no more. Big damned cave on Venus." Demarco smiled. "Welcome to the Planet of Love, Brooklyn Lamontagne."

"Hard to keep track. Guess there's hundred-fifty, hundred-seventy of us here now." Demarco rubbed his chin. "Might be more somewheres else. Lotta room on Venus."

"Nearly the size of the Earth," Milk said. "There could be a lot more."

"Can't exactly get to the surface to look." Demarco leaned against the counter. "Professor dug up some shit up backs the We-On-Venus theory, but I s'pose we could be in a whole 'nother galaxy. Far, far away from the cool green hills of Earth."

"Venus makes more sense," Milk said. "And at least we know where it is."

"The fuck would aliens from Mercury stick us on Venus?" Brooklyn said.

"Yeah, that's where it gets interestin'," Demarco glanced at Milk, "we figure this is where they really from. Right next door to good old planet Earth."

A phone rang in the next room. Milk ducked out to take the call.

Brooklyn eyeballed the room for hidden cameras. More spy shit maybe. Charlie and the Angels could have grabbed him off the *Baron*. Might be a test. Might be... *Who fuckin knows*. He made his face blank "How'd they get you?"

Demarco did something with a blender, his back to the sickbed. "Jerked off, went to sleep in my bunk on Eisenhower. Woke up here in the dark. Swear to God, thought I was in Hell." The sound of pouring. "This ain't gonna be the worse thing you've ever tasted, but it'll be close."

He helped Brooklyn sit up.

"What is it?"

"A milkshake that only dreamt of a cow. Drink up. Doctor's orders."

"How do I know it ain't drugged?"

"Drink it myself if it was." He helped Brooklyn drink.

"That's horrible." His gorge rose.

"Like cold cream of mushroom soup, lemon juice, and semen, or so I've been told. Drink the rest."

"No way."

"You gotta eat, babe. Be a couple days yet until you can do solid food."

Brooklyn managed to finish the stuff and washed it down with a glass of orange drink, its citrusy taste barely there. "Can you put some more powder in?"

"Nah. Shit's worth its weight in gold 'round here. Cost you an arm and your first-born child for an unopened can of Tang. You sit tight a minute while I tidy up." He rinsed the glasses out at the sink. Brooklyn's vacsuit was sprawled in the corner, and Demarco gathered it up. Something fell to the floor when he moved the boots. "Lucky charm?"

"What is it?"

Demarco brought it over to the bed. "Appears to be a soft-tip .38-caliber round." He held it up to the light. "Been fired."

"It was in the suit?"

"Left boot." He put the round in Brooklyn's hand.

"Never seen it before. Only worn that vacsuit a couple of times."

"Suit got a hole in it right here," Demarco patted his own chest, "but since there no hole in you... Maybe somebody else's lucky charm. You want it?"

"No."

Demarco reclaimed the slug and tossed it in the trash. He hung Brooklyn's vacsuit in the waiting room outside.

"Makes you think the aliens are from Venus?" Brooklyn was tired, downright exhausted, but there was no way in hell he was going to sleep. *Gotta keep poking till I find the holes in this.*

"You might want to wait till Milk comes back to hear that. She the voice of reason in these parts."

"Just wish the fuck somebody would tell me what happened to my ship."

Demarco grunted and dragged a stool over to Brooklyn's bedside. He filled a glass of water from the tap and sat down. He took a long drink. "Tell you what I know and what I surmise. Let you know when one becomes t'other, OK?"

Brooklyn nodded.

"The Chiggers, that's what I call them, dump a load of supplies, mostly trash, here every so often. Based on the newspapers and magazines we dig out, we sorta know what's goin' on in the world, what year it is. We got wrist watches and calendars ta keep it sorta clear. Get me?" He cleared his throat. "I went off shift at 1800 Tuesday, March 3, 1958 on Eisenhower Station. You been there?"

"Trained there a couple of weeks before going to Freedom."

"The Moon." Demarco took another sip of water. "So, I went out in 1958, had a couple of beers, came back to my bunk to sleep. Woke up here."

"That's..." Brooklyn's eyes narrowed.

"You getting the picture now. Woke up here six years ago, after going to sleep fourteen years before that. That's a long-ass nap. What's the last day you remember?"

"Friday. February something. 1978."

"Milk got nabbed in '68. Wasn't even in space. Got her right off the ground. California somewheres."

"Said she's been here only four years."

"Interestin' isn't it?" He untucked his shirt and lifted the hem to show his stomach. A scar ran from his navel to his sternum. "Didn't have that scar when I went to sleep. Milk has one like it here." He touched the back of his neck. "Lot of things like that around here. Know a guy woke up missing his whole leg. Meanwhile, and I can't prove it 'cuz I don't have a picture or nothing, I'm pretty sure I don't look twenty years older than I did on Eisenhower.

"Are you saying you time traveled or something?" *The bullshit just keeps getting deeper!*

"Here's where I start surmising. One, the Chiggers are scoopin' us up and studyin' us like we would a butterfly. Two, they got some way to freeze us till they need us or get done with us. Once they done, they dump us here. Fair number of us are military, but a lot ain't. None of us got took in a battle or went down fighting, but we pretty much all woke up with scars or missing pieces. It ain't sequential, neither. The professor got here before me but got picked up after."

"What's all that got to do with me?"

"Maybe you and Robinson the only ones from your ship the Chiggers took. Rest might be floatin' along wondering where the fuck you is."

Milk checked Brooklyn's pulse and blood pressure when she returned that evening. "Decompression rash is fading fast. I must be a medical genius."

"Still itches."

"Give it a few." She dropped onto the bedside stool. Her eyes were red and raw. She was either truly tired or a great actor. "Accident up at the Dig. Usual small shit. Sprains and stitches. One concussion."

"What are they digging for?"

"The past." She folded her arms. "Demarco told me he threw some of his theories at you this morning."

"Morning, huh. Was that when it was? Hard to tell with time slipping around like it does here."

"There's a clock in my office that says it's 5:30pm. One just like it at the Dig. Another one at the Boneyard. They all say it's 5:30. No slippage."

"Just because they're all set the same don't mean they're right."

"Doesn't it? Time's a natural thing. We're the ones who mathed it out into seconds and hours. We all agree it's 5:30, it's 5:30." She looked at her watch. "Five-forty now. But this runs a little fast."

"So, Demarco was telling the truth."

"Probably. Unless he was bragging about his sexual exploits.

When he's off shift you can find him with a drink in front of him and his nose in a book, not poon."

"Venus books."

"Nope. Shitty little shed full of scavenged paperbacks. Lot of Westerns and Romance. Old newspapers, magazines. Surprising number of STD pamphlets."

Brooklyn dragged himself into a sitting position. "How'd I get here?"

"Same way we all did. Aliens dropped you off with the other trash, and we toted you back here. Hooked you up to an IV and waited. You woke up, and we said 'howdy'."

"So you seen actual aliens. Tentacles, googly eyes, the works."

"Just the ships. They come down every forty-five days. Drop shit off. Pick up a load from the Dig and head back out."

"A load of what?"

She adjusted his IV tube. "Artifacts. One of the first groups here was a bunch of archaeologists. Harvard, Oxford types. Tweed and tea time. They're the ones who figured out where we are based on some old mosaics they found."

"An' next to Venus was a big 'You are Here' label."

"Pretty much. Theory is they evolved here. Crawled out of the sea, had a big high-tech civilization."

"And then fucked it all up." Demarco entered through the waiting-room door. "Came by to see if I broke your brain."

"Gave me lot to think about."

"Handling it better than I did. Got here I screamed myself stupid." Demarco thrust his hands into his pockets. "Dark up, down, and sideways for days. Still get the nightmares."

Milk rubbed absently at the scar tissue on her forehead and cheek. "Venus was habitable until seven hundred million years ago, back when Earth was just a big useless ice ball."

"Got a case of the greenhouse gasses," Demarco said. "The same thing going on Earth now, but the Chiggers were better at it."

"The team at the Dig believe they packed everything up and headed to another solar system."

"And now they're coming back to the old neighborhood?" Brooklyn nearly laughed.

"Something like that," Milk said. "The surface of Venus is uninhabitable, but Earth is probably enough like Old Venus now to make it attractive."

"A lot of people on Earth say it's all a, whatayacallit, a conspiracy. UN, Kennedy-Johnson, all in on it. One big snow job to scare people straight."

"People been saying shit like that since the '50s," Demarco said. "Knew a coupla guys in the Easy who said the first Moon landing was faked."

"I heard Nixon destroyed Cleveland to make sure he got re-elected."

Milk chuckled. "Still can't believe he got elected the first time. Nixon's a son of a bitch, but I doubt even he would have gone that far."

"'Sides." Demarco pulled a bedpan off a hook on the wall and tossed it toward the ceiling. It fell slower than it would have on Earth, not much slower but undeniable. He caught it with a flourish, and tossed it to Brooklyn. It flew straight, with none of the weird sideways arcing it would have gotten from spin, and landed lightly in Brooklyn's lap. "Nixon mighta gone to China, but I betcha he never made it here."

Brooklyn gulped. "Doc, how 'bout some of that morphine?"

TWENTY-EIGHT

Demarco held out an armload of clean clothes: jeans, socks, underwear, a T-shirt, and a pair of work boots. "I came in looking like you, they'd have to blast me out of bed with a grenade."

"Must be all that clean living." Brooklyn's joints still ached but nothing like the pain he felt the day before. He pushed himself up. "Can't drink any more of those shakes. Don't get something better in me for dinner, might as well die."

Demarco busied himself with paperwork on the other side of the room while Brooklyn dressed. The clothes the older man picked out fit decent, right down to the Chevy T-shirt and the denim jacket.

"Temperature don't change much here, but a jacket's never a bad idea. Extra pockets if nothin' else."

"'Preciate it," Brooklyn said. "Be good to get up and move around some."

Outside was the darkest night he had ever seen. Overcast, starless, moonless... none of those words compared to the blackness above and around. The lighting outside the clinic barely beat it back. Tired and yellow, strings of bulbs arrayed like junkyard Christmas and crude pole lights set up every fifteen feet or so.

Brooklyn looked up to where the thin light was swallowed by darkness. "Far underground are we?"

"Coupla miles at least. Atmospheric pressure on the surface would crush you like a bug and broil the paste," Demarco said. "In here you could shoot a round straight up, an' you won't hit anything until it comes back on ya."

Brooklyn's hand floated to his mouth. His throat threatened to close. Demarco let him be quiet awhile.

"Spent the last month on a spaceship, and I lived on the Moon a year," Brooklyn finally choked out. "Don't know why the idea of being on another planet is fucking with me so much. Sorry 'bout–"

"Sorry 'bout nothin', man. Not a day gone by I ain't wondered if I lost my damned mind somewhere."

Milk's clinic was at the center of a cluster of ramshackle huts, De Milo's living quarters and amenities. Demarco pointed out the important sites as they walked: the Shop, a bar called Toad Stools, the De Milo Public Library, and the showers.

"None of this was around when the Chiggers left me here," Demarco said. "I wandered in darkness, felt like hundred years, before I found the professor. Thought I was dead."

Demarco got nods and greetings from the few passersby. He introduced them all to Brooklyn. Everyone in De Milo looked worn and tired, thin but not abused. They all showed signs of hard work.

"Geneva Convention says POWs can't be used as slave labor," Brooklyn said.

"Don't believe the Chiggers ever been to Geneva." Demarco lit a hand-rolled cigarette. "'Sides, most of the work we do is for ourselves. We don't work, we don't eat so good. Lemme show you the greenhouse."

Twenty-five yards past the spread of huts was a cleared area filled with boxes and racks with lights of every description trained on them. "Hope you like mushrooms," Demarco said. "That's the staple. Potatoes and beets sometimes, when we can spare a few more lights. Green peppers. Chiggers left us a grain sorta thing grows OK. We can make bread with it." He pointed.

"Boneyard's that way about two miles. Eyes get a little more accustomed, you can probably see the glow. I got to work there tomorrow." He shifted his aim about forty-five degrees. "Cemetery, maybe a quarter mile out." He shifted again. "The Dig. You thirsty?"

Mushroom wine was nearly drinkable, but mushroom beer was the pits. Brooklyn welcomed every glass.

"Shit probably cures cancer," Demarco said. "Milk, we ever have anyone die of cancer here?"

The doctor was at the other end of the bar with her own glass. "Not in my time."

"Point made," Demarco said. "Drink up."

The residents had rigged up a sound system, and the *Shaft* soundtrack was playing tinnily on it. There were about twenty others crowded into the bar. They'd swarmed Brooklyn like wasps looking for news about the war, about Earth, about the World Series. Brooklyn took a long swallow of beer. It tasted like dirt, but it was helping with the joint pain. Milk said he had the Bends.

As part of the tour, Demarco had led him to a large storage locker near the clinic and pronounced it Brooklyn's new home. Inside, there was just enough space for a battered acceleration couch, a bucket, a set of metal shelves, and a lamp. Now, half drunk, sick, and over-stimulated, Brooklyn was feeling the pull of the couch. Dinner had been a mushroom burger on strange, grayish bread, and it was sitting funny in his stomach.

"Might want to go easy on the beer." Milk slid down the bar toward them. "It's going to take a while for your gut to get used to everything, and there's no sense spending your first few days back on your feet squatting over a bucket."

Brooklyn pushed his glass to the side. "Who runs De Milo?"

"Ranking officer is a Soviet, a captain lieutenant named Kasparov. But we run it as council. Anyone who's interested can get together, argue things out, and we go from there.

Kasparov mostly runs the Boneyard, though." She pointed. "He's over there."

The Soviet officer had a glorious beard, but he looked as pale, thin, and worn as everyone else. He was playing chess with a bald woman and drinking–

"Is that real vodka?" Brooklyn said. The Soviet's bottle very clearly said Smirnoff.

Milk squinted. "Maybe. He might have salvaged it from one of the wrecks. He's the first one to see whatever comes in."

Wrecks... "Wish the hell I knew what happened with the Baron. Were we shot down?"

"If so, you'd be the first one here I know of who'd been taken in battle," Milk said. "Most of the rest of us were stolen right from our beds."

"Had friends there. Just wanna know."

"We all had friends before." She stood. "Fuck your stomach. Let's see if we can cadge some of that vodka from Kas and drink to them."

Brooklyn stretched and nearly fell off his acceleration couch. It was not well suited for sleeping, but the vodka had shut him down like malfunctioning hardware and maybe killed off some of the Venusian microbes that had been making his stomach flop. All in all, he felt better. He pulled on his clothes and went in search of breakfast. He was a new face and on doctor-prescribed rest for the next few days, so no one looked askance when he filled his plate from the communal buffet and joined a noisy table.

"How big is this place?" he asked his tablemates after they'd exchanged greetings and probed him for news.

"De Milo or cave?" said a strong-looking woman with a shaved head. The Soviet hammer and sickle was crudely tattooed above her left ear.

"The cave," Brooklyn said.

"I once packed bag, picked direction, started walking." She pointed toward the door. "Two and a half days later I turned back. That big. Bigger."

"De Milo at the center of it?"

"No way a-knowin'," said a one-eyed man named Jack Wilson. "We all done our share of trampin' 'round. Never foun' the edge."

"It ain't the Dark Ages," Brooklyn said. "Never found any radar or radios in the junkyard?"

"I work the kitchen. You wanna know somethin' technical, talk to someone works in the Boneyard." Wilson cracked his thick knuckles. "You're from New York, huh? My daddy always said it was full of demons and sinners."

"It sure is," Brooklyn said, "but there's no place better on Earth."

Brooklyn rested and wandered for the remainder of the morning before heading back to the clinic for a check in with Milk. She was taping up a sprained ankle when he entered the rough little building and pointed him to a seat. "Tai here stepped in a hole. Only take a minute." Her hands were practiced and strong as they wound the bandage over and around. She patted the man's leg. "I love it when you bring me something I actually know how to fix. You want any painkillers?"

The man grunted a negative.

"Stay off it for a few days then come back slow. I'll let the kitchen know you're on light duty."

Tai slid off the table and pulled a package out of his coat pocket. He handed it to Milk.

"That from Kas? Tell him I said thank you."

Brooklyn watched her open the package. "What's that?"

"Salvage." She held up one of the bottles inside. "This one's an antibiotic." She held up another. "I don't know what this is. Have to look it up in the book." She set the package aside. "How are you feeling?"

"Hung over. Gut's better though."

Milk waved him to the examination table. "Hop up. Any dizziness or mental fuzziness?"

"Not since last night. How're you feeling?"

"I'm the one with the keys to the aspirin supply." She took his pulse and blood pressure and examined his eyes. "I don't think you're dying today. Still itchy?"

"Nope."

"Lemme ask you something else." She opened a cabinet door and pulled out a set of folded up coveralls. "You had these on when we found you." She unfolded them on the examination table. "Notice something."

He touched the dark stain. "That blood?"

She nodded. "And I believe that's a bullet hole. Got anything you want to tell me?"

"Don't remember getting shot."

"You remember shooting anyone and stealing their clothes, maybe?"

Brooklyn tapped the nametag sewed onto the breast pocket of the coveralls. "Says my name, right there."

"Unless you stole that, too."

"Didn't– Don't think I killed anyone." He rubbed the bloodstain with his fingertips. "Doctor on the *Baron* did something to me. Helped me adjust to the spin. Made me heal faster."

"I'd like to believe you. There's probably worse than murderers here. Back stories don't mean much in a situation like this, but I like to know who I'm dealing with."

Brooklyn held out his wrist. "Cut me."

"What?"

"Cut me. Bandage it up, and it'll be healed in a couple of days."

"First line of my resumé says 'do no harm'." Her mouth firmed. "Come back in on," she looked at the calendar on the wall, "Thursday. I'll clear you for work."

"That calendar is out of date by at least two years," Brooklyn said.

"It might not even be Tuesday anywhere else but right here."

"Any idea what I should do next? Already hit all the hot spots, and I ain't seen a computer that needs fixing."

"There's a library."

"Not much of a reader."

"The Shop?"

Junk room more like. The proprietor, a one-legged man named Turk, took payment in trade or labor, which usually involved helping him clean or repair the junk. "Been there, done that," Brooklyn said.

Milk washed her hands. "Well, you can't hang around here bugging the shit out of me. Demarco's off today. Right about now, he'll probably be thinking about hitting the bar. Go find him and tell him I told him to take you to see the Trolls."

"Trolls?"

"That's just what we call them." She arched her only eyebrow. "You see, Brook, we aren't the only ones living in this cave."

TWENTY-NINE

"She said that?" Demarco laughed.

"What's the joke?"

"No joke. Just her way of gettin' you from under her feet and makin' sure I don't spend my day off at the Toad Stool."

Demarco's shack was little bigger than the one Brooklyn was staying in, but homier. He'd put a mattress on a raised platform in one corner with a nightstand and a light. There was a book on the nightstand. Demarco followed Brooklyn's gaze. "Read that one three times already 'cause the library's so skinny. Kasparov and his crew are still going through the mess that came in with you. Hope they find some more."

"Don't really have to go anywhere," Brooklyn said. "I'm just edgy. I can head back to my place and sit on my hands. Maybe take a nap."

Demarco heaved himself to his feet. "Naw, we can go. Better to walk than to stew on shit you can't fix. Probably a good idea to check on them anyway."

"Who are the Trolls?"

"You see them you'll be asking, 'what the hell are they?'" Demarco reached behind the door and pulled a helmet off a hook there. "You got one of these yet?"

Brooklyn shook his head.

"Not a bad idea to trade for one or rig one up for yourself.

Every once awhile something falls from the ceiling. Most times it will kill you whether or not you're protecting your head, but there's this." He put the helmet on and flicked a switch sending a cone of light from the light mounted on it onto the wall opposite. "Flashlight on the table over there. Grab it, and we'll head out."

The ground under their feet was gritty sand, the result of 750 million years of rock decay from the ceiling above.

"Professor says the Chiggers dug these caves out and lived down here after they fucked up the planet." He pointed at an irregular stone that had made a crater in the grit, clearing it down to the matte stone floor below. "Watch your step."

"Hard to believe the caves have lasted that long." Brooklyn shone his flashlight all around. The beam faded out before it hit anything.

"What are men to rocks and mountains?" Demarco said. "Anyways, Chiggers found a way out, left all this behind. Hold up a minute and cut your light." He reached up and turned off his headlamp.

Brooklyn had believed he knew what darkness was, but he'd known nothing until that moment. It was darker than dark. Smothering dark. Squeezing dark. His heart sped up.

"Give it a couple of minutes," Demarco said. "Let your eyes adjust. This is all I saw when I first got here. Days and days of it."

Brooklyn forced himself to relax and slowly the quality of the darkness changed.

Demarco put his hand on Brooklyn's shoulder to direct him. "See that little glow?"

"Maybe." He absolutely could not.

"That's the Trolls. Now turn around." Demarco kept his hand on Brooklyn's shoulder. "See that one? It's brighter."

Brooklyn strained to see and slowly he could, or believed he could. A softening of the darkness, right at the horizon.

"That's De Milo. We maybe two miles outta town. If you

need to get back, just follow that glow." Demarco turned his light back on, careful to keep it out of Brooklyn's face. "'Bout a mile to go. Let's keep on."

They covered the last mile in about twenty-five minutes. Brooklyn's knees were aching, and Demarco's helmet light was panning over a dimly-lit ring of low domes.

Brooklyn drew a sharp breath. "What are they?" The Trolls were roughly human-shaped but short and thick like fireplugs. Curled ram's horns grew from the sides of their heads, and their heavily muscled bodies looked gray under the light.

"We put that light there." Demarco pointed at a battery-powered light strung up between two poles. "They don't need it. Probably can't even see it." He pulled a flask out of his pocket and handed it to Brooklyn. "Ready for some more could-be bullshit? We figure they's aliens, too. Not Chiggers but from somewheres else. Somewhere with high gravity."

Brooklyn unscrewed the top of the flask and tasted the contents. "Can they hear us?"

"No idea. Maybe. Maybe they just don't care."

Five or six of the Trolls were clustered around a pot, using their fingers to eat from it.

"What are they doing here?"

"Same as us, maybe. Working, surviving, digging up things for the Chiggers." Demarco reclaimed his flask and took a drink. "We tried to trade with them a few times, brought over some stuff we didn't need. Nothing. They didn't acknowledge our existence. We could walk right in there, and they wouldn't look twice at us unless we got in their way."

"And then what?"

"They'd move around us and get on with their business."

Brooklyn started counting and gave up at fifty-seven. "How many of them are here?"

"What you see plus some more. Can't tell you how many more. Can't tell you how long they been here. Can't tell you what music they like." Demarco swept his hand in an arc that covered the entire village. "There you go, man. The Trolls."

Brooklyn felt dizzy again, but he was fairly sure it wasn't decompression sickness this time. He'd lived on the Moon and onboard a spaceship, and now he was a prisoner on Venus, but none of that had felt as alien as seeing the Trolls up and moving around. They were real, right before his eyes, and plainly inhuman.

"Ready to go back, man," he said. "Think I'm gonna be sick."

Brooklyn met the children of De Milo at dinner that evening. There were a dozen of them, the oldest around eight years old. "Why'd the aliens take kids?"

"That's the first thing you thought of?" Milk said. "Kids are here, so the aliens must have taken kids? See, Brook, when a Mommy and a Daddy love each other very much…"

Brooklyn flushed. "Birth control in short supply then?"

"Some people wanted to start families. The first native-born Venusian humans." She looked thoughtful. "Wonder how that affects citizenship."

"Trolls having kids, too?"

"If they are, they aren't telling me about it." She pointed out one little boy. "That's Chumo. He wasn't born here. Aliens dropped him off about a year ago.

There was nothing particularly special about the boy, other than he had two teeth missing in the front.

"Near as we can tell he's South American. He was a toddler and didn't speak much when he showed up." She moved the food around on her plate. "Have you met Jack Wilson?"

"Guy who works in the kitchen? Yeah."

"He's from Alabama. They took him off his tractor in 1948. Flew right over the field. He woke up here three years ago short an eye."

Brooklyn had the creeping horrors, wondering what the aliens might have done to him while he was asleep. "Is that how…" Brooklyn touched his face. "Is that how you got hurt?"

"That happened a few months after I got here. An accident at the Dig. I drove a pick right into a pocket of acid gas. Demarco saved my eye and did the best he could with the rest." She cleared her throat. "You should go up to the Boneyard tomorrow and meet Kas. That's probably where you'll be the most use."

"I hear he prefers Russians."

"Kas is particular about who he works with and protective of his people. If you don't want to be assigned to the Dig or the greenhouse full-time, make sure he likes you."

The woman with the hammer-and-sickle tattoo directed Brooklyn to Kasparov's office, but Brooklyn found the man deep in the yard itself, tearing into an HVAC unit.

"Those things are all over Freedom Base," Brooklyn said.

The Russian put down his wrench. "Do you know how to fix them?"

"No. I've just seen a bunch. I do computers. Hardware mostly."

Kasparov pulled a rag from his pocket and ran it over his face. "Have you seen many computers in use in De Milo?"

"Not a one."

"Can you think of a good reason to use computers here?"

"Not right off, but…" Brooklyn could tell he was losing ground. "I'm pretty good with tools overall, and I learn quick."

"Do you speak Russian?"

"No, but I work cheap, and I've killed every plant I ever touched. Don't want me at the greenhouse."

"The Dig always needs more workers."

"Shame to put that training to waste. You wanna sweeten the deal, I can build you a still. Made the best vodka on the Moon. Even the Admiral drank it."

"Jillian still has you on light duty." He picked up his wrench. "Speak to me when you are well."

* * *

"Boneyard's the best job in De Milo, if you can get it." Demarco tipped his chair back and leaned against the wall. A scattering of empty glasses dotted the small table between them.

"How so?"

"Everything that comes in comes in there. Tech, clothes, food, real booze," he ticked the examples off on his fingers, "books, music... You name it. Russians get the first look."

"Thought all that was supposed to be divided up equal or sent to the Shop." Brooklyn's stomach had adapted to the mushroom beer, and he'd almost enjoyed the fungi sandwich he'd had for dinner.

"All Venusians are equal, but some more equal than others. They work hard over there. No one's going to squawk much if Kas and his crew skim a little." He grinned. "Me, I got a key to the medicine cabinet and know where Milk hides the good drugs."

Brooklyn toyed with his glass. "Alright, think I got my mind around the whole Venus POW thing. Was on the fence for awhile about the aliens, but I see that's real, too."

Demarco spread his arms. "Exhibit A, my friend. No downtown bus goes this far out."

"Yeah." He drank some beer and set the glass down carefully. "So, what's the plan?"

"Plan?"

"For getting the fuck out of here. Getting home."

"Ah. You seem cool, so I forgot you new to this." He put his elbows on the table and leaned in to whisper. "There's no plan."

"Come on. You can tell me."

The chair creaked as Demarco leaned back. "We first got here we talked about it all the time. How we gonna get home. Figure things out, bide our time, be good boys and girls until the aliens stopped paying attention to us, and then bust out."

"And?"

"They ain't paying attention, man. There's no guards to overpower. No fences to cut through. No keys to swipe. No need. Temperature up top high enough to melt lead, and we one-hundred and fifty million miles from home on a good day. No escape, and no big rescue, either, 'cause Earth don't know we're here, and they don't have the tech to get through the atmosphere anyway. Get it now?"

"I–"

"You don't, yet. See it in your face." He sucked his teeth. "Only going to say this one time. We don't talk about leavin' no more. It's the ultimate cock-blocking killjoy. Forgetting that liable to get you punched in the head. Getting a little heated my own self."

Brooklyn's jaw tightened.

"You got it?"

"Sure."

Demarco's eyes narrowed. "The hell you do. But you'll figure it out. Why doncha go get us some more beers."

THIRTY

Brooklyn converted a hot plate and a lamp to DC current in exchange for five clean T-shirts, a half-pound of laundry detergent, and use of the tubs and makeshift washboards in the clothes-washing station behind the building.

"Where does the water come from?"

"Reservoir." Turk, the guy who ran the Shop, talked like Johnny Rotten and looked like a scarecrow with delusions of royalty. "Big tank over there."

"Before that?"

"Underground lake somewheres. Piped in."

"What about the air?"

"Same, pretty much. I first got here it was shite thick and full of acid, and not the good kind. Kasparov and his boys rigged purifiers from a bunch of ship junk. It's better now."

"How long have you been here?"

Turk rubbed his face. "What year is it?"

"Nineteen seventy-eight."

"Six years then. I came along early."

"RAF?"

He scoffed. "Went to sleep in the car park after a Zeppelin concert in Surrey. Woke up here."

"Is that where you lost the leg?"

"Nah. Lost that in a lorry accident. Chiggers took my appendix and my left bollock."

"Bollock?"

He gripped his crotch. "Testes. Testicles."

The next day, Milk ran Brooklyn through the gauntlet and pronounced him fit for work. "I'd give a foot for your metabolism," she said.

The scarring made it hard to figure her age. Brooklyn put his shirt back on. "Told you I heal fast."

"If I were more awake, I'd ask you for a blood sample and do a screening."

"Just tell me when." Brooklyn slid off the exam table. "Help you with anything 'fore I go?"

"How about a vacation somewhere with sunlight?"

He winced. "Must get pretty bad being the only doc in town."

"Oh, this isn't bad. We had a suicide epidemic about three years ago. That was bad. Nearly didn't make it myself."

Brooklyn struggled into his T-shirt. "What happened?"

"Lot of people lost hope at the same time. Realized that we were all here for the long haul and couldn't take it."

"What stopped it?"

"People. Aliens dropped off five new ones. All nabbed in '73. It had been a while since we had new blood, and they gave us a recharge. Next best thing to a letter from home."

"So when I showed–"

"Yep, proof that the world's still going. It's nice to know."

Kasparov's face furrowed in a scowl. "Trial basis only." He summoned the tattooed woman. "This is Yeva Topolski. Your boss." He jabbed his finger at Brooklyn, then turned his frown on Topolski. "Show him the ropes."

Topolski led Brooklyn to a clear area among the piles of scrap. "Here are the ropes. Pay attention, please." She pointed toward the unseeable ceiling of the cave. "Every forty-five days, it glows blue up there and a ship comes down here." She pointed at the ground. "It leaves garbage, supplies, and sometimes people." She pointed off toward the Dig. "Ship flies to the Dig where it picks up old shit and takes it back to the blue glow. Those are the ropes."

"And you guys go through the garbage and salvage anything useful. When is the next ship due?"

"Thirty-seven days. You were part of the last garbage drop. Usefulness yet unproven."

Brooklyn cracked his knuckles. "Point me at a pile, and I'll get started."

A lot of scrap came down with every drop and sorting through it was a multi-stage process. Bigger pieces – hull plates, decking, etc. – went into a pile designated as construction material. Smaller bits were sorted into piles of tech, food, entertainment, reading material, toys, appliances, housewares, furniture... After that, the smaller piles were broken up again into piles labeled – in Cyrillic – "working" or "not working", "broken" or "intact", "edible" or "spoiled". It didn't take long for Brooklyn to find something he had no idea what to do with. He wrapped it in his jacket and went to find Topolski.

"Need to see Kasparov," he said.

"For what?"

"Found something I think he should see."

"He is in the machine section," she jerked a thumb over her shoulder, "that way."

Brooklyn found him working on another HVAC system. "Think you should see this." He unwrapped the object. "The safety's on."

Kasparov picked up the rifle and turned it in his hands. "M16A1 rifle. 5.56 millimeter ammunition."

"Clip's full. All thirty rounds."

Kasparov handed the gun back to Brooklyn. "You know how to make it safe? Remove the clip? Eject the round?"

"Sure."

"Do that. Then dismantle it, and throw it in the 'scrap' pile."

"Shouldn't we hide it somewhere in case we need it?"

"Need it?" Kasparov smoothed his beard. "Who would we shoot? Rocks? The Trolls? Each other? Ourselves?" He pushed the gun against Brooklyn's chest, forcing him back a step "There are no enemies here." His voice rose. "Remember that. No war to fight."

Brooklyn held the rifle in one hand.

"If I could, I would melt that down and make something useful." He gestured toward the sorting area. "It's no use to us."

Brooklyn worked four days in the yard, sorting scrap and being ignored by his coworkers. On the morning of day five, he drew from the community-chore jar and spent his workshift baking bread and preparing meals with Wilson and his crew. According to Milk's calendar, the next day was a Tuesday, but it hardly mattered. For some, it was the start of their five-day work cycle so they called it Monday. Others just gave it a number. Whatever it was, it marked the start of Brooklyn's weekend, so he slept in then went to see what Demarco was up to.

The older man was outside the yard loading up a three-wheeled cart with insulated wire and poles. "Playing electrician today," Demarco said. "Going out to the Dig to string some lights. You can keep me company if you like."

"I've seen all the movies at the Heights," Brooklyn said, "and the boob tube don't work. Might as well waste my day off following you around."

Demarco pulled his flask out of his pocket and passed it to Brooklyn. "You drive."

The liquor was sour and thin but warming. "This is terrible." Brooklyn took another pull.

"Pruno – used to call it toilet wine – minus the usual botulism. Maybe that's the flavor you're missing."

Brooklyn handed back the flask and climbed into the cart. He inspected the controls. "The hell is this thing?"

"Part genuine Melex golf cart." Demarco took the passenger seat. "Have to ask the Russians where the rest of it came from." He pointed ahead. "Let's get to getting."

There was a real road between De Milo and the Dig, packed down from years of back-and-forth travel, about four miles long. Demarco propped his foot up on the dashboard of the golf cart. "Been a couple weeks since I been out here. Wonder if they've turned up anything new."

"What are they looking for?" The golf cart tended to veer right, so Brooklyn kept his eyes on the road.

"Anything. This whole place was city once. Chiggers want some shit to remind 'em of home, I guess. Look there." He pointed.

The headlights of the little cart touched on a dome-shaped structure, about fifteen feet tall, to the left of the road. "What is it?" Brooklyn said.

"House, maybe. Two floors, empty. Been here since before we came out the ocean."

"Can we go in?"

"Suit yourself."

Brooklyn parked the cart. He had a helmet now, and his own flashlight. He walked around the dome until he found an opening, about seven feet high and circular. "Is it safe?" he said.

"Been here near a billion years and ain't collapsed yet," Demarco said. "Today might be the day, but I doubt it."

Inside, the dome was empty to the walls, which were undecorated. Brooklyn shone his light around the floor and then up to the ceiling. A round hole there cut through the second floor. "How'd ya get up there?"

"Nothing up there," Demarco said. "Same as down here, but smaller."

"Yeah, OK, but how?" Brooklyn shone the light around. "A ladder, stairs? Hell, a rope?"

Demarco opened his flask. "Maybe they flew."

"So, they're about our size, and they like domes. What else we know about them?"

"Our size 'bout a billion years ago. Maybe," Demarco said. "This could have been a kid's playhouse. Even a dollhouse."

Brooklyn ran his hand along the wall. It was smooth, and his hand came away covered in dust. "What the hell lasts a billion years? Diamonds?"

"Let's keep on, and I'll show you."

The Dig was a bit further on and its glow on the horizon showed well before the site did. Brooklyn parked where Demarco told him. Several more of the domed buildings were visible in the electric lights.

"Grab that wire and a couple poles and follow me." Demarco led the way to a rectangular trench dug into the ground. Inside it, at least two dozen people were working with brushes and trowels. "Good morning!" Demarco called out. "Where's the professor at?"

One of the women in the trench stood and waved. "Just in time! We've extended the trench another six feet and need all the light we can get."

"Just point us, and we'll get it done!" Demarco lowered his voice. "Professor Yarrow is a bona fide Oxford University-trained archaeologist. She was one of the first ones here."

The professor met them at the top of the ladder leading into the trench. Her short bob of hair was just beginning to gray. "This way," she said. "We have a few others coming over to help."

With the extra help the work was easy. They erected five light poles, strung them with the insulated wire, and connected them to the Dig's power supply, a mini-reactor similar to the ones Brooklyn had encountered on the Moon. Professor Yarrow caught him studying it and smiled. "It was behind me, still in the crate, when I woke up here."

"It doesn't look right," Brooklyn said.

"It's a copy of one of ours. There are four of them in the Dig, and we have no idea how they work. They never need refueling or maintenance."

"Not made by us, then," Brooklyn said. The ones he'd seen on the Moon needed near constant attention.

"One at the Boneyard, one in De Milo, and one here," Demarco said. "We keep one spare."

"What do the Trolls use, I wonder," Brooklyn said.

"Drop by and ask 'em someday," Demarco said. "Professor Yarrow, this is Brooklyn Lamontagne," he almost had the pronunciation right, "the LOD."

"The last one down!" The professor's eyes lit up. "It's been a year since we had one of those. What's happening on Earth?"

Demarco slapped Brooklyn on the chest. "Don't say nothin' until she agrees to trade. Answer all her questions in return for lunch and a tour." He smiled at the professor. "Brook wants to know what sort of things y'all find out here."

Professor Yarrow's questions ran heavily to politics, which Brooklyn was a little thin on, and to music, which he was more than happy to answer. The last live concert she'd seen was the Beatles at Candlestick Park in San Francisco so she was saddened but not surprised to learn the group had broken up.

"They were too good to last," she said.

"You missed a lot of their best stuff," Brooklyn said. "*Sergeant Pepper, The White Album, Abbey Road...*"

"I had *Sgt Pepper's Lonely Hearts Club Band* for about a month before I was taken. Nearly wore it out!" Her eyes went dreamy. "I don't suppose you have any marijuana."

Brooklyn blinked. "I don't. Sorry."

"Worst thing about being here. No reefer." She tapped her teacup. "Mushroom tea is my substitute. This blend has a slight hallucinogenic effect. Puts just the slightest glow on things and keeps my mind open." She sighed. "Anyway, I suppose it's my turn to answer questions."

Demarco stretched his legs out under the table and poured

himself a cup of the professor's tea. "Tell him how you got here. That's always a good story."

"You just like the bit about the party I was at before it all happened, you wicked man!" She smiled. "Just for that, I will skip ahead."

Demarco grunted. "Sounded like a good party. Flower children, skinny dipping, and all the free love you could carry home."

"Someday I will write it all down for you, and you can read about it to your heart's content. Anyway," she took a sip of the tea, "I was teaching at Berkeley at the time. At some point during the party, I passed out. I woke, with a smashing headache, in a silver chamber. A voice informed me that I had been chosen to study an ancient civilization and that it would be my life's greatest work. When I woke again, I was here with eleven others, all trained archaeologists and anthropologists, and we eagerly began our study."

"Just like that," Brooklyn said.

Her mouth twisted. "There was an adjustment period, of course. We'd been supplied food, water, lights, power, tools. Initially, there was some resistance – confusion and panic, really – but we soon realized we had nothing better to do than study the site. We're the ones who started calling it the Dig."

"What are you supposed to be looking for?"

"Evidence, I suppose, of what they were. A billion years is *such* a long time. I imagine the Venusians have changed so much they hardly recognize themselves. A billion years ago, humans were still microbial!"

"Meanwhile, there was a whole civilization living next door." Demarco ran his hand slowly over the back of his head. "Something to think about."

"Earth was the first planet the Venusians visited once they achieved spaceflight. We know that." The professor's face was flushed with excitement. "I imagine they went to all of them, eventually, but Earth was theirs well before anything native crawled or swam there."

"Some of the professor's people think it's possible the Chiggers mighta done something to give evolution a push." He cleared his throat. "Might be we owe our existence to them."

"You found anything that says that?" Brooklyn said.

"It's mostly been bits and pieces," the professor said. "Shards and tiles. We've found a roadway made, we think, of synthetic diamond. Crystals that might have been decorative or might have been some kind of storage medium. Pieces of metal from what might have been tools. Fossils of what we believe were livestock or pets. Some of the bones are... interesting."

"Any idea what the hell they want now?" Brooklyn said.

"Want what's theirs," Demarco said. "What they found and claimed before anyone else was 'round."

"Just because? Got bored one day and said, 'Let's check out the old apartment'?"

"Something like that. I don't believe they want to hurt us." The professor folded her napkin. "It's a good thing, too, because I don't believe there is any way in the world we could stop them."

THIRTY-ONE

It took three weeks of hard work, and the recovery of a mostly intact radar system from a junked Japanese robocab, to net a grunt of approval from Kasparov.

"Not much range," he added.

Brooklyn had also put in another day's work in the kitchen, spent a shift shoveling compost at the greenhouse, and did a day at the Dig that consisted of using a toothbrush to remove ancient cement-like dirt from ceramic shard. The cleaning revealed part of a symbol that the professor and her team had oohed and ahhed over for hours, entirely forgetting Brooklyn was there. At the end of the shift, he'd left them to it and caught a ride home on the supply cart. But, be it ever so humble, the Boneyard was the place he felt most comfortable. He turned to the last pallet of the day.

"Hell's this shit coming from?" he said. "That's a 351 Cleveland V8, and ain't no way the aliens found it in space."

Topolski worked a kink out of her right shoulder with the opposite hand. "The Moon, maybe."

"No way. Every vehicle up there runs on batteries." He prodded the engine block with his foot. "This is Michigan-made, American steel, and the aliens had to go to Earth to get it."

"Much of this comes from Earth." She raised and dropped her shoulders a few times. "We find labels with addresses of warehouses. Maybe the aliens do not want us to get homesick. Here." She bent and pulled a battered stuffed animal out of the pile. The toy was wearing a white suit, and its head was encased in a clear plastic bubble. "Laika. First dog in space. She traveled to the Moon and back in 1949."

"That's not Laika. It's Snoopy. He's from a cartoon."

"Take it home to cuddle, and your discontent will fade. For now, work. I am tired and hungry."

Brooklyn was hungry, too, and he'd almost started to look forward to the lukewarm, musty taste of mushroom beer. He put the toy aside. "Maybe one of the kids will want it. I'll bring it to the Shop later."

Brooklyn stretched himself awake. "Good morning," he said.

The stuffed dog beside the bed didn't answer. It was no Karla Conway, but Brooklyn had spent hours watching *The Snoopy Chronicles* cartoon as a kid. The little dog had gotten himself lost in space and spent every episode trying to get back home to Charlie Brown. David had mocked the show, thought it was funny that every planet Snoopy landed on had breathable air and aliens who spoke English.

"Ever tell Topolski that I brought you home instead of dropping you at the Shop, and you and me are gonna have words, little dog," Brooklyn said.

The toy's only expression was "worried", so Brooklyn took it as agreement. He ran his fingers through the patchy hair on his face. He needed to trade for scissors and a razor or find someone in De Milo who barbered. *Maybe I'll just grow it all out like a caveman.*

Fucking cave. Aside from the food, the beer, and being the captive of an alien species, the worst part of being in De Milo was the lack of sunlight. Every moment of the day was as dimly lit as every other, and above it all hung inky darkness. It felt like a physical weight, and Brooklyn had caught himself slouching under it. It felt better anyplace with a roof, which was probably why everyone spent so much of their free time at the bar.

Brooklyn sat on the edge of his couch and pulled on the fresher of his two pair of pants. It was his Sixthday, the first morning of his weekend, but his new still wasn't going to try itself out. If it worked, the days and nights at the bar might feel a little more civilized and the mornings come with fewer headaches and less nausea. It would be Brooklyn's greatest contribution to De Milo since his salvaged radar proved the cave was dome-shaped and the ceiling at least six miles high at its center. The results of the survey were barely talked about anymore, and why would they be? The information changed nothing. Good booze would.

He shoved his feet into his boots, shrugged into a clean shirt, and wrapped his toolbelt around his waist. Forty-five days since he'd woken up in De Milo. Day off or not, still test or not, he wouldn't miss seeing an alien spacecraft.

The kitchen was still out of coffee, another point in favor of life away from Venus. The withdrawal headaches had been hell. The options in front of him now included mushroom juice, mushroom tea, or a ration of Tang from a bin zealously guarded by Jack Wilson and his staff. Brooklyn opted for the tea and sipped it while eating his "omelet"– a scoop of dehydrated eggs with sliced mushrooms – and a side of alien toast. He'd save the Tang as a mixer if the still worked.

"Merry Christmas!"

The exclamation was followed by a mighty slap on his back. Brooklyn had prepared himself for it, so he had nothing in his mouth to choke on or spew, and he tried not to wince. "Morning, Top," he said. "Join–"

The bald Russian hadn't waited for the invitation. She never did. She slid comfortably into the seat across from him and reached for the salt shaker in the middle of the table. She salted everything she ate, including that morning's bowl of mushroom-and-alien-grain porridge.

"What will Christmas Father bring us today?" It was Top's day off, too, but anyone who could find or create an excuse to hang around the Boneyard would be there to see what the aliens had for them.

"Hoping for a pony. You?"

"Da, meat would be nice, but I prefer a cattle." She brightened. "Today is also day you blind us all!"

Brooklyn's mash – alien grain, mushrooms (of course), and a single potato for luck – had been quietly fermenting for two weeks. Anticipation was building among those in the know.

"Dumb enough to drink the foreshots, you deserve what you get," Brooklyn said. The methanol content of the first thirty-five percent of a run was good for cleaning machine parts or fueling a camp stove and not much else. "I wouldn't advise it."

"Americans are a weak people." Topolski rubbed the side of her head. She never stubbled up, and Brooklyn was about to ask her who cut her hair when she looked at her watch. "We should go. I want to be in the front to see."

They signed out a couple of the community bicycles and pedaled toward the Boneyard. As they went, Brooklyn practiced his rudimentary Russian skills, but Topolski's shouts of laughter soon put him out of the mood. A crowd had already assembled, but coworkers had saved them a space near the front. Brooklyn took a slug from the flask being passed around– mushroom wine fortified with gin, maybe – and settled in to wait. Topolski launched into a story, speaking in Russian, and he was happy to note he could catch every third word or so. Chumo and the other kids played soccer in the clearing. *It's like a picnic or an outdoor show.*

The blue glow was a cold light, miserly with illumination, but sharp. The alien ship emerged from it and approached slowly, a near subsonic hum its only sound. Adults hustled the kids out of the clearing and turned to watch the thing float down to hover fifteen feet or so off the ground. It was saucer-shaped, matte gray, about the size of a destroyer. The cargo door irised open. Several tons of garbage fell to the ground with a dusty *thwump* and clatter. Next the more delicate goods came. Foodstuffs and any new POWs. Seven large crates floated slowly to the ground.

The cargo door irised closed, and the ship slid off toward the Dig.

Topolski pointed toward the crates. "The one with the lights. New people."

"That how I got here?"

"No. You were lying in the trash. We assumed you were dead and did not look for several hours."

"Several *hours*?"

She shrugged. "A corpse will always be a corpse. We had lightbulb shortage. Priorities."

Milk and her medical crew approached the lighted vessel. It was less a crate than a cylinder, and it reminded Brooklyn of the *Baron*'s damage-control pod. Milk and Demarco levered it open. They stared into it for what seemed like an unusually long time.

"What are they doing?" Topolski said.

Demarco waved his arms over his head and raised his voice to be heard over the crowd. "Is Lamontagne here? If he's here, tell him to get his ass down here!"

THIRTY-TWO

She was tall, easily six feet, and dressed in plain coveralls. Her hair was thick and cropped close to her scalp. Her skin was a pleasant shade of leaf green.

"She some kind of a Troll?" Demarco said. "Maybe got off the wrong stop?"

"Too tall," Milk said, "and not bulky enough. The Trolls are a low-gravi–"

"I am an ambassador." The stranger sought out Brooklyn's face. "You are the last one here?"

Brooklyn glanced behind him. "Nobody else got called d–"

"We think she means you're the most recent arrival to De Milo," Milk said.

"True but–"

"I require your assistance." The woman's eyes were fixed on Brooklyn. "American English is your preferred language?"

"Been trying to learn Russian–"

She unleashed a rapid string of Russian consonants and vowels; Brooklyn got almost none of it.

"If you slow it down, maybe I could–"

"We will use American English." She turned to Milk. "Thank you. Your assistance is no longer needed."

Milk drew herself up. "Hold on a fucking min–"

"Come with me." The tall woman took Brooklyn's arm

and led him away from the others. "What is your name?"

"Brooklyn."

"Brooklyn is a borough of New York City in the state of New York in the country called the United States," she said, "population two-point-six million."

"Sure, but–"

Milk and Demarco came up behind them. "The Chiggers send her?" Demarco said.

The stranger's brow furrowed. "'Chiggers' is a colloquialism for the larva of the *Trombiculidae* mite. The larva inject digestive enzymes into the human dermis, usually at the groin and armpit. The result is intense itching and reddened pustules." She frowned. "I was not sent by chiggers."

"Who did send you?" Milk said.

"I was sent by the First."

"Who are the First?" Demarco said.

"The First was the first claimant to the planet you call Earth. Your species are the Third."

"Hell happened to the Second?" Brooklyn said.

"The Second no longer exist or no longer matter." She took Brooklyn's arm again, her grip nearly painful. "We are wasting time here when we should be working. My mission is to identify problems with resettlement, establish the appropriate relationships, make use of those relationships, and move on to the next problem. You are to teach me how to establish relationships."

Brooklyn tried and failed to pull his arm away. "How'd I get roped into this?"

"You are the most recent arrival," she said.

"No," Milk put her hand on the woman's arm, "you're the most recent arrival, and it's my job to make sure you're healthy. And safe. Let's go down to the clinic and get you checked out, then you and Brooklyn can start working. Any objections?"

Brooklyn said, "Yes" and the ambassador said, "No" in near unison.

"Fine," Milk said. "Let's go."

* * *

Brooklyn and Demarco waited outside while Milk examined the new arrival.

"The hell is happening?" Brooklyn said.

Demarco unscrewed his flask. "She in the pod when we opened up. Relaxed as can be. Like she was riding the bus. Started talking as soon as she could see us and insisted on seeing you."

"She asked for me by name?" Brooklyn put his hand out for the flask.

"She asked for the LOD, and said she wouldn't talk to anyone else. That's you. You ever see anything like her before?"

Brooklyn screwed up his face at the sweetened-sweat-sock taste of the fortified mushroom wine. "Hell would I have seen something like her?"

Demarco shrugged. "Don' know your life, man. Could have been anywhere before you got here. Could be a Chigger spy."

"I'm not a spy."

"That's what a spy would say." He scratched his head. "You help her out, it's probably treason."

"I know the drill. Name, rank, and serial number."

"She's cute though. For an alien menace." He cleared his throat. "Milk's coming out."

Milk was drying her hands on a worn towel. "She's getting dressed."

"The hell is she?" Brooklyn said. "And don't give me any shit about doctor-patient confidentiality."

"She's not human," Milk sighed. "She's not a Troll, either."

"How can you be sure she's not a Troll?"

Milk and Demarco exchanged a glance. "I dissected one a couple of years back. If I had to, I'd say she's some kind of hybrid. Human and something else."

"What else?" Demarco said.

"Whatever a First is, maybe? I've really no idea. Her body

temperature is few degrees higher than ours, her heartbeat is slower. She has breasts but no nipples. I didn't get much further than that."

"How many arms she have?" Brooklyn said.

Milk looked at him strangely. "Two."

"She dangerous?" Demarco said.

"She's not carrying a gun and doesn't appear to have claws, razor teeth, or hidden spikes. I'm not sure what else to look for." She rubbed her upper arms. "She has orange blood."

"Like orange orange?" Demarco said.

"More like a reddish orange. Kind of like a tomato. Or a persimmon." Milk nodded toward the door. "She's coming out."

The ambassador joined them. "I trust that will be the final delay and that Brooklyn and I can get to work."

"What's this work you keep talking about?" Brooklyn said.

"Assimilation of knowledge and acclimation to human culture in order to improve my work as an ambassador," she said. "I require you to assist me."

"Why me?" Brooklyn said. "I'm no one special."

"You are not special," she said, "but by virtue of being the most recent arrival you are best equipped help me to assimilate and acclimate."

"Who will you be conducting relations for?" Milk said.

"I will mediate among the First, the Third, and the Designed."

"This making my head hurt," Demarco said. "Who the Designed?"

"I am Designed, and there are other Designed here in the Refuge."

"No one here but us and the…" Demarco's eyes widened. "Other Designed are the Trolls. And if you Designed and they Designed that means–"

"I'm going to need more than that flask of yours to get through this," Brooklyn said. "Let's go get a drink."

"Should we let people see her?" Milk said.

"Everyone's seen her already. The only people not at the Boneyard were the professor and her people."

"What if alcohol is poison to her kind of people?" Milk said.

Problem solved then. "I'll drink hers," Brooklyn said.

The bar was full but the way cleared for the new arrival and they had no problem finding a seat. "Feel like I'm on display." Brooklyn frowned into the dozens of eyes watching. "Da fuck you lookin' at? Mind ya business!"

It worked on a few people, but the majority went right back to staring.

"Would you like me to remove them?" the ambassador said.

"Jesus, no! Just... Just sit. And don't hurt nobody." Brooklyn ordered a round of drinks.

Demarco looked intently at the ambassador. "You genetically-engineered, aren't you? Like in that science-fiction story 'Call Me Joe'." He flushed under the looks he got from Brooklyn and Milk. "What? Had a subscription to *Astounding Science Fiction*. I like that shit."

The ambassador sniffed her drink. "This is ethanol, made from the fermentation of yeast, sugars, and starches."

"Yeah," Brooklyn said, "it helps with stressful situations."

"My genome was indeed engineered by the First. In what way is this situation stressful, Brooklyn, and how does the word 'fuck' fit into the question you asked when we entered this room? Are you a Christian?" Her sentences ran together with hardly a pause.

"Ah, shit." Brooklyn gulped down half of the sickly sweet drink in his glass.

"Looks like the work has started," Milk said. "Nobody say anything else for a minute." She frowned and focused her attention on the ambassador. "Your mission, as I understand it, is to get better at communicating with us so you can serve as a bridge between the people who made you, the people of

Earth, and the other Designed living here. Is that correct?"

"Correct," the ambassador said.

"And you asked for Brooklyn because his knowledge of Earth culture is fresher than anyone else's here." She paused. "Demarco, what's a better way to say fresher?"

"More current," he said.

"I ain't been on Earth in more than a year!" Brooklyn said.

"You asked for Brooklyn because his knowledge of Earth culture is the most current of anyone here. Is that correct?"

"Correct."

"Ask her why I should help her." Brooklyn stared mournfully into his mostly empty glass. "Got plenty to do already."

"I was getting to that," Milk said. "Ambassador, you were sent here by our enemy. The ones you call the First have destroyed our cities and killed many of us. We are here," she took in the others around the table, "because we are prisoners of the First. Do you understand that?"

"The First have not destroyed cities, and you are not prisoners."

"Been here a long time, babe," Demarco said. "Feeling pretty damned imprisoned."

Milk shushed him. "We were put here by the First without our permission, and we cannot leave."

"True," the ambassador said.

"By our understanding of that action, you represent our enemy. If Brooklyn helps you, he will be helping our enemy. He will be committing treason. Do you know that word?"

"I know all of the words in the Oxford English Dictionary, including the supplementary volumes published in 1933 and 1972."

Milk blinked several times. "Good. Brooklyn is under oath as a member of the Extra-Orbital Forces, and, as such, treason is a crime that can be punished by death."

"I have prepared for this argument," the ambassador said. "In assisting me, Brooklyn may be committing treason, but to do otherwise could result in the end of all human life on Earth."

"Time out." Brooklyn's heart hammered, and the mushroom-based booze in his gut threatened to rebel. "Milk. You, me, outside."

Brooklyn paced. "Should have just gone to Attica. No Moon, no space battles, no caves, no Venus, no Trolls, no fucking alien chicks asking me for shit."

Milk leaned gingerly against a light post. "I think you have to do it, Brook. We need to know more, and she's the only chance we've had to communicate with the aliens since Yarrow and her bunch got here."

"Assuming that wasn't just an acid trip. Yarrow could have been talking to a fondue pot." Brooklyn paced some more. "Why me? You'd be better at this. Can't we just tell her that we made a mistake and that you're the last one down?"

"It's too late for that. Anyway, I can't imagine they're not keeping track of when people get here. There can't be so many humans here that they couldn't keep tabs on who goes where."

"Ain't a fan of this plan."

"You'll be making history, Brook."

"Don't wanna make history. Don't even want to know it." He tapped the bar's crude-looking sign with the side of his fist. Breaking it would have been more satisfying, but community rules said he'd be the one responsible for fixing it.

"She seems to be pretty free with her answers, almost to the point of naivety," Milk said. "Just be careful about what you tell her about Earth's defenses."

"Don't know nothing about them!"

Milk put her hand on his upper arm. "This will be easy then. You, me, and Demarco – maybe Kas, too – will get together every day and talk about what you've learned. If we feel like you're getting too far into the weeds, we'll pull you out and take her to the Trolls. She can be their problem."

"Still don't like it."

"You don't need to like it. Just do it." She smiled. "I'll be happy to testify at your court martial."

"Real funny."

"Best I can do," she said. "Let's get back to the bar before Demarco teaches the ambassador how to really drink."

Brooklyn palmed his eyes. When he lowered his hands, the green woman was still on the other side of the table. "How is this s'posed to work? Do you need me to get a chalkboard and hold classes or something?"

"Classes should not be required," the ambassador said. "We will spend time together. I will ask you questions, and you will provide answers."

"And you'll answer my questions?" Brooklyn said. "Anything I ask."

"Yes, provided I know the correct response."

"Correct or allowed?" Demarco had kept drinking while Brooklyn and Milk talked over the situation, and he swayed comfortably in his seat.

"I do not understand the question," the ambassador said. "Please elaborate."

"'Correct' means you'll give the answer no matter what," Demarco said, slurring slightly. "'Allowed' means you'll only tell us what your bosses say is OK for us to know."

"The First have no secrets. I will tell you whatever I know."

Demarco looked blearily at Milk. "Got any idea how to tell when a genetically-modified alien lady lies to your face? I sure as hell don't."

"I don't either," Milk said. "I suppose time will tell. I have patients. So, I am going to let Brooklyn get on with his work." She stood. "Coming?"

Demarco rose carefully and tossed a salute to the ambassador. "Going to grab a nap. Maybe see you cats at dinner."

Brooklyn watched them leave before reluctantly returning his attention to the ambassador. "Now what?"

"Would you like to have sex?"

"What? No!" It was about the last thing he expected on top of a day full of surprises.

"You inferred that you were drinking ethanol to help with the stress of this situation. In my experience, sexual activity can also help with stress."

"Get that from the dictionary, too?"

"I also learn from life experience. I have engaged in sexual activity 1,253 times."

"Babe, this ain't that kind of movie." Brooklyn slumped. "Look, just ask me some questions or something."

"In what way is this situation stressful? Why do you use the word 'fuck' in so many different ways? Do you follow the teachings of Jesus Christ?"

Fuckin A.

THIRTY-THREE

"Anyone know what an adverb is?" Brooklyn said.

Kasparov's eyes widened. "Is part of speech. Describes how, when, or where action takes place, or it can intensify adjective."

"As in 'the very hungry man angrily sat down to the breakfast he'd hoped to enjoy alone'," Demarco said. He pulled his arm out of Brooklyn's grasp. Brooklyn had caught him in the buffet line and towed him to the table where Milk and Kasparov were eating. "How the hell you not know that?"

"Had better things to do than study parts of speech." Brooklyn's hair was on end, and he was wearing the previous day's T-shirt. "Andy kept me up all night talking about the Bible and all the ways you can use the word 'fuck'."

"Sounds interesting," Milk said.

"For you, maybe." Brooklyn rubbed his eyes. "Not cut out for this, guys. Gonna cause a war or something."

"We already at war," Demarco said. "You and the alien lady on a first-name basis. That's something."

"Ain't her real name." Brooklyn slumped into an empty seat. "Got sick of calling her ambassador and just gave her a name. Andromeda. Andy for short."

Demarco hummed. "Andromeda. Sacrificed to the gods to pay for her mother's sin."

"Thought it was just a constellation," Brooklyn said. "My dad showed it to me."

"It's a whole damned galaxy, man!"

"Demarco, sit." Milk pointed at the last empty chair. "Where is she now?"

"Sleeping. Found her a place to crash. Says she needs 'precisely eight hours sleep a night'." Brooklyn looked at his watch. "If that's true, we got about two hours 'fore she wakes up. Lucky I didn't drag you all out of bed soon as she conked."

"What did you find out?" Milk said.

"Lot of Yarrow's ideas are right. First put a claim on Earth back before we ever existed, and the bill's come due. Plan is to relocate us here."

"Not a chance," Demarco said. "They 3.6 billion with a B people on Earth. No way to get them all up here even if they'd fit."

"Told her that. She said there's plenty of room and the First are real patient. Got a scheme to build up our space-flight capacity and get everyone off the planet in a few generations."

"Then our grandkids and everyone after them live like mole people on Venus, forever and ever, the end." Demarco cursed. "Knew I shouldna got up this morning."

Brooklyn shook his head. "Think the idea is we'd get sick of it, like they did, and go somewheres else."

"Earth's population went from two billion to more than three in the last forty years." Milk frowned. "Two generations will be double."

Kasparov tugged at his beard. "It will require population control. Laws on how many children are allowed. Forced sterilization, perhaps."

Brooklyn raised his hands. "Only know what she said."

"Did you sleep?" Milk said.

"Not much. Way too wired."

"Try to grab a nap before she wakes up." She moved her plate aside. "Meantime, here's what you're going to ask her about today."

* * *

Brooklyn lit the burner under the stainless-stainless steel pot. "Now we wait."

Andy looked closely at the flame and traced the piping from the pot to the thump keg to the worm box. "Please elaborate."

"Wanna know how it works?" Brooklyn said. Kasparov said there was no way in hell he was letting Brooklyn build a still in the Boneyard, so the site was about a hundred yards outside. Brooklyn and Demarco had hauled in the pieces and set up the lights.

"No. The process is fucking simple." She pointed at the pot. "The alcohol turns to vapor there. The vapor is purified here then it goes into this box, which I assume is the condenser."

Brooklyn nodded.

"As I said, a fucking simple process. Why do you undertake it? There appears to be no shortage of ethanol here."

"My ethanol will be the best," Brooklyn said, "and once I make it, I can trade it."

"What will you trade for? Everything here is communal, or nearly so. Even the Shop only requires that you do something of use before you take what you require."

"That works fine for ordinary shit."

"What other shit is there?"

"I don't..." Brooklyn took a breath. "Look, this is one of the two or three things I'm good at. There's not much need for a computer tech here, and I don't like the idea of busting my balls digging holes or weeding mushrooms for the rest of my life. If I make the best booze in De Milo, I can do my thing and everyone will leave me alone. Got it?"

Andy nodded as if she had learned the motion the night before, which she had. "Why do you desire to be alone?"

"Not, like, alone alone," Brooklyn said. "Just tired of like, owing people. If I gotta do something, I want to do it because I want to not because I owe it to someone. You dig?"

"I do not."

"You're a pain in the ass. Let's call it my turn to ask questions for a while."

"Certainly." Andy sat on a nearby crate. "Proceed."

Brooklyn ran Milk's questions through his head and picked the most obvious one. "The First blew up Cleveland, Freeport, and some city in Russia. How does that square with what you said about not wanting to kill us?"

"The First did not blow up those cities."

"Fine." Brooklyn was getting used to her semantics. "The First destroyed Cleveland, Freeport, and some city in Russia by chucking meteorites at them. How does that square with your kumbaya Joan Baez shit?"

"The First did not destroy those cities. Their destruction was either accidental or a plot by Earth governments."

Brooklyn rubbed his mouth. *Duke was wrong about there being aliens, there's no way in hell he was right about that.* "You're lying."

"No, I am fucking not."

Brooklyn was out of breath when he dumped his bike at the clinic and pushed into Milk's office. "Emergency meeting!"

Milk looked up from the paperwork on her desk. "Where's the ambassador?"

"Back watching my still." He gulped air. "I asked her about Cleveland. She says the aliens didn't do it. Says the US government mighta."

"Don't forget who she is and who she represents."

"Ain't the only one I heard say something like that. Nixon was running behind McGovern in '72 until the meteorite hit and everyone started worrying 'bout aliens again."

Milk rubbed her forehead, right where the scar tissue took over from the smooth skin. "Did she say anything else?"

"I booked it right over here when she told me about Cleveland."

"You need to be calm. Don't freak out every time she says something strange. Ask her the rest of the questions, but don't believe anything she says."

"She's pretty convincing, Milk."

"That's her job. Your job is to make her slip up enough that we get something useful. Get it?"

Andy was adjusting the burner flame under the pot when Brooklyn returned.

"The hell you doing?" Brooklyn pulled her hand away from the gas tap.

"Reducing the heat. The boiling point of methanol is one-hundred and forty-eight point five degrees Fahrenheit. Acetone boils at one-thirty-three degrees."

"Ain't my first rodeo, sister. Why were you screwing with my still?"

"Ethanol boils at one-hundred and seventy-three degrees, brother. With the flame so high you were increasing the length of time your process would produce ethanol contaminated with–"

Brooklyn held up his hand. "Alright, alright... I get the picture."

"It's fucking simple science."

Brooklyn checked the temperature on the pot. The ambassador had made the right call. "You don't have to say 'fucking' every damned time you mean 'very' or 'really'. Just when you're pissed off. Or trying to be a wise ass, maybe." He checked the temperature again, buying a second or two to collect his thoughts. "What about the abductions? We got plenty of people here say they were taken right off Earth."

"I am not familiar with the origin of everyone in this facility, but no doubt that is true. There are several possible reasons for such takings." She fell silent and turned to regard the still.

Brooklyn rolled his eyes. "And the reasons for the abductions are?"

"Originally, it was research and experimentation. Those taken during that period were examined and released or examined and held in storage."

"Guy runs the shop says the First cut off one of his nuts, his testicles. One in the kitchen says they took his eye."

"Some of the early studies were crude in contrast to later efforts, and not all First scientists use the same methods. I can assure you, though, that none of the subjects felt pain."

"You want to check on that yourself? I can introduce you."
Her expression didn't change. "I would like that."

"Alright, so you took people to experiment on. Why else?"
She shook her head. "I took no one."

"But you're totally with those guys, right? A loyal soldier." Brooklyn gave himself a mental pat on the back for sneaking another one of Milk's questions in. "Andy and the First, one big happy family of alien overlords."

"I am no more First than are you," she said. "I am Designed. I was created by the First to fulfill a purpose."

"The Trolls are Designed, too." *Another question off the list!* "What were they made for?"

"They rebuilt the Refuge before you arrived."

"The cave."

"The systems that supply atmosphere and water. The caves were here, but they needed to be repaired and modified to support human life."

"And now what are the Trolls doing?"

"They are waiting until they are needed again."

"They don't seem too happy about it."

"It is what they were made for."

Brooklyn touched the thump tank. It was warming up nicely off the heat of the pot. "Why else did you – sorry, the First – kidnap people?"

"Human scholars were taken to provide evidence of the

First's claims to your planet. Some believed that your leaders would be more willing to accept the notion were it backed by human scholars. Others were taken to be replaced by Designed serving as agents of the First."

"Spies?"

She nodded. "Among other purposes. For example, US presidential candidate George Stanley McGovern was replaced by a Designed in 1971 to promote the demilitarization of space and prepare for the First's arrival."

"McGovern was an alien?!"

"A Designed. Approximately ninety-nine percent human. If he had won the presidency, the First would likely have approached your world three years ago."

"But Cleveland happened." *And the military build up and now I'm on Venus talking to a fucking alien who looks like Julie Andrews if she was playing the Jolly Green Giant.* The thump keg burped like a percolator. "There it goes. You got them jars ready for me?"

Andy rose to her feet. "I will bring them over."

THIRTY-FOUR

Brooklyn lined the jars up on the bar at Toad Stools. "Made the first run small, but there's enough here for everyone to get a taste." He jabbed his finger at the bartender. "See anyone mixing my booze with pruno or some other shit, shoot them."

The bartender flipped his towel onto his shoulder. "Out of my hands, man. You find a guitar for me, yet?"

Bruce the bartender said he'd been an up-and-comer on the New York folk scene in the mid-60s before finding himself on Venus minus two toes and a kidney.

"Haven't been to work since the last load came down." Brooklyn pointed over his shoulder at the ambassador, who was watching the humans around her intently. "Been a little distracted."

"She's got a lot of people nervous," Bruce said. "Think she's dangerous?"

"Works for the assholes who put us here. What does that tell you?" Brooklyn snagged a full jar of liquor off the bar and carried it over to the table where Milk and Kasparov were sitting. "Some?"

"Yes, please!" Milk held out a highball glass. Brooklyn poured a careful two fingers.

"Boss?" he said.

"I will see if Jillian survives," Kasparov said. "Then, possibly."

"Your loss." Brooklyn sipped straight from the jar. "She fill you in about McGovern?"

Kasparov nodded. "If the ambassador is telling the truth, it opens up many possibilities."

Brooklyn took another sip and handed the jar to Kasparov. "It's like 'Attack of the Bodysnatchers'."

"*Invasion of the Bodysnatchers.*" Milk held her glass out for a refill. "If they could replace a presidential candidate, they could replace anyone. Hell, Brook, you could be a Designed."

"Not me." Brooklyn rubbed his face. "Not sure about the rest of you, though. Demarco's a pretty strange cat."

"Wonder if Andy can tell who's Designed and who's not." Milk chewed her lip and watched the ambassador trying out various facial expressions a couple of tables away, most of them friendly.

Brooklyn followed the doctor's eyes. "Add it to the list."

"What are we doing this morning, Brooklyn? I predict that it is too early to run the still again."

Brooklyn signed out a couple of the community bicycles. If they busted or a tire went flat or something, he was responsible for the repairs. "Take Your Ambassador to Work Day. Kas said you came down with all kinds of good garbage." He threw his leg over the bike.

Andy looked at her bike, a small, puzzled smile on her face.

"What are you waiting for?"

"I do not know how to use this," she said. "Perhaps we should walk as we did yesterday."

"Yesterday we walked about the length of a football field. Boneyard's miles away." He got off his bike. "It's easy. Just like… doing something easy. Here."

He listed the parts of the bike, pointing them out as he went. Andy soaked it up like a sponge.

"It is a fucking efficient design," she said. "I don't understand how your planet got so polluted if these were available."

"Back on Earth, bikes are for kids. Soon as you get money, you get a car and move farther out so it makes sense to have one. Get it?"

"Not at all."

Brooklyn climbed on his bike again. "Do like I do. It's all about keeping the thing moving so you can balance."

Andy hoisted the heavy air-conditioning unit over her head. "Where would you like me to put it?"

He pointed. "There's a pile over there with a sign. *Dlya diagnostiki*, or something like that. Russian writing."

"'To diagnose'. I see it." Andy carried the unit to the designated area and came back.

Brooklyn continued to sort through the trash. He tossed a broken hockey stick to the side. "I wonder where the First gets this shit."

"Some of it is wreckage, as you have seen," Andy said. "Much of it comes from junkyards and foreclosed warehouses. The First often uses them as operations bases."

"For deploying fake people."

"Reproducing the human phenotype is not difficult. There are likely thousands on Earth already. Some are agents. Many are embodied First who are simply curious about living as a human."

"All ready to spring out for your master plan."

She sighed. "It is not my plan. I have told you this. I am a very small part of it."

"Any other Designed look like you? Talk like you?"

"Many." She picked through a pile of paper goods – a mix of magazines, books, packages of napkins, cardboard boxes. "My phenotype is a mélange of human and what humans should see as positive alien traits. If I were too human, I might not be taken credibly. If I were too alien, I might not be relatable. I could easily have looked like this." She held up a science-fiction magazine with what appeared to be an evil toad in a turtleneck on the cover. "Special Women's Issue", it said.

"Set that aside for Demarco. He loves that shit. Think there are any First here in De Milo?"

"Possibly. Unless they identify themselves to me, I would have no way of knowing without an examination of their genetic code."

Brooklyn ran his hand through his hair. "Wish like hell I knew whether you were lying to me."

"There is no reason for me to be anything but candid. You are making a mistake by thinking of this as a war. It is not. It was over as soon as the First decided they wanted to return. You have no weapon that can harm them. No defense." She added another magazine to the pile she was making for Demarco. "If they wanted, they could have outlasted you. If the First had not revealed itself in 1961, there is a seventy-seven percent chance you would have exterminated yourself with nuclear weapons by now."

"Nice of them to care."

"They do not. They are a billion years ahead of you in terms of evolution, technology, culture, art, and motivation. You are a microorganism by comparison."

"The fuck they want my planet for?"

"Some of them want to remember what it was like to live as physical beings. It has been so long that they have forgotten." She stood to stretch. "Think about it like this. By remembering, maybe they will understand you better and perceive you as more than an annoyance."

"Ain't gonna work, Andy. People get cranky you tell 'em what to do and where to go."

"You need to stop believing you have a choice. I grew up on an artificial planet the First built, as part of a species they created as the means to fulfill a curiosity, a whim."

"Just saying they coulda asked."

"Does the tide ask if it is OK to rise and fall?"

PART TEN
Flash Light

April 1978

THIRTY-FIVE

"Said you could talk to the Trolls, right?" Brooklyn said.

"It is one of the languages I learned."

"Learned." Brooklyn hummed. "Thought you mighta been, like, programmed or somethin'."

Andy frowned. She was getting good at it. "I prepared for 28.7 Earth years for this assignment. There were no short-cuts."

"Be nice if there were. Just dump a bunch of knowhow in your head, send you on your way." Brooklyn reinstalled the platter of the Phillips record-player he was repairing for Turk. Both he and Andy needed new clothes, and Turk had strongly suggested getting the turntable up and running again would be required. Brooklyn put the floppy slipmat in place and switched the player on. He looked up at the man behind the counter. "There you go, pal. Not that I've seen many records since I been here. Obsolete tech."

"I keep 'em all for myself," Turk said. "Go ahead and take what you need."

Brooklyn snagged a pair of blue jeans and a couple of T-shirts and used the dressing room to change. Andy opted for a pair of patched bell bottoms and a fringed leather vest. Brooklyn put his denim jacket back on. He hardly needed it in the cave but liked having the extra pockets. "Fit OK?" he said.

"OK enough," Andy said. "Why are you asking about the Trolls?"

"Kas gave me the rest of the day off. Figured we'd go over to Troll Town and say hello to your relatives."

"That would be enjoyable," Andy said.

"Turk." Brooklyn snapped his fingers to drag the man's attention away from the turntable. "Lemme borrow a couple of those big flashlights for a few hours."

"What are you gonna do for me?"

"Just want to borrow them."

Turk crossed his arms over his chest.

"I'll bring you back something nice from Troll Town."

The big lights made the going safer but no more interesting. Brooklyn panned his in a slow half circle in front of them as they walked. "This is a shit hole. Can't imagine the First were happy about moving down here."

"They barely survived the first millennium," Andy said. "Birth rates dropped. Sensorum addiction soared."

"That some kind of drug?"

"It was similar to television but more immersive. It played to all of the senses and allowed the user to pretend they were elsewhere."

"Don't blame them." He moved the cone of light overhead. "A thousand years down here. Can't fucking imagine it."

"A thousand years was just the beginning." She flicked her own flashlight around. "Records from the Second Age show the creation of an artificial sun – fusion-powered – that simulated the day-to-night cycle. Life improved after that."

"First didn't think to change the bulb on it before throwing us down here? Seems like it would have been a good selling point."

"Perhaps they are waiting for you to find it and set it alight yourself as proof of growth," she said. "Not all of the returning First support the human relocation plan. Some advocated for extermination."

"Guess we should be glad the Democrats won."

They walked on in silence for a few minutes.

"Miss the sky," Brooklyn said. "Any sky. Earth sky or Moon. It's like it gives your thoughts somewhere to go. Feel like I'm trapped in here with everything bouncing back at me."

"I lived most of my life inside an arti-planet that orbits your sun directly opposite Earth," Andy said. "Somewhat larger than your Moon. It was created as a laboratory and home for the Designed."

"No sky?"

"The surface is covered with solar-power collectors. There was seldom any reason to go out and see."

"Any brothers or sisters?"

"Creche groups. We studied and trained together."

"Boyfriend? Girlfriend?"

"Several."

There was something in her voice. "You miss them," Brooklyn said.

She smiled. "I see them."

"Your boyfriends?"

"The Refuge workers… your Trolls." She jogged ahead, the cone cast by her flashlight bobbing in front of her feet.

Brooklyn followed as quickly as he could. His night vision had improved during his time in the cave, but he had nothing on Andy. When he arrived at the village, she was surrounded by wildly gesturing Trolls. Brooklyn couldn't get close to her, so he stood on the outskirts of the scrum.

"How come they're not saying anything?" he said.

"What?" She started. "They… They are using a hand language." Her own hands made several sharp motions. "This Design often works in environments where sound does not carry. They say they are pleased to see me and are asking if I have any assignments for them."

"Do you?"

"My only instructions regarding the Refuge workers is to

provide translation between them and the human population."
She frowned. "It is strange that they would ask me for
assignments. They should be receiving them directly from the
arti-planet."

"Tell 'em I say hello," Brooklyn said, "and 'welcome to the
neighborhood'."

"Hello, definitely," Andy said, "but a welcome would be
a century late. You are the new arrivals." She watched the
hand gestures of one of the Trolls. "They offer greetings and
welcome."

Brooklyn scratched his head. "How come they didn't try
to talk to us before? Demarco says there've been a bunch
of attempts to talk and trade. Been here a couple of times
myself."

"Strictly speaking, you don't exist to them. You have nothing
they want, and their work does not directly involve you.
They do not hear, and they see in a different visual spectrum.
If anything at all, to them you are rocks with an annoying
tendency to move."

"How 'bout now?" Brooklyn waved his arms like a baseball
empire. "Show me how to say 'hello'."

She shook her head. "They still won't see you as something
– as someone – to interact with. That may change with time,
but for now…"

"Can you ask them if they need anything? Scrap? Hooch?
Mushrooms? Blue jeans?"

Andy spoke at length with one of the largest Trolls. "They say
they don't. However, they are curious about a site," she pointed
in the opposite direction of De Milo, "about twenty miles that
way. It is also recent and not part of their instructions."

"You fill them in?"

"I could not answer the question. I am not aware of anything
that would be there. Are you?"

* * *

"I was a happier man before our tall, green friend dropped out of the sky," Demarco said.

Milk frowned. "You were self-medicating and spending all your free time in the bar or curled up with a book."

"See?" Demarco spread his hands. "Happy. Now, I got to pay attention and think all kinds of bad thoughts."

"Andy didn't say this other thing was dangerous," Brooklyn said. "Just doesn't know what it is."

"Maybe it's another group of humans," Milk said.

"Could be. We ain't usually that out that far to see. Found the Trolls and pretty much stopped there." Demarco sucked his teeth. "But why don't your girlfriend know about them, then? She the assigned mediator."

"More Designed?" Brooklyn said.

"Same problem. Your lady ought to know."

"Or she may be lying," Kasparov crossed his arms, "which again casts doubt on everything else she's told us."

THIRTY-SIX

"This is better." Andy tapped her glass. "Fewer toxins, less of a," she hesitated, "rotten-fruit taste." It had taken a lot of booze to make it happen, but she was finally getting a little slushy.

Brooklyn thrust his fists in the air. "Heard it from the genetically-enhanced lady's mouth, Demarco. Brooklyn's Best beats the local swill in every blind taste test."

Demarco inspected the cloudy liquid in his glass. "Bet this has more vitamins and minerals though." He took a long drink. "Probably got some protein, too."

"Sore loser." Brooklyn mixed a round of Tang screwdrivers for Andy and himself. "Alright, here's something I been thinking about. Growing up, we all heard the aliens had tentacles and fangs right?"

"Missed that part," Demarco said. "Attack came after I was taken. Only evil aliens I saw were on magazine covers. Green men with laser guns." He nodded to Andy. "No offense."

"None taken."

"Bear with me," Brooklyn said. "When I was stationed at Freedom, I met a woman. Some kind of EOF special agent."

"She hot?" Demarco said.

"Yeah, but ain't that kind of story." Brooklyn considered. "Could be, but that's not the point. Point is, she said she'd seen an alien. With her own eyes. A dead one. Said they were squishy, multi-armed. Traveled in metal pod things. That's ain't how I picture the First."

Andy frowned. "It's not at all like them."

"More Designed, maybe," Demarco said, "or propaganda? Scarier than a floating brain. Maybe spy lady was lying. Maybe her superiors lied to her."

"I know of no reason why the returning First would need such a phenotype," Andy said. "I have certainly never seen one."

"Well then," Demarco laughed, "maybe they two sets of alien conquerors."

Andy caught Brooklyn as he was coming out of his shed the next morning. "I need to see the Trolls, and I would like you to accompany me."

"I'm down." Brooklyn covered a yawn. "Demarco is off today, an' I know he's like to try sayin' 'hello'. Mind him coming?"

"He should. Something he said last night stuck with me."

The Trolls greeted Andy's return with enthusiasm and acknowledged Brooklyn and Demarco's existence with a new hand signal. Andy showed them how to return it.

"Progress," Demarco said. "We'll be selling 'em beads and firewater in no time."

"I've told them that I need to visit their library," Andy said. "We will have to follow them into their tunnels."

Brooklyn's shoulders crept up. He'd been living underground for months, but the idea of going even lower felt wrong. "Will we fit? They're about half our size."

"Easily," Andy said. "They'll take us through the main door."

They followed two of the Trolls for about a hundred yards before stopping in front of a dome with a door set into it. One of the Trolls made a hand gesture, and the door opened like an elevator. Inside, a wide tunnel led into darkness.

Demarco grunted. "Forgot they don't see like we do. Good thing I ain't afraid of the boogeyman."

"Good thing we brought lights," Brooklyn said.

The Trolls led them down the tunnel and into an area that the sound of their footsteps suggested was much larger.

"Can you see like they can?" Brooklyn asked Andy.

"Not nearly as well," she said. "I believe we're in their equivalent of the Boneyard. This way."

Brooklyn lost track of the turns they made. He got the sense that there were multiple chambers on either side of the new tunnel, which was smaller than the one they'd used to come down from the surface.

"We are in their living quarters now," Andy said, answering his unspoken question. "Cafeteria. Apartments. Theater."

"Theater?" Demarco said.

Andy spoke to their guides. "It is their primary entertainment. They perform plays for each other about technical problems they've encountered."

The route led to a circular chamber with a four-foot tall pillar in the middle. "Here it is." Andy touched the pillar. It responded with a soft glow. Symbols blinked over the surface. "I have temporarily configured it for our use."

"Some kind of a computer?" Brooklyn said.

Demarco squinted at the symbols. "Those supposed to be words?"

"Just a minute." Andy poked the pillar again, and the symbols changed to English letters. They spelled out "Ready. Not connected."

Andy hummed and poked some more. "It's lost its connection to the arti-planet."

"Like a modem?" Brooklyn said.

"It should be connected, entangled really, at the subatomic level. An instantaneous connection. But the connection is broken." She frowned. "I am asking it to present a summary, with visuals, of any information available in this terminal about a species we call the Second." Andy worked the machine in silence for a few seconds. She laughed. "It keeps trying to interface with you, Brook."

"Must be a bug." He moved further away from the computer.

The pillar projected several paragraphs of text and a grainy three-dimensional image of a jellyfish-like creature, multi-armed, working outside an underwater building. "That is a Second. The original native intelligence of your planet," Andy said.

Demarco whistled. "Alien Invasion, Part Two."

"We need to see that other site," Milk said.

"Trolls say they can show us where it is." Brooklyn lifted himself to a seat on her examination table. "About twenty miles past their village, so we'll need to take a cart."

"And extra batteries. Even then it will be difficult." Kasparov drummed his fingers. "You believe the ambassador knows nothing about it."

"S'what she said. As far as she knew, the Second warred and pillaged themselves to death millions of years ago." He fanned a sheaf of papers. "Got the history right here. She printed it off for us."

"Earth's first intelligent species was a jellyfish." Milk tapped her lips with her index finger. "The Creationists will have a fit when they find out."

"Computer said they left Earth just before a big meteor hit, like sixty million years ago," Brooklyn said. "Andy said it's the real reason dinosaurs died out."

"Makes more sense than that damned volcano theory." Demarco had his own copy of the printout and was leaning against the wall leafing through it. "Troll computer gets an F for grammar and syntax, but pretty clear the Second are not peaceful folks. Planets strip mined, civilizations destroyed, spelling-bees cheated at... They really like dropping space rocks on folks. Wonder where they got that idea."

"Could some have come to Venus to escape the asteroid?" Milk said. "Maybe they've been here all along."

"Trolls said the caves were sealed when they came to open it up for us," Brooklyn said. "'Sides, they said the site was new."

"I will draw up plans for an expedition," Kasparov said.

"How the First not know they here?" Demarco said. "For all-powerful beings, they sure in hell miss a lot of shit."

"Maybe they knew," Milk said. "Maybe they're just too powerful to care."

THIRTY-SEVEN

Brooklyn propped his elbows on the bar. "Wish we had a movie theater. Be great to see an action movie. Something with a car chase."

"Like *Bullitt*," Andy said.

"You've seen *Bullitt*?"

"And *The French Connection*." She was on her second vodka gimlet, a half a teaspoon of Tang substituting for lemon juice. "I would like to go to the movies. I could use the distraction."

"You think we're 'bout to find out some bad shit."

She traced the rim of her glass with her finger. "Few of the scenarios I am considering have positive outcomes."

"Name one."

"Well-provisioned explorers from a highly aggressive advanced civilization have come here for a picnic and will be happy to share the Refuge with humans."

"We'll just drop by for a beer and a hot dog." Brooklyn rubbed his face. "Sounds like a stretch."

"Thus my need for a distraction." She sighed. "Tell me the rest of your story."

"Which one?"

"The one about the spy. Tell me the 'that kind of a story' part."

Brooklyn flushed. "Uh... we did some work on the defense-grid computers and she left."

"That's it?"

"Had sex a couple of times, and she threatened to steal my rover if I didn't give her a ride back to her ship."

"Somewhat better. Brook, I am feeling a great deal of stress tonight, and I would like to have sex to alleviate it."

Brooklyn gulped. "With me?"

"That would be my preference, but I am not inclined to be choosy."

"How would we? I mean… I never had sex with… someone like you before."

"My anatomy is fully compatible with a human's," she said. "I doubt there will be any problems."

Brooklyn downed the rest of his drink. "OK then."

"Excellent. Your shed or mine?"

Andy pulled Brooklyn into a kiss on the way out of the bar. Her lips were warm, and her skin smelled like something homey. Turnips, maybe, plus candle wax. She was tall enough that Brooklyn had to stand on tiptoe to make it work.

"How was that?" she said.

Brooklyn felt his pulse in his ears. "Good. This part of your ambassador training?"

"Extracurricular pastime. You are my first human." She took his hand. "Come on."

Their next stop was the alley between the shop and the library. Brooklyn slid his hand into her coveralls.

"No nipples," he said. "Milk said something about that."

"Unnecessary. Designed are creche-born. No suckling or ovarian gestation required. My breasts are purely cosmetic."

"Does it still feel good when I…?" He gestured.

"I will tell you if you do something I do not enjoy. I expect you to do the same."

"You know, my place is closer."

"I have a better sleeping platform."

Andy had decorated since Brooklyn had set her up with the shed. She'd hung up travel posters and pictures of Earth landscapes. There was barely room for two people to help each other out of their clothes, but they managed.

"Do it like this?" Brooklyn said somewhat later.

She adjusted his hand. "Somewhat harder and faster."

Brooklyn was dazzled. He had never had a lover who was so blunt and clear about what she wanted. It was exciting. He buried his face in her neck. Something touched his wrist. He glanced down. "The fuck is that?"

She followed his gaze. "A penis. Much like yours in shape and function, but slightly smaller and fully retractable."

"But you're..."

"I am Designed. I have a penis and a vagina, and at the moment both are stimulated. Consider it a testament to your effectiveness as a lover."

"I..."

She took his face in both hands. "Can we talk about this later?"

It had been a long time since the Moon.

"Yeah. Just don't... poke me with it."

Demarco was the only one at the breakfast table. He held out his hand. "Slip me some skin, man. Heard you got a piece off an alien last night."

"News gets around." Brooklyn slapped Demarco's hand, but there wasn't much energy in it. He slumped into a seat.

"She not shy with her vocalizations, friend. Half De Milo heard her."

"She has a dick."

Demarco burst out laughing. "Man, yo face!" He wiped his eyes. "Yeah, first time that happens blows the mind somewhat. Mine was a lady I met in the Quarter. Tall, graceful, long hair, sweet as pie. You look at her, and you'd never guess, but when the panties came off... *BOING!* Sharde was her name."

"First time?"

"I seen some things, junior. Curl your hair and turn it white. Most of it was a lot of fun." He shook his head. "It's all just bodies and parts and moving around right. You can scratch an itch with just 'bout anything."

"Has a muff, too."

"Really?" His eyes widened. "Never seen that. You should write it up and send it to the magazines. 'My Girlfriend was a Space Alien'. Something like that."

Brooklyn ran his hands over his face. "She said she cycles between male and female a couple times a year. Three-quarters the way to female now. Makes her more sexually aggressive." He turned his head and winced at pain he found there. "Stronger, too."

"If you lucky, maybe she'll keep you 'round." Demarco pushed the pitcher of mushroom tea across the table. "Took the liberty. One of the professor's blends. It will wake you up and keep you sharp."

It tasted like woodsy dirt, but it cleared Brooklyn's head.

"Colors seem a little sharper," he said.

"That's the psilocybin."

"'Bout to go confront an alien menace and you drugged my tea?"

"Calm down." Demarco patted the air with his hand. "Professor says it's a warrior mix. Won't see nothing that's not there. You'll just see everything better."

Milk and Kasparov entered the room together and headed for the table.

"Don't drink the tea," Brooklyn said.

Demarco shrugged. "Your loss."

"The vehicle is ready," Kasparov said. "Will the ambassador be joining us?"

Brooklyn looked at his watch. "She has about fifteen minutes left on her sleep schedule. Said she'd meet us at the Boneyard."

"Topolski is there already, finishing preparations."

Milk poured herself a mug of tea. "Did Andy drop any new bombs last night?"

Demarco giggled. "Nothing that will blow up in *your* face."

"Don't listen to him." Brooklyn shot Demarco a warning look. "Let's grab some sandwiches and hit the road."

Most of the powered vehicles used in De Milo were tiny, repurposed electric golf carts and handmade rovers. The expedition vehicle was a massive thing, all military camouflage and enormous tires.

"M3 Scout Car," Kasparov said. "Post-war American. We decided this trip was worth dipping into the petrol supply."

"It runs?" Brooklyn said.

"It came though mostly intact. Engine was fine. We had to reconstruct part of the frame."

Topolski showed up with her arms full of long guns and ammo slings. "Take what you like."

"Thought you didn't like guns," Brooklyn said.

"This is from Demarco's stash," Kasparov said.

"I ain't just here for comic relief, chum," Demarco said.

Brooklyn had practiced with an M16 in basic training, so that's what he grabbed. He ran the rifle through its standard function check.

Demarco picked up an M14 and inspected it. "Hopin' we don't need these today."

"Best to be prepared." Topolski slung her rifle over her shoulder. "You, Brooklyn, and alien girl will ride in the back."

Andy came around the vehicle. Brooklyn waved at her awkwardly, and she answered with thinned lips and a tight nod.

"Will you take a weapon, Ambassador?" Kasparov said.

Andy inspected the guns. "I have not practiced with any of these."

"Get yourself that one there," Demarco pointed, "and step back here with me. Give you a quick lesson."

"Lot of firepower," Brooklyn said.

"I destroy most of them. Our suicide rate is high enough. But as Topolski said, it is best to stay prepared. Demarco drew the short straw." Kasparov picked up the last gun. "Kalashnikov AKM. Hideous thing." He ran it through a functions check, barely looking at his hands, and slid in a clip. "Are we ready?"

Demarco and Andy returned to the side of the M3. "This is a M1 Garand," she said. "Thirty caliber. Effective at five-hundred yards."

"Your girl a quick study," Demarco said. "Time we get this show on the road."

Brooklyn felt a surge of dizziness and everything in his eyesight seemed to vibrate. The lights on the poles left streaks in the air. *Real-life aliens & astronauts. Weird times. Long, long way from Queens.* He rubbed his eyes. "Let's do this."

Somebody had installed an eight-track player in the armored car, and Topolski plugged in a tape. It was hard to hear over the big engine and churning wheels, and Brooklyn asked her to turn it up. Black Sabbath. "You know the guitarist on this is missing fingers," he said.

"That explains much," Kasparov said. "We will play Pesniary next."

"The one with all the accordions and whistles and shit?" Demarco groaned. "The last thing I need is to have that in my ears as some alien rips my head off."

Kasparov didn't relent, and they pulled up to Troll Town listening to him and Topolski singing along to a song called "I Dreamt of You in Spring".

Andy spoke animatedly to three Trolls who'd met them. "They have volunteered to come with us. I expect it is the only way we will find the site."

"Do they like Pesniary?" Demarco said.

"I doubt they've ever heard of it," Andy said.

"Works for me."

"If they are to be guides, one of them should sit in the front with me," Kasparov said, "with the ambassador beside it to translate."

Andy took the front passenger seat and one of the Trolls squeezed into the cab beside her. The other two joined Brooklyn, Demarco, and Topolski in the back.

"Wonder how they navigate." Demarco nodded at the Trolls. "No magnetic field to make a compass work, no light…"

Brooklyn propped his feet up on the seat opposite. "Once we're all buddies we can ask." He leaned back in the seat as much as it allowed. "Wake me up when we get close."

The nap was not to be. Past Troll Town, the going grew rough. Rocks and other debris appeared suddenly at the edge of the headlights and disappeared just as quickly behind. The armored car rocked and swayed as it clawed forward at three to five miles per hour. Thick darkness hemmed them in on each side. Kasparov had ordered them to save their lights, so the only illumination that reached the back of the truck came from the small instrument cluster in the cab.

"Feel like I seen this movie," Demarco said. "Next scene, one of us goes off to take a piss and don't come back."

"Not good movie." Topolski wrapped her fingers around the stock of her rifle. "We will piss in teams. Always one to stand guard."

"You reckon the Trolls piss and shit like we do?" Demarco said. "Do they eat?"

"Ambassador eats," Topolski said. "She has a good appetite."

"But she's part human," Demarco said. "Right, Brook? She's got human parts."

Brooklyn frowned even though he knew Demarco couldn't see it. "Maybe we shouldn't talk about them like they ain't here."

"Just passing the time," Demarco sucked his teeth. "Could play I Spy."

"Could play shut the hell up."

"Could. Not much fun, though." He shifted. "Top, you got any fun Russian games?"

"Chess. Have you ever played by memory?"

"Never. But I'll give it a try."

"Visualize board. I will take black."

"Brook, you back me up case she tries to cheat. Uhm, king's knight to… b3."

Brooklyn made an effort to follow the game but lost track after a few moves. He couldn't keep the board in his head the way Demarco and the Russian could. Still, being left to his thoughts was better than being razzed about Andy.

Kasparov called a stretch break within an hour or so, and as Topolski suggested, bathroom breaks were on the buddy system. Brooklyn stood guard for both Demarco and Kasparov then had his own turn, pissing in a spot where no water had fallen since well before mankind started walking erect. Topolski passed out rations, and they climbed back into the truck.

"Where were we?" Topolski said.

"You'd just moved your bishop," Demarco said. "G5, I think."

Two matches later, Kasparov killed the engine and the lights. "Our guide says we have about a mile and a half to go. We walk from here."

"How we going to find the truck again?" Demarco said.

Brooklyn stretched his back. "The Trolls can probably help us."

"Just in case." Kasparov pulled something out of the cab. "Topolski will carry ultraviolet light, and I will blaze every fifty feet or so." The satchel he slung over his shoulder was filled with strips of white cloth.

Andy and the Trolls led the way, navigating by whatever strange means they had. Within a half mile, the horizon had lightened subtly. "They using lights," Demarco said. "Make it easier for us to creep up and take a look-see."

Topolski pulled out a roll of tape from somewhere, and they all used it to reduce the cones of their flashlights.

"Keep them on the ground," she demonstrated, "no waving around."

Leaving the truck behind ramped up Brooklyn's tension. The vehicle had masked the death-like silence of the cave, the churn of its engine a promise of life. Now there were only slivers of light, puffs of breath, and the unseen scrape of boot soles on ancient rock.

Kasparov called another halt. "We will take a first look from here," he whispered. "Binoculars and scopes."

They were about a hundred yards out, and Brooklyn found the camp easily through the scope on his rifle. Machinery, crates, lights, and tanks that looked like they might be made for holding liquid. Demarco grabbed his arm. "Over there," he breathed.

Brooklyn swung his rifle in the direction Demarco indicated and focused the scope. A cluster of tall, human-like bodies filled the ocular. "They naked?"

"Try these." Demarco handed Brooklyn his binoculars.

It took Brooklyn a minute or two to adjust the binoculars to his face, find the right spot again, and thumb it clear with the focus wheel. There were fifteen or twenty of the standing figures, immobile. No time had been spent on making anything below the neck more than vaguely human shaped, but their faces, thin and sickly-looking, had been carefully made.

"Brook! Goddamn it, I can't hold him!"

The green flash.

David.

Brooklyn's heart sped up, and he took in a lot of shuddery air to slow it down. "Seen one of those before. On Earth."

"Are they Second?" Demarco said.

"They ain't us. That's the important thing." Brooklyn reached over to tap Kasparov's shoulder. "Let's go back. Think we've seen enough."

Kasparov nodded. "Slow and very quiet."

Topolski unlimbered the UV lamp, and they followed the blazes back to the truck.

"What are they?" Kasparov said.

Brooklyn looked at Andy. Worry was plainly etched on her face.

"They're trouble."

THIRTY-SEVEN

Kasparov insisted they put a few more miles between themselves and the site before sitting down to compare notes. They squeezed into the back of the truck and turned on one of the electric lanterns so they could see each other's faces.

Brooklyn told them about the tapes and David's going-away party.

"What was on the tapes?" Demarco said.

"Military software? Maybe they needed it to figure out how our computers work. Doubt their operating system is compatible with ours."

"What do we know about their tech?" Kasparov said.

"They evolved after the First left the solar system, and there was minimal contact after that," Andy said. "Obviously, they can travel through space."

"They can sorta pass for people. One I met looked sick, that was about it. I never suspected he was something else."

"It was an exoskeleton," Andy said. "The Second was inside. They had them, although a different design, when the First encountered them several million years ago."

"What was the nature of that encounter?" Kasparov said.

"They attacked and then offered a parley, which they then violated with another attack. The First held them off with little difficulty."

Brooklyn rubbed his mouth. "Makes sense with what Sierra told me, that the Second are the ones we really been fighting with."

"Surprised they not more advanced," Demarco said. "You said it millions of years since the last scrap. Why they not disembodied brains, too?"

"They are stupid," Topolski said.

"It could be a matter of relativity," Andy considered. "If the Second are limited to relativistic speeds, from their perspective the conflict with the First might have been a few thousand years ago. If they used some kind of hibernation tech–"

"Could be the same guys the First sent packing all those years ago," Demarco said. "Come running back home with they tentacles tucked."

"We're just speculating now," Kasparov said. "Let's drop the Trolls off and head back to town."

"I need a drink." Milk perched on the edge of her examination table. "Anybody holding? Demarco? Even the shit you make is better than facing this completely lucid."

"I'm empty." Demarco hauled himself to his feet. "Lemme run over to the Toad Stool."

He walked out the door, passing Kasparov who was leaning against the wall next to the eye chart. The Russian cleared his throat. "Professor Yarrow is back at the Dig?"

Milk nodded. "They opened up another six feet of trench. Where's the ambassador?"

"Andy and Top drove the truck to the Boneyard to unpack it," Brooklyn said.

"So, it's just us chickens." She sighed. "Are we in any immediate danger, Kas?"

Kasparov pushed his shoulders against the wall. "I don't think they spotted us."

"Left a pretty clear trail coming back though," Brooklyn said. "Truck ain't exactly sneaky."

"Two sets of alien invaders. I did not see that coming." Milk looked at Brooklyn. "We're sure they're not working together? Andy could be lying about there being two separate groups."

"She's the one told us about it," Brooklyn said. "Only thing I know for sure is one of those exoskeleton things was on Earth and killed my best friend."

Demarco came back through the door with a quart of vodka and a pitcher of Tang. Brooklyn chewed on his thoughts while the drinks were distributed.

"Our evidence is circumstantial," Kasparov said. "One face-to-face interaction, lots of hearsay, and history so old it might as well be myth. We need more information."

"I say we don't wait," Demarco said. "We rolled in quiet today. I say we roll in loud tomorrow, get out the truck, smile a big smile, and say 'howdy'. Brook said they speak English."

"What if they start shooting?" Milk said.

"Then they intentions are clear." Demarco made a finger gun and leveled it at her. "An' we shoot them right back."

"Twice this time." Andy kissed Brooklyn's cheek and rolled off him. "I am glad you waited up."

Brooklyn was covered in sweat. Andy's body was a few degrees warmer than his, and her small shed steamed up quickly. "You don't think going out there tomorrow is a good idea."

"I'm seldom in favor of deliberate violence," she said.

"Won't be deliberate on our end." He ran his hand through her thick hair. The brush cut she'd shown up with was growing in fast. "A big smile and 'howdy' is all we're offering."

Her mouth twisted. "Provided you ignore the guns hidden in the back of the truck and the twenty-person backup force in the shadows."

"They don't make a move, the backup might as well not

exist." Brooklyn rose to his elbows. "Got a better idea, I'll take it to Milk right now. I won't even stop to put on pants."

"They attacked a parley." She rolled to face away from him. "Some of you will be killed."

"That was the old Second."

"They killed your friend, and they would have killed you." Brooklyn rubbed her back. "It's going to be fine."

"Shots will be fired, and David won't be there to save you this time."

Brooklyn climbed into the truck with Topolski and two others from Kasparov's crew, two bulky square-headed guys who looked like they could crack walnuts with their lips. Each was armed with a Kalashnikov. Brooklyn stuck with the M16. After performing three nervous function checks, he set it on the floor of the truck.

The big men were whispering to each other in Russian and one of them described Brooklyn as "the alien lover". Brooklyn was prepared. "*Chtob u tebya hui vo lbu vyros,*" he said. *May a dick grow on your forehead.*

The men looked startled. Brooklyn waved to them. "*Dobroye utro, rebyata.*" *Good morning, boys!* He hoped that would be the end of the hazing. He understood more Russian than he spoke, but even that was nothing to brag about.

Demarco climbed into the cab with Kasparov and the truck lurched into motion, following the tracks it had left the day before. This time there'd be no stop to pick up a guide. Finding their way back to De Milo, if anyone remained left to return, would rely on tracks in the dirt and the radio beacon they'd set up in the Boneyard.

Andy's place in the expedition had been the subject of much argument, which she'd settled that morning by deciding not to go. Brooklyn missed her. He planted his feet and tried to get comfortable in the swaying truck bed.

Past Troll Town, Kasparov crept the M3 along, both to make sure they didn't lose the tracks and to allow the fleet of smaller vehicles behind them to keep up. At hour nine, they stopped to make camp.

"Get the generators started and top off all the batteries," Kasparov said. "We don't want to be out of juice if we must leave quickly."

Brooklyn took charge of the rations, hauling the crate to the center of camp and getting everyone something to eat. Kasparov had put the kibosh on bringing booze along, but flasks and jars were ubiquitous among the small groups of men and women clustered around battery-powered lanterns.

Brooklyn brought his own meal back to the M3 and slumped against one of its enormous tires to eat. Demarco had the same idea.

"Wonder where all the carbon monoxide will go." Brooklyn stretched his legs out and looked into the darkness overhead.

"Probably nowhere. It's all hanging around at ceiling level." Demarco shifted his position. "One of the reasons, early on, we decided to avoid burning much of anything here. Wood, fuel, cigarettes, et cetera. No telling where the smoke went. Liable to fill up the space and kill us all in our sleep."

"Worse ways to go," Brooklyn said. "Gotta cousin who offed himself that way. Ran a hose from his tailpipe and breathed hisself to sleep."

"Sounds to me like you nervous."

Brooklyn seesawed his hand. "Never been in a real firefight before."

"Still haven't. Might not even be an issue."

"Andy thinks it will be."

"That why she not here?"

"Maybe. She got kind of upset last night. Well, upset for her. Said she was going back to Troll Town to do more research."

"Bet she got a way there to talk to the First. Can't be a bridge unless you know what your boss wants and can tell him what the other side has in mind."

"I didn't think of that."

"Milk has. You been invited to her secret morning meetings, but she goes to *all* the hush-hush powwows."

"Doesn't trust me."

"You OK. She not so sure about Andy. Maybe the pretty alien has the power to cloud men's minds and make them do her wicked will."

"She doesn't have any powers."

"Exactly what a man with a clouded mind might say."

"Why do you get to go to all the secret meetings?"

Demarco grinned. "Maybe I the mastermind behind the whole thing."

"Yeah, right." Brooklyn yawned. "I'm going to try to get some sleep."

"Sweet dreams, babe."

Kasparov handed Brooklyn a cup of coffee. "I took two men and scouted the Second site last night. Nothing has changed. The exoskeletons have not moved."

"How close did you get?"

"Close," the Russian said. "Maybe fifty feet. No sign of activity. Just a low hum from the tanks."

"Maybe no one's home," Brooklyn said. "It might be abandoned or a supply depot or something."

"Then why leave lights on?" Kasparov rubbed his eyes. "We'll see in a couple of hours."

Brooklyn finished his coffee and checked his weapon again. His job was to stay quiet and low in the back of the truck unless the aliens started shooting. *I can do that. Probably.*

Kasparov set the convoy back in motion about thirty minutes later. The M3 pulled ahead, leaving the backup fleet to keep pace a hundred yards back.

The square-headed Russians sharing the truck with Brooklyn chatted quietly.

"They are making bets," Topolski said. "Ony," she pointed, "says you will be the first to run. Grisha thinks you will be the first to die."

"How do you say, 'Go fuck yourself' in Russian?"

She told him. Brooklyn relayed the message, prompting laughter.

"Ony now agrees with Grisha," Topolski said.

Brooklyn gripped his rifle more tightly.

Demarco slid open the window between the cab and the bed. "Down and quiet," he said. "We almost there."

Topolski used her flashlight to relay the message to the backup fleet then crawled into the shadow of the tarp with Brooklyn. There was barely enough light to see her teeth flash. If anyone wanted the shooting to start it was her.

Brooklyn felt the truck come to a halt. The passenger side door creaked as Demarco opened it and stepped out.

"Hello!" he called. "We just dropping by to say 'howdy'."

"What's happening?" Brooklyn hissed.

Topolski held up her hand. She had the best view through the M3's windshield.

The driver-side creaked open, and Kasparov climbed out of the cab. He left the big engine running.

"Four of the robot men are moving toward a tank of water," Topolski said. "They are climbing into it."

Demarco shouted more words of greeting. The plan was for him to stop well short of the tanks and wait for Kasparov to come up behind him.

"They are emerging from the tanks," Topolski said.

Greet light flared. *ZARK!* Demarco swore and Kasparov opened up with his rifle.

"Up and over!" Topolski said. "Brooklyn, signal the backup!"

Brooklyn lunged for the signal light as the Russians got into position. Ony and Grisha stood on the running boards and used the open doors for cover. Topolski got behind the wheel and put the truck between Demarco and the exosuits.

ZARK! The green light flashed again. Brooklyn was supposed to be firing from the truck bed, but he couldn't see over the side.

"Brooklyn!" Topolski said. "Stand up!"

His back wouldn't straighten, and his knees refused to unlock. He had a white-knuckle grip on his rifle. Somebody screamed.

"More robots are moving toward the tanks!" Topolski said. "Brooklyn, get your ass up and check Demarco."

He could do that maybe. Moving toward the open back of the truck didn't require standing, and neither did dropping to the ground below. The green lights were at the front of the truck, and Brooklyn was now safely behind.

Demarco wasn't moving. Brooklyn headed toward him at a fast crawl.

ZARK! ZARK!

The Russians' rifles replied. Single shots and full-auto bursts.

Brooklyn reached Demarco, who was bleeding from the head. No other signs of injury. Brooklyn put his hands under the man's armpits and dragged him back to the truck. Kasparov was already there.

"How badly is he hurt?" the Russian said.

"Head wound." Brooklyn panted. He couldn't get enough air.

"Help me get him into the truck."

Lifting Demarco over the tailgate, Brooklyn finally regained his ability to stand. He used it to brace his rifle on the truck cab and look over the top. A few of the robot men lay still, leaking something dark onto the ground. Others were still firing.

ZARK!

"Where's the backup!" Brooklyn said. "Why aren't they coming?"

Kasparov looked at him strangely. "It's only been less than a minute. They will be here."

Brooklyn took a deep breath and held it. He let it go slowly and aimed his M-16 like he learned in training. He squeezed the trigger.

ZARK! ZARK!

THIRTY-EIGHT

"I froze, man."

"Least you unfroze and made yourself useful. I took myself out on a rock." Demarco winced. The side of his head was bandaged. "We get 'em all?"

"Took a few prisoners. Sorting through the rest of the exoskeletons now. Just came over 'cause I heard you were awake."

"Wanted to look at your handiwork?" He hummed. "Kasparov told me you pulled me out. Much appreciated."

"Looked kinda stupid lying there bleeding on yourself." Brooklyn put his hand on the older man's shoulder. "Sit tight, and get some rest. I'll come back and fill you in later."

He tried not to look too closely at the others in the triage center. Grisha was short an arm and had been drugged unconscious. Six shrouded bodies were laid out off to the side, and another of the wounded would likely join them soon. Milk and one of her Russian recruits were working over her, but there wasn't much hope in their eyes. Brooklyn left the area to avoid the bad news.

The Second didn't look happy out of the water, so Kasparov was tossing any survivors into a tank that Brooklyn had isolated by cutting the power lines leading to it. Cutting the power had the added benefit of making the tanks transparent, and five of the multi-armed bastards were floating inside like pissed-off aquarium exhibits. As Brooklyn watched, one of the critters grabbed at a fish analog swimming in the tank and stuffed it into its mouth.

Kasparov was standing over one of the felled exoskeletons about a dozen yards away. He called Brooklyn over. "This is what you encountered on Earth?"

Brooklyn looked down at the thing. Its face showed no reaction to the damage done to the rest of its body. "Could be its twin brother," he said. The exoskeleton was essentially an armored tank of water with arms, legs, and head. This one had been shot several times in the abdomen and the Second inside shredded. "Find anything useful?"

"One of the exoskeletons is damaged but still functional. We disarmed it and rendered it somewhat less functional. Topolski is attempting to communicate with it."

"That the only one?"

"I am told there is one more survivor for the tank. We took them by surprise, and our weapons proved more accurate over the distance."

"Milk says Grisha's going to make it," Brooklyn said. "I'll go check in with Topolski."

Kasparov waved him away.

Topolski and Ony had the torso of an exoskeleton propped against a rock. The machine was missing an arm and both legs.

"It talking?" Brooklyn said.

"We are not sure it is still alive," Topolski said.

Ony rattled off a string of syllables. Brooklyn caught the word "electricity".

"Ony suggests we try to wake it up with jumper cables." Topolski laughed.

Brooklyn knelt to get a better look. The faces of the exoskeletons were identical: thin, waxy, with teeth like cheap dentures. This one blinked abruptly, and Brooklyn nearly fell backward in surprise.

"What do you want with us?" he said, recovering his balance. "Why are you here?"

The exoskeleton turned its head to look at him but said nothing. Brooklyn stood. A sixth alien had been added to the holding tank. "I bet they're talking about us in there." He prodded the exoskeleton with his toe. "Answer some questions, and we'll put you in the tank with your friends. You can eat little fish and talk all the shit you want."

The exoskeleton's remaining arm stabbed out, clamping a steely hand around Brooklyn's ankle. "Jumper cables. Fuck you," it said.

Brooklyn's muscles seized, every molecule in his body vibrating like a speaker head with too much bass. His teeth slammed together, and his chest cramped. His heart burst.

The exoskeleton let go his ankle, and Topolski caught his body as he fell.

PART ELEVEN
Boy From New York City
Still May, Probably

THIRTY-NINE

Something was covering his face, but Brooklyn couldn't move to push it away. His brain and body were not on speaking terms.

Should have gotten that toe! (who the fuck said that). Flame-colored trumpet notes wheezed in and out. The worst Miles Davis solo ever. The Purple Lady laid down some alto sax above and around the simple rhythm. *Everyone has trauma.*

Light built in his chest, warming and waking the rest of his body. He shivered. *David won't be there to save you this time.*

The covering was not only on his face, it was head to toe. He struggled to remember how to take a breath. His diaphragm flexed once. Twice. Went back to work and filled his lungs with the eggy, tangy air of the Venus underground. Brooklyn's eyes fluttered open, but there was nothing to see.

There a towel on my face?

Brooklyn's arms still wouldn't work. A strangled gurgle came out of his mouth instead of the call for help he'd been planning.

It worked anyway. Rapid footsteps. The cloth on his face flew away. Demarco stood over him with red eyes. His head was bandaged.

"The fuck, man?" he said. "You s'posed to be dead!"

* * *

The simple respirator breathing for the woman across the room continued to wheeze, in and out. Milk took Brooklyn's vitals again.

"He was stone dead, I swear," she said. "We covered him up and moved him to the morgue side more than twelve hours ago."

Kasparov tugged on his beard. "Could you have made a mistake?"

"If she fucked up, I did, too. But I know dead, and my boy here was cold." Demarco smiled. "Not that I ain't glad you got better."

"Me, either." Brooklyn said. "What'd you do to yourself?"

Demarco looked askance. "Head injury at the start of the fight. You pulled me back onto the truck. You don't remember that?"

"We win?"

"Lost six people but achieved part of the objective. Guess that a win. Still don't know what the Jellies doin' here."

Milk pulled the rest of Brooklyn's shroud away.

"Hey!" He expected to be naked underneath, but he was only bare-chested. One leg of his jeans had been cut off at the thigh. There was a band of new pink skin around his ankle.

Milk examined it. "That was a third-degree burn. A real mess." She ran her fingers along Brooklyn's sternum. "Pretty sure we broke some ribs doing CPR, too." She prodded. "Any pain when I do this?"

"Little tender. Mostly I just feel tired."

Milk's eyes narrowed. "We're going to run those blood tests as soon as we get back to De Milo."

Brooklyn's throat felt like sandpaper. "Meantime, can I get some water?"

"Water and then sleep." Milk checked his pulse for the fifth time. "And don't you fucking die on me again."

* * *

The surviving Second glowered from the holding tank. The little fish things were keeping their distance.

"The Jellies eat the little suckers," Demarco said. "Little pod over there is full of them, frozen. Drop them in the water, they start swimming around."

"Have they said anything?" Brooklyn moved stiffly toward the tank. Milk couldn't come up with a good reason to keep him prone, but he'd had to lie a little to make it happen.

"Don't think they can do American without their people suits."

The other tank was empty except for the little fish, and the sides were still opaque. Brooklyn hung over the edge and tried to get a look at the inside walls.

"What's going on?" Milk said.

"Think the insides of the tank are some kind of television screen," Brooklyn said. "Probably shut the other one off when I cut the cables."

Milk stood beside Brooklyn and looked into the tank. "All I see are colors and shadows."

"We ain't in the tank, and we ain't jellyfish," he said.

"We can solve one of those problems. What about the other?"

"One thing at a time. There a way to make sure that," he pointed at the liquid in the tank, "is actually water and that the little fish things aren't flesh-eating or poisonous?"

A few minutes later, Brooklyn stripped down to his briefs and slid the makeshift goggles over his eyes.

Topolski leered at him. "You are better built than I expected, American." She handed him the end of the hose that he'd be using as a snorkel. "Any last requests?"

"Yeah, if you see a feeding frenzy start, pull me out. Milk's not a hundred percent sure about those fish." He climbed the ladder and stuck his foot into the water to test the temperature. It was cold, but he slid the rest of the way in.

The snorkel-hose tasted like gasoline, not unexpected as it

had come from the toolbox and probably had been used as a siphon. Brooklyn floated in the tank and waited for his body and eyes to adjust.

The images on the tank walls changed constantly. Symbols, charts and maps, maybe, but they were out of focus. Brooklyn touched one of the symbols and it changed. Another touch, another change. *It's a computer, but what the hell am I seeing?*

He poked experimentally at a green dot, and it expanded into a square about the size of his chest. A blurry blob with tentacles swimming with smaller versions of itself. Children maybe. A home movie. Maybe a message from the folks back in the Land of Angry Jellyfish.

Brooklyn surfaced and pulled himself out of the tank. "Something there," he said. "We need Andy."

Andy arrived the next day on one of Turk's rental carts. She had two Trolls with her.

"Rigged you a mask and snorkel," Brooklyn said.

"I won't need it." She looked brittle. "They told me you were killed."

"Got better, I guess. Glad you're here. I'm just… so over my head in all of this."

She nodded tightly. "We'll talk about it later. I've been using the Trolls' library to learn what little is there about the Second's language and culture.

The three Designed followed Brooklyn to the tank and, after a brief conversation, climbed in and sank to the bottom.

"She can breathe underwater?" Demarco said.

"Guess so," Brooklyn said.

Minutes ticked by. From outside the tank, Brooklyn could see Andy touching the screens and having animated conversations with the Trolls. *Sign language does come in handy.* He'd learned a few of the Trolls' basic signs, but wasn't far past "hello", "goodbye", and "thank you."

Demarco wandered off and came back with two MREs. Brooklyn didn't take his eyes off the tank while he ate.

"I think someone's sweet on the alien lady," Demarco said.

"Yeah, maybe." Brooklyn's mouth twisted. "Don't even know if she has feelings."

"White-man's biggest blunder. Assumin' that 'cause someone has titties, or dark skin, or two sets of genitals they don't think about or want the same things you do." Demarco pulled his flask out. "We all people, babe. You, me, even the Jellies." He spread his arms. "Just tiny lifeforms floating in a vast uncaring universe trying to get by and find a little love. Prick us, do we not bleed?"

"Quit preaching, and let me have a drink."

Andy and the Trolls surfaced in another hour or so. Brooklyn had a towel ready for her, and a change of clothes. The Trolls weren't wearing anything and showed no sign of discomfort. "You want something hot to drink, warm you up?" he said.

"We have a problem, Brook. A large one."

FORTY

"They're going to drop a meteor on New York City?" Milk paled.

"That part is certain," Andy said. "What I am..." She looked at the Trolls who were also part of the circle. "What we're not sure about is the motive."

"An incitin' incident," Demarco said. "Cock-blocking the First. First comes to say hello in '61, Jellies drop a rock on Kansas. First candidate about to win the '72 election, Jellies give Cleveland the Boot. Now..."

"The timing suggests they want to start a war between our people and yours," Kasparov said. "If the city is destroyed immediately before the First delegation arrives, who will the EOF blame?"

"Your weapons pose no danger to the First," Andy said. "How could a war be anything more than a distraction?"

"If nothin' else, it would make it harder to get the planet," Demarco said. "First would win, but they'd have kicking and screaming humans to deal with every step of the way."

"That might give the First's Kill-All-the-Humans Party something to change hearts and minds with," Milk said.

"Assuming the First have hearts," Brooklyn said.

"Love's in the mind, babe. Heart's just a muscle that moves blood around."

"What about the oceans?" Kasparov said. "I doubt the Jellies would want to live on land. If the First destroys us quickly, there could be room for two alien species on the planet."

"Get a message to the First, Andy. You gotta have a way," Demarco said. "Way you talk about them says they could shut down those multi-armed motherfuckers pretty quick."

"I should have a direct neural link to the arti-planet, but like the Trolls, my connection has been severed. I suspect the Second may have something to do with it."

Demarco worried his left ear. "If the Jellies can do that, wonder if they got somethin' else lets him hide from the big brains."

"That's it then," Milk said. "Our hands are tied."

"Perhaps not all of them." Kasparov caught Demarco's eye. "We need to get back to De Milo."

"Plan V." Demarco rubbed his hands together.

Brooklyn peered into the tank. The surviving Jellies looked surly. "Gonna do with them?"

"Drain tank," Topolski said. "Leave them to gasp out shame and regret."

"Negative." Kasparov considered. He raised his voice. "Ony, my friend, when you were a boy, did you ever want to maintain and guard an aquarium?"

They followed the tracks and radio beacon back to De Milo. Most went to their beds to sleep or to the bar to plan funerals for the men and women killed in the assault. Milk and Demarco took Grisha to the clinic for surgery. Brooklyn and Andy parked the M3 with Kasparov and followed him to the far side of the Boneyard. The Russian closed an unobtrusive knife switch, and a string of pole lamps woke to illuminate a path leading away from the yard.

"It's not far," he said.

In a quarter mile or so, the path of lights doubled back on

itself to form a rough circle with a looming, irregular shape in the middle.

Brooklyn spotted the lettering on the hull: *Victory*. Neurons fired and misfired, rerouted. Awareness dawned. "No fucking way."

"It was here before we arrived." Kasparov folded his arms. "Pure chance we found it."

"Any sign of Carson?"

"The pilot? Maybe he did not come with it. Maybe," the Russian gestured at the darkness surrounding the little oasis of light, "maybe his bones lie just outside."

"Big movie came out about him few months before I joined up. Ship in it didn't look much like this one." The movie ship had looked sleek and sure, powerful. The real ship looked like something thrown together in an amateur hotrodder's garage, the hull cut and twisted, deformed to make room for the Oppenheimer engines. "Looks like a fucked-up garbage truck."

"How old were you when the invasion started?" Kasparov said.

"Ten," Brooklyn said.

"I was twenty-four. It feels like a century ago." Kasparov tugged his beard. "She's not a fighter. She's a utility vehicle. Armed, yes, but mostly used for search-and-rescue operations."

"It run?"

"Demarco and I worked on it in the early days, when we still harbored ideas of escape. We patched the hull, did some rewiring, made general repairs. The reactor is sound." He put his hand on the hull. "Perhaps it would fly."

"I sense a 'but'."

"Several of them," Kasparov said. "Vessels of this kind require a booster sled to launch from a planet's surface. We don't have one."

"The Oppenheimers–"

"If we tried to launch with the Oppenheimers we would likely destroy De Milo and slam the ship into the ceiling of the cave. They are simply too powerful. Moreover, by luck or planning, we have no pilots among us. A beautician and two sculptors, a baker, a typewriter repairwoman, a telephone operator, a horse farrier, but no pilots."

"Don't get it, then," Brooklyn said. "Why you showing us this?"

"The ship has a computer, an autopilot, really, that until recently we've had no one to program."

"It's impossible." Brooklyn leaned back into the cracked leather seat and covered his aching eyes.

"Is it?" Andy asked.

"Yes. No. I don't know. Maybe." He knuckled the autopilot. "Runs on punched cards. Don't have a keypunch."

"Or cards."

"I could probably make those." He scratched his head. "Maybe I could hand punch them. This thing probably uses FORTRAN III. It was big in the late 50s, early 60s."

Kasparov poked his head into the cockpit. "Governments usually run several years behind private industry."

Brooklyn waved the punched card he'd removed from the machine. "Tell me something I don't fucking know. I was replacing these things on the Moon a few months ago, and they'd been obsolete for more than a decade."

"Can you do it?" Kasparov said.

"Does it matter?" Brooklyn said. "You already told me we can't get it in the air without a booster sled. Don't even have the fuel for one of them."

"I have an idea for that," Andy said. "A fucking simple process."

FORTY-ONE

There was no sun to come up, no dawn, but it didn't matter. None of them had gone to bed, and the conference table was covered in coffee cups and snack plates.

"Tight, tight, tight," Demarco said. "Twenty-seven days until the next trash dropoff, and we can't leave, assuming all this shit comes together, until one after that."

"The First delegation arrives on Earth in eighty-six days, provided they keep to the schedule." Milk glanced at Andy.

"Ballistics and orbital mechanics don't lie," Andy said, "and the First are seldom tardy."

"Any reason we can't just flag down the trash ship and tell them what the problem is?" Brooklyn said.

"The Designed piloting the ships are single-minded. Pickups and dropoffs are all they are taught. They will ignore any attempts to signal them."

"So we launch in seventy-two days and head toward Earth screaming our heads off that the First are walking into a trap and there's a giant meteor heading for Manhattan we hope they'll take care of for us." Demarco put his palms flat on the table. "Like I said, tight."

Kasparov nodded. "And before then, Brooklyn must program the autopilot, and my crew must design and build a launch booster."

"Could use a few people to help me out," Brooklyn said. "Andy is going to be busy at the still."

"Rocket fuel does not distill itself," Andy said. "I also will be procuring liquid oxygen with the Refuge workers."

"Alright, we get Brook a little nerd crew." Demarco leaned back in his chair. "Who gonna be in the ship when it blasts off?"

Milk frowned. "Andy needs to go. We'll need her as proof of all of this."

"Do that violate her mission, being ambassador, at all?" Demarco said.

"My mission is moot if there are no humans to resettle," Andy said. "I believe you will stand a better chance communicating with the First ambassadors if I am there to speak for you."

"Ship's got room for two," Demarco said. "Who been here the longest?"

"Professor Yarrow, but I don't think she'd want to go. We should get her to write up a report of her findings, though," Milk said. "I don't think we ought to decide based on seniority. Kas has rank and record. He shows up, they'll listen."

"Decision made then? Kas and Andy?" Demarco looked around the table. "Any bullshit remaining? Any new bullshit? Seeing none... meeting adjourned."

Milk peered into the microscope at a slide smeared with Brooklyn's blood. "There's something there. Come and see."

"Was only a few injections." Brooklyn pulled his shirt back on. "Doc said the radiation I soaked up on the Moon mighta made 'em work better." He crossed the room and looked into the oculars. "What am I looking at?"

"You see how your cells look... fuzzy?"

"No."

"It's like there's something in them or on them. I can't get enough magnification on this damned thing to see. Maybe if I had an electron microscope..."

"Keep an eye out for one in the Boneyard."

"Is there anything else it could be? Immaculate conception, maybe? Were you kissed by an angel as a child?"

Brooklyn snorted. "No angel was going to touch me." He rolled his shoulders. "Gonna sound crazy. I did, like, an alternative therapy with some hippy-dippy types 'while ago. Shrooms and acupuncture. Chakras. It kind of... opened me up. Ever since, I get dreams about this purple alien lady watching over me."

Milk quirked her eyebrow. "You sure she's not green?"

Brooklyn flushed. "Ain't Andy. Purple Lady is bigger somehow. Cosmic." He scoffed. "Just bullshit acid-trip stuff."

"Probably. And it doesn't tell us what you are."

Brooklyn leaned against the exam table. "Guy from Queens."

"Who came back from the dead. Maybe not for the first time, either. I bet you were dead when they dropped you here. That's why they dumped you with the trash instead of putting you in a transport pod."

Brooklyn laughed. "So I'm immortal now? Can't die?"

"Only way to know for sure is to kill you again, but I'd feel awfully stupid if you didn't come back. Might be only a two-time thing. Maybe you have nine lives like a cat. Maybe you just got really fucking lucky."

"Most of my luck is bad," Brooklyn said. "More likely I wasn't dead as you thought."

"And the quick healing?"

"Chock that up to Doc Carruthers and his magic medicine. Asked me if he could cut my finger or toe off to see if it grew back." He held up his hand. "Don't get any ideas."

Milk tapped her lips with her thumb. "I bet they have better gear in Troll Town."

"Maybe." Brooklyn pushed himself to his feet. "Ain't got time to waste on it. Got a planet to save."

* * *

"Earth is fucked." Brooklyn got up to pace the work area he'd created in the Boneyard. A rough assortment of desks and drafting boards played host to the Calculator Squad, made up of anyone in De Milo who'd gotten past basic algebra. "Can't write a program without parameters, and won't have that until it's too late to write the program."

Bruce's chair creaked as he rocked back on two of its legs. "Negative vibes won't get you anywhere, man. Take a walk. Smell the mushrooms. We got this."

"Bring us back some snacks," Topolski said. "And drinks."

Brooklyn's jaw ached from clenching it. It had taken the better part of two weeks to figure out how the *Victory*'s computer was wired and what parts of the booster sled and ship it needed to control. From there, he'd had to transform the ancient thing from a simple timer with engine-firing and limited attitude control to something that could make several maneuvers in a short time, in atmosphere, at a gravity that was ninety-one percent of what it was programmed for. Then, he'd need to put all kinds of course data on a punch card and hope the jury-rigged autopilot didn't choke on it. *No fucking problem! Glad it ain't me going up in that thing.*

He crossed the yard to the fuel-processing area formerly known as his distillery. He barely recognized it. Andy had torn it apart and rebuilt, adding more pots and kegs and filters until he was no longer sure he could puzzle it out. Whatever was coming out of the pipe was undrinkable but undeniably explosive.

Andy waved. "You just missed Demarco. He brought some books over for you."

Brooklyn studied the titles. *A Guide to FORTRAN Programming* by Daniel D McCracken, published in 1961, and *FORTRAN IV with Watfor and Watfiv* by Wes Graham, 1968. "Might help." He set the books to the side. "You know, I'm really more of a hardware guy, if you wanted to–"

"I don't know much about computers, Brook. My training

was in Earth history, urban planning, languages, and human psychology." She took a step back. "Besides, my hands are full with the fuel project. This shit isn't going to make itself."

"Milk tell you to say that?"

"The answer is mine, but she coached me on the syntax." She smiled. "But if you want, we can start looking at the texts together tonight."

Brooklyn picked the books back up. "Drop 'em off at your place. Grabbing lunch for everyone. You want anything?"

"A couple of sandwiches would be nice." She considered. "And a beer."

Brooklyn snagged one of the communal bikes parked at the gate and pedaled back to town. His programming skills would be a moot point if they couldn't get the data they needed off the First garbage run. His project was just a link in a chain that needed to go perfectly if humanity had a chance at survival. *No pressure at all. Sorry, Ma.*

FORTY-ONE

"I have waited long enough," Andy said. "We will both sleep better if you pause your studies and knock boots with me."

Lies. You sleep like a rock every night, eight hours without fail. "Knock boots? Where'd you hear that one?"

"We traveled to the builder settlement today to pick up some liquid oxygen. One of the drivers said it. I realize it is not entirely appropriate for this situation since neither of us are wearing–"

"Got the picture." Brooklyn closed the programming manual and put it on the floor near the bed. "Put mine back on if–"

"Shut up now and come here," she said.

Later, they lay together entangled, content. The clock was nearing midnight, about the time Andy would abruptly fall asleep.

"Don't know if I can do this," Brooklyn said. "Feels like the whole world is hangin' on me, and I didn't even go to college."

"Ah, talking." She rose to her elbow. "It's true, you are not a superior example of humanity. You are of average height and weight. Your musculature and many other functions seem heightened, but not to the extent of many Designed. Still, you are capable of the task before you. I believe you can succeed." She yawned. "Does that make you feel better?"

Brooklyn kissed her on the mouth. "Some."

She lowered herself to the mattress and rolled over. "Good night."

"These guys gonna be pissed when we use radar on them?" Brooklyn checked his watch. Five minutes until the blue glow would appear.

"The ambassador says the Designed that pilot the ships are barely more intelligent than insects. Likely they won't notice." Kasparov shifted his weight carefully. The radar tower they'd thrown together from scrap metal, on paper at least, could handle the weight of two men and the salvaged radar, but neither of them trusted it. A hundred feet was a long, long way to drop. "I used it on them the last time they came. Just a test near ground. There was no reaction."

"Maybe they like it when we show initiative," Brooklyn said. "Big test to see if we're worth adding to the galactic empire or whatever."

"You'd be wise to spend more time with your punch cards and less time with Demarco," Kasparov sighed. "We had all these debates when we first arrived and came to the conclusion that it didn't matter. Test, prison, colony, science experiment... our options aren't different."

"We knew it was a test or an experiment, we'd know how seriously to take it."

"And prejudice the results? Then we'd be a failed experiment, and there'd be no point keeping us around." A bell sounded from the ground below. "Showtime."

The glow appeared, high and to the right. "What if the tunnel doesn't show up on radar?"

"The ship will. Just be ready."

A blip appeared on the radar screen, and both men started transcribing numbers, tracing the course of the alien spacecraft as it emerged from the glowing aperture and descended to the Boneyard. "Looks like we got it," Brooklyn said.

"Keep tracking it."

The ship made its drop and continued on to the Dig.

"Now, let's get off this fucking thing," Kasparov said. "We can compare the figures at the bottom."

Brooklyn presented the data to his team the next morning. "If we can rig the autopilot to go from here," he pointed to the crude drawing in the blackboard, "to here, we can put *Victory* right into the glow, straight up the chute, and get it the fuck out of here."

Bruce and a couple of the other calculators exchanged glances. "We been talking, man," Bruce said. "What if the glow ain't a tunnel like we hope? What if it's, like, a portal? Go in one side and pop out somewhere else."

"Like a wormhole?" Brooklyn shook his head. "Andy said it would take decades to get to the First home planet. If they could make wormholes, they could just go right through, right?"

"Maybe." Bruce frowned. "How long does it take to travel through folded space? If their home planet is, like, really, really far away, it might take years to get through the fold."

Brooklyn examined the figures on the board. "Don't know. I'll ask Andy. Doubt she'd send herself a billion miles away to drift until their air runs out while New York City becomes a crater and humanity runs itself off a cliff. Satisfied?"

Bruce was pale. He nodded.

"Alright, let's get to work. The clock is really ticking now."

The next day, the team in charge of making punch cards, one at a time by hand, had to toss everything they'd made because of a tracing error.

The first test of Brooklyn's program fifteen days later resulted in a nearly perfect simulated launch and a devastating simulated crash a few hundred yards off target. The teams ran the numbers and made adjustments. Test two, resulted in a simulated crash, too, one hundred yards wrong the other way. *Data error? Programming error?* Brooklyn didn't sleep that night.

A fire at the fuel refinery destroyed the machinery that kept the liquid oxygen cold. Andy stayed awake all night. Brooklyn hadn't known she could do that.

Two days later a test of the rocket booster killed two members of Kasparov's crew. No one slept.

"I think we got it, Brook!" Bruce scrawled math on the chalkboard. "This is where the problem is!"

Brooklyn tried to rub away a headache. "Just tell me what numbers to put in."

The next simulation was nearly in the acceptable range.

The day nothing failed, no one died, and nothing blew up, Kasparov organized a gathering, inviting everyone who'd worked on the project and anyone else who was interested. He dipped into his personal booze stash for the event and set up a video projector in front of Brooklyn's blackboard.

"This will either inspire you or cause you to drink." He held up his glass. "Fortunately, we are prepared for either."

Topolski unrolled the projector screen.

"Kas and I pulled this out years ago when we found *Victory*. It's a failsafe. Supposed to launch and head toward Earth if the ship gets destroyed. Apparently it never got that far." Demarco hit "play".

The image on the screen was black-and-white and grainy,

but clear enough to make it obvious that Jet Carson looked nothing like the actor who'd played him. He was jowly and balding, looking more like a cop holding out for retirement than an action hero.

"This is Lt Commander Jethro Carson of the United States Air Force and the National Air and Space Administration. It's February 9, 1961, and this is my final message." His jaw tightened. "I was part of a joint task force, American and Soviet, sent out to confront an alien invasion force, and, as far as I know, I am the sole survivor. We lost four ships en route, one Soviet and three American. Their engines failed under acceleration."

"Did you know any of these guys?" Brooklyn asked Kasparov.

"I met Yuri Grishuk in training once. Shook his hand." Kasparov pointed at the screen. "Watch."

"The invasion force was a single ship, and we had orders to destroy it. We began our attack run as soon as were in range. Thirty seconds into the run, my ship shut down. All systems. Nothing worked. Looking out my cockpit windows I determined that the other ships in the task force were in similar condition. Inertia kept us moving along our final courses, and most of the ships drifted out of my sight within hours. My efforts to restore power to the ship's systems have failed. The reactor is inert."

"What the hell happened?" Brooklyn said.

"Some weirdo First weapon," Demarco said. He was kicked back in his chair, feet propped on a box. "Shut 'em all down before they could fire a shot."

Carson's face on the screen looked pained. "The mission was a failure, obviously. But that's not the worst part. The worst part is not knowing what happened next. If anyone finds this, give Betty my love." He reached to touch something, and the screen went blank.

"Drinking, definitely drinking," Brooklyn said.

Demarco held up his flask. "Way 'head of you."

PART TWELVE
Take a Chance on Me

July 1978

FORTY-TWO

It wasn't a noise, but something woke Brooklyn in time to see the exoskeleton standing over him raise a weapon. The sleeping bag he'd spread out on the floor of his work area tangled around his feet and rendered him immobile. The business end of the plasma weapon was the biggest thing he had ever seen. *David? Ma?*

The gun jerked skyward, and the green flash dissipated harmlessly overhead. There was a cracking, metal-tearing sound, and he was drenched in cold, fishy-smelling water. The exo fell stiffly sideways revealing Topolski grinning, clutching a mangled jellyfish in her fist. She dropped it at the foot of Brooklyn's sleeping bag and sat down next to him.

"Yes, I am First," she said. "You are very surprised, and grateful I saved your life. Merry Christmas!"

"That was–"

"An assassin sent here to kill all it could and sabotage tomorrow's launch." She rubbed her bloodied knuckles. "There were two. Now there are none."

"You're First."

"Yes, as I have said."

"Gotta get Kas–"

She waved her hand. "Let him sleep. Tomorrow will be a large day. Will still be First in the morning and tell him then. Waiting will change nothing."

The dying Jelly spasmed and released a foul-smelling fluid. Brooklyn pulled his feet up. "Was it from the camp we attacked or–"

"Different one. We left none of the exoskeletons at the site functional." Her nose wrinkled. "I smell piss."

"That's me. I–"

"No shame. Body was preparing for battle or death. Out of control. But should change pants." She stood.

Brooklyn slid out of the sleeping bag, careful to avoid the mangled alien. "What about...?"

"Dead or good as. No danger. Come."

Brooklyn followed her to the Boneyard locker room, where he took a quick shower and put on fresh clothes.

"Nice body. Good thighs," she said. "Aroused? Hungry?"

"No." Brooklyn dizzied and nearly fell, the adrenaline rush of near death giving way to weakness. "Could use a drink."

She opened her locker and tossed him one of the bottles inside. "Real Russian vodka." She opened another and took a swig. "Yours is better."

"Lot of the real stuff is distilled from petroleum." Brooklyn took a seat on a bench and unscrewed the bottle top. "If you're First, the fuck you doin' in De Milo?"

"Parents said Earth, Moon, or Venus. I chose here." Topolski slapped herself in the forehead. "Parents is not correct word. Human brains are so small. What is word for removing small piece of self and sending piece away to learn and experience?"

"Don't know that there is a word. Maybe Demar–"

"Good idea. I will ask him after the launch."

"Are you spying on us?"

She laughed. "Spying! What is there to spy? Eating, whining, walking about?" She leaned closer. "Did you know Kasparov and Milk have sex often? They think it is a secret. First doesn't care."

"You supposed to stop the launch?"

"Launch, don't launch." She took a drink from her bottle.

"If you're First, why are you doing any of this?"

Topolski frowned. "Is very boring being an immortal disembodied consciousness. Easy to lose perspective." She slapped her thigh. "Now I have food, and drinking, and sex. Killing. Joyful fighting. Hangovers, Comrades." She smiled. "Feelings! Life!" She jabbed her finger at him. "You should sleep. Large day tomorrow."

"I don't know if I –"

"Consume more vodka. I will keep watch." She took a gulp of the cheap booze as if to show him how. "Remind this one to tell Milk how to turn on the sun. Darkness is very depressing."

Milk drove down from town at seven.

"Got a problem," Brooklyn said.

"Get in line," Milk said. "We–"

"Topolski's a First."

She blinked. "I didn't see that coming. Is it a bigger problem than the Jellies we got coming at us?"

"Doubt it. She killed two of them last night. Says the First don't care if we launch. She's off telling Kas now."

"Can she warn her people about the meteorite?"

"Says the Jellies cut the link between her and her… parent."

Milk climbed out of the cart. "Put her at the bottom of the list then. Ony radioed in and said a bunch of those exoskeletons showed up and rescued their buddies. They're headed our way now."

Brooklyn rubbed his face. "They want to stop us."

Milk consulted her watch. "They have three hours to do it. We better get ready."

Two hours before launch, Brooklyn climbed to the top of the rickety radar tower.

"No sign of them yet. Not that I can see shit." Milk rested

her binoculars. "Gotta tell ya, Brook. This was not how I saw my life going. Up here on watch. Living in a fucking cave. Figured I'd join up, serve a couple of terms, get some money for medical school, get a Porsche, date a movie star..."

"Top says you and Kas are a thing," Brooklyn said.

"It's not all terrible." She glanced at him. "My family would disown me if they knew I was sleeping with a Red."

"Good thing they aren't here," Brooklyn said. "Seem OK with letting him go."

"I'm scared shitless. Shooting him into space in that piece of shit?" She cleared her throat. "But saving the world versus my hurt feelings? Yeah, I'm OK."

Brooklyn picked up her binoculars. "This ain't in my plans, either."

"Disappointed how it came out?"

"Food's probably better in Attica." He scanned the darkness, barely held back at bay by a line of lights set up about fifty yards out. "Kas wants to do a quick meeting before we start the clock. Fifteen minutes. Sending someone up to take your spot."

"I am not going." Kasparov leaned against the desk in his office, his beard falling heavy on his chest. "I should be here to repel the Second's attack."

"That the only reason?" Demarco winked at Milk.

She rolled her eyes. "Topolski tell you, too?"

"Naw. Figured it out myself couple of years ago. Small planet, babe."

Milk glared at Kasparov. "I told you it didn't make any damned sense to keep it a secret!"

Kasparov colored. "But fraternization–"

"We are way outside any chain of command, Yuri! We've been sneaking back and forth for three years when we could have–"

"Perhaps this should be discussed later," Andy said.

Milk folded her arms and nodded.

Kasparov cleared his throat. "We have new information from Ony. The Jellies killed five of our people in the escape. He says there are at least twenty-five exoskeletons headed our way in two groups. Ony believes one group will attack the Boneyard while the other attacks the town."

"Divide and conquer," Milk said.

"Hard to focus on protecting the *Victory* when someone setting fire to your house," Demarco said.

Kasparov nodded. "So we split up. Milk, I need you back in the village in case of casualties. Demarco will set up a field station here. I'll run defense. Grisha will run it back at the village."

"He's only got one arm, Kas," Milk said.

"He can handle it."

"We sending Andy up alone?" Brooklyn said.

"Nyet," Kasparov said. "It is my belief that our computer autopilot should be tended by a computer expert."

Brooklyn swallowed hard. "Me?"

"Pro Terra."

FORTY-THREE

More than half the telltales on the ship's control panels were yellow or red. Switches and bypasses were labeled with masking tape and scrawl, much of it Brooklyn's.

He shifted uncomfortably on the cracked leather of the pilot's couch. "This thing is a wreck."

"Don't tell it that," Andy said. "We may have it fooled."

Brooklyn ran another systems check. Nothing had changed in the four minutes since the last one.

"Here." Andy pushed a tape into the eight-track Brooklyn had hastily wired into the power system. "James Taylor will calm you."

"Great. I'm going to explode listening to *Fire & Rain*. Perfect."

She shrugged. "It's either that or Don McLean. Kasparov only had the two tapes in his office."

The countdown was at fifteen minutes. "I gotta take a leak." Brooklyn unstrapped and crawled backward to the ladder leading down to the refresher unit. The *Victory* was balanced on her tail for the launch, and it took him a minute or two to suss out how to use the plumbing in that orientation. He lingered, face buried in his hands, feeling more than hearing the vibration of the power plant.

"Five minutes, Brook!" Andy announced.

He crawled back up the ladder and strapped back in. The

telltales looked no healthier than they had before. He tapped one with his knuckle. It flickered from yellow to red.

Andy frowned. "You're making it worse!"

Kasparov crackled into their headsets. "Top says the Jellies got through her. They're about to begin their attack."

Top had gleefully volunteered to take a handful of people out on the M3 to meet the Second's advance on the Boneyard. Kasparov had agreed but only after she'd written out detailed instructions for relighting the sun.

Brooklyn strained up to peer out the *Victory*'s narrow port window. *Was that a green flash?*

"Three minutes," Andy said.

Far above them the blue glow appeared. *Victory* would launch when the First ship lowered itself into the junkyard.

"Junk ship is in sight," Kasparov said.

Least something is going according to plan.

Green light flared, and the *Victory* rocked.

"The Jellies just took out the junk ship!" Kasparov crackled. "Launch now! I repeat launch now!"

Andy stabbed the red button that bypassed the countdown, and the sled's rocket boosters roared to life. Brooklyn was pushed hard into the acceleration couch, as *Victory* leapt into the air for the first time in nearly two decades.

"Supposed to shake like this?" Brooklyn clutched the arms of his seat.

"Doubtful," Andy said. "Look!"

The blue glow grew ahead of them. Larger. Larger. Then they were inside.

Brooklyn tried not to think about the diagrams and data on his chalkboard. The atmosphere of Venus at its surface was ninety times heavier than that of Earth. Surface temperature was nearly 900 degrees Fahrenheit. The temperature dropped to Earth normal about thirty miles above the surface, but the clouds up there were made of acid and traded lightning bolts for fun.

The blue glow, Andy said, was a force-field, a corridor meant to protect the junk ship in its descent from orbit. Stood to reason that it would protect the *Victory* on the way up.

"The field is collapsing!" Andy said. "The destruction of the garbage ship must have triggered something."

The glow of the forcefield was thinning, turning a muddy brown as it revealed more of the orange of the planet's sky.

The old ship really started shaking. "I'm going to goose it!" Brooklyn jabbed the emergency booster button. More telltales went into the red. He groped and found Andy's hand. She squeezed back and nearly broke his fingers.

Twenty-three thousand miles per hour, give or take, was the speed *Victory* needed to be going to achieve escape velocity. Sparks burst like fireworks from a panel near Andy's head. She flinched away from it. Brooklyn had no idea what the electronics under the panel were for. *As long as the engine keeps firing.*

Twenty miles up. Twenty-five. The ship's hull screamed. Thirty miles up. *'Course, the engines could keep firing, and we could still die.*

G-forces pinned Brooklyn's arms to his sides. Andy dropped her hand and did something to the controls. The Oppenheimers kicked them forward like a football, throwing them into a mad tumble at sixty thousand miles per hour. Brooklyn thought he might explode like a stepped-on grape.

The *Victory* burst into blackness and stars.

Andy cut the engines. "We're up!" She was laughing. "We're up!"

The long expired anti-nausea drugs he found in his seat compartment were not helping. Brooklyn dry-heaved into the space-sickness bag and quietly hated Andy who appeared untroubled. The control surfaces in the cockpit were a mass of blinking, screaming red.

Brooklyn scowled, then gulped as Venus again rolled into view in the front windows. They were tumbling badly, speeding away from the planet toward a destination unknown. "Can't you get us stabilized?" he whined.

She wanted to kill him just then. He could see it on her face. "I'm not a pilot, Brook! Either go down to the sleeping berth and strap yourself in or do something useful!"

"Like what?"

"Run the message. It's already loaded up. It just needs to be transmitted."

Brooklyn nodded. He scanned the control boards looking for something familiar. He hadn't expected to be on the mission and hadn't taken part in many of the flight trainings.

"There! Look where I'm pointing!" Andy jerked her thumb toward the panel Brooklyn had seen explode with sparks. The edges were dark with scorch marks.

"Uhm…" he began.

The fury in her eyes silenced him.

"Never mind." There was a tool belt underneath his seat. He remembered that much. Brooklyn strapped it around his chest and gingerly made his way across the rolling cabin.

Andy got the ship steadied about the same time Brooklyn gave up on the long-range transmitter. "It's fried," he said. "Power surge from the force field, maybe. Looks like someone jammed a fork in it then threw it in a bathtub with a toaster."

Andy didn't answer. Her hair was sticking out in every direction, and she looked like she'd run a marathon. Still, the ship was stable on every axis, nose pointed firmly away from Venus, moving away from the planet at nearly seventy-nine times the speed of sound.

"Where are we heading?" Brooklyn said.

"Not toward Earth, I can tell you that much." She sighed. "Are we leaking anywhere?"

He shook his head. "Did a fog test when I went down to the engine room for parts. We're sound. How's life support?"

She seesawed her hand. "That's as specific an answer I can give you until I can run some diagnostics."

"Let me do those," Brooklyn said. "Go back and grab a nap."

"Just an hour, though. That will be enough." She unstrapped and floated to the rear of the cockpit and grabbed a handhold near the door. "I didn't think we were going to make it."

"All your doing, babe. Couldn't even lift my arms."

She nodded. "Happy to help."

Brooklyn had done enough time in space to know his way around a life-support system. The one on the *Victory* was less robust than the *Baron*'s, but it had a few redundancies, and he got it working at about fifty percent of capacity. Good enough to keep it comfortable for a while. The long-range transmitter was more than a total loss. The power loop had melted open and was wasting juice by electrifying the outer hull. Brooklyn pulled the entire unit, nearly electrocuting himself again in the process. He floated the whole mess down to the compact workstation in the engine room and was poking dubiously at it with a circuit tester when Andy woke up.

"What do we have that works?" she said.

Brooklyn wiped his forehead. "Life support sorta checks out. Booster sled failed to eject and is now twisted around us like a garter belt." He paused to collect his thoughts. "Oppenheimers are down, and nobody packed toilet paper."

"The transmitter?" She nodded at the wreck in front of them.

Brooklyn made a finger gun and shot the transmitter with it. "Paperweight. Ugly paperweight."

"Got any ideas?"

"One."

James Taylor made the ultimate sacrifice. Brooklyn cracked

open the case, shortened the tape to a five-minute loop, and recorded over "Sweet Baby James" and "Lo and Behold" to make a message to send out via the short-range radio. *This is Brooklyn Lamontagne. Earth is in danger. There are two sets of aliens. Prisoners on Venus. If anyone hears this, please get a hold of blah-blah.* Brooklyn added every comm code he could think of, including Sierra's ID. "It'll get there. Whether there's anything left to understand…"

Then it was his turn to sleep. As some point, Andy joined him in the bunk. It wasn't big enough for two, but microgravity helped. The morning, or whatever it was, found their circumstances unchanged, but they were better able to face them. Brooklyn made breakfast then lunch then dinner. Andy worked out a plan to slow them down and change their direction while listening to "American Pie" on repeat.

"Here are the calculations." She handed Brooklyn a stack of paper and hit the fresher for a shower.

Over the next couple of days, Brooklyn wrote a new program for the autopilot while Andy made punch cards from whatever scrap she could find. When the program tested out, he slid the cards into the computer. The maneuvering thrusters engaged, giving them direction and a semblance of gravity. The program, if it worked at all, would park them right in high Earth orbit.

"Gonna take a month to get us slowed down enough to head in the right direction, then at least seven months of travel time," Brooklyn said. "First delegation is going to be in Earth orbit in ten days."

"I'm open to suggestions."

He had none. He taught Andy how to play chess and wasn't at all surprised when, after two games, she stopped losing.

FORTY-FOUR

Eight days before the First were to arrive on Earth, the short-range radio crackled. "Hey, white boy. Knew you were too cool to be dead."

Docking with the little scout ship meant Brooklyn had to take a spacewalk in his patched vacsuit to clear the airlock. He used Jet Carson's ancient cutting torch to slice through the booster sled in three places and set Kasparov's hard work adrift.

He was out of the suit in time to see Dee come through the inner door.

"Brother Brooklyn!" Dee pulled Brooklyn into a bear hug. "Damned good to see you, man! Heard you were dead I just about–"

"Heard anything from Tommy? He was aboard the *Baron* when–"

"Got a message from him couple of weeks ago. We s'posed to get together and mourn your ass." The airlock cycled again. Dee took a step to the side. "Believe you've met my old lady."

"He means 'his boss'," Sierra said, making her own entrance through the hatch. "We relayed your message up the food chain. Smart move to put my code on it, but we're going to need something to back it up."

"Like what?" Brooklyn said.

"Her." Sierra jabbed her finger at Andy.

"Alien lady." Dark Side blinked. "Hot alien lady."

"Ambassador," Andy said.

"Doesn't change a thing I just said."

Sierra rolled her eyes. "Can these 'First' stop the asteroid?"

"Provided they can find it," Andy said. "The Second has a way of disrupting First communications and possibly hiding them."

"Then here's what we'll do," Sierra said. "Ambassador, you're coming with us. We can get you to Earth in less than six days and put you in front of the United Nations. Meanwhile, you will help us get a message to the First delegation asking for help with the asteroid. Sound good?"

"Scout ship can't handle four," Dee considered. "Can't really do three, but we can probably force it. Someone's gonna need to stay here."

"In this wreck?" Brooklyn said. "Take more than eight months for it ta get back to Earth."

"Can't be helped." Dee's mouth firmed. "Brook, you seen both sets of aliens. Make sense that I stay behind, let you go back an' make the case."

"Whole boat's on its last legs, man."

"I know a few tricks. An' as soon as you get back, I'm counting on you to send someone out here to get my ass."

"We gotta go if we're making this work," Sierra said. "Wheels up in ten."

"Lemme show Dee aroun' and see what he's up against," Brooklyn said.

"Twenty. No longer."

"Look here." Brooklyn tapped the indicator. "Life-support's running at about fifty-three percent."

"What's that mean?" Dee said.

"Hot and stuffy. Headaches from too much carbon dioxide. Best bet is to seal up as much of the ship as you can and make a little cave. Haul food and water up to the cockpit."

Dee nodded. "Good thing I brought some books."

"Thing hasn't flown in twenty-seven years, man. No telling what's gonna break down next. You don't have the knowhow to—"

"Challenge accepted!" Dee grinned. "What's this flashing light over here?" He moved to the far wall, catching his artificial foot on the work bench, dragging the remains of the long-range transmitter with him.

Brooklyn moved quick and caught the thing before it could pin Dee against the wall with its mass.

"Whoo! Glad you were there." Dee worked the prosthesis, setting it straight.

Stop being a selfish prick, Brook. Captain Computer Jockey had a better chance of keeping the life support running than the deep-space scout. *Not doing this again. Not adding another ounce of guilt and debt to my fuckin' sleep cycle.* "I'm staying," Brooklyn said. "Andy knows everything you need about the First an' the Jellies."

"Now who's gonna die?" Dee said.

"Maybe no one." *Hope that shit the Doc injected me with is worth at least three lives.* "I got a trick, too. Andy can fill you in on the way."

They went back up to the airlock and announced the decision.

Sierra kissed Brooklyn on the cheek. "Good to see you, Moon boy. Sorry to leave you in the lurch."

She floated back through the hatch to her ship.

"Lemme get some things for you." Dee followed her

Brooklyn pulled his eyes off the hatch and found Andy. "So, this is it."

"Are you sure about this?" she said.

"I'm sure. Mostly sure." *Better get the fuck out of here 'fore I change my mind.*

"I have enjoyed our time together."

Establish a relationship, make use of the relationship, move on to the next problem. Is that all this is? "Me too."

Dee glided back in with a ship's bugout bag. "Got this for you, too." He held up a plastic gadget, about the size of a textbook. "Sierra picked it up last time we were on Mars. It's an e-reader. Uses these cassette-tape things. Each one has three or four books on it. I put some extras in there." He tossed the bag to Brooklyn. "Put some music in there, too. Mix tapes. They'll play on the reader." He looked at Andy. "We gotta go."

She nodded.

Dee tossed Brooklyn a sloppy salute. "Soon as we get things under control, we'll send someone out to grab you. Cut some time off your trip."

Andy pulled Brooklyn into a long kiss. "Find me on Earth."

She followed Dee through the hatch and closed it behind her. Brooklyn felt the rumble of the scout ship's engines as they uncoupled and began the return trip. He completely changed his mind about staying and made it to the window just in time to watch them accelerate away.

"Well, fuck."

Brooklyn dismantled the emergency message and recorded a new one – name, rank, ship status, request for rescue, and set it in motion. He took a shower and ate some lunch. He filled a bag with MREs and all the containers he could find with water and loaded them into the cockpit. He shoved a bucket with a tight lid behind the copilot's seat. He carried Dee's bugout bag up there, too, closing doors and sealing vents as he went.

Brooklyn powered up the e-reader and explored the tapes. *Slapstick* by Kurt Vonnegut. *The Deep* by Peter Benchley. *Lady Oracle* by Margaret Atwood. He vaguely recognized Vonnegut's name. The mixtapes were marked by hand, some in Dee's looping scrawl, others in a hand he assumed was Sierra's. He picked one at random and pushed it into the slot.

Keith Richards' guitar work jangled through the ship.

Brooklyn laughed. "Dead Flowers", off the *Blistered Fingers* LP. 1971. Seven years past its day on *Hit Parade*.

Fucking song is following me. Brooklyn took a deep breath. *Just looking to get home, man. Not too much to ask. See the big blue marble rise up, just like that time on the Moon.*

The life support indicator on the console turned yellow and dropped to forty-nine percent. He leaned back on the acceleration couch to listen to the music and watch space roll by.

Rapture

March 13, 1981

The *Burra* was a blend of VW Bus, shipping container, and cherry picker, brought together and made mostly functional with First Tech. It corkscrewed into orbit rather than punched, lifted from its pad in Chihuahua City and protected en route by the aliens' mysterious blue-glow force field.

"What's next for you?" The ship's new owner Luis checked the crude instrument cluster to ensure they were still on course, not that it was all that important on the way up. Coming back, navigation would be the key to landing safely at home or ending up in the wrong state or, *dios no lo quiera*, the wrong country.

Luis's long-time friend and the former owner of the *Burra* Antonio leaned back in the VW's co-pilot seat. "Home to pack. Then, I hope my friends will throw a going-away party for me."

Antonio's family was going to the New World. A place where a *familia* could still make a good living off hard work. Let the Americans screw around and waste time protesting the inevitable. Venus meant opportunity and a chance at a better life. It made sense to get there early.

"Rosa will be cooking all day," Luis said. "All your favorites." Had Rosa had her way and her restaurant made more money, they'd be headed to Venus, too. But Antonio had sold him the *Burra* for a song, almost a gift, and it would only take a year or two of hard work to pave their way to prosperity. If the timing worked out, Juana, their oldest, would have her *quinceanera* in a new family compound below the surface of Venus.

Antonio tapped one of the indicator dials on the dashboard. The needle sluggishly swung into its proper position. "Let's go a little higher today. Pickings are getting thin in the lower orbits."

The space race had littered the gravity well with probes and satellites, lost tools, spare parts, broken ships, and forgotten experiments. The First wanted it cleaned up, and while the members of the UN Security Council wasted time talking and shaking their fists at the new boss, more practical peoples had rolled up their sleeves and gotten to work. Antonio had paid off his debts, built up a good nest egg, and covered his family's fare to Venus in less than twelve months. His cousin Ramon was close to doing the same with his cleanup work on the Pacific Ocean, near where the Jellies were settling.

"Yesterday was a good day," Luis said. "I hope we have another."

The day before, they'd harvested an intact vacsuit and a Soviet space capsule with a mummified dog inside. They'd added the vacsuit to the *Burra*'s equipment closet and sold the tiny ship at a good price.

"*Que los astros te sean propicio!*" Antonio said.

"Right now the stars and the magnetometer say there is something big ahead. Going higher was a good idea!" Luis gripped the wheel. The van's transmission shifter no longer changed gears. Luis used it and the steering wheel deftly to bring the *Burra* into orbit next to the mysterious object. He flipped on the headlights.

Antonio whistled. "It's a ship. An old one."

"*El Norte.*" Luis pointed through the windshield at the faded American flag painted on the hull. The ship tumbled slowly. "Looks intact."

He returned his attention to the controls, working the steering wheel, shifter, and pedals to bring the *Burra*'s crude airlock into contact with the derelict's.

"Looks good," Antonio said. He'd moved to the rear of the

VW to check the seal. "I'm opening the doors. You should hire someone to help you when I am gone."

"Juana is coming up to work with me. It's good to work with family."

Luis watched the Earth turn outside the driver's side window. Blue, green, and beautiful, but seldom fair. Her bounty had never been shared equally among her people. He turned on the radio to catch the morning show from Mexico City. The world had changed, the dee jay said, so much since the First ambassadors arrived with the American patrol ship as escort, just in time to destroy a meteorite that could have wrecked the entire planet. Was it any wonder the people of Earth were grateful?

Antonio and Luis floated into the American ship. The air was thin, refreshed only by the tanks and scrubbers on board the *Burra*. A ladder led down into the engine room and up into what was probably the cockpit. They went down first, cataloging their finds.

"That's a third-generation Oppenheimer," Antonio said. "Twenty-five years old at least."

"Good for parts if nothing else," Luis said. "Plenty of good steel and other recyclables, too. Bet the computer is an antique, though."

They poked their heads into the small living quarters and continued up to the cockpit. A frost-rimmed face frowned blankly at them from the pilot's couch.

"*Dios!* What a sight!" Antonio said. "A human *paleta*!"

Luis reached past the stiff to brush ice off the ship's nameplate. "*La Victoria*," he said. "That seems familiar. Maybe we'll get more money if we return this to the US."

"Could be." Antonio pushed "play" on the e-reader wired into the console in front of the pilot. The end of "Jungle Boogie" by Kool & the Gang poured out of the ship's speakers. "I like this song."

"That supposed to be Mary?" Luis pointed to the crudely

drawn figure of a woman, outlined in purple on the wall.

"Maybe his girlfriend," Antonio said.

Luis gasped.

"What?" Antonio scanned the control board looking for notification of an O_2 or radiation leak.

"*Hijole*!" Luis's face was pale. "The paleta just started breathing!"

ACKNOWLEDGEMENTS

I'm a space guy. Always have been, and I grew up frustrated that NASA ended manned Moon missions in 1972, when I was way too young to do anything about it. When NASA cancelled the shuttle program in 2011... Well, that was the last straw. I sat down and wrote a story about the Apollo 1 astronauts – Gus Grissom, Ed White, and Roger Chaffee – giving them a death in the stars instead of on the launch pad, a pyrrhic victory against impossible odds shoulder to shoulder with Soviet cosmonauts. So, yeah, when you read 'Jet Carson' think 'Gus Grissom', because that's where this all started.

My thanks to Sara Megibow, literary agent to the stars (and me), for all her work making this book and its younger siblings happen. We are not done with Brooklyn, yet, nor, I suspect, is he done with us. Without Angry Robot Books' CPU, its circuits and servos, its batteries and RAM, this page and the last few hundred would not have been possible, and I am grateful to my editor Eleanor Teasdale, guru Gemma Creffield, standard-bearers Caroline Lambe and Ailsa Stuart, cover-designer David Leehy, and face-savers Andrew Hook and Paul Simpson.

Thanks also to Nick Alhelm for putting the bug in my ear about turning a short story into a novel, to my pal Merle Drown for reading the thing, and to my writing groups – The #TranspatialTavern and The Bigfoot Appreciation Society – for keeping me stable. I am deep in debt to Brenda Noiseux, spouse and life support, for helping me find my way through this book and putting critique into words that I could understand.

Finally, to the book bloggers, reviewers, Tweeters, Instagrammers, and readers, thanks so much for the time, energy, and support. Pro Terra!

Liked what you read? Good news!
We've got a sequel coming
27th June 2023

Read the first chapter of
EARTH RETROGRADE
here...

JUNE 4, 1987

"Hey there, LA!"

Brooklyn's mouth twisted. Los Angeles deejays were weirdly chipper in the face of possible extinction.

"The Center for Disease Control has released some new dope on the so-called alien flu. They're talking a ninety-seven percent infection rate, world-wide! Everyone's gonna get it! Symptoms include fever, aches, and temporary weakness. You'll feel like BEEEEP! Good excuse to take a couple of days off and stay home, amirite! Now, here's one from Falco, his new 'Rock Me Amadeus,' to kick off a thirty-minute KROQ B-B-Block!"

Brooklyn punched the next preset on the van radio and caught the back half of a new Tina Turner song instead. The deejay had skipped the lede entirely, but reminding listeners of that part would kill the buzz of an ad-free rock block for sure. Scowling Dan Rather would do the dirty work on the eleven o'clock news. The flu was a delivery system for planetary-scale gene therapy. Nearly fifty percent of the infected could wave bye-bye to any plans of ever having children. Permanent sterilization for half the people on Earth, courtesy of the First.

Kids suck anyway. Brooklyn peeked at the scrap of paper he was crushing against the steering wheel. A right at the Nity Nite Motel – where particolored block lettering promised color TVs,

AM/FM radios, adult movies, and water beds. Past Shipwreck Joey's Topless Cabaret. Park beside the next warehouse on the left.

The rental van squeaked to a stop and rattled out of gear. Piles of pallets and dented trash bins warred with abandoned blankets for attention, half-shadowed and half-jaundiced by the shitty lighting. Brooklyn twisted the key back in millimeter increments and killed the engine. It ticked at him, cooling after the long drive from his storage unit in Avenal. *Cheap, but not as cheap as your girlfriend.* He fumbled in his pocket for the penknife he'd taken to carrying there and opened its sharpest blade. He pulled it across his forearm, mouth firming at the pain. He wiped the blood away with his shirt tail and made a fist to feel the pull of the already healing skin. *Good to go.*

Brooklyn put the key ring in his pocket and locked the van door behind him. The air was warm and thick but cleaner than it had any right to be. The laws and tech the First were deploying against the human stain were doing their jobs. Mostly. Brooklyn pointed his chin at the man who'd just stepped out of a shadowed doorway. "You Big Tony?"

"I fucking look like Big Tony?" the man said.

The guy looked pretty average-sized, but there was no telling where people picked up the their nicknames. "Whack-Whack said I could find him here."

"Whack-Whack." The guy hummed. "Whadaya want Tony for?"

Brooklyn flipped an over-the-shoulder thumb at the van. "Got a load of flat TVs. Jelly Tech. Whack-Whack said you guys might be interested."

"How many?"

"Twenty. Converted for standard voltage and ohm connectors. Hook 'em right up to your VCR or cable box."

The doorway turned into a portal of light as the man reached inside the warehouse and flipped the switch to open the metal roll-up. An aging electric motor strained to comply. "Drive on in."

The roll-up was fully open before Brooklyn retraced his steps to the van. The lighting was better in the warehouse, but there were still plenty of ambush-friendly shadows. Big Tony was an unknown. Might be the type to offer a bullet or pipe to the head if he thought it would save him some money. He drove the van inside and killed the engine again.

He walked around to the back, hands low and ready. The shadowy guy had rezzed into a ropy-looking white dude in a gray suit. The dude lit a cigarette. "Tony's in the office over there. He'll want to see the merchandise."

Each flatscreen weighed nearly one-hundred and seventy pounds. "You got a cart or something I can use?"

Gray Suit flicked his eyes to the right, where a four-wheeled cart strained under the weight of a couple dozen cases of chicken-noodle soup.

"Gonna help me out?" Brooklyn said.

"Nah." Gray Suit took a drag on his cigarette. "Just put 'em off to the side there."

Brooklyn pushed the cart a few inches to test the weight. Properly motivated, he could have tossed the whole thing at Gray Suit's head. "Thanks a bunch." He lifted the first three cases off the cart and set them on the floor.

Gray Suit whistled while Brooklyn worked. "I know you, pal? Your face rings a bell."

"Saved the world few years ago." Brooklyn moved the last box of soup and put his hands to the small of his back. "Want an autograph?"

The thug snorted. "Move your ass. Ain't got all night."

Brooklyn loaded the cart with one of the flatscreens. He could have lifted it easily, but the size and shape of the thing made it hard to handle alone. He locked the van again and pushed the cart into the office.

The fence's nickname didn't originate in subtlety. Bastard had to weigh close to three-hundred. Thick head of hair. Rosy cheeks. Piggy eyes. Tattooed hands resting atop a battered metal desk. Lit cigar resting in a ceramic ashtray. He had a voice like a sewer. "Whack said you was coming. Set it up over there."

Brooklyn balanced the flatscreen on a couple of folding chairs and hooked it up to a Sony Betamax Big Tony pointed out. "Got a tape you want to look at?"

The fence grunted toward a shelf of tapes along the wall. Brooklyn grabbed one at random and slid it into the Betamax. The image swam up on the flatscreen, nearly big as life. Meaty thwacks, grunts, and whimpers spilled from the built-in speakers.

"The fuck's it so blurry?" Gray Suit said. "Can barely see what's happening."

Brooklyn reached into his jacket and pulled out three narrow cases. "Forgot these." He handed a case each to Big Tony and Gray Suit. "Put 'em on. Jellies don't see like we do. These make up the difference."

Brooklyn donned the third pair of glasses. The images shivered into focus. On screen, Gray Suit, minus the suit and with his shirt sleeves rolled up to the elbow, rammed his fists into the face of a man tied to a chair.

"I remember this," Gray Suit said. "Didn't know you recorded it."

"Jackie Bananas. Owed us ten Gs."

Brooklyn removed the glasses. Wearing them for more than a few minutes gave him an 80-proof migraine. "Whadaya think?"

"Whatcha asking?" the fence said.

"A G per set. I'll throw in four pairs of glasses each one."

"Give you $500 each."

"Eight hundred fifty. I got twenty."

Big Tony rubbed his face with one big hand. "You can get more of them?"

"Take me longer if I have to do the conversions myself, but yeah."

"Give you sixteen-thousand for all of them, and you come see me when you have more."

"Deal."

"Throw in the van," Gray Suit said. "It's a rental, whaddaya care?"

"The fuck am I s'posed to get back to town?" Brooklyn said.

"These will sell fast." Big Tony slid the glasses to the end of his nose and peered over them at the screen. "Rumor goin' round the First can send, like, death rays through Earth TVs. Kill everyone in the house without scorchin' the wallpaper." He switched between looking over the glasses and looking through them a few times. "Go next store to the poon show. Tell the guy at the door I sent you, and he'll comp you in. Call yourself a cab at the bar." He looked through the glasses at Gray Suit. "Gerry, get the man his money and chase me down a couple of aspirin. Think I'm getting a headache."

People hear the world's ending, and they just start dancing faster. Brooklyn stared moodily at the ice in his highboy glass. He'd walked right past the Topless Cabaret and taken a prepaid robocab to the Sunset Strip in West Hollywood. Ditching the van had been in the cards from the start, and tracing it would only lead to a fake name and a hacked cash-cart. By the time Big Tony and Gerry Gray Suit figured out most people couldn't watch their new TVs without painkillers, it would be too late.

The party bustled around him. LA in all its colors and flavors getting high off sexual tension, ego, desperation, and any number of complicated chemical chains. Three months in the city, he'd gotten a good idea of the surface of the city and sussed out that surface was pretty much all it was.

Brooklyn drank some of his Old Fashioned, angry about maybe burning Whack-Whack as a contact and angrier at letting the Jelly computers – each with fifty times the number-crunching power of a Cray-2 but incompatible with any computer made on Earth – go as television sets. *Like selling a Porsche 911 as a cigarette lighter.* He looked at his watch, a bulky digital with a homemade band. Ten minutes before the exchange.

"You know Motley Crue had their debut show right up the block?" The voice came out of a douchey-looking guy wearing a pair of Ray Ban aviators and a black watch cap. "All started right here, dude."

Or maybe he'll be early. The guy's name was Henry something. He was way too old for the word 'dude,' and it was way too hot for a fucking hat like that

"Hey, whadaItellyouboutthisplace?" Watch-Cap Henry pulled a mirror out of his breast pocket and laid it on the bar. "Totally tubular, right?"

The dark-haired woman on stage was whipping around to Donna Summer's "She Works Hard for the Money," and a guy who might have been Charles Bukowski was sleeping at the end of the bar. "It's groovy," Brooklyn said

Watch-Cap powdered the mirror with a small vial and used a razor blade to sculpt three lines on its surface. "They don't say 'groovy' anymore, dude. Now it's 'radical.' Or 'gnarly,' maybe." He rolled a fifty-dollar bill into a straw. "Some?"

Brooklyn shook his head. "Don't let me stop you."

"I won't." He snorted one of the lines. "You got my money?"

"Got my codes?"

Watch-Cap made the 'wait' gesture with his left hand and used his right to hold the fifty. He snorted another line. "You're from the Big Apple, right? Probably why you didn't do so good here. Too uptight, dude. Gotta take a chill pill." He cleaned the mirror with his finger and rubbed the powder into his gums. "Look at these assholes. All the shit happening this week, and they make like it's another excuse to party."

"You got kids?"

"Two. Teenagers. Live with their mother." He slid the mirror back in his pocket. "They really talk like that, you know.

'Tubular' and all that shit. All a sudden, like they learned it in school."

"MTV."

"Really? That music show?" He shrugged. "You got kids? You don't look old enough."

"Good genes. Nah, no kids for me."

"Probably for the best, world the way it is." Watch-Cap looked tired. "Yeah, I got your codes," he patted the pocket the mirror had come out of, "right here."

"Let's get this over with, man. Earth gravity makes my knees ache."

"That's right, you're the fucking starman. Likes looking down on the rest of us from orbit." He dabbed at his nose. "How'd you get there, second star from the right and straight on until you fuck someone else over?"

"Didn't fuck Conrad over," Brooklyn said. "Made the introduction just like he wanted. Wasn't my fault it didn't come out for him. Told him the First ain't interested in money."

"They burned our entire organization, dude. Killed everyone. I'm the only one left."

"Conrad shoulda taken 'no' for an answer. Kidnapping an Ambassador was a real bad idea. Shooting them was worse." Brooklyn finished his drink. "I got your money. Ten large. You give me the codes to my ship, and we'll be shut."

Watch-Cap looked right and left. "Not here. We'll go 'round back of the building, make the exchange there."

"Don't see why we gotta do it on the sly, man." Brooklyn pulled a twenty from his money clip and laid it on the bar. "Let's just do it here."

Watch-Cap's face was red, his heart rate speeding up from anger or the coke. "I got your fucking codes, dude. We do it my way, or you never see your ship again."

Brooklyn raised his hands in mock surrender. "Your town, your rules, man. Lead the way."

Brooklyn followed the crook to the back of the club and

through a door that led to the alley outside. It was deserted, trash strewn, and filled with dumpsters. *Great place for a murder.* The Moon hung low overhead, full and bright in the way-less-than-usual light pollution. The First didn't put up with it anymore than they'd put up with Conrad's shit.

Brooklyn took a rolled-up paper bag out of his pocket. "You want to count it?"

"It can wait." Light glinted off the butterfly knife that had flicked its way into Watch-Cap's hand. He swept the blade across Brooklyn's chest, cutting through his shirt and skin.

The bag of money hit the ground. Brooklyn took a long step back and made a pistol shape with his right hand. He dropped his thumb like a hammer. ZEEK! Blue light flashed from Brooklyn's watch, along his hand, and followed a concealed wire along his pointer finger to the end. The light hit Watch-Cap in the neck, and he collapsed like a felled tree. His top and bottom teeth came together with a crack

"Fuck!" Brooklyn flailed at the watch's catch until he got it unfastened and let the thing drop to the ground. It burst into flames, and Brooklyn didn't bother to stamp them out. The watch was never meant to be anything but a one-shot holdout. "God damn it."

He lifted his shirt to get a look at the knife wound in the rum light of the alley. It was long, but not deep, and neck and neck with the burns on his hand and wrist for the evening's Gold Medal of Pain. Brooklyn squatted beside Watch-Cap Henry and checked his pulse. The neural disruptor he'd built into the watch was designed to keep an adult harmless for three or four hours, but First Tech sometimes had unexpected effects on people. Watch-Cap was breathing smooth and slow, and he'd pissed himself. Brooklyn grimaced and went through the crook's pockets. He found the cartridge with the unlock codes in the hood's blazer, along with the rest of his cocaine.

The coke made the pain a distant thing. The dumpster looked plenty big enough to hide an unconscious thug in, so

Brooklyn grabbed Watch-Cap by the back of his pants and his collar to hoist him up. The thug's hat slipped off. The top of his head looked like a Jiffy-Pop, domed over with tinfoil. *What the fuck?* Brooklyn peeled the foil off to see what was underneath. It was all head, pink and shaved down to stubble.

Watch-Cap grunted, and a flare of heat and light made Brooklyn jerk back and shield his eyes. When he could see again, he balled the tinfoil up and threw it to the side. The thug's body was gone, a thin film of greasy ash on the ground. The First didn't take prisoners or coffee breaks. *Glad I got the money first.*

The alley smelled like rotting garbage and burned fat. Brooklyn pondered the Moon, wondering what the hell to do and if anyone he knew was still up there. *Maybe Whack-Whack isn't a lost cause.* Brooklyn zipped his jacket up over his ravaged shirt and went back inside to find a payphone.

A richer man by five grand, Whack-Whack dropped Brooklyn at the shipyard. He was a reliable info broker when he wasn't going through a depressive phase, and getting on his bad side would have cost far more. Brooklyn gave Whack-Whack a sloppy, two-fingered salute. "Back in a coupla months, pal."

"Call first." The toothpick in Whack-Whack's mouth moved from one corner of his frown to the other. "Let you know if it's safe ta show your face."

When the taillights of Whack-Whack's low-end electric Ford were out of sight, Brooklyn walked to the security gate. Conrad had enjoyed a lot of pull with the local authorities until he'd gotten the bad idea to offer the First a deal and the far worse plan to try to twist their nonexistent arms when they rejected him. He'd gotten the cops to lock Brooklyn's ship and refused to give up the keys until the deal was in hand. Watch-Cap had inherited the codes when Conrad's plans went south and put his own spin on Brooklyn's troubles.

Brooklyn slid the cartridge into the lock and mentally crossed his fingers. Magnetic storage and high-energy discharges were not the best of friends.

The lock beeped twice and clicked open. Brooklyn slipped through as soon as the door was wide enough.

The *Victory*, was the oldest and dumpiest of the dozen or so ships in the hanger, but one of the few capable of breaking orbit. Brooklyn's eyes lingered over the others: smooth curves, matte-black aerodynamic planes, designed around First Tech. Far, far beyond his budget and probably well outside his ability to steal. He tapped his numbers into the *Victory*'s battered outer airlock door and went inside.

The ship was obsolete, much-modified military surplus, and after three months on standby, the air inside was stuffy and still, an oily mix of locker room and machine shop. Brooklyn woke the reactor and flipped on the fans. It didn't look like anyone had been on board, but he checked his stashes to be sure. The cash in his pocket barely made up for the yard and refueling fees.

The water in the shower tank was just this side of tepid, but he used it anyway. His shirt was a total loss. The skin on his hand and around the knife slash was still tender, but the wounds were mostly healed. Brooklyn donned a set of the coveralls he liked to wear onboard. He shoved his feet back into his boots but left them untied and clomped up the corridor to the cockpit.

The *Victory*'s original punch-card computer had given way to a K-Mart Special Atari 800XL with a 19-inch color Magnavox as the monitor. Brooklyn plucked the navigation-control program from the co-pilot's seat and slid it into the Atari's cartridge slot before tapping the computer's power button. He'd written the program himself and burned it to the chip, but had yet to tie any of the ship's fly-by-wire options into the Atari.

The monitor flickered. "Hello, Brook." The words were

barely recognizable as such, only the roughest approximation of the sexy-secretary analog he'd been trying to program.

"New York City. LaGuardia." Brooklyn said the destination aloud even as he typed it in, even though the program was even further away from voice recognition than it was from speech. He'd lick the problem eventually, but relying on it now would plot a course to First knows where.

"Execute?" The prompt appeared in standard eight-bit ASCII, but the answer was nothing like as clear. The narrow bunk room he'd passed while moving through the ship was tempting far beyond the merits of the thin mattresses inside. Sleep, food, more sleep, a pot of coffee seemed a friendlier order of operations. The *Victory* had lain dormant for months, and there was no telling what sort of gremlins had crept into its antique and arcane systems.

Against all of that was one simple fact: Brooklyn was sick of LA. His finger found the "y" key, and he hit 'return.'

The fuck outta here, man.